Great Expe

By Charles Dickens

Abridged by Evan Galt

Cover Artwork by Sabat Pirriyadi

Dedicated to my wife, Von, for inspiring me to actually make this book a reality

Table of Contents

About Charles Dickens and "Great Expectations" (source: Wikipedia, Dec 2020)

Charles Dickens was born in 1812 in Portsmouth, England, and died in 1870. In those 58 years he wrote some of the world's most well known and loved stories, including "A Christmas Carol", "Oliver Twist", "A Tale of Two Cities", and of course this story, "Great Expectations".

His writing reflected his critical views of the Victorian Era he grew up in and lived through in England, with its oppressive class structure, debtor's prisons, and where the poor and children were often treated harshly by society.

"Great Expectations" showcases all of these conditions, as well as more general themes of life. He wrote it from 1860 to 1861. It was released in segments in a British literary magazine titled "All the Year Round", which Dickens founded and owned. "Great Expectations" had a different original ending, but it was changed due to complaints from friends prior to publication. You can find it online, so I will not spoil the fun in this book.

Author's Foreword

If you are anything like me, then you don't normally read the foreword, so if you skip this, then no hard feelings. But if you are curious why I made this book, please read on, and Thank You!

And for the TL,DR crowd:

1. This abridgment contains the full plot
2. The wording is simplified but mostly his
3. Use this book as the gateway to reading the real thing

For the rest of you, normally somebody other than the author would write the foreword, but I feel I should since I didn't write "Great Expectations", and I wanted to let you know why I created an abridged version of this classic story for you.

First, because I wanted it to be more accessible to all. The language and humour Dickens uses in it are what drew me in, and he has a way with words I could never have. I've read the story at least twenty times since I first read it in high school, and I always find something new in it that I missed before, even if it's just a small detail.

However, that beautiful language comes at a price. His writing can be very flowery, with extensive descriptions of things; it also uses very uncommon words by today's general standards (Exhort? Denunciation?); and it includes the names of some things that people don't use anymore (ever use a "boot-jack"? or heard of a "coiner"?)

Therefore, sometimes I literally did not know what he was talking about. I remember when I first read it that I would often finish a page and only have some vague idea of what I just read. That's not a good recipe for enjoying a book, and I'd have to re-read what I just read, or look up words, or just try to guess what they meant by the context. If nothing else, it disrupted the story's flow. But I still enjoyed the plot and his humour. Then, after finishing it and writing whatever report I had to write for class, I mostly forgot about the book. Thankfully, some years later, I decided on a whim that I wanted to re-read it, and at that point I fell in love with it.

So, after reading it twenty-plus times over twenty-plus years, and knowing others' frustrations with getting into this great story, I decided I wanted to make a more accessible version. I simplified many things in it, but not all of it; the charm of the story is the humor and the general tone he uses throughout. I kept as much as I could, and what I simplified I tried to write in the same tone as his. The chapter structure is also the same as his.

Secondly, I made this because other abridged versions fell much too far short of the original. They cut entire characters and story arcs out of the book, which ruins the experience. They seem to be intended for children, when this is not a children's story; nobody younger than high school age has any business reading this book. If Dickens' story was a full Thanksgiving turkey dinner with the trimmings, then the abridged versions I've researched were only some of the bones with a little stuffing. I felt there needed to be a version in between, and I humbly hope I succeeded, as this version includes the entire plot.

And third, because of these reasons, I wanted to write a version that people would instantly grasp, then be incentivized to read the original book. This version is roughly half the size of the original, and is not meant to replace it; it's meant to draw you in and enjoy the story enough that you want to read the real thing.

So, I hope you enjoy reading this book as much as I enjoyed crafting it. Thank you, Mr. Dickens, and thank you, dear reader.

Chapter 1

My name is Philip Pirrip, but as a toddler the closest I could come to saying my name was "Pip". So, I called myself Pip, and eventually other people called me that as well and it became my name.

As a child, there were two reasons that I knew my last name was Pirrip. First, because it was engraved on my parents' tombstone, and second, because of my sister, who was twenty years older than I and married to the town blacksmith, Joe Gargery. I never knew what my parents looked like since they died when I was very young and long before photographs existed. Next to their tombstone were five other smaller tombstones, one for each of five brothers of mine that died as infants, and of course I had never known them, either. Except for my sister and Joe, I was all alone. We lived in the marsh country of England, by the river, within twenty miles of the sea.

One of my earliest memories was on Christmas Eve, near evening, when I was seven years old. I was kneeling among the tombstones of my family in the town cemetery, which was all overgrown with weeds and nettles. I knew the desolate wilderness around the cemetery with a few cattle, small hills, and dykes were the marshes. I knew the dark line beyond that was the river, and that the cold wind blowing in from it was from the ocean. And I knew that the lonely, small, shivering child growing afraid of it all and beginning to cry, was me.

"Stop that noise!" cried a terrible voice, as a man got up from among the nearby graves by the side of the cemetery. "Keep quiet, you little devil, or I'll cut your throat!"

He was a scary looking man, wearing tattered grey clothes and worn-out shoes, and with an iron band on his leg that only a prisoner would have. Every part of him and his clothes looked to be stained and covered with mud. He wore no hat but instead had an old rag tied around his head. He was shivering and sore from the cold and wet, and looked like he was as angry at the world as the world had been angry at him.

He came over and grabbed me by the chin, forcing my head up so he could see me. "Please don't cut my throat, sir!" I pleaded in terror.

"Tell me your name" said the man. "Quick!"

"Pip, sir," I barely squeaked out.

"Once more," said the man. "Speak up!"

"Pip. Pip, sir".

"Point to where you live" said the man.

I pointed to where our village was, a mile or so from the cemetery.

The man suddenly grabbed me and turned me upside down, emptying my pockets. I had nothing but a piece of bread, which he took. He then turned me right side up and placed me sitting on top of a tombstone, and ate the bread ravenously.

"You young dog," said the man as he ate, "what fat cheeks you've got. Darn me if I couldn't eat 'em, and I've got half a mind to do it!"

I earnestly expressed my hope that he wouldn't, and held tighter to the tombstone on which he put me.

"Where's your mother?" said the man.

"There, sir" said I, pointing.

He looked surprised, turned and staggered away a few steps, then stopped to look over his shoulder, expecting my mother and who-knows-who else to be there with her.

"There, sir" I timidly explained, still pointing at her tombstone. "'Georgianna'. That's my mother."

"Oh." said he, limping back to where he had put me. "And is that your father, with your mother?"

"Yes, sir."

"Who do you live with? That is, supposing I let you live."

"My sister, sir – Mrs. Joe Gargery – wife of Joe Gargery, the blacksmith, sir."

"Blacksmith, eh?" said he, and looked down at his leg where the iron was.

After considering something in his mind for a moment, he came closer to the tombstone he had sat me on, pinned my arms to my sides, and tilted me back so he towered over me and I looked up helplessly at him.

"Now, listen. The question being whether I'll let you live or not. Do you know what a file is?"

"Y-Yes, sir."

"And do you know what food is?"

"Yes, sir."

He went on threateningly, "Early tomorrow morning, you bring me a file and food. You bring 'em both to where the old cannons are mounted on the shore of the river, and don't say a word to anybody, and I'll let you live. If you fail or tell anybody, then your heart and liver will be torn out, roasted, and eaten. Now, I'm not alone out here; there's a man hidden nearby, and compared to him, I'm an angel. He hears what I'm saying, and he has a secret way to get at a boy. You may think yourself safe and hidden, locked in your house, and with your warm bed sheets covering your head, but that man will softly creep in, and tear you open and get your heart and liver. So, what do you say?"

Shaking in fear, I said that I would get him the file and what food I could, and I would bring them to him tomorrow morning.

"Now," he pursued, "you remember what you've agreed to. You remember the man that will hunt you down if you don't do it, and you get home!" With that, he released me, and turned to make his way towards the short cemetery wall.

"Goo-good night, sir," I faltered, still sitting terrified on the tombstone he had sat me on.

"Bah!" said he, glancing about him over the cold wet flat land. "I wish I was a frog. Or an eel!"

He then hugged his shuddering body and limped off, picking his way among the tombstones and nettles. He looked to my young eyes like he was trying to evade the hands of dead people, stretching up out of their graves to pull him in. I was so frightened that I jumped down off the tombstone and made the best use of my legs, running all the way home without stopping.

Chapter 2

My sister, Mrs. Joe Gargery, had established a great reputatio ... herself and the neighbors because she had brought me up "by hand". I didn't know what that meant, but I knew she had a hard and heavy hand, and that she hit her husband with it as often as she hit me.

My sister was not a good-looking woman, and I had a general impression that she had made Joe marry her by hand, too. She had black hair and eyes, and such red skin that I sometimes used to wonder if she washed herself with a cheese grater instead of soap. She was tall and bony, and almost always wore a rough apron that was stuck full of pins and needles. She wore the apron as a sort of badge, like a uniform she felt compelled to wear to show the world what she had to endure living with Joe and me. Joe was a fair man, with blond hair and blue eyes. He was a mild, good-natured, foolish dear fellow, and extremely strong from his craft.

Joe's blacksmith forge was attached to our house, which was a small simple wooden one as most were in our village. When I ran home from the cemetery, I saw that the forge was closed up, and Joe was sitting alone in the kitchen by the fire. As Joe and I were fellow-sufferers under my sister, the moment I entered the kitchen he advised me, "Mrs. Joe has been out a dozen times looking for you, Pip. And, what's worse, she's got Tickler with her." Tickler was a wooden stick, worn smooth by my sister repeatedly hitting me with it.

"She got up, she grabbed Tickler, and she Ram-paged out. That's what she did," said Joe, "she Ram-paged out, Pip."

"Has she been gone long, Joe?" I always treated him as a larger type of child than me, and as no more than my equal.

"Well," said Joe, glancing at the clock, "she's been on the Ram-page, this last time, about five minutes, Pip. Oh, she's coming! Get behind the door, old chap, and put the towel between you two."

I took his advice. My sister threw the door open, and finding an obstruction behind it, immediately assumed the cause, and applied Tickler to investigate. She finished by throwing me at Joe, who passed me onto a small stool in the chimney corner and quietly fenced me in with his big leg.

"Where have you been, you young monkey?" said Mrs. Joe, stamping her foot. "Tell me right now what you've been doing to make me so worried, or I'll get you out of that corner even if you were fifty Pips and he was five hundred Gargerys!"

"I've only been to the cemetery," said I, crying and rubbing my wounds from Tickler.

"Cemetery!" repeated my sister. "If wasn't for me you'd have been to the cemetery long ago, and stayed there. Who brought you up by hand?"

"You did," said I, sheepishly.

"And why did I do it, I should like to know?" exclaimed my sister.

I whimpered, "I don't know."

"I don't either!" said my sister. "I'd never do it again! I may truly say I've never had this apron of mine off since you were born. It's bad enough to be a blacksmith's wife without having to be your mother, too! Cemetery, indeed! The two of you will drive me to the cemetery one of these days, and oh, what a pr-r-recious pair you'd be without me!" She put Tickler back and went to work in the kitchen. She made me and Joe each a slice of bread and butter for dinner.

Though I was hungry, I dared not eat my slice. I needed food for the dreaded convict and his still more dreaded friend that would eat my heart and liver if I failed. I knew Mrs. Joe's housekeeping was strict and I would not find extra food lying around. Therefore, I decided to hide my bread and butter down the leg of my pants.

This would already be a tough feat to accomplish without being seen doing it, but it was made even tougher because of Joe. In his good-natured companionship with me, it was our evening habit to compare the way we bit through our slices by holding them up to each other's admiration. Tonight, Joe several times invited me to enter our friendly competition by holding his rapidly shrinking slice up for me to see. But each time he found me with my untouched bread-and-butter on my plate. At last, seeing an opportunity when nobody was looking, I stuffed my bread and butter down my pants.

Joe was chewing his bread slowly and thoughtfully now, staring off into space, apparently uncomfortable over my lack of appetite and wondering why I wasn't playing our usual game. He was about to take another bite when he happened to look at me again and noticed my bread and butter was gone.

The wonder and awe on his face when he stopped in mid bite was too obvious for my sister to miss.

"What's the matter now?" said she, sharply, as she put down her cup.

"I say, you know," muttered Joe with concern. "Pip, old chap! It'll stick somewhere. You can't have chewed it. If you can cough any of it up, I'd recommend you to do it. Manners is manners, but still; your health's your health."

"Been inhaling his food, has he?" cried my sister. She pounced on me and said, "You come along and be dosed."

Some awful doctor had revived Tar-water in those days as being a fine medicine, and Mrs. Joe always kept a supply of it in the cupboard, having a belief that its effectiveness must match its nastiness. At times, she poured so much of this elixir down my throat that I smelled like a new fence. On this particular evening the urgency of my case required a pint of this stuff, which was poured down my throat, supposedly for my comfort, while Mrs. Joe clamped my head under her arm like a vice. She also made Joe drink half a pint "because he had had a turn." From judging Joe's reaction to drinking it, I should say he certainly had a turn afterwards, if he hadn't had one before.

After dinner I had to stir the pudding for the next day's Christmas festivities, from seven to eight o'clock. The bread and butter down my leg was a constant reminder of what I was doing. The knowledge that I was going to rob our household, coupled with the necessity of always keeping one hand on the hidden bread-and-butter in my pants until I could get alone, almost drove me out of my mind. In every little noise I heard the convict or his friend, coming for their food and file now rather than waiting until morning. Or the convict's friend losing patience and coming for my heart and liver before my time was up. Finally, I was able to slip away for a minute and put the bread-and-butter in my attic bedroom, then return to finish my stirring duties.

With my kitchen chores complete, I was warming myself in the chimney corner before being sent up to bed when I heard a distant but powerful booming sound outside; "What was that, Joe?"

"Ah!" said Joe. "There's another convict off."

"What does that mean, Joe?" said I.

"Escaped. Escaped." said Mrs. Joe snappishly, serving the definition like she served Tar-water.

"A convict escaped last night," said Joe, "after sunset. And they fired warning of him. And now, it appears they're firing warning of another".

"Who's firing?" said I.

"Drat that boy," interjected my sister, frowning at me over her work, "what a questioner he is. Ask no questions, and you'll be told no lies."

She was not very polite to herself, I thought, to imply that she would tell me lies if I asked her questions. But she was never polite, unless there was company.

"Mrs. Joe," said I, "I should like to know – if you wouldn't much mind – where the firing comes from?"

"Lord bless the boy!" exclaimed my sister, as if she really meant quite the opposite. "From the Hulks!"

"And please, what are Hulks?" said I.

"That's the way with this boy!" exclaimed my sister, pointing at me with her needle and thread, and shaking her head at me. "Answer him one question, and he'll ask you a dozen directly. Hulks are prison-ships, on the river across the marshes."

My thoughts drifted to the convict and his friend, and the robbery I was committing for their benefit. Not asking anybody in particular, but thinking aloud, I said, "I wonder who's put into prison-ships, and why they're put there?"

It was too much for Mrs. Joe, who immediately got up. "I tell you what, young fellow," said she, "I didn't bring you up by hand to badger people's lives out. People are put in the Hulks because they murder, and rob, and forge, and do all sorts of bad things; and they always begin by asking questions. Now, you get along to bed!"

I was never allowed a candle to light my way to bed, and, as I went upstairs in the dark, I felt it must be my destiny that the Hulks were so nearby; I was clearly on my way there. I had begun by asking questions, and I was going to rob Mrs. Joe.

Since that time, I have often thought that few people know what secrecy there is in the young, under terror. I was in mortal terror of the convict with the iron on his leg; I was in mortal terror of his friend who wanted my heart and liver; I had no hope of help from my sister; I am afraid to think of what I might have done, if needed, in the secrecy of my terror.

I was afraid to sleep, even if I had been able to, for I knew that at the first faint dawn of morning I must rob the pantry. When the time came, I got up and went down stairs. Every board on the way creaked with my steps, seeming to call out, "Stop thief!" and "Get up, Mrs. Joe!"

Once in the pantry, I had no time to spare. I stole some bread, some cheese, about half a jar of mincemeat (which I tied up in my pocket-handkerchief with my last night's bread-and-butter), a pork pie, and some brandy from a stone bottle. I added water from a jug in the kitchen to the stone bottle so it would not appear any brandy was missing.

There was a door in the kitchen, joining the house with the forge. I quietly unbolted that door and got a file from among Joe's tools. Then, I re-bolted that door, and opened the one at which I had entered when I ran home last night, shut it, and ran for the misty marshes.

Chapter 3

It was a damp, cold, quiet morning. The marsh-mist was so thick that the wooden finger on the post directing people to our village was invisible to me until I was quite close to it. Then, as I looked up at it, while it dripped dew, it seemed to my conscience like a ghost pointing me to the prison ships that surely awaited me.

The mist was heavier yet when I got out upon the marshes, so that instead of my running at everything, everything seemed to run at me. This was very disagreeable to a boy with a guilty conscience. Cattle, gates, and dykes burst at me through the mist as I ran, as if accusing me, "A boy with somebody-else's pork pie! Stop him! Young thief!"

I was getting on towards the river; but however fast I went, I couldn't warm my feet up, to which the damp cold seemed riveted, as the iron was riveted to the leg of the convict I was running to meet. I knew my way to where the old cannons were by the river shore, for I had been down there on a Sunday with Joe, and Joe, sitting on an old gun, had told me that when I was apprenticed to him as a blacksmith we would have such Larks there! However, in the confusion of the mist, I found myself too far to the right, and had to walk back along the river edge.

Making my way along as best and fast as I could, I had just crossed a ditch which I knew to be very near the old cannons, when I saw the man sitting in front of me. His back was to me, he had his arms folded, and was nodding forward, with sleep. I went forward softly and touched him on the shoulder. He instantly jumped up, and it was not the same man, but another man!

And yet this man was dressed in grey, too, and had a great iron on his leg, and was lame, and hoarse, and cold, and was everything that the other man was; except that he had not the same face, and had a flat broad-brimmed felt hat on. All this I saw in a moment, for I had only a moment to see it in: he swore at me, tried to hit me – it was a weak punch that missed me and almost knocked himself down, for it made him stumble – and then he ran off into the mist, stumbling twice as he went, and I lost sight of him.

"It must be the convict's friend!" I thought, feeling my heart race as I identified him. I dare say I should have felt a pain in my liver, too, if I had known where it was.

I was soon at the old cannons, and there was the right man, hugging himself and limping to and fro, as if he had never all night stopped hugging and limping, waiting for me in the cold. His eyes looked so awfully hungry, too, that when I handed him the file and he laid it down on the grass, it occurred to me that he would have tried to eat it if he had not seen my bundle. He did not turn me upside down this time, to get at what I had, but left me right side up while I opened the bundle and emptied my pockets.

"What's in the bottle, boy?" said he.

"Brandy," said I.

He was already handing mincemeat down his throat in the most curious manner – more like a man who was putting it away somewhere in a violent hurry, than a man who was eating it – but he stopped long enough to drink some of the brandy. He shivered all the while, so violently, that it was all he could do to keep the neck of the bottle between his teeth without biting it off.

"It's bad out here," I told him. "You've been lying out on the marshes, and they're dreadful."

"I'll eat my breakfast before they're the death of me," said he.

He was gobbling mincemeat, bread, cheese, and pork pie, all at once: staring distrustfully while he did so at the mist all around us, and often stopping – even stopping his jaws – to listen. Some real or imagined sound now gave him a start, and he said, suddenly fixing his eyes on me:

"You're not a deceiving imp? You brought no one with you?"

"No, sir! No!"

"Well," said he, "I believe you. You'd be a fierce young hound indeed, if at your age you could help to hunt a wretched varmint like me!"

Pitying his desolation and watching him as he gradually settled down upon the pie, I said sheepishly, "I am glad you enjoy it."

"Did you speak?"

"I said I was glad you enjoyed it."

"Thankee, my boy, I do."

I had often watched a large dog of ours eating his food; and I now noticed a definite similarity between the dog's way of eating, and the man's. The man took strong sharp sudden bites, just like the dog. He swallowed, or rather snapped up, every mouthful; and he looked sideways here and there while he ate, as if he thought there was danger in every direction of somebody's coming to take the pie away.

"I am afraid you won't leave any of it for him," said I, timidly. "There's no more to be got where that came from."

"Leave any for him?" said the convict, stopping in his crunching of pie-crust. "Who's 'him'?"

"Your friend that you spoke of. That was hid with you and would hunt me if I didn't come back here."

"Oh, ah!" he returned, with something like a gruff laugh. "Him? Yes, yes! He's not hungry."

"I thought he looked as if he was," said I.

The man stopped eating, and looked at me with the keenest scrutiny and the greatest surprise. "Looked? When?"

"Just now."

"Where?"

"Yonder," said I, pointing; "over there, where I found him nodding asleep, and thought it was you."

He grabbed me by the collar and stared at me so, that I began to think his first idea about cutting my throat had returned to him.

"Dressed like you, you know, only with a hat," I explained, trembling; "and - and" - I was very anxious to put this delicately - "and with the same reason for wanting to borrow a file. Didn't you hear the cannon last night?"

"Then, there was firing!" he said to himself.

"I wonder you shouldn't have been sure of that," I returned, "for we heard it up at home, and that's further away, and we were shut in besides."

"Why, see now!" said he. "When a man's alone on these flats, with a light head and a light stomach, perishing of cold and hunger, he hears nothin' all night but guns firing and voices calling. But this man, did you notice anything about him?"

"He had a badly bruised face," said I, recalling what I hardly knew I knew.

"Not here?" exclaimed the man, striking his left cheek hard with his hand.

"Yes, there!"

"Where is he? Show me the way he went. I'll pull him down, like a bloodhound. Curse this iron on my sore leg! Give me the file, boy."

I indicated in what direction the mist had covered the other man, and he looked up at it for an instant. But then he was down on the wet grass, filing at his iron like a madman, and not minding me or minding his own leg, which had an old wound upon it and was bloody, but which he handled as roughly as if it had no more feeling in it than the file. I was very much afraid of him again, now that he had worked himself up into this fierce frenzy, and I was also very much afraid of keeping away from home any longer. I told him I must go, but he took no notice of me, so I thought the best thing I could do was to slip off. The last I saw of him, his head was bent over his knee and he was working hard with the file, muttering impatiently at it and at his leg. The last I heard of him, I stopped in the mist to listen, and the file was still going.

Chapter 4

I fully expected to find a policeman in the kitchen, waiting to arrest me. But not only was there no policeman there, the robbery had not yet been discovered. Mrs. Joe was busy getting the house ready for the festivities of the day, and Joe had been put out of the kitchen to keep him out of the way.

"And where the deuce have you been?" was Mrs. Joe's Christmas greeting to me.

I said I had been down in the village to hear Christmas carols being sung. "Ah! Well!" observed Mrs. Joe. "You might have done worse." Not a doubt of that, I thought.

"Perhaps if I wasn't a blacksmith's wife, and a slave with her apron never off, I should have been to hear the carols, too," said Mrs. Joe. "I'm fond of carols, and that's the best reason why I never get to hear any."

We were to have a superb dinner, consisting of a leg of pickled pork and greens, and a pair of roast stuffed fowls. A handsome mince-pie had been made yesterday morning (which accounted for the extra mincemeat not being missed), and the pudding was already boiling. These extensive arrangements caused Joe and I to be cut off from having breakfast; "for I ain't," said Mrs. Joe, "a-going to have either of you make a mess with what work I've got before me today, I promise you!"

So, we had our bread-and-butter slices served out as if we were soldiers on a forced march instead of a man and boy at home; and we took gulps of milk and water from a jug on the dresser. In the meantime, Mrs. Joe put clean white curtains up, and tacked a new flowered piece of fabric across the wide chimney to replace the old one, and uncovered the little formal dining room across from the kitchen, which was never uncovered at any other time of year.

My sister, having so much to do, sent Joe and I to church alone. In his working clothes, Joe was a well-knit characteristic-looking blacksmith; however, in his holiday clothes he was more like a scarecrow than anything else. Nothing that he wore fitted him or seemed to belong to him. This morning, after changing into his suit, he emerged from his room looking miserable. As for me, when I was taken to have a new suit of clothes, the tailor had orders to make them like a kind of tight prison, and on no account to let me have the free use of my arms or legs.

Yet, what I suffered outside was nothing compared to what I suffered within. The terror that I had felt whenever Mrs. Joe had gone near the pantry was only to be equaled by the guilt of knowing that I had committed a robbery there. Under the weight of my wicked secret I wondered whether the Church would be powerful enough to shield me from the vengeance of the convict's terrible friend if I confessed my crime there.

We were having company for Christmas dinner that day. Mr. Wopsle, who was the clerk at church; Mr. Hubble the wheelwright and Mrs. Hubble; and Uncle Pumblechook (Joe's uncle, but Mrs. Joe had appropriated him), who was a well-to-do livestock feed merchant in the nearest town, and drove his own horse cart. The dinner hour was half-past one. When Joe and I got home, we found the table laid, Mrs. Joe dressed, and everything most splendid looking. And still, not a word of the robbery.

The dinner time came, and the company came. I opened the door first to Mr. Wopsle, next to Mr. and Mrs. Hubble, and last of all to Uncle Pumblechook. It's worth mentioning that I was not allowed to call him "uncle", under the severest of penalties.

Mr. Wopsle had a large nose and a large shining bald forehead. He also had a deep voice which he was uncommonly proud of and liked to show off in church services whenever he could.

Mrs. Hubble was a little sharp-edged person who had married Mr. Hubble when she was much younger than he. And Mr. Hubble was a high-shouldered stooping old man who smelled like sawdust, and whose legs were extraordinarily wide apart, so that I always saw miles of open country between them when I met him coming up the lane.

Mr. Pumblechook was a large, hard-breathing, middle-aged, slow man, with a mouth like a fish, dull staring eyes, and sandy hair that stood upright on his head, so that he looked as if he had just been choked nearly to death.

"Mrs. Joe," said Mr. Pumblechook, "I have brought you, as the compliments of the season, a bottle of sherry wine, and I have brought you a bottle of port wine."

Every Christmas Day he presented himself with exactly the same words, and carrying the two bottles like dumb-bells. Every Christmas Day, Mrs. Joe replied, as she now replied, "Oh, Un - cle Pum - ble - chook! This IS kind!" Every Christmas Day he replied, as he now replied, "It's no more than your merits. And now are you all in good spirits! And how's Sixpennorth of halfpence?" meaning me.

We dined on these occasions in the kitchen, and afterward moved to the parlour for nuts and oranges and apples. My sister was uncommonly lively on the present occasion, and indeed was generally more gracious when Mrs. Hubble was a guest.

Among this good company I was always in a bad position. Not because I was squeezed in to only a few inches of the table-cloth with Mr.

Pumblechook's elbow in my eye; not because I was not allowed to speak (I didn't want to speak); not because I was given the worst of the food there was to go around. No; I should not have minded any of that, if they would have only left me alone. But they wouldn't leave me alone. They seemed to think the opportunity lost if they failed to direct the conversation at me, and stick the point into me.

It began the moment we sat down to dinner. Mr. Wopsle said grace with theatrical flair showcasing his voice, and ended, saying that we might be truly grateful. Upon which my sister fixed me with her eye, and said, in a low reproachful voice, "Do you hear that? Be grateful."

"Especially," said Mr. Pumblechook, "be grateful, boy, to them which brought you up by hand."

Mrs. Hubble shook her head and looked at me with a mournful expression, signifying that I would amount to no good, and asked, "Why is it that the young are never grateful?" This moral mystery seemed too much for the company to answer until Mr. Hubble tersely solved it by saying, "Naturally vicious." Everybody but Joe then murmured "True!" and scowled at me in a particularly unpleasant and personal manner.

Joe's position and influence were even less (if possible) when there was company, than when there was none. But he always aided and comforted me when he could, and he always did so at dinner-time by giving me gravy, if there were any. There was plenty of gravy that day since it was Christmas, so Joe spooned onto my plate about half a pint.

A little later on in the dinner, Mr. Wopsle unfavorably reviewed the sermon from that day's church service, and mentioned what kind of sermon he would have given them if he had had the opportunity. He said that he considered the subject of the sermon ill-chosen, when there were "so many better subjects going about."

"True again," said Mr. Pumblechook. "You've hit it, sir! Plenty of subjects going about. Look at Pork, there's a subject! If you want a subject, look at Pork!"

"True, sir. Many a moral for the young in that subject," returned Mr. Wopsle, and I knew he was going to pull me into his sermon somehow.

("You listen to this," said my sister to me, in a severe parenthesis.)

Joe gave me some more gravy.

"Swine," pursued Mr. Wopsle, in his deepest voice, and pointing his fork at me as if Swine were my name; "Swine were the companions of the wasteful. The gluttony of Swine is put before us, as an example to the young." (I thought this was pretty ironic of him, as he had been praising the pork for being so plump and juicy.) "What is detestable in a pig, is more detestable in a boy."

"Besides," said Mr. Pumblechook, turning sharp on me, "think what you've got to be grateful for. If you'd been born a Squeaker--"

"He was, if ever a child was," said my sister, most emphatically.

Joe gave me some more gravy.

"Well, but I mean a four-footed Squeaker," said Mr. Pumblechook. "If you had been born as such, would you have been here now? Not you--"

"Unless looking like that," said Mr. Wopsle, nodding towards the dinner.

"But I don't mean in that form, sir," returned Mr. Pumblechook, who had an objection to being interrupted; "I mean, he wouldn't be enjoying himself with his elders and betters, and improving himself with their conversation, and rolling in the lap of luxury. Would he have been doing that as a pig? No, he wouldn't. And what would have been your destination?" turning on me again. "You would have been sold for so many shillings, and the butcher would have come up to you as you lay in your straw and he would have shed your blood and had your life. No bringing up by hand then!"

Joe offered me more gravy, which I was afraid to take.

"He's been a world of trouble to you, ma'am," said Mrs. Hubble, comforting my sister.

"Trouble?" echoed my sister; "Trouble?" and then she began a long list of all the illnesses I had been guilty of, and all the things I had done to make her lose sleep, and all the high places I had fallen from, and all the low places I had fallen into, and all the injuries I had done to myself, and all the times she had wished me in my grave and I had stubbornly refused to go there.

She finished, and after a pause said, "Have a little brandy, uncle."

O Heavens, it had come at last! He would find the brandy was weak and I would be caught! I grabbed and held tight to the leg of the table under the cloth with both hands and awaited my fate.

My sister left the table and came back with the stone bottle full of brandy (with the water I had added to it to make up for what I gave the convict), and poured him some. The wretched man played with his glass - picked it up, looked at it through the light, put it down - prolonging my misery. He picked it back up, admired the glass some more, smiled, and finally drink the brandy off in one gulp. Instantly, he sprang to his feet, turned around several times in an appalling spasmodic dance, and rushed out the door. He was visible through the window, violently coughing and spitting, making the most hideous faces, and apparently out of his mind.

I held on tight to the hidden table leg in front of me while the guests were all alarmed and confused, and Mrs. Joe and Joe ran outside to him. I didn't know how I had done it, but I had no doubt I had murdered him somehow. He was brought back inside and sank down into his chair with the one significant gasp, "Tar!"

I had filled up the bottle from the tar-water jug by mistake.

"Tar!" cried my sister, in amazement. "Why, how could Tar be in there?"

But Mr. Pumblechook, who was the ruler in that kitchen, didn't want to discuss the word or the subject and imperiously waved it all away with his hand, and asked for hot gin-and-water. For the time being at least, I was saved.

Little by little, I became calm enough to release my grasp of the table leg and had some pudding along with the rest of the company when things had settled down. I began to think I should survive the day, when my sister said to the guests, "You must finish with such a delightful and savoury pork pie!" I immediately clutched the table leg again and felt that this time I really was gone, since the pork pie was gone.

The guests murmured their compliments. Mr. Pumblechook said – quite enthusiastically, all things considered – "Well, Mrs. Joe, we'll do our best; let us have some of this pie."

My sister went out to get it. I saw Mr. Pumblechook get his knife ready. I saw a re-awakening appetite in Mr. Wopsle. I heard Mr. Hubble remark that "a bit of savoury pork pie could finish any dinner, and do no harm," and I heard Joe say, "You shall have some, Pip." I could bear no more, and had to run away. I released the leg of the table, got up, and ran for my life.

But, I ran no further than the house door, for when I threw it open I ran head first into a party of soldiers with their muskets, one of whom held out a pair of handcuffs to me, saying, "Here you are, look sharp, come on!"

Chapter 5

The appearance of a group of soldiers with their loaded muskets on our door-step caused the dinner-party to rise from the table in confusion, and caused Mrs. Joe re-entering the kitchen empty-handed to stop and stare before the missing pork pie could be discussed.

It was the sergeant who had spoken to me, and he was now standing in the kitchen looking around at the dinner guests, with his handcuffs invitingly extended towards them in his right hand, and his left on my shoulder.

"Excuse me, ladies and gentleman," said the sergeant, "but as I mentioned at the door to this smart young lad" (which he hadn't), "I am on a chase in the name of the king, and I need the blacksmith."

"And what might you need with him?" retorted my sister, quick to resent Joe being needed at all.

"Missis," returned the gallant sergeant, "speaking for the king, I need a little job done."

"You see, blacksmith," continued the sergeant, who had by this time picked out Joe from the guests, "we had an accident with these handcuffs, and the lock doesn't work. As they are needed for immediate service, will you take a look at them?"

Joe took a look at them and said that the job would require him to fire up the forge and would take about two hours.

"Will it? Then will you begin at once, blacksmith?" said the sergeant, "as it's on his Majesty's service. And if my men can lend a hand anywhere, they'll make themselves useful." With that, he called to his men, who came trooping into the kitchen one after another and piled their guns in a corner and then stood around, as soldiers do.

I was beginning to understand that the handcuffs were not meant for me, and that the appearance of the military in our house had so far been more important than the missing pie, so I was able to collect a little more of my scattered wits.

"What time is it?" said the sergeant to Mr. Pumblechook.

"It's just half-past two."

"That's not so bad," said the sergeant, reflecting; "even if I was forced to wait here two hours, that'll do. How far might you say you are from the marshes? Not more than a mile, I bet?"

"Just a mile," said Mrs. Joe.

"That'll do. We'll begin to close in on them about dusk."

"Convicts, sergeant?" asked Mr. Wopsle, in a matter-of-course way.

"Ay!" returned the sergeant, "Two. We're pretty sure they are out on the marshes still, and they won't try to escape them before sunset. Anybody here seen two such men?"

Everybody confidently said no, except me. Nobody thought of asking me.

"Well!" said the sergeant, "they'll find themselves trapped in a circle sooner than they count on."

Joe had changed out of his Sunday suit and put his work clothes and leather apron on, and went into the forge. The soldiers helped Joe get the fire going and then he began to hammer and clink and we all looked on.

The excitement of the upcoming chase was infectious, and even made my sister generous. She poured a pitcher of beer from the cask for the soldiers, and invited the sergeant to have a glass of brandy. But Mr. Pumblechook said, sharply, "Give him wine, Mum. I'll bet there's no tar in that" so, the sergeant thanked him and said that since he preferred his drink without tar, he would have some wine instead. When it was given to him, he drank his Majesty's health and Compliments of the Season, and drank it all in one mouthful and smacked his lips.

"Good stuff, eh, sergeant?" said Mr. Pumblechook.

"I'll tell you something," returned the sergeant; "I'd bet that wine was provided by you."

Mr. Pumblechook, with a conceited sort of laugh, said, "Ay, ay? Why?"

"Because," returned the sergeant, clapping him on the shoulder, "you're a man that knows what's what."

"Do you think so?" said Mr. Pumblechook, with the same laugh. "Have another glass!"

"With you," returned the sergeant. "To your health. May you live a thousand years, and never be a worse judge of men than you are now!"

The sergeant downed his glass again and seemed quite ready for another glass. I noticed that Mr. Pumblechook appeared to forget that the wine was a present for Mrs. Joe, but instead took the credit of handing it out in a gush of festivity. Even I got some. Mr. Pumblechook was so free with the wine that he even took the other bottle and handed that about in the same manner when the first was gone.

As I watched them while they all stood clustering about the forge, I thought what terrible great sport for a dinner party my fugitive friend on the marshes was. They had not enjoyed themselves half so much before the entertainment he provided.

At last, Joe's job was done, and the hammering and roaring fire stopped. As Joe got on his coat, he proposed that some of us should go with the soldiers and see what came of the hunt. Mr. Pumblechook and Mr. Hubble declined, but Mr. Wopsle agreed. Joe and I never would have received permission to go, I am sure, except Mrs. Joe was curious and wanted to know all about it and how it ended. As it was, she merely warned Joe, "If you bring the boy back with his head blown to bits by a musket, don't look to me to put it together again."

Mr. Wopsle, Joe, and I received strict orders from the sergeant to stay in the back, and to speak no word after we reached the marshes.

We passed the wooden finger-post I had seen just that morning, and went straight on to the church and cemetery. There we stopped a few minutes while two or three of the sergeant's men examined the graves and the church porch. They came back again without finding anything. Then we headed out for the open marshes, and Joe picked me up and carried me on his back.

I now wondered with great dread, if we found them, would my particular convict suppose that I had brought the soldiers? He had asked me if I was a deceiving imp, and he had said I should be a fierce young hound if I joined the hunt against him. Would he believe that I was both, and had betrayed him?

It was no use asking myself this question now. There I was, on Joe's back, and there was Joe beneath me, charging ahead like a hunter, and inspiring Mr. Wopsle to keep up with us despite his hard breathing and wheezing. The soldiers were in front of us, extending into a pretty wide line with large spaces between them. We were heading the same way I had that morning. The sun was setting and everything had a watery grey colour to it.

The soldiers were moving on in the direction of the old cannons by the shore, and we were following a little way behind them, when, all of a sudden, we heard a shout. It was a long distance away, but we could tell it was loud. There seemed to be two or more shouts together.

The sergeant and the nearest men had stopped and were speaking under their breath, when Joe and I came up. The sergeant, a decisive man, ordered that the shouts should not be answered, but that our course should be changed, and that his men should head towards it "at the double." So, we slanted to the right towards the sound, and Joe ran away so fast that I had to hold on tight to keep my seat.

Down banks and up banks and splashing through mud, as we came nearer to the shouting it became more and more apparent that it was made by more than one voice. After a while, we had come close enough that we could hear one voice calling "Murder!" and another voice, "Guard!

This way for the runaway convicts!" Then both voices would seem to be stifled in a struggle, and then would break out again.

The sergeant ran in first, and two of his men ran in right behind him. The other soldiers' guns were cocked and aimed when the rest of us caught up.

"Here are both men!" panted the sergeant, struggling at the bottom of a ditch. "Surrender, you two wild beasts!"

Water was splashing, and mud was flying along with foul language, and punches were being thrown, when some more soldiers went down into the ditch to help the sergeant. They dragged out, separately, my convict and the other one. Both were bleeding, panting, swearing, and struggling; but of course I knew them both immediately.

"Mind!" said my convict, wiping blood from his face with his ragged sleeves, and shaking torn hair from his fingers: "I got him! I give him up to you! Keep that in mind!"

"Small detail," said the sergeant; "it won't do you any good, my man, being in the same situation yourself. Handcuffs there!"

"I don't expect it to do me any good," said my convict, with a greedy laugh. "I got him. He knows it. That's enough for me."

The other convict was a mess to look at, and, in addition to the bruised left side of his face I saw that morning, seemed to now be bruised all over. He could not get his breath to speak until they were both separately handcuffed, and he had to lean on a soldier to keep himself from falling over.

"Take notice, guard – he tried to murder me," were his first words.

"Tried to murder him?" said my convict, disdainfully. "Try, and not do it? I captured him, and turned him in; that's what I done. I not only kept him from getting off the marshes, but I dragged him here – dragged him this far on his way back. He's a gentleman, if you please, this villain. Now, the Hulks has got its gentleman again, because of me. Murder him? Not worth my while, when I could make it worse for him and drag him back!"

The other fugitive, who was evidently extremely afraid of his companion, repeated, "He tried to murder me. I should have been a dead man if you had not arrived."

"He lies!" said my convict, with fierce energy. "He's a liar born, and he'll die a liar. Look at his face; ain't it written there? Let him turn those eyes of his on me. I defy him to do it."

The other, with an effort at a scornful smile looked at the soldiers, and looked about at the marshes and at the sky, but certainly did not look at the speaker.

"Do you see him?" pursued my convict. "Do you see what a villain he is? Do you see those groveling and wandering eyes? That's how he looked when we were tried together. He never looked at me."

The other, working his dry lips and turning his eyes restlessly about him far and near, did at last turn them for a moment on the speaker, with the words, "You're not much to look at," and with a half-taunting glance at his bound hands. At that point my convict became so enraged that he tried to rush at him, requiring several soldiers to block him. "Didn't I tell you," said the other convict then, "that he would murder me, if he could?" And anyone could see that he shook with fear.

"Enough of this talk," said the sergeant. "Light those torches."

As one of the soldiers lit some torches, my convict looked around him for the first time, and saw me. I had gotten down from Joe's back on the edge of the ditch when we arrived, and had not moved since. I looked at him eagerly when he looked at me, and slightly moved my hands and shook my head. I had been waiting for him to see me, that I might try to assure him of my innocence. I couldn't tell if he understood my intention, for he gave me a look that I did not understand, and it all passed in a moment.

The soldier soon lighted several torches, took one himself and passed out the others. It had been almost dark before, and now it was quite dark. A few soldiers fired twice into the sky, signaling the hunt was over. We had not gone far when three cannons were fired ahead of us with a sound that seemed to burst something inside my ear. "You are expected on board," said the sergeant to my convict; "they know you are coming. Don't straggle, my man."

The two were kept apart, and each walked surrounded by a separate guard. I had hold of Joe's hand now, and Joe carried one of the torches. Mr. Wopsle had wanted to leave, but Joe was determined to see it through to the end, so we went on with the soldiers. There was a reasonably good path now, mostly on the edge of the river. Our lights warmed the air about us, and the two prisoners seemed rather to like that after being so cold, as they limped along surrounded by soldiers. We could not go fast, because of their lameness; and they were so tired that two or three times we had to halt while they rested.

After an hour or so of this walking, we came to a rough wooden hut by the shore and a landing dock for boats. We went into the hut where there was a smell of tobacco, a bright fire, a gun rack, and a low wooden group of beds capable of holding about a dozen soldiers. The sergeant made some kind of report, and some entry in a book, and then the much-bruised convict was sent off with his guard to go on board first.

My convict never looked at me, except that one time. While we stood in the hut, he stood before the fire looking thoughtfully at it. Suddenly, he turned to the sergeant, and said:

"I wish to say something regarding this escape. It may prevent some people from being under suspicion along with me."

"You can say what you like," returned the sergeant, standing coolly looking at him with his arms folded, "but you have no need to say it here."

"I know, but I want to. A man can't starve; at least I can't. I took some food, up at the village over yonder."

"You mean stole," said the sergeant.

"And I'll tell you where from. From the blacksmith's."

"Halloa!" said the sergeant, staring at Joe.

"Halloa, Pip!" said Joe, staring at me.

"It was some bits of food – that's what it was – and a bit of liquor, and a pie."

"Have you happened to miss a pie, blacksmith?" asked the sergeant.

"My wife did, at the very moment when you came in."

"So," said my convict, turning his eyes on Joe, and without the least glance at me; "so you're the blacksmith, are you? Then I'm sorry to say, I've eaten your pie."

"God knows you're welcome to it – so far as it was ever mine," returned Joe. "We don't know what you have done, but we wouldn't have you starved to death for it, poor miserable fellow-creature. Would us, Pip?"

The convict turned back to looking at the fire. The boat had returned, and his guard were ready, so we followed him to the landing-place made of rough stakes and stones, and saw him put into the boat, which was rowed by a crew of convicts like himself. No one seemed surprised to see him, or glad, or sorry, or spoke a word, except that somebody in the boat growled, as if to dogs, "Give way, you!" which was the signal for the rowers to begin. By the light of the torches, we saw the black Hulk lying out a little way from the mud off the shore, like a wicked Noah's ark. We saw the boat go alongside, and we saw him taken up and disappear. Then, the ends of the torches were flung into the water, hissing as they went out, as if it were all over with him.

Chapter 6

I was very sleepy by this point, so Joe took me on his back again and carried me home. Mr. Wopsle must have had a tiresome journey of it, for he was in such a very bad mood when we got back to the kitchen that I'm sure if he had been allowed to give the sermon at Church he probably would have excommunicated the whole expedition, beginning with Joe and myself. During the journey, he kept sitting down in the wet ground to such an insane extent that when his coat was taken off to be dried at the kitchen fire, even his pants were mud-stained and soaked.

By that time, I was staggering on the kitchen floor like a little drunkard, due to having been set upon my feet after having fallen asleep on Joe's shoulders for the walk back home. As my senses returned (with the aid of a heavy thump between my shoulders from my sister, and her healing words "Yah! Was there ever such a boy as this!"), I found Joe telling them about the convict's confession, and all the visitors were suggesting different ways by which he could have got into the pantry.

Mr. Pumblechook theorized, after carefully surveying the kitchen, that the convict had first got up on the roof of the forge and had then let himself down the kitchen chimney by a rope made of his bedding cut into strips. And since Mr. Pumblechook was very positive about this, and since he was the only one of the party to own a horse cart, it was agreed that that must be what happened. Mr. Wopsle, cried out "No!" with the feeble voice of a tired man; but, since he had no theory of his own, and no coat on, he was unanimously rejected – and not to mention that his smoking behind, as he stood with his back to the kitchen fire to dry his pants off, was not a sight that inspired confidence.

This was all I heard that night before my sister got hold of me and assisted me up to bed with such a strong hand that I seemed to have fifty boots on, and to be dangling them all against the edges of the stairs. Once in bed and quietly alone, my mind was free to trouble me.

Having any suspicion of the robbery removed from me by the convict's false confession made it much easier to be around my sister, since I wasn't fond of her anyway and no longer had to hide the robbery from her. However, I loved Joe, and regarding him, my inner self was not so easily settled. I wanted to tell Joe the whole truth, especially when I first saw him looking around for his file. Yet, I did not, and for the reason that I thought that if I did, he would think me worse than I was and I would lose his friendship and trust. In a word, I was too cowardly to do what I knew to be right, as I had been too cowardly to avoid doing what I knew to be wrong.

Chapter 7

When I was old enough, I was to be apprenticed to Joe to be a blacksmith, and until I could I was not to be what Mrs. Joe called "Pompeyed," (or, as I translate it, pampered). Therefore, I not only helped around the forge, but also if any neighbor happened to want an extra boy to frighten birds, or pick up stones, or do any odd job, I was picked for the employment. A money-box was kept on the kitchen shelf, into which it was made known by my sister that all my earnings were deposited. I wasn't sure what the money was going to be used for, but I knew I had no hope of any personal gain from what I earned.

When I wasn't working, I went to school. Mr. Wopsle's great-aunt kept an evening school in the village, which I attended to further my education. More accurately, she was a ridiculous old woman of limited abilities who used to go to sleep from six to seven every evening surrounded by young kids who each paid twopence per week for the opportunity of seeing her do it.

Mr. Wopsle's great-aunt, besides running this Educational Institution, also had – in the same room – a little general shop. She had no idea what stock she had, or what the price of anything in it was; but there was a little greasy notebook she kept in a drawer which served as a Catalogue of Prices, and with this book Biddy ran the store. Biddy was Mr. Wopsle's great-aunt's granddaughter; I confess I'm quite unable to figure out how she was related to Mr. Wopsle. She was an orphan like myself, and about my age; and, like me, had been brought up by hand. Her hair always needed brushing, her hands always needed washing, and her shoes always needed mending. However, this description is for week-days only; on Sundays she went to church very well put together and detailed.

More by the help of Biddy than of Mr. Wopsle's great-aunt, I struggled through the alphabet as if it had been a bramble-bush, getting considerably scratched by every letter. After that, I studied those thieves, the nine numbers, who seemed every evening to do something new to disguise themselves and baffle me. But, at last I began to read, write, and do math at the most basic level.

One night I was sitting in the chimney-corner with my slate, spending great effort to write a letter to Joe. I think it must have been a year after our hunt upon the marshes, for it was a long time after and was winter again, so I must have been about eight years old. With an alphabet on the hearth at my feet for reference, I worked for an hour or two to print and smear this note:

"MI DEER JO i OPE U R KR WITE WELL i OPE i SHAL SON B HABELL 4 2 TEEDGE U JO AN THEN WE SHORL B SO GLODD AN WEN i M PRENGTD 2 U JO WOT LARX AN BLEVE ME INF XN PIP."

There was no need for my communicating with Joe by letter, since he sat beside me and we were alone. But, I delivered this written communication (slate and all) with my own hand, and Joe received it as a miracle.

"I say, Pip, old chap!" cried Joe, opening his blue eyes wide, "what a scholar you are! Ain't you?"

"I should like to be," said I, glancing at the slate as he held it, with a doubt that my writing looked rather hilly.

"Why, here's a J," said Joe, "and a O as good as any! Here's a J and a O, Pip, and a J-O, Joe."

I had never heard Joe read aloud to any greater extent than this one word, and I had observed at church last Sunday when I accidentally held our prayer-book upside down that it seemed to suit him quite as well as if it had been right side up. Wanting to find out whether in teaching Joe I should have to start at the beginning, I said, "Ah! But read the rest, Joe."

"The rest, eh, Pip?" said Joe, looking at it with a slowly searching eye, "One, two, three. Why, here's three Js, and three Os, and three J-O, Joes in it, Pip!"

I leaned over Joe and, with the aid of my finger, read him the whole letter.

"Astonishing!" said Joe, when I had finished. "You ARE a scholar."

Pursuing the subject, I asked: "Did you ever go to school, Joe, when you were as little as me?"

"No, Pip."

"Why not?"

"Well, Pip," said Joe, picking up the fire poker, and settling himself to his usual habit when he was thoughtful, of slowly raking the coals between the lower bars: "I'll tell you. My father, Pip, he were a drinker, and when he was drunk he hammered away at my mother, most unmerciful. It was almost the only hammering he did, except at me. And he hammered me with a vigour only to be equaled by the vigour with which he didn't hammer at his anvil. - You're a-listening and understanding, Pip?"

"Yes, Joe."

"'Consequently, my mother and me we ran away from my father, several times; and then my mother she'd go out to work, and she'd say, "Joe, now, please God, you shall have some schooling, child," and she'd put me to school. But my father were that good in his heart that he couldn't bear to be without us. So, he'd come and make such a noise at the doors of the houses where my mother and I was that they used to be obligated to give us up to him. And then he took us home and hammered us. Which, you see, Pip," said Joe, pausing in his meditative raking of the fire and looking at me, "were a drawback on my learning."

"Certainly, poor Joe!"

“However, my father didn't make objections to my going to work; so I went to work at my present job, which were his too, if he would have done it. And I worked tolerable hard, I assure you, Pip. In time I were able to provide for him, and I did till he died in a purple-leptic fit. And it were my intentions to have had put on his tombstone that ‘Whatsumever the failings on his part, remember reader, he were that good in his heart’."

Joe recited this phrase with such obvious pride and carefulness that I asked him if he had made it himself.

"I made it," said Joe, "my own self. It was like striking out a horseshoe complete, in a single blow. I never was so much surprised in all my life – couldn't credit my own head. As I was saying, Pip, it were my intentions to have had it carved on his tombstone; but poetry costs money, and it were not done. All the money that could be spared were needed for my mother. She were in poor health, and quite broke. She followed soon after, poor soul, and her share of peace come round at last." Joe's blue eyes turned a little watery.

"It was lonesome then," said Joe, "living here alone, and I got acquainted with your sister. Now, Pip;" Joe looked firmly at me, as if he knew I was not going to agree with him; "your sister is a fine figure of a woman."

I could not help looking at the fire in an obvious state of doubt.

"Whatever family opinions, or whatever the world's opinions on that subject may be, Pip, your sister is," Joe tapped the top bar with the poker after every word following, "a – fine – figure – of – a – woman!"

I could think of nothing better to say than "I am glad you think so, Joe."

"So am I," returned Joe, “When I got acquainted with your sister, it were the talk how she was bringing you up by hand. Very kind of her too, all the folks said, and I said, along with all the folks. When I offered to marry your sister, I said to her, 'And bring the poor little child. God bless the poor little child,' I said to your sister, 'there's room for him at the forge!'"

I broke out crying and begging pardon, and hugged Joe round the neck, who dropped the poker to hug me, and to say, "Ever the best of friends, ain't us, Pip? Don't cry, old chap!"

When this little interruption was over, Joe resumed:

"Well, you see, Pip, and here we are! Now, when you take me in hand in my learning, Pip (and I tell you beforehand that I'm awful dull, most awful dull), Mrs. Joe mustn't see too much of what we're up to. It must be done, as I may say, on the sly. And why on the sly? I'll tell you why, Pip."

He had picked up the poker again; without which, I doubt if he could have proceeded in his explanation.

"Your sister is given to government."

"Given to government, Joe?" I was startled, for I had some vague idea (and I am afraid I must add, hope) that Joe had divorced her and given her to the Treasury.

"Given to government," said Joe. "Which I mean to say, the governing of you and myself."

"Oh!"

"And she's not in favor of having scholars on the premises," Joe continued, "and in partickler would not be in favor of my being a scholar, for fear as I might rise. Like a sort or rebel, don't you see?"

I was going to reply with a question, and had got as far as "Why--" when Joe stopped me.

"Wait a moment. I know what you're a-going to say, Pip! I don't deny that your sister does drop down heavy on us, like when she's on the Rampage, Pip. So, why don't I rise? That were your question when I broke it off, right Pip?"

"Yes, Joe."

"Well," said Joe, "I want to say very serious to you, old chap – I see so much of my poor mother in her, of a woman drudging and slaving and breaking her honest heart and never getting no peace in her mortal days, that I'm dead afeerd of going wrong in the way of not doing what's right by a woman, and I'd far rather of the two go wrong the other way, and be a little ill-convenienced myself. I wish it was only me that got put out, Pip; I wish there wasn't no Tickler for you, old chap; I wish I could take it all on myself; but this is how it is, Pip, and I hope you'll overlook shortcomings."

Young as I was, I believe that I had a new admiration of Joe from that night. We were equals still; but, afterwards at quiet times when I sat looking at Joe, I knew that I was looking up to him in my heart.

"However," said Joe, rising to replenish the fire; "It's about eight o'clock, and she's not come home yet! I hope Uncle Pumblechook's horse hasn't slipped on a piece of ice, and gone down."

Mrs. Joe made occasional trips with Uncle Pumblechook on market-days, to assist him in buying such household goods as required a woman's judgment, since he was a bachelor. This was market-day, and Mrs. Joe was out on one of these trips.

Joe made the fire and swept the hearth, and then we went to the door to listen for Mr. Pumblechook's horse cart. We soon heard the sound of the mare's iron shoes upon the ground, as she came along at a much quicker trot than usual. We stirred up the fire that they might see a bright window, and took a final look around the kitchen to make sure nothing was out of place. They drove up, wrapped to the eyes to ward off the bitter cold, and Joe and I went out to help them. We were all soon in the kitchen, bringing so much cold air in with us that it seemed to drive all the heat out of the fire.

"Now," said Mrs. Joe, unwrapping herself with haste and excitement: "if this boy ain't grateful this night, he never will be!"

I tried to look as grateful as any boy possibly could who had no idea why he ought to look that way.

"It's only to be hoped," said my sister, "that he won't be pompeyed. But I have my fears."

"She's not like that, Mum," said Mr. Pumblechook. "She knows better."

She? Joe and I looked at each other, making the motion with our lips and eyebrows.

"She?" said my sister sarcastically, catching Joe in the act. "And she is a she, I suppose? Unless you call Miss Havisham a he. And I doubt if even you'll go so far as that. She wants this boy to go and play at her house. And of course he's going. And he had better play there," said my sister, shaking her head at me, "or I'll work him."

I had heard of Miss Havisham – everybody for miles around had heard of Miss Havisham – as an immensely rich and grim lady who lived in a large and dismal house up town that was barricaded against robbers, and who led a life of seclusion.

"Well, to be sure!" said Joe, astounded. "I wonder how she come to know Pip!"

"Noodle!" cried my sister. "Who said she knew him?"

"I believe," Joe politely hinted, "that somebody here mentioned that she wanted him to go and play there...?"

My sister retorted, "Isn't it just barely possible that Uncle Pumblechook may be a tenant of hers, and that he may sometimes go there to pay his rent? And couldn't she then ask Uncle Pumblechook if he knew of a boy to go and play there? And couldn't Uncle Pumblechook, being always considerate and thoughtful for us – though you may not think it, Joseph," in a tone of the deepest reproach, as if he were the worst of nephews, "then mention this boy, standing prancing here" - which I swear I was not doing - "that I have for ever been a slave to?"

"Well put!" cried Uncle Pumblechook. "Good indeed! Now Joseph, you know the case."

"No, Joseph," said my sister, still in a reproachful manner, "you do not yet. For you do not know that Uncle Pumblechook, knowing that for anything we can tell this boy's fortune may be made by his going to Miss Havisham's, has offered to take him into town tonight in his own horse cart, and to keep him tonight, and to take him with his own hands to Miss Havisham's tomorrow morning. And Lord-a-mercy me!" cried my sister, casting off her bonnet in sudden desperation, "here I stand talking to two idiots, with Uncle Pumblechook waiting, and the mare catching cold at the door, and the boy grimed with dirt from the hair of his head to the sole of his foot!"

With that, she pounced on me, like an eagle on a lamb, and my face was squeezed into wooden bowls in sinks, and my head was put under taps of water, and I was soaped, and kneaded, and toweled, and thumped until I really was quite overwhelmed.

I was put into the stiffest, tightest, and most uncomfortable suit I had. I was then handed over to Mr. Pumblechook, who formally received me as if he were the Sheriff, and said to me the speech that I knew he had been dying to make all along: "Boy, be forever grateful to all friends, but especially unto them which brought you up by hand!"

"Good-bye, Joe!"

"God bless you, Pip, old chap!"

Up in the horse cart I went. I could see the stars twinkling, but they shed no light on the questions of why on earth I was going to play at Miss Havisham's, and what on earth I was expected to play at.

Chapter 8

I arrived at Mr. Pumblechook's house in the market area of town and had been sent straight to bed in an attic with a sloping roof, which was so low in the corner where the bed was that I swear the roof tiles were within a foot of my eyebrows.

In the morning, Mr. Pumblechook's premises struck me as peppercorny and starchy, as the premises of a seed seller should be. I noticed that Mr. Pumblechook appeared to conduct his business by looking across the street at the saddler, who appeared to transact his business by keeping his eye on the coach-maker, who appeared to get on in life by putting his hands in his pockets and watching the baker, who folded his arms and stared at the grocer, who stood at his door and yawned at the chemist. The watch-maker, intently leaning over a little desk with a magnifying glass at his eye, seemed to be the only person in the market area whose job engaged his attention.

Mr. Pumblechook and I had breakfast at eight o'clock in the parlour behind his shop, while his employee had his in the shop. Mr. Pumblechook was wretched company. Besides giving me as much crumb as possible in combination with as little butter, and putting so much warm water into my milk that it would have been better to have just left the milk out altogether, his conversation consisted of nothing but math. On my politely bidding him Good Morning, he said, pompously, "Seven times nine, boy?" And how should I be able to answer, harassed in that way, in a strange place, on an empty stomach! I was hungry, but before I had swallowed a morsel, he began a running sum that lasted all through the breakfast. "And seven?"

"And four?"

"And eight?"

"And six?"

"And two?"

"And ten?"

And so on. And after each figure was answered, it was as much as I could do to get another bite before the next came; while he sat at his ease guessing nothing, and gorging himself on bacon and hot roll.

For these reasons I was very glad when ten o'clock came and we left for Miss Havisham's; though I was not at all at ease regarding what I was to do there. Within a quarter of an hour we came to Miss Havisham's house, which was made of old brick and looked dismal. Some of the windows had been walled up; of those that remained, all the lower ones were rustily barred. There was a court-yard in front, and that was barred with a gate; so, we had to wait, after ringing the bell, until someone should come to open it. While we waited at the gate, I peeped in (even then Mr. Pumblechook said, "And fourteen?" but I pretended not to hear him), and saw that at the side of the house there was a large brewery. No brewing was going on in it, and none seemed to have gone on for a long time.

A window was raised in the house, and a clear voice demanded "What name?" To which my conductor replied, "Pumblechook." The voice returned, "Quite right," and the window was shut again, and a young lady opened a side door and came across the court-yard, with keys in her hand.

"This," said Mr. Pumblechook, "is Pip."

"This is Pip, is it?" returned the young lady, who was very pretty and seemed very proud; "come in, boy."

Mr. Pumblechook started to come in, too, when she stopped him with the gate.

"Oh!" she said. "Did you wish to see Miss Havisham?"

"If Miss Havisham wished to see me," returned Mr. Pumblechook, uncomfortably.

"Ah!" said the girl; "but you see, she doesn't."

She said it so finally, and in such an undiscussible way, that Mr. Pumblechook, though his dignity was ruffled, could not protest. But he eyed me severely – as if I had done anything to him! – and departed, saying reproachfully: "Boy! Let your behavior here be a credit to those that brought you up by hand!" I wouldn't have been surprised if he had come back to exclaim through the gate, "And sixteen?" but he didn't.

The young lady locked the gate, and we went across the court-yard. It was paved and clean, but grass was growing in every crack. A fork in the path led to the brewery buildings which were all empty and no longer used.

She saw me looking at it, and she said, "Better not try to brew beer there now, or it would turn out sour, boy; don't you think so?"

"It looks like it, miss," said I, in a shy way.

"Not that anybody wants to try," she added, "for that's all done with, and the place will stand as silent as it is til it falls. As for beer, there's enough of it in the cellars already to drown the Manor House."

"Is that the name of this house, miss?"

"One of its names, boy."

"It has more than one, then, miss?"

"One more. Its other name was Satis; which is Greek, or Latin, or Hebrew, or all three – all the same to me – for 'Enough'."

"Enough House," said I; "that's a curious name, miss."

"Yes," she replied; "but it meant more than it said. It meant that whoever had this house could want nothing else. They must have been easily satisfied in those days. But don't loiter, boy."

Though she called me "boy" so often, and with a carelessness that was far from nice, she was about my own age. She seemed much older than I, of course, being a girl, and was beautiful and self-possessed; and she was as scornful of me as if she had been twenty-one and a queen.

We went into the house by the side door she had come out of – the big front entrance had two chains across it outside – and the first thing I noticed was that the passages were all dark, and that she had left a candle burning there. She picked it up, and we went through more passages and up a staircase, and still it was all dark, and only the candle lighted us.

At last we came to the closed door of a room, and she said, "Go in."

I answered, more in shyness than politeness, "After you, miss."

To this, she returned, "Don't be ridiculous, boy; I'm not going in", and scornfully walked away, and – what was worse – took the candle with her.

Standing in the dark hallway alone was very uncomfortable, and I was half afraid. However, I did the only thing I could do and I knocked at the door, and was told from within to enter. I entered and found myself in a pretty large room, well lighted with wax candles. No glimpse of daylight was to be seen in it. It was a dressing-room, as I supposed from the furniture, though much of it was of types and uses then unknown to me. But prominent in it was a draped table with a large gilded mirror, and that I could tell at first sight was a fine lady's dressing-table.

In an arm-chair, with an elbow resting on that table and her head leaning on that hand, sat the strangest lady I have ever seen, or shall ever see.

She was dressed in rich materials – satins, lace, and silks – all of white. Her shoes were white. And she had a long white veil hanging from her hair, and she had bridal flowers in her hair, but her hair was white. Some bright jewels sparkled on her neck and on her hands, and some other jewels lay sparkling on the table. Dresses, less splendid than the dress she wore, and half-packed trunks, were scattered about. She had not quite finished dressing, for she had only one shoe on – the other was on the table near her hand – her veil was half arranged, her watch and chain were not put on, and some lace for her dress lay with those trinkets, and with her handkerchief, and gloves, and some flowers, and a prayer-book, all confusedly heaped about the mirror.

But, I saw that everything within my view which was supposed to be white, had been white long ago, and had lost its luster, and was faded and yellow now. I saw that the bride within the bridal dress had withered like the dress, and like the flowers, and had no brightness left but the brightness of her sunken eyes. I saw that the dress had been put upon the rounded figure of a young woman, and that the figure upon which it now hung loose, had shrunk to skin and bone. Once, I had been taken to see some ghastly wax statue at the Fair, and another time I had been taken to see a skeleton that had been dug out of a vault under the church pavement. Now, waxwork and skeleton were combined and seemed to have dark eyes that moved and looked at me. I would have cried out in fright, if I could.

"Who is it?" said the lady at the table.

"Pip, ma'am."

"Pip?"

"Mr. Pumblechook's boy, ma'am. Come... to play."

"Come nearer; let me look at you. Come close."

Avoiding her eyes, I saw that her watch had stopped at twenty minutes to nine, and that a clock in the room had stopped at twenty minutes to nine, too.

"Look at me," said Miss Havisham. "You are not afraid of a woman who has never seen the sun since you were born?"

I regret to say that I was not afraid of telling the enormous lie in the answer "No."

"Do you know what I touch here?" she said, laying her hands, one upon the other, on her left side.

"Yes, ma'am, your heart."

"Broken!"

She said the word with an eager look, and with strong emphasis, and with a weird smile that had a kind of boast in it.

"I am tired," said Miss Havisham. "I want diversion, and I'm sick of men and women. Now, play."

I think it would be agreed by all that she could hardly have directed an unfortunate boy to do anything in the whole world more difficult under those circumstances.

"I sometimes have sick fancies," she went on, "and I have a sick fancy that I want to see some play. There, there!" with an impatient movement of the fingers of her right hand; "play, play, play!"

For a moment, with the fear of my sister's working me going through my mind, I had a desperate idea of going around the room pretending to be Mr. Pumblechook's horse cart. But, I felt myself so unable to perform that I gave the idea up, and stood looking at Miss Havisham in what I suppose she took for a stubborn manner, since she said, after we had taken a good look at each other, "Are you sullen and obstinate?"

"No, ma'am, I am very sorry for you, and very sorry I can't play just now. If you complain about me I shall get into trouble with my sister, so I would play if I could; but it's so new here, and so strange, and so fine – and melancholy--." I stopped, fearing I might say too much, or had already said it, and we took another look at each other.

Before she spoke again, she turned her eyes from me and looked at the dress she wore, and at the dressing-table, and finally at herself in the mirror.

"So new to him," she muttered, "so old to me; so strange to him, so familiar to me; so melancholy to both of us! Call Estella."

As she was still looking at the reflection of herself, I thought she was still talking to herself, and kept quiet.

"Call Estella," she repeated, flashing a look at me. "You can do that. Call Estella. At the door."

To stand in the dark and mysterious hallway of an unknown house bellowing 'Estella!' to a scornful young lady who was neither visible nor answering was almost as bad as being ordered to play. But, she answered at last, and her light came along the dark hallway like a star.

Miss Havisham beckoned her to come close, took up a jewel from the table, and tried its effect upon her fair young bosom and against her pretty brown hair. "Your own, one day, my dear, and you will use it well. Let me see you play cards with this boy."

"With this boy? Why, he is a common labouring-boy!"

I thought I overheard Miss Havisham answer – only it seemed so unlikely - "Well? You can break his heart."

Estella turned to me and said, with the greatest disdain, "What do you play, boy?"

"Nothing but beggar my neighbour, miss."

"Beggar him," said Miss Havisham to Estella. So, we sat down to cards.

It was then I began to understand that everything in the room had stopped, like the watch and the clock, a long time ago. I noticed that Miss Havisham put down the jewel exactly on the spot from which she had picked it up. As Estella dealt the cards, I glanced at the dressing-table again and saw that the shoe upon it, once white and now yellow, had never been worn. I glanced down at Miss Havisham's foot from which the shoe was missing, and saw that the silk stocking on it, once white, was now yellow and worn ragged.

So she sat, corpse-like, as we played at cards; the frillings and trimmings on her bridal dress looking like ancient wispy paper. She looked as if the natural light of day would have struck her to dust.

"He calls the knaves, Jacks, this boy!" said Estella scornfully, before our first game was finished. "And what coarse hands he has! And what thick boots!"

I had never thought of being ashamed of my hands before, but her contempt for me was so strong that it became infectious, and I caught it.

She won the game, and I dealt. I misdealt, naturally, when I knew she was waiting for me to make a mistake, and she declared that I was a stupid, clumsy labouring-boy.

"You say nothing of her," remarked Miss Havisham to me, as she looked on. "She says many bad things of you, but you say nothing of her. What do you think of her?"

"I don't like to say," I stammered.

"Tell me in my ear," said Miss Havisham quietly, bending down.

"I think she is very proud," I replied, in a whisper.

"Anything else?"

"I think she is very pretty."

"Anything else?"

"I think she is very insulting."

"Anything else?"

"I think I'd like to go home."

"And never see her again, though she is so pretty?"

"I am not sure about that, but I should like to go home now."

"You shall go soon," said Miss Havisham, aloud. "Play the game out."

I played the game to an end with Estella, and she beggared me. She threw the cards down on the table when she had won them all, as if she despised them for having been won from me.

"When shall I have you here again?" said Miss Havisham. "Let me think."

I was beginning to remind her that today was Wednesday, when she stopped me with an impatient movement of the fingers of her right hand.

"There, there! I know nothing of days of the week; I know nothing of weeks of the year. Come again after six days. You hear?"

"Yes, ma'am."

"Estella, take him down. Let him have something to eat, and let him roam and look about while he eats. Go, Pip."

I followed the candle down, as I had followed the candle up, and she placed it where I had first seen it when we entered the house. Until she opened that entrance I had assumed, without thinking about it, that it must be night-time. The rush of the daylight quite surprised me, and made me feel as if I had been in the candlelight of the strange room many hours.

"You are to wait in the courtyard, boy," said Estella; and disappeared and closed the door.

I took the opportunity of being alone there to look at my coarse hands and my common boots. They had never troubled me before, but they troubled me now. I determined to ask Joe why he had ever taught me to call those picture-cards Jacks, which ought to be called knaves. I wished Joe had been more genteelly brought up, and then I should have been, too.

She came back, with some bread and meat and a little mug of beer. She put the mug down on the stones of the yard, and gave me the bread and meat without looking at me, as if I were a disgraced dog. I was so humiliated, hurt, spurned, offended, angry, sorry – I cannot find the right name for the feeling – that tears came to my eyes. The moment they sprang there, Estella looked at me with a quick delight as having been the cause of them. This gave me the power to keep them back and to look at her. So, she gave a contemptuous toss of her hair and left me.

When she was gone, I looked around for a place to hide my face in, and got behind one of the gates in the brewery-lane, and leaned my sleeve and forehead against the wall there and cried.

In the little world in which children have their existence, there is nothing so strongly perceived and felt as injustice. It may be only small injustice, but the child is small, and its world is small. I had known, from the time when I could speak, that my sister was unjust to me. I was positive that her bringing me up by hand gave her no right to bring me up by jerks. Through all my punishments and disgraces I had kept this belief, and, from my thinking about it so much in a solitary way, it led me to become morally timid and very sensitive.

I got rid of my injured feelings for the time by crying them out, and then I smoothed my face with my sleeve and came out from behind the gate. The bread and meat were acceptable, and the beer was warming and tingling, and I was soon in a better mood to look around the premises.

It was definitely a deserted place. There were no horses in the stable, no pigs in the sty, no malt in the store-house, no smells of beer in the vat. In a side yard there were many empty casks strewn about. Behind the furthest end of the brewery was an overgrown garden with pathways around and through it.

I returned to the courtyard, and I soon saw Estella approaching with the keys to let me out, and that helped me feel a bit better. She would have a good reason for looking down on me, I thought, if she saw me hurt still; and I didn't want her to have that reason.

She gave me a triumphant glance in walking by me, as if she were thrilled that my hands were so coarse and my boots were so thick, and she opened the gate, and stood holding it. I was walking out without looking at her, when she touched me with a taunting hand.

"Why don't you cry?"

"Because I don't want to."

"Yes you do," said she. "You have been crying till you are half blind, and you are near crying again now."

She laughed contemptuously, pushed me out, and locked the gate behind me. I went straight to Mr. Pumblechook's, and was very relieved to find him not at home. So, leaving word with his employee on what day I was wanted at Miss Havisham's again, I set off on the four-mile walk to our forge. I pondered, as I went along, on all I had seen, and felt deeply that I was a common labouring-boy; that my hands were coarse; that my boots were thick; that I had fallen into a terrible habit of calling knaves Jacks; that I was much more ignorant than I had considered myself last night, and generally that I was in a low-lived bad way.

Chapter 9

When I reached home, my sister was very curious to know all about Miss Havisham's, and asked many questions. And I soon found myself getting heavily pushed around and having my face shamefully shoved against the kitchen wall because my answers were too short.

I felt convinced that if I described Miss Havisham's as I had seen it, I would not be understood. Not only that, but I felt convinced that Miss Havisham herself would not be understood; and I believed that it would be rude to discuss her as she really was (let alone Miss Estella) in front of Mrs. Joe. So, I said as little as I could, and had my face shoved against the kitchen wall as a result.

The worst of it was that bullying old Pumblechook, who had a devouring curiosity to know all I had seen and heard. He rode his cart to our house at tea-time to have all the details out of me. The mere sight of the wretch, with his fishy eyes and open mouth full of math, made me more determined to say as little as possible.

"Well, boy," Mr. Pumblechook began, as soon as he was seated in the chair of honour by the fire. "How did you get on up town?"

I answered, "Pretty well, sir," and my sister shook her fist at me.

"Pretty well?" Mr. Pumblechook repeated. "Pretty well is no answer. Tell us what you mean by pretty well, boy?"

I thought about it for some time, and then answered as if I had discovered a new idea, "I mean, pretty well."

My sister with an exclamation of impatience was going to attack me – I had no hope of defense since Joe was busy in the forge, but Mr. Pumblechook stopped her with "No! Don't lose your temper. Leave this lad to me, ma'am." Mr. Pumblechook then turned me towards him, as if he were going to cut my hair, and said: "First (to get our thoughts in order): Forty-three pence?"

I thought of the consequences of replying "Four Hundred Pounds," and decided they would not be good, so I said as near the right answer as I could – which was about eightpence off. Mr. Pumblechook then put me through my pence-table from "twelve pence make one shilling," up to "forty pence make three and fourpence,"

"Now boy! What is Miss Havisham like?" Mr. Pumblechook began again, folding his arms tight on his chest.

"Very tall and dark," I told him.

"Is she, uncle?" asked my sister.

Mr. Pumblechook winked agreement to her; from which I at once knew that he had never seen Miss Havisham, for she was nothing like that.

"Good!" said Mr. Pumblechook conceitedly. ("This is the way to have him! We are beginning to get somewhere, Mum.")

"I am sure, uncle," returned Mrs. Joe, "I wish you had him always; you know so well how to deal with him."

"Now, boy! What was she doing, when you went in today?" asked Mr. Pumblechook.

"She was sitting," I answered, "in a black velvet coach."

Mr. Pumblechook and Mrs. Joe stared at one another – as they well might – and both repeated, "In a black velvet coach?"

"Yes," said I. "And Miss Estella – that's her niece, I think – handed her in cake and wine at the coach-window, on a gold plate. And we all had cake and wine on gold plates. And I got up behind the coach to eat mine, because she told me to."

"Was anybody else there?" asked Mr. Pumblechook.

"Four dogs," said I.

"Large or small?"

"Immense," said I. "And they fought for veal cutlets out of a silver basket."

Mr. Pumblechook and Mrs. Joe stared at one another again, in utter amazement. I was a reckless witness under their torture, and would have told them anything.

"Where on earth was this coach?" asked my sister.

"In Miss Havisham's room." They stared again. "But there weren't any horses to it." I added this saving detail, right before I had the idea of adding four richly decorated horses to the carriage.

"Can this be possible, uncle?" asked Mrs. Joe. "What can the boy mean?"

"I'll tell you, Mum," said Mr. Pumblechook. "My opinion is, it's a sedan-chair. She's flighty, you know, quite flighty enough to pass her days in a sedan-chair."

"Did you ever see her in it, uncle?" asked Mrs. Joe.

"How could I," he returned, forced to tell the truth, "when I've never seen her in my life!"

"Goodness, uncle! And yet you have spoken to her?"

"Why, don't you know," said Mr. Pumblechook, testily, "that when I have been there I have been taken up to the outside of her door, and the door has stood ajar, and she has spoke to me that way. Anyway, the boy went there to play. What did you play at, boy?"

"We played with flags," I said. (I have to mention that I'm still amazed when I remember the lies I told on this occasion.)

"Flags!" echoed my sister.

"Yes," said I. "Estella waved a blue flag, and I waved a red one, and Miss Havisham waved one sprinkled all over with little gold stars, out at the coach-window. And then we all waved our swords and shouted 'Hurrah!'"

"Swords!" repeated my sister. "Where did you get swords from?"

"Out of a cupboard," said I. "And I saw pistols in it – and jam – and pills. And there was no daylight in the room, but it was all lighted up with candles."

"That's true, Mum," said Mr. Pumblechook, with a grave nod. "For that much I've seen myself." And then they both stared at me.

If they had asked me any more questions I would have surely given myself away, for I was even then on the brink of mentioning that there was a hot air balloon in the courtyard and a bear roaming around the brewery. However, they were so pre-occupied in discussing the marvels I had already told them that they stopped asking me any more questions. They were still discussing the subject when Joe came in from his work to have a cup of tea, to whom my sister shared my pretended experiences.

Now, when I saw Joe open his blue eyes wide and roll them all around the kitchen in amazement, I felt guilty; but only towards him, not in the least towards the other two. To Joe, and Joe only, I considered myself a young monster, while they all sat debating what results would come to me from meeting Miss Havisham and having her approval. They had no doubt that Miss Havisham would "do something" for me. My sister thought I (meaning her) would get "property." Mr. Pumblechook believed there would be a handsome reward for binding me apprentice to some genteel trade – say, the corn and seed trade, for instance. Joe disgraced himself in their eyes for offering the suggestion that I might only be given one of the dogs who had fought for the veal-cutlets. "If your fool's head doesn't have a better opinion than that," said my sister, "and you've got any work to do, you had better go and do it." So he went.

After Mr. Pumblechook had driven off, and when my sister was washing up, I snuck into the forge to see Joe, and remained by him until he had finished for the night. Then I said, "Before the fire goes out, Joe, I'd like to tell you something."

"OK" said Joe, taking a seat on his shoeing-stool near the forge. "Tell me then. What is it, Pip?"

"Joe," said I, "you remember all that about Miss Havisham's?"

"Remember?" said Joe. "I believe you! Wonderful!"

"It's a terrible thing, Joe; it ain't true."

"What are you talking about, Pip?" cried Joe, falling back in the greatest amazement. "You don't mean to say it's--"

"Yes I do; it's lies, Joe."

"But not all of it? Why, you mean that there was no black velvet coach?"

I stood shaking my head.

"But at least there was dogs, Pip? Come, Pip," said Joe, persuasively, "if there weren't no veal-cutlets, at least there was dogs?"

"No, Joe."

"A dog?" said Joe. "A puppy at least?"

"No, Joe, there was nothing at all of the kind."

Joe contemplated me in dismay. "Pip, old chap! This won't do, old fellow! I say! Where do you expect to go to?"

"It's terrible, Joe; ain't it?"

"Terrible?" cried Joe. "Awful! What possessed you to lie?"

"I don't know, Joe," I replied, sitting down in the ashes at his feet, hanging my head; "but I wish you hadn't taught me to call Knaves at cards Jacks; and I wish my boots weren't so thick, nor my hands so coarse."

And then I told Joe that I felt very miserable, and that I hadn't been able to explain myself to Mrs. Joe and Pumblechook who were so rude to me, and that there had been a beautiful young lady at Miss Havisham's who was dreadfully proud, and that she had said I was common, and that I knew I was common, and that I wished I was not common, and that the lies had come of it somehow, though I didn't know how.

"There's one thing you may be sure of, Pip," said Joe, after some thought, "namely, that lies is lies. However they come, they didn't ought to come, and they come from the father of lies. Don't you tell no more of 'em, Pip. That ain't the way to get out of being common, old chap. And as to being common, I don't agree at all. You are uncommon in some things. You're uncommon small. Also, you're a uncommon scholar."

"No, I'm ignorant and backward, Joe."

"Why, how about that great letter you wrote last night! Wrote in print even! I've seen letters from gentlefolks that I'll swear weren't wrote in print," said Joe.

"I have learnt next to nothing, Joe. You think much of me. It's only that."

"Well, Pip," said Joe, "be it so or be it not, you must be a common scholar before you can be a uncommon one. The king upon his throne can't sit and write his acts of Parliament in print without having begun with the alphabet. And begun at A too, and worked his way to Z. And I know what a thing that is to do, though I can't say I've exactly done it myself."

There was some hope in this piece of wisdom, and it rather encouraged me.

"Lookee here, Pip, at what is said to you by a true friend. If you can't get to be uncommon through going straight, you'll never get to do it through going crooked."

"You are not angry with me, Joe?"

"No, old chap. I'd advise discussing them in your prayers tonight. That's all, old chap, and don't never do it no more."

When I got up to my little room and said my prayers, I did not forget Joe's recommendation. And yet, I thought long after I laid down, how common Estella would consider Joe, a mere blacksmith: how thick his boots, and how coarse his hands. I thought how Joe and my sister were then sitting in the kitchen, and how Miss Havisham and Estella never sat in a kitchen, but were far above the level of such common doings. I fell asleep remembering what I "used to do" when I was at Miss Havisham's, as though I had been there weeks or months instead of hours; and as though it were quite an old subject, instead of one that had happened only that day.

That was a memorable day, for it made great changes in me. But, it's the same with any life. Imagine one particular day removed from it, and think how different that life's course would have been without it. Pause, you who read this, and think for a moment of the long chain of iron or gold that would have never bound you, but for the creation of the first link on one memorable day.

Chapter 10

The idea occurred to me a morning or two later after my discussion with Joe that the best first step I could take to making myself uncommon was to have Biddy teach me everything she knew. I certainly wasn't going to improve myself by just attending class, as I had been.

The Educational Course provided by Mr. Wopsle's great-aunt may be summarized as follows. The students ate apples and put straws down each other's backs until Mr. Wopsle's great-aunt collected her energies and made a random tottering swing at one of them with a birch-rod. After this, the pupils formed in line and passed a single ragged book from student to student. The book had an alphabet in it, some numbers, and a little spelling – that is to say, it had had those things in it at one time in the past. As soon as this book began to circulate around the students, Mr. Wopsle's great-aunt fell asleep in her chair. The pupils then entered into a competition among themselves with the goal of seeing who could stomp on whose toes the hardest. This mental exercise lasted until Biddy made a rush at them and distributed three tattered Bibles, more illegibly printed than any books I have since seen, and having various insect specimens smashed between their pages. Biddy gave out the number of a page, and then we all read aloud what we could – or what we couldn't – in an awful chorus, with Biddy leading in a high-pitched monotonous voice, and none of us having the least notion or care of what we were reading about. When this horrible noise had lasted awhile, it mechanically awoke Mr. Wopsle's great-aunt, who would stagger at the nearest boy and pull his ears. This meant the Course had ended for the evening and we emerged outside with shrieks of intellectual victory.

I believed it would take a long time to become uncommon under those circumstances. When I saw Biddy next at Mr. Wopsle's great-aunt's, I mentioned to her that I had a particular reason for wishing to improve my prospects in life, and that I would be very grateful if she would teach me what she knew. Biddy, who was always helpful, immediately said she would, and began to carry out her promise within five minutes. She shared some information from her little catalogue of prices, and lent me, to copy at home, a large old English letter 'D' which she had imitated from the heading of some newspaper, and which I thought was the design for a belt buckle until she told me what it was.

There was a public house in the village called the Three Jolly Bargemen, and Joe liked to smoke his pipe there sometimes, as he was on this particular day. I had received strict orders from my sister to go and get him that evening, on my way home from school, and bring him home, or else. So, of course I went.

I entered the common room at the end of the establishment where there was a bright large kitchen fire. Joe was smoking his pipe with Mr. Wopsle and a stranger, seated at a table with a few benches around it. Joe greeted me as usual with "Halloa, Pip, old chap!" and the moment he said that, the stranger turned his head and looked at me.

He was a secret-looking man whom I had never seen before. One of his eyes was half shut up, as if he were taking aim at something with an invisible gun. He had a pipe in his mouth and, looking hard at me, nodded greeting. So, I nodded to him, and sat down next to Joe on the opposite bench.

"You was saying," said the strange man, turning to Joe, "that you was a blacksmith."

"Yes," said Joe.

"What'll you drink, Mr. Gargery? At my expense?"

"Well," said Joe, "to tell you the truth, I ain't much in the habit of drinking at anybody's expense but my own."

"Habit? No," returned the stranger, "but every so often. Come! Put a name to it, Mr. Gargery."

"I wouldn't wish to be bad company," said Joe. "Rum."

"Rum," repeated the stranger. "And what will the other gentleman have?"

"Rum," said Mr. Wopsle.

"Three Rums!" cried the stranger, calling to the landlord. "Glasses round!"

The stranger, with a comfortable kind of grunt over his pipe, put his legs up on the bench that he had to himself. He wore a broad-brimmed traveller's hat, and under it a handkerchief tied over his head like a cap, so that he showed no hair. As he looked at the fire, I thought I saw a cunning expression, followed by a half-laugh, come into his face.

"I am not familiar with this country, gentlemen, but it seems solitary towards the river. Do you find any tramps or vagrants of any sort out there?"

"No," said Joe; "none but a runaway convict now and then. And we don't find them, easy. Eh, Mr. Wopsle?"

Mr. Wopsle, with a remembrance of old discomfort, agreed.

"It seems you have been out after such people?" asked the stranger.

"Once," returned Joe. "Not that we wanted to capture them, you understand. We went out as lookers on; me, and Mr. Wopsle, and Pip. Didn't us, Pip?"

"Yes, Joe."

The stranger looked at me again – still cocking his eye, as if he were taking aim at me with his invisible gun – and said, "He's a likely young parcel of bones, that one. What is it you call him?"

"Pip," said Joe.

"First name Pip?"

"No, not christened Pip."

"Last name Pip?"

"No," said Joe, "it's a kind of family name that he gave himself when a toddler, and is called by."

"Son of yours?"

"Well," said Joe, thoughtfully – not, of course, that it was necessary to think about the question, but because it was customary at the Jolly Bargemen to consider deeply about everything that was discussed over pipes; "well – no. No, he ain't."

"Nephew?" said the strange man.

"Well," said Joe, "he is not – no, not to deceive you, he is not – my nephew."

"What the Blue Blazes is he?" asked the stranger, a little unnecessarily strong, I thought.

Mr. Wopsle answered, as one who knew all about relationships, and explained the ties between me and Joe.

All the while, the strange man looked at nobody but me, and looked at me with his half-closed eye as if he were determined to take a shot at me, and bring me down. But he said nothing after offering his Blue Blazes comment, until the glasses of rum-and-water were brought; and then he made his shot, and a most extraordinary shot it was.

He stirred his rum-and-water pointedly at me, and he tasted his rum-and-water pointedly at me. And he stirred it and he tasted it; not with the spoon that was brought to him, but with a blacksmith file.

He did this so that nobody but I saw the file; and when he had done it he wiped the file and put it in a breast-pocket. I knew it was Joe's file, and I knew that he knew my convict, the moment I saw it. I sat gazing at him, spell-bound. But he now reclined on his bench, taking very little notice of me, and talking mainly about turnips.

The rum-and-water finished, Joe got up to go, and took me by the hand.

"Stop half a moment, Mr. Gargery," said the strange man. "I think I've got a bright new shilling somewhere in my pocket, and if I do, the boy shall have it."

He took it out from a handful of small change, folded it in some crumpled paper, and gave it to me. "Yours!" said he. "Mind! It's your own."

I thanked him, staring at him longer than was polite, and holding tight to Joe. He bid Joe and Mr. Wopsle good-night as we got up from the table.

On the way home I was speechless by this turning up of my old misdeed and old acquaintance, and could think of nothing else.

My sister was in a decent temper when we arrived in the kitchen, and Joe was encouraged by that unusual situation to tell her about the bright shilling. "A bad one, I'll bet," said Mrs. Joe triumphantly, "or he wouldn't have given it to the boy! Let's look at it."

I took it out of the paper, and it proved to be a good one. "But what's this?" said Mrs. Joe, throwing down the shilling and grabbing the paper it was wrapped in. "Two One-Pound notes?"

Nothing less than two fat one-pound notes were in her hand. Joe got his hat on again, and ran with them to the Jolly Bargemen to return them to their owner. While he was gone, I sat down on my usual stool by the kitchen fire, feeling pretty sure that the man would not be there.

Soon, Joe came back, saying that the man was gone, but that he had left word at the Three Jolly Bargemen for the man. Then my sister sealed them up in a piece of paper, and put them under some dried rose-leaves in a tea-pot in the parlour. There they remained, a nightmare to me, many a night and day.

I slept badly that night, thinking of the strange man taking aim at me with his invisible gun, and of the coarse and common thing it was to be on secret terms of conspiracy with convicts. I was haunted by the file too. I had a feeling that when I least expected it, the file would reappear. I managed to fall asleep by thinking of Miss Havisham's, next Wednesday; and in my sleep I saw the file coming at me out of a door, without seeing who held it, and I screamed myself awake.

Chapter 11

At the agreed-to time I returned to Miss Havisham's, and Estella met me at the gate after I rang. She locked it after letting me in, as she had done before, and again led me into the dark side entrance passage where her candle stood. She took no notice of me until she had the candle in her hand, when she looked over her shoulder, disdainfully saying, "You are to come this way today," and took me to a different part of the house.

The dark passage was a long one, and at the end of it she stopped, and put her candle down and opened a door to the outside. Here, I found myself in a small paved court-yard, at the opposite side of which was a separate house that looked as if it had once belonged to the manager of the derelict brewery. There was a clock in the outer wall of this house. Like the clock in Miss Havisham's room and like Miss Havisham's watch, it had stopped at twenty minutes to nine.

We crossed the courtyard and went in at the wide open door of this dwelling, which opened to a hallway that led into a gloomy room with a low ceiling. There were some guests standing in the room, and Estella said to me as she joined them, "You are to go and stand there, boy, till you are wanted."

"There", being by the window, I walked over to it, and stood "there," in a very uncomfortable state of mind, looking outside into a miserable corner of the neglected garden.

I figured out that my arrival had stopped the conversation in the room, and that its other occupants were looking at me. I could see nothing of the room except the reflected shining of the fire in the window I was looking out of, but my joints all stiffened with the feeling that I was being closely inspected.

There were three ladies in the room and one gentleman. Before I had been standing at the window five minutes, they somehow conveyed to me that they were all toadies and humbugs, but that each one of them pretended not to know that the others were toadies and humbugs; because if they did, that would have made themselves out to be toadies and humbugs, too.

They all seemed to be waiting for somebody, and the most talkative of the ladies had to repress a yawn. This lady, whose name I later discovered was Camilla, very much reminded me of my sister, with the difference that she was older and more bland looking.

"Poor dear soul!" said this lady, with a tone quite like my sister's. "Matthew is nobody's enemy but his own!"

"It would be much better to be somebody else's enemy," said the gentleman; "far more natural."

"Cousin Raymond," observed another lady, "we are to love our neighbours."

"Sarah Pocket," returned Cousin Raymond, "if a man is not his own neighbour, who is?"

Miss Pocket laughed, and Camilla laughed and said (stifling another yawn), "The idea!"

The third lady, who had not spoken yet, said gravely and emphatically, "Very true!"

"Poor soul!" Camilla presently went on (I knew they had all been looking at me in the meantime), "he is so very strange! Would anyone believe that when Tom's wife died, Matthew actually could not be made to see the importance of her children being all dressed up splendidly for their mourning? 'Good Lord!' says he, 'Camilla, what does it matter so long as the poor little things are in black?' So like Matthew! The idea!"

"Matthew has good points in him," said Cousin Raymond; "Heaven forbid I should deny there are good points in him; but he never had, and he never will have, any sense of the proprieties."

"You know I had to be firm," said Camilla, "I said, 'It WILL NOT DO, for the credit of the family.' I told him that, without all the accessories, the family would be disgraced. I upset my stomach, crying about it from breakfast till dinner. And at last he flung out in his violent way, and said, with a capital D, 'Then Do as you like.' Thank goodness it will always make me feel good to know that I instantly went out in a pouring rain and bought the things."

"Matthew paid for them, didn't he?" asked Estella.

"It's not the question, my dear child, who paid for them," returned Camilla. "I went out and got them. And I shall often think of that with peace, when I wake up in the night."

The ringing of a distant bell interrupted the conversation and caused Estella to say to me, "Now, boy!" On my turning around, they all looked at me with the utmost contempt, and, as I went out to the hall with Estella, I heard Sarah Pocket say, "Well I am sure! What next!" and Camilla add, with annoyance, "Was there ever such a fancy! The i-de-a!"

We left that house, crossed the courtyard, and returned to the long dark passageway of the main house. As we were going with our candle along the dark hallway, Estella stopped all of a sudden, and, turning around, said in her taunting manner with her face quite close to mine:

"Well?"

"Well, miss?" I answered, almost falling over her.

She stood looking at me, and, of course, I stood looking at her.

"Am I pretty?"

"Yes; I think you are very pretty."

"Am I insulting?"

"Not so much as last time," said I.

"Not so much?"

"No."

She turned red when she asked the last question, and when I answered it, she slapped my face quite hard.

"Now?" said she. "You coarse little monster, what do you think of me now?"

"I shall not tell you."

"Because you are going to tell up-stairs, is that it?"

"No," said I, "that's not it."

"Why don't you cry again, you little wretch?"

"Because I'll never cry for you again," said I. Which was, I suppose, the single biggest lie I've ever told, for I was inwardly crying for her then, and I know what pain she cost me later.

We went on our way up-stairs after this episode, and, as we were going up, we met a gentleman groping his way down in the darkness.

"Whom have we here?" asked the gentleman, stopping and looking at me.

"A boy," said Estella.

He was a burly man, with a very large head and correspondingly large hands. He took my chin in his large hand and turned up my face to have a look at me by the light of the candle. He was bald on the top of his head, and had wild, bushy black eyebrows. His eyes were disagreeably sharp and suspicious. He had a large watch chain, and strong black dots where his beard and whiskers would have been if he had let them grow.

"Boy of the neighborhood, eh?" said he.

"Yes, sir," said I.

"Why are you here?"

"Miss Havisham sent for me, sir," I explained.

"Well! I have a pretty large experience with boys, and you're a bad set of fellows," said he, biting the side of his big forefinger as he frowned at me, "you behave yourself!" With those words, he released me – which I was glad of, for his hand smelled like scented soap.

We were soon in Miss Havisham's room, where she and everything else were just as I had left them. Estella left me standing near the door, and I stood there until Miss Havisham looked at me from the dressing-table.

"So," she said, without being startled or surprised; "the days have worn away, have they?"

"Yes, ma'am. Today is--"

"There, there, there!" with that impatient movement of her fingers. "I don't want to know. Are you ready to play?"

I had to answer in some confusion, "I don't think I am, ma'am."

"Since this house strikes you old and grave, boy," said Miss Havisham, impatiently, "and you are unwilling to play, are you willing to work?"

I could answer this question much easier than I had been able to answer the other question, and I said I was quite willing.

"Then, go into that opposite room," said she, pointing at the door behind me with her withered hand, "and wait there till I come."

I turned around behind me on the landing between the rooms and entered the one she indicated. From that room, too, the daylight was completely excluded, and the air was stale. A fire had been recently made in the damp old-fashioned grate, and it seemed to want to go out more than it wanted to burn. A few candles on the high chimneypiece faintly lighted the chamber. It was spacious, and I bet had once been beautiful, but everything in it was covered with dust and mold and was falling apart. The most prominent object in the room was a long table with a tablecloth spread on it, as if a feast was being prepared when the house and the clocks had all stopped together. A centerpiece of some kind was in the middle of this table; it was so heavily covered with cobwebs that I couldn't tell what it was.

As I looked along the table out of which the centerpiece seemed to grow, I saw speckled-legged spiders running in and out of that object as if something of the greatest importance had just happened in the spider community. I heard mice, too, rattling behind the wall panels, as if the same topic were important to them as well. But, the black beetles on the hearth didn't seem to notice or care about this activity, and went about their business ponderously.

I was fascinated by these crawling things as I watched them from a distance, when Miss Havisham laid a hand on my shoulder. In her other hand she had a crutch on which she leaned, and she looked like the Witch of the place.

"This," said she, pointing to the long table with her stick, "is where I will be laid when I am dead. They shall come and look at me here."

With some vague idea that she might get up on the table right then and there and die at once, I shrank under her touch.

"What do you think that is?" she asked me, pointing with her stick at the centerpiece; "that, where those cobwebs are?"

"I can't guess what it is, ma'am."

"It's a great bridal cake. Mine!"

She glaringly looked all around the room, and then said, "Come, come, come! Walk me, walk me!"

I deduced from this that the work I had to do was to walk Miss Havisham round and round the room. So, I started at once, and she leaned on my shoulder, and we went away at an impatient speed, which led me to believe that we were going fast because her thoughts went fast. After a while she said, "Call Estella!" so I stepped out the door and roared her name as I had done previously. When her light appeared, I returned to Miss Havisham, and we started away again going round and round the room.

I would have felt nervous enough if it was only Estella that had come to be a spectator of our parade; but, since she brought with her the three ladies and the gentleman whom I had seen in the detached house, I didn't know what to do. In my politeness I would have stopped; but, Miss Havisham twitched my shoulder with her hand and we marched on, with me feeling guilty that they would think it was all my doing that we ignored them.

"Dear Miss Havisham," said Miss Sarah Pocket. "How well you look!"

"I do not," returned Miss Havisham. "I am yellow skin and bone." Camilla brightened when Miss Pocket was met with this retort, and she murmured, "Poor dear soul! Certainly not to be expected to look well, poor thing. The idea!"

"And how are you?" said Miss Havisham to Camilla, as we walked on around the table.

"Thank you, Miss Havisham," she returned, "I am as well as can be expected."

"Why, what's the matter with you?" asked Miss Havisham, with exceeding sharpness.

"Nothing worth mentioning," replied Camilla. "I don't wish to make a display of my feelings, but I have been dwelling on you anxiously quite a bit in recent nights."

"Then don't dwell on me," retorted Miss Havisham.

"Very easily said!" remarked Camilla, repressing a sob, "Raymond is a witness what medication I have to take at night when I think of those that I love. If I could be less affectionate and sensitive then I'm sure I'd have an iron set of nerves. But, to not be concerned about you – The idea!" Here, a burst of tears.

The Raymond she referred to I assumed was the gentleman with her, and he was apparently Mr. Camilla, her husband. He came to her rescue at this point, and said in a comforting and complimentary voice, "Camilla, my dear, it is well known that your tender feelings are gradually undermining your health to the extent of making one of your legs shorter than the other."

"I am not aware," observed the third lady whose voice I had heard but once, "that to think of any person is to somehow own them, my dear."

Miss Sarah Pocket, whom I now saw to be a little dry brown old woman, with a small face that might have been made of walnut shells, and a large mouth like a cat's without the whiskers, agreed with this claim by saying, "No, indeed, my dear. Hem!"

"Oh, yes, yes!" cried Camilla, "It's all very true! It's a weakness to be so affectionate, but I can't help it. No doubt my health would be much better if it was otherwise, still I wouldn't change the way I am if I could. It's the cause of much suffering for me, but it's a consolation to know I possess it, when I wake up in the night." Here another burst of feeling and tears.

Miss Havisham and I had never stopped all this time, but kept going round and round the room.

"And then there's Matthew!" said Camilla. "Never visiting any family, never coming here to see how Miss Havisham is! I have had to lay on the sofa for hours, insensible, on account of Matthew's strange conduct, and nobody has thanked me."

"Well, my dear," added Miss Sarah Pocket, "the question to put to yourself is, who did you expect to thank you?"

"Without expecting any thanks, or anything like it," resumed Camilla, "I have remained in that state, hours and hours, and Raymond is a witness to it."

When this Matthew was mentioned, Miss Havisham stopped me and herself, and stood looking at the speaker. This change had a great influence in bringing Camilla to be suddenly healed and sensible.

"Matthew will come and see me at last," said Miss Havisham, sternly, "when I am laid on that table. That will be his place – there," striking the table with her stick, "at my head! And yours will be there! And your husband's there! And Sarah Pocket's there! And Georgiana's there! Now you all know where to take your seats when you come to feast on me. And now leave!"

At the mention of each name, she had struck the table with her stick in a new place. She now said, "Walk me, walk me!" and we went on again.

"I suppose there's nothing to be done," exclaimed Camilla, "but comply and depart. It's so good to have seen the object of one's love and duty, for even so short a time. I will think of it with a melancholy satisfaction when I wake up in the night. I wish Matthew could have that comfort, but he's defiant. I am determined not to make a display of my feelings, but it's very hard to be told one wants to feast on one's relations, and then be told to go. The bare idea!"

Mr. Camilla interposed and escorted the ever-feeling Mrs. Camilla out. Sarah Pocket and Georgiana (who I had figured out by now was the third lady) quietly fought for who should remain last; but, Sarah was too cunning to be outdone, and ambled around Georgiana with artful slipperiness, so that Georgiana had to say her goodbye's first. The only remaining toady, Sarah Pocket then said, "Bless you, Miss Havisham dear!" and with a smile of forgiving pity for the weaknesses of the other guests that had left.

While Estella was away seeing them off downstairs, Miss Havisham still walked with her hand on my shoulder, more slowly, and then stopped before the fire, and said, after muttering and looking at it several seconds:

"This is my birthday, Pip."

I was going to wish her many happy returns, when she lifted her stick.

"I don't want it to be spoken of. I don't let those who were here just now, or anyone, speak of it. They come here on the day, but they dare not mention it."

Of course, I made no further effort to mention it as well.

"On this day of the year, long before you were born, this heap of decay was brought here," pointing with her crutch at the pile of cobwebs that used to be a cake on the table, "It, and I, have worn away together. The mice have gnawed at it, and sharper teeth than that have gnawed at me."

She held the head of her stick against her heart as she stood looking at the table; she in her once white dress, all yellow and withered; the once white cloth, all yellow and withered; everything around, looking like it would crumble under a touch.

"When the ruin is complete," said she, with a ghastly look, "and when they lay me dead, in my bride's dress on the bride's table – which shall be done, and will finish the curse upon him – so much the better if it is done on this day!"

She stood looking at the table as if she stood looking at her own figure lying there. I remained quiet. Estella returned, and she too remained quiet. It seemed to me that we continued this way for a long time. Eventually, snapping in a moment out of her distraught state, Miss Havisham said, "Let me see you two play cards; why have you not begun?" With that, we returned to her room across the hall and sat down like last time. I was beggared, like last time; and again, Miss Havisham watched us all the while, directing my attention to Estella's beauty, and made me notice it the more by trying her jewels on Estella's breast and hair.

Estella, for her part, also treated me like before; except that she did not even condescend to speak to me. When we had played about 6 games, a day was decided for my return, and I was taken down into the yard to be fed in the previous dog-like manner as last time. There, too, I was again left to wander around as I liked.

I went to the ruined garden and walked all around it. It was quite a wilderness, and I eventually found myself in the dismal corner of it that I had seen from the window of the detached house. I looked in that house through another window and found myself, to my great surprise, exchanging a stare with a pale young gentleman with red eyelids and light hair.

This pale young gentleman quickly disappeared, and re-appeared beside me. He had been studying at his books when I had found myself staring at him.

"Halloa, young fellow!" said he.

Halloa being a general greeting which I had usually observed to be best answered by repeating, I said, "Halloa!" politely omitting the 'young fellow' part.

"Who let you in?" said he.

"Miss Estella."

"Who gave you permission to prowl about?"

"Miss Estella."

"Come and fight," said the pale young gentleman.

What could I do but follow him? I have often asked myself the question since, but, what else could I do? His manner was so final and I was so surprised, that I followed where he led, as if I had been under a spell.

"Stop a minute, though," he said, turning around to face me before we had gone very far. "I should give you a reason for fighting. Here it is!" In a most irritating manner he instantly slapped his hands together, daintily flung one of his legs up behind him, pulled my hair, slapped his hands again, dipped his head, and butted it into my stomach.

This insult was particularly disagreeable after having just eaten bread and meat. I therefore hit out at him and was going to hit out again, when he said, "Aha! Would you?" and he began dancing backwards and forwards, and skipping from leg to leg in a manner quite unlike any I had seen in my limited experience while I looked helplessly at him. "Laws of the game!" said he, "Regular rules! Come to the ground, and go through the preliminaries!"

I was secretly afraid of him when I saw how dexterous he was, but, I felt convinced that his light head of hair had no business being rammed into my stomach. Therefore, I followed him without a word to a small corner of the garden formed by two walls and blocked off by some rubbish. He asked me if I was satisfied with the area, and on my replying Yes, he politely excused himself for a moment, and quickly returned with a bottle of water and a sponge dipped in vinegar. "Available for both," he said, placing them against the wall. And then he started to take off not only his jacket and waistcoat, but his shirt too, in a manner that was all at once light-hearted, businesslike, and bloodthirsty.

Although he did not look very healthy – having pimples on his face – his dreadful preparations quite appalled me. I judged him to be about my own age, but he was much taller, though his elbows, knees, and wrists were considerably more developed than his muscles.

My courage failed me when I saw him assume a fighting stance and studying me as if he were carefully choosing his target. I've never been so surprised in my life as I was when I made the first blow and saw him lying on his back, looking up at me with a bloody nose.

But, he was on his feet immediately and, after sponging himself off, began squaring again. The second greatest surprise I have ever had in my life was seeing him on his back again, looking up at me out of a black eye.

I greatly respected his spirit. He seemed to have no strength, and he never once hit me hard, and I always knocked him down. But, he would be up again in a moment, sponging himself or drinking out of the water-bottle, and then would come at me with a zeal that made me believe he really was going to get me at last. He got heavily bruised, for I am sorry to admit that the more I hit him, the harder I hit him; but, he came up again and again and again, until at last he had a bad fall, hitting the back of his head against the wall. Even after that, he got up and turned around confusedly a few times, not knowing where I was; but finally fell to his knees and tossed the sponge up in the air, at the same time panting, "That means you have won."

He seemed so brave and innocent, that although I had not suggested the fight, I felt no satisfaction in my victory. I got dressed, and I said, "Can I help you?" and he said "No, thankee," and I said "Good afternoon," and he said "Same to you."

When I got into the court-yard, I found Estella waiting with the gate keys. But, she neither asked me where I had been, nor why I had kept her waiting; and there was a bright red flush on her face, as though something had happened to delight her. Instead of going straight to the gate, too, she stepped back into the house side entry, and beckoned me.

"Come here! You may kiss me, if you like."

I kissed her cheek as she turned it to me. I think I would have gone through a great deal to kiss her cheek. But, I felt that the kiss was given to the coarse common boy as a piece of money might have been, and that it was worth nothing, and she still behaved as cold as ice to me.

After a day of Miss Havisham's birthday visitors, and with playing cards, and with the fight, my stay had lasted so long that when I neared home, I could see Joe's furnace was flinging a path of light across the road against a black night sky.

Chapter 12

I was very nervous regarding the pale young gentleman. The more I thought of the fight, and remembered him on his back in various stages of defeat, the more certain it appeared that I would be punished. I didn't know the penalties I would face, but it was still clear to me that village boys could not go prowling about the country and beating up the young gentlemen of England without earning severe punishment. I didn't tell Joe or anybody else about it, and for several days I even kept close to home and looked out the kitchen door with great caution before going on an errand, in case the officers of the County Jail should pounce on me. I had cut my knuckles on his teeth, and in my imagination I devised incredible ways of explaining away that evidence when I would be brought before the Judges. The closer it got to the day I had to return, the more nervous I became.

However, go to Miss Havisham's I must, and go I did. And behold! there were no consequences from the fight. It was not mentioned in any way, and no pale young gentleman was to be seen there. I explored the garden, and even looked in at the windows of the detached house, but all was still and lifeless. Only in the corner where the combat had taken place could I find any evidence of the young gentleman's existence. There were traces of his blood there, and I covered them with garden-mold.

On arriving in the usual manner to that landing between Miss Havisham's room and that other room in which the long table was laid out, I saw a wheelchair. It had been placed there since my last visit, and I now entered on a regular job of pushing Miss Havisham in this chair (when she was tired of walking with her hand on my shoulder) around her own room, across the landing, and around the bridal feast room. Over and over again we would make these journeys, and sometimes they would last as long as three hours at a time. I mention these journeys as being numerous, because it was decided that I should return every other day at noon for these purposes, and because I am now going to sum up a period of several years.

As we began to be more used to each other, Miss Havisham talked more to me and asked me such questions as what had I learnt and what was I going to be? I told her I was going to be apprenticed to Joe; and I informed her of my wanting to know more and learn as much as I could, in the hope that she might offer some help. But, she did not; on the contrary, she seemed to prefer my being ignorant. Neither did she ever give me any money – or anything but my daily dinner – nor ever stipulate that I should be paid for my services.

Estella was always about, and always let me in and out, but never told me I could kiss her again. Sometimes, she would coldly tolerate me; sometimes she would be condescending to me; sometimes she would be quite friendly with me; sometimes she would explosively say that she hated me. Miss Havisham would often ask me in a whisper, or when we were alone, "Does she grow prettier and prettier, Pip?" And when I said Yes (for indeed, she was), Miss Havisham would seem to enjoy it greedily. Also, when we played at cards Miss Havisham would look on, relishing Estella's moods, whatever they happened to be. And sometimes, when her moods were so many and so contradictory of each other that I was puzzled what to say or do, Miss Havisham would hug her with excessive emotion, murmuring something in her ear that sounded like "Break their hearts my pride and hope, break their hearts and have no mercy!"

What could I become with these surroundings? How could my character help but be influenced by them? Should anybody be surprised if my thoughts were dazed, as my eyes were, when I came out into the daylight from those dark rooms?

That initial desire to not discuss Miss Havisham and Estella grew with time. I didn't confide in anybody but Biddy; but, I told poor Biddy everything. Why it came natural to me to open up to her, and why she was deeply concerned about everything I told her, I didn't know then, though I think I know now.

Meanwhile, councils were held in the kitchen at home over my prospects with Miss Havisham and what she would "do" for me. That ass, Pumblechook, used to often come over for these discussions with my sister; and I really do believe (even now, with less guilt than I should feel), that if I could have taken the linchpin out of his horse cart, I would have done it.

The miserable man could not discuss my prospects without having me standing in front of him, and he would drag me up from my stool (usually by the collar) where I was quiet in a corner and would begin by saying, "Now, Mum, here is this boy! Here is this boy which you brought up by hand. Hold up your head, boy, and be forever grateful unto them which did so. Now, Mum, about this boy!" Then, he and my sister would wildly speculate about what Miss Havisham would do for me. It was all I could do to not burst into tears and pummel Pumblechook all over. In these discussions, my sister spoke to me to only hammer morals into me with every reference; while Pumblechook acted as if he was my disappointed owner; like he was the architect of my fortunes who thought he was wasting his time with a pointless job that would never amount to anything.

Joe had no part in these discussions. But during them, he was often talked at by Mrs. Joe, who suspected he was not in favor of my being taken away from the forge so often to go to Miss Havisham's, as I was old enough now to be apprenticed to Joe. All these discussions ended the same way. All of a sudden, my sister would catch herself in a yawn, and glance at me as if by accident, and would swoop down on me with, "Come! That's enough of you! You get along to bed; you've been enough trouble for one night!" As if I had asked them as a favor to drag me before them and plot my life out.

We went on this way for a long time, and it seemed likely that we would continue, when one day, when I was about twelve, Miss Havisham stopped as she and I were walking, with her leaning on my shoulder; and said with some displeasure:

"You are growing tall, Pip."

She said no more at the time; but, she soon stopped and looked at me again, and after that she was frowning and moody. On the next day when our usual exercise was over and I had returned her to her dressing table, she beckoned me to wait a moment before I left: "Tell me again the name of that blacksmith of yours."

"Joe Gargery, ma'am."

"And he's the master you are to be apprenticed to?"

"Yes, Miss Havisham."

"Well, you had better be apprenticed at once. Do you think Gargery would come here with you, and bring your indentures?"

I replied that I had no doubt he would take it as an honour to be asked.

"Then let him come."

"At any particular time, Miss Havisham?"

"There, there! I know nothing about times. Let him come soon, and come along with you."

When I got home that night and delivered this message for Joe, my sister "went on the Rampage," in a more alarming degree than I'd ever seen. She asked me and Joe whether we supposed she was a doormat under our feet, and how we dared use her like that, and what company we thought she was fit for if she couldn't come with us? When she had spit out a river of such questions, she threw a candlestick at Joe, burst into loud sobbing, got out the dustpan – which was always a very bad sign – put on her coarse apron, and began cleaning up every little thing. Not satisfied with just a dry cleaning, she took a pail and scrub-brush and cleaned us out of house and home, so that Joe and I had to stand shivering in the back-yard. It was ten o'clock at night before we crept inside again, and then she asked Joe why he hadn't just married a Negress Slave? Joe offered no answer, poor fellow, but stood feeling his whiskers and looking sadly at me, as if he thought it really might have been a better idea to have done that.

Chapter 13

Joe decided he needed to dress in his Sunday suit to accompany me to Miss Havisham's. His shirt collar stuck up so far in back that it made the hair on his head there stand up like a tuft of feathers. I felt bad to see him dressed that way, for he looked far better in his working clothes, and he made himself so very uncomfortable entirely on my account.

At breakfast time my sister declared that she was going to town with us, and would wait at Uncle Pumblechook's for us "when we had done with our fine ladies". The forge was shut up for the day, and Joe wrote in chalk upon the door (as he usually did on the very rare occasions when he was not at work) the single word HOUT, with an arrow supposed to be pointing in the direction he had taken.

When we had walked to Pumblechook's, we left my sister there to await our return. As it was almost noon, Joe and I went straight on to Miss Havisham's house. Estella opened the gate as usual, and, the moment she appeared, Joe took his hat off and stood weighing it by the brim in both his hands, as if he had some urgent reason to know its weight to within half a quarter of an ounce.

Estella ignored both of us and led the way that I knew so well. I followed next to her, and Joe came last. When I looked back at Joe in the long passage, he was still weighing his hat with the greatest care.

Estella told me we were both to go in, so I took Joe by his coat-cuff and led him into Miss Havisham's presence. She was seated at her dressing-table, and turned to us immediately.

"Oh!" said she to Joe. "You are the husband of the sister of this boy?"

I could hardly have imagined dear old Joe looking so unlike himself, or so much like some unusual bird, standing there as he was, speechless, with his tuft of feathers ruffled and his mouth open, as if he wanted a worm.

"You are the husband," repeated Miss Havisham, "of the sister of this boy?"

It was quite infuriating, but throughout the interview Joe insisted in talking to me instead of to Miss Havisham.

"As you know, Pip," Joe said in a formal, and a bit argumentative, manner, "I did marry your sister, and I was at the time what you might call a single man."

"Well!" said Miss Havisham. "And you have raised the boy with the intention of taking him for your apprentice; is that so, Mr. Gargery?"

"You know, Pip," replied Joe to me, "as you and me were ever friends, and your apprenticeship were looked forward to between us as being calculated to lead to larks."

"Has the boy," said Miss Havisham, "ever made any objection? Does he like the trade?"

"Which it is well known to yourself, Pip," returned Joe, "that it were the wish of your own heart." (I saw the idea suddenly dawn on him that he could adapt his father's tombstone epitaph to this occasion, before he went on to say) "And there weren't no objection on your part, and Pip it were the great wish of your heart!"

I tried in vain to make him speak to Miss Havisham instead of me. The more I made faces and gestures to him to do it, the more argumentative and polite he persisted in being to me.

"Have you brought his indentures with you?" asked Miss Havisham.

"Well, Pip, you know," replied Joe, as if the question was a little unreasonable, "you yourself see me put 'em in my hat, and therefore you know they are here." He then took them out and gave them to me, not to Miss Havisham. I was ashamed of the dear good fellow when I saw Estella standing at the back of Miss Havisham's chair, and that her eyes laughed mischievously. I took the indentures out of his hand and gave them to Miss Havisham.

"You expected," said Miss Havisham, as she looked them over, "no premium with the boy?"

Joe stood there silently. "Joe!" I urged, "Why don't you answer--"

"Pip," returned Joe, cutting me short as if he were hurt, "which I mean to say that's not a question requiring an answer between yourself and me, and which you know the answer to be No. You know it to be No, Pip, and so why mention it?"

Miss Havisham glanced at him as if she understood what he really was, better than I had thought possible, and picked up a little bag from the table beside her.

"Pip has earned a premium here," she said, "and here it is. There are twenty-five pounds in this bag. Give it to your master, Pip."

As if he were absolutely out of his mind with the wonder of her strange appearance and the strange room, Joe persisted in addressing me.

"This is very generous on your part, Pip," said Joe, "and it is as such received and grateful welcomed, though never looked for; far, nor near, nor nowheres. And now, old chap, may we do our duty! May you and me do our duty, both of us by one and another, and by them which your liberal present – have conveyed – to be – for the satisfaction of mind – of them – as never--" here Joe had lost his path, until he triumphantly rescued himself with the words, "and from myself far be it!" These words had such a convincing sound for him that he said them twice.

"Good-bye, Pip!" said Miss Havisham. "Let them out, Estella."

"Am I to come again, Miss Havisham?" I asked.

"No. Gargery is your master now. Gargery! One word!"

Calling him back as I went out of the door, I heard her say to Joe, in a distinct emphatic voice, "The boy has been a good boy here, and that is his reward. Of course, as an honest man, you will expect no other and no more."

How Joe got out of the room, I have never been able to determine; but, I know that when he did get out he turned to go up-stairs instead of coming down, and wouldn't listen to any directions until I went after him and got ahold of him. In another minute we were outside the gate, and it was locked, and Estella was gone.

When we stood in the daylight alone again, Joe backed up against a wall, and said to me, "Astonishing!" And there he remained, saying "Astonishing" every few moments, so that I began to think his senses were never coming back. Eventually, he extended his remark to "Pip, I do assure you this is as-TONishing!" and so, by degrees, he became himself again and we were able to walk away.

Joe's senses may have been shaken up by the encounter he had just endured, but it seemed to help him devise a plan to soothe Mrs. Joe's wounded pride. I say this because of what took place when we arrived at Pumblechook's, where my sister sat with that detested seedsman in his parlor.

"Well?" cried my sister, addressing us both at once. "And what's happened to you? I wonder you condescend to come back to such poor company as me!"

"Miss Havisham," said Joe, with a fixed look at me, like an effort of remembrance, "made it very particular that we should give her compliments to Mrs. J. Gargery--"

"Much good they'll do me!" observed my sister; but rather gratified too.

"And wishing," pursued Joe, with another fixed look at me, like another effort of remembrance, "that the state of her health were such as would have allowed her to have the pleasure of ladies' company," said Joe. And drew a long breath.

"Well!" cried my sister, with a relieved glance at Mr. Pumblechook. "She might have had the politeness to send that message at first, but it's better late than never. And what did she give young Rantipole here?"

"She give him," said Joe, "nothing."

Mrs. Joe was going to break out, but Joe went on.

"What she give," said Joe, "she give to his friends. 'And by his friends,' were her explanation, 'I mean into the hands of his sister Mrs. J. Gargery.' Them were her words: 'Mrs. J. Gargery.'"

My sister looked at Pumblechook, who nodded at her, as if he had known all about it beforehand.

"And how much have you got?" asked my sister, laughing. Positively laughing!

"What would present company say to ten pounds?" demanded Joe.

"They'd say," returned my sister, curtly, "pretty well. Not too much, but pretty well."

"It's more than that, then," said Joe.

That impostor, Pumblechook, immediately nodded, and said, as he rubbed the arms of his chair: "It's more than that, Mum."

"Why, you don't mean to say--" began my sister.

"Yes I do, Mum," said Pumblechook; "but wait a bit. Go on, Joseph. Good in you! Go on!"

"What would present company say," proceeded Joe, "to twenty pounds?"

"Handsome would be the word," returned my sister.

"Well, then," said Joe, "It's more than twenty pounds."

That hypocrite, Pumblechook, nodded again, and said, with a patronizing laugh, "It's more than that, Mum. Good again! Follow her up, Joseph!"

"Then to make an end of it," said Joe, delightedly handing the bag to my sister; "it's twenty-five pounds."

"It's twenty-five pounds, Mum," echoed that worst of swindlers, Pumblechook, rising to shake hands with her; "and it's no more than your merits, and I wish you joy of the money!"

If the villain had stopped here his case would have been sufficiently awful, but he worsened his guilt by proceeding to take my arm into custody.

"Now you see, Joseph and wife," said Pumblechook, as he held me by the arm above the elbow, "I am one of them that always finishes with what they've begun. This boy was brought up by hand; he must be bound by hand. That's my way. Bound by hand."

"Goodness knows, Uncle Pumblechook," said my sister (clutching the money), "we're deeply beholden to you."

"Never mind me, Mum," returned that diabolical corn-chandler. "A pleasure's a pleasure, all the world over. But this boy, you know; we must have him bound. I said I'd see to it, to tell you the truth."

The Judges were sitting in the Town Hall nearby, and we at once went over to have me bound apprentice to Joe. I say we went over, but really I was pushed over by Pumblechook, exactly as if I had that moment committed a crime. Indeed, it was the general impression of those in Court that I had been caught red-handed, for, as Pumblechook shoved me before him through the crowd, I heard some people say, "What's he done?" and others, "He's a young one too, but looks bad, don't he?" One kind person even gave me a scripture book decorated with a picture of an evil looking young man, titled "TO BE READ IN MY CELL".

The Hall was a weird place, I thought, with higher pews in it than a church – and with people hanging over them watching all that was going on – and with mighty Justices leaning back in chairs with folded arms, or going to sleep, or writing, or reading the newspaper. Here, in a corner, my indentures were signed and authenticated, and I was "bound"; Pumblechook was grasping me by the arm the whole time, as if he had been forced to stop by on our way to the hanging scaffold to have those little preliminaries taken care of.

When we had come out again we went back to Pumblechook's. And there my sister became so excited by the twenty-five pounds that she decided we must have a dinner from that windfall, at the Blue Boar, and that the Hubbles and Mr. Wopsle should accompany us.

It was agreed; and I had a miserable evening. They all asked me from time to time – in short, whenever they had nothing else to do – why I didn't enjoy myself. And what could I possibly do then, but say I was enjoying myself, when in reality I wasn't.

That swindling Pumblechook, glorified as the benefactor of the whole occasion, actually sat at the head of the table; and, when he addressed them on the subject of my being bound apprentice, he placed me standing on a chair beside him, to illustrate his remarks.

My only other remembrances of the great dinner are that they wouldn't let me go to sleep, but whenever they saw me dropping off, they woke me up and told me to enjoy myself. That, and I remember that when I finally got into my little bedroom I was truly wretched, and had a strong conviction that I would never like Joe's trade. I had liked it once, but once was not now.

]

Chapter 14

It is a most miserable thing to feel ashamed of home. Home had never been a very pleasant place for me, because of my sister's temper. But, Joe had made it a worthy place, and I had believed in it. I had believed in the best parlour as a most elegant room; I had believed in the kitchen as the purest of sanctuaries; I had believed in the forge as the glowing road to manhood and independence. But, within a few years, all of this was changed. Now, it was all coarse and common, and I would not have had Miss Havisham and Estella see it for any reason.

Once, I had believed that when I at last rolled up my shirt-sleeves and went into the forge as Joe's apprentice that I would be proud and happy. Now that the reality was here, I only felt that I was covered with common coal dust, and that I had a weight on my mind so heavy that it made the forge's anvil seem like a feather in comparison. There have been times in my life (as in most lives, I suppose) when I felt as if a thick curtain had fallen over all my interests and desires; to shut me out of enjoying life, and instead having to merely just endure it. Never has that curtain dropped so heavy as when my road in life lay stretched out straight before me through the road of apprenticeship to Joe.

How much of my ungracious state of mind was my own fault, how much Miss Havisham's, and how much my sister's, doesn't matter. The change was made in me; for better or worse, the thing was done.

I am glad to know that I never breathed a word of these feelings to Joe while my apprenticeship lasted. It's about the only thing I am glad to know of my behavior regarding that time. I know very well that any good that came from my apprenticeship came from plain contented Joe, and not from restless discontented me.

What I wanted, who can say? How can I say, when I didn't even know? What I dreaded was, that in some unlucky hour, I would be at my grimiest and commonest and would lift up my eyes and see Estella looking in at one of the windows of the forge. I was haunted by the fear that she would sooner or later find me out, with my black face and hands, doing the coarsest part of my work, and would mock me and despise me. Often after dark, I would look towards the dark windows of the forge and would imagine that I saw her face just leaving, and would believe that she had come at last to gloat.

After that, when we went in to supper, the place and the meal would have a more common look than ever, and I would feel more ashamed of home than ever, in my own ungracious heart.

Chapter 15

As I was getting too big for Mr. Wopsle's great-aunt's school, my education under that preposterous female ended. Not, however, until Biddy had taught me everything she knew; from the little catalogue of prices, to a comic song she had once bought for a halfpenny.

Whatever I learned, I tried to pass on to Joe. This statement sounds so nice that I cannot in good conscience let it go unexplained. Really, I wanted to make Joe less ignorant and common; that he might be worthier of my company and less likely for Estella to look down on.

The old cannon mound out on the marshes by the river's shore was our place of study, and a broken slate and a short pencil were our educational tools, to which Joe always added a pipe of tobacco. I never knew Joe to remember anything from one Sunday to the next, or to learn any piece of information from me at all. Yet he would smoke his pipe out there with a far more learned air than anywhere else, as if he considered himself to be advancing immensely. Dear fellow, I hope he did.

It was pleasant and quiet out there, with sailboats on the river. Whenever I saw the ships heading out to sea with their white sails spread, I somehow thought of Miss Havisham and Estella; and whenever the light struck just right on a cloud or a green hill-side, it was just the same. Miss Havisham, Estella, and the strange house and the strange life were somehow tied together in my mind with all things picturesque.

One Sunday when Joe and I were out there, I was laying on the mound, day dreaming of Estella and that other life, until at last I made my mind up to discuss an idea that had been on my mind for a while.

"Joe," said I; "do you think I ought to pay Miss Havisham a visit?"

"Well, Pip," returned Joe, slowly considering. "What for?"

"What for, Joe? What is any visit for?"

"Well, visits can have different purposes. In regard to visiting Miss Havisham, she might think you wanted something – expected something from her."

"Don't you think I might say that I did not, Joe?"

"You might, old chap," said Joe. "And she might believe it. Similarly, she might not."

Joe felt, as I did, that he had made a point there.

"You see, Pip," Joe pursued, "Miss Havisham done the handsome thing by you. When Miss Havisham done the handsome thing by you, she called me back to say to me as that were all."

"Yes, Joe, I heard her."

"ALL," Joe repeated, very emphatically.

"Yes, Joe. I tell you, I heard her."

"Which I mean to say, Pip, it might be that her meaning were – Make an end of it! Me to the North, and you to the South!"

I had thought of that too, and it was very far from comforting to me to find that he had also thought of it, for it seemed to make it more likely.

"But, Joe..."

"Yes, old chap."

"Here I am, getting on in the first year of my apprenticeship, and, since the day of my being bound, I have never thanked Miss Havisham, or asked after her, or shown that I remember her. I was thinking, since we aren't very busy right now, if you would give me a half-holiday tomorrow, I think I would go up-town and make a call on Miss Est - Havisham."

"Which her name," said Joe, gravely, "ain't Estavisham, Pip, unless she's changed it."

"I know, Joe, I know. It was a slip of mine. What do you think of it, Joe?"

In short, Joe thought that if I thought well of it, then he thought well of it. But, he was particular in stipulating that if I were not well received, or if I were not encouraged to repeat my visit, then this experimental trip would be the last. With these conditions I agreed.

Now, Joe had a journeyman in the forge whose name was Orlick. He was a broad-shouldered fellow of great strength, was never in a hurry, and was always slouching wherever he went. He never seemed to come to the forge on purpose, but would slouch in, as if by accident. He lived at a gate-keeper's house out on the marshes. On Sundays he mostly lay all day on the marshes or leaned against barns.

This sullen journeyman did not like me at all. When I was very small and timid he told me that the Devil lived in a dark corner of the forge, and that he knew the fiend very well. Also, that it was necessary to make up the forge fire once every seven years with a live boy, and that I might consider myself fuel for it. When I became Joe's apprentice, Orlick's suspicions were confirmed in his head that I would replace him, so he liked me even less. Not that he ever said or did anything openly showing hostility; I only noticed that he always beat his sparks in my direction.

Orlick was at work the next day when I reminded Joe of my half-holiday. Orlick said, leaning on his hammer, "Now, master! Surely you're not going to favour only one of us. If young Pip has a half-holiday, do as much for Old Orlick." I suppose he was about twenty-five, but he usually spoke of himself as an ancient person.

"Why, what'll you do with a half-holiday, if you get it?" said Joe.

"What'll I do with it? What'll HE do with it? I'll do as much with it as him," said Orlick.

"As for Pip, he's going up-town," said Joe.

"Well then, as for Old Orlick, he's a-going up-town," retorted Orlick. "Two can go up-town. It's not only one that can go up-town."

"Don't lose your temper," said Joe.

"I shall if I like," growled Orlick. "Some people and their up-towning! Now, master! Come. No favouring in this shop."

"OK then, since you do your work as well as most men," said Joe, "let it be a half-holiday for all."

My sister had been standing silent in the yard, within hearing – she was quite a spy and listener – and she instantly looked in at one of the windows.

"Just like you, you fool!" said she to Joe, "giving holidays to lazy idiots like that. You must be a rich man to waste wages that way. I wish I was his master!"

"You'd be everybody's master, if you could," retorted Orlick, with a wicked grin.

("Leave her alone," said Joe.)

"I'm a match for all noodles and all rogues," returned my sister, beginning to work herself into a mighty rage. "And I couldn't be a match for the noodles without being a match for your master, who's the king of the noodles. And I couldn't be a match for the rogues, without being a match for you, who are the worst rogue between here and France!"

"You're a foul shrew, Mother Gargery," growled the journeyman. "If that makes somebody a judge of rogues, you ought to be a good one."

("Leave her alone, will you?" said Joe.)

"What did you say?" cried my sister, beginning to scream. "What did that fellow Orlick say to me, Pip? What did he call me, with my husband standing by? O! O! O!" Each of these exclamations was a shriek, "What was the name he gave me in front of the man who swore to defend me? O! Hold me!"

"Ah-h-h!" growled the journeyman, between his teeth, "I'd hold you, if you was my wife. I'd hold you under the water pump, and choke it out of you."

("I tell you, leave her alone," said Joe.)

"Oh! To hear him!" cried my sister, with a clap of her hands and a scream together – which was her next stage of working herself up. "To hear the names he's giving me! That Orlick! In my own house! Me, a married woman! With my husband standing by! O! O!" Here my sister, after a fit of clapping and screaming, beat her hands upon her bosom and upon her knees, threw her cap off, and pulled her hair down – which were the last stages on her road to frenzy. Being by this time a perfect Fury, she made a dash at the door, which I had fortunately locked.

What could poor Joe do now, after his ignored parenthetical warnings to Orlick, but stand up to his journeyman, and ask him what he meant by interfering between himself and his wife; and further, whether he was man enough to back it up with his fists? Old Orlick felt that the situation required backing it up. So, without even taking off their leather aprons, they went at one another, like two giants. But, there was no man in that neighbourhood that could stand up long against Joe. Orlick, as if he had been no stronger than the pale young gentleman, was very soon on his back among the coal-dust, and in no hurry to come out of it. Then, Joe unlocked the door and picked up my sister, who had fainted at the window (but who had seen the fight first, I think), and carried her into the house and laid her down and tended to her. I went up-stairs to dress myself for my visit up-town.

When I came down again, I found Joe and Orlick sweeping up the forge, without any traces that something had happened, other than a slit in one of Orlick's nostrils. A pot of beer had appeared from the Jolly Bargemen, and they were sharing it by turns in a peaceable manner. This quiet time had a calming and philosophical influence on Joe, who followed me out into the road to say, as a parting observation that might do me good, "On the Rampage, and off the Rampage, Pip – such is Life!"

I went to Miss Havisham's with a whirlwind of different emotions. I passed and repassed the gate many times before I could make up my mind to ring it, but I finally mustered the courage to do so.

Miss Sarah Pocket came to the gate. No Estella.

"How, then? You here again?" said Miss Pocket. "What do you want?"

When I said that I only came to see how Miss Havisham was, Miss Pocket apparently debated in her head about whether or not she should send me away. But, unwilling to make that decision, she let me in, and presently brought back the sharp message that I was to "come up."

Everything was unchanged, and Miss Havisham was alone.

"Well?" said she, fixing her eyes upon me. "I hope you want nothing? You'll get nothing."

"No, indeed, Miss Havisham. I only wanted you to know that I am doing very well in my apprenticeship, and am always much obliged to you."

"There, there!" with the old restless fingers. "Come now and then; come on your birthday. - Ay!" she cried suddenly, turning herself and her chair towards me, "You are looking around for Estella?"

I had, in fact, been looking around for Estella – and I stammered that I hoped she was well.

"Abroad," said Miss Havisham; "educating to become a lady; far out of reach; prettier than ever; admired by all who see her. Do you feel that you have lost her?"

There was such a cruel enjoyment in her saying those last words, and she broke into such a disagreeable laugh, that I was at a loss what to say. She spared me the trouble by dismissing me. When the gate was closed on me by Sarah Pocket, I felt more than ever dissatisfied with my home and with my trade and with everything.

As I was loitering along the market street, looking dejectedly in at the shop windows and thinking what I would buy if I were a gentleman, who should come out of the bookshop but Mr. Wopsle. He was holding a book that he intended to read with his booming theatrical voice to Mr. Pumblechook over tea. He insisted I accompany him to grow his audience, and since I knew it would be miserable at home, and almost any companionship on the road was better than none, I agreed. Therefore, we turned into Pumblechook's shop just as the street was lighting up for evening.

Mr. Wopsle read from the book with dramatic flair, and, of course, every moral lesson and failing in the book was pointed at me. Even after Mr. Wopsle had closed the book, Pumblechook sat staring at me, shaking his head, and saying, "Take warning, boy, take warning!"

It was a very dark night by the time I set out with Mr. Wopsle on the walk home, and there was a heavy mist out. The turnpike lamp was only a blur through this mist, when we came upon a man, slouching under the turnpike house.

"Halloa!" we said, stopping. "Orlick, there?"

"Ah!" he answered, slouching out. "I was waiting a minute, hoping for some company."

"You are late," I remarked.

Orlick naturally answered, "Well? You're late, too."

We all went on together. I asked him presently whether he had been spending his half-holiday up and down town?

"Yes," said he, "all of it. I come in behind you. I didn't see you, but I must have been pretty close behind you. By-the-way, the guns is going again."

"At the Hulks?" said I.

"Ay! There's some of the birds escaped from their cages. The guns have been going since dark, about. You'll hear one presently."

We had not walked much farther when the well-remembered Boom came towards us, deadened by the mist.

"A good night for escaping in," said Orlick. "We'd be puzzled how to bring down a jail-bird tonight."

The subject brought back memories for me, and I thought about it in silence. Orlick, with his hands in his pockets, slouched heavily at my side. It was very dark, very wet, very muddy, and so we splashed our way to the village. The route by which we approached took us past the Three Jolly Bargemen, which we were surprised to find in a state of commotion, since it was now eleven o'clock. Mr. Wopsle dropped in to ask what was the matter, and came running out in a great hurry.

"There's something wrong," said he, without stopping, "up at your place, Pip. Run all!"

"What is it?" I asked, keeping up with him. So did Orlick, at my side.

"I couldn't quite understand. The house seems to have been violently entered when Joe Gargery was out. Supposedly by convicts. Somebody has been attacked and hurt."

We were running too fast for more to be said, and we made no stop until we got into our kitchen. It was full of people; the whole village was there, or in the yard. There was a surgeon, and there was Joe, and there was a group of women, all on the floor in the middle of the kitchen. The bystanders drew back when they saw me, and so I saw my sister – lying alive, but not moving, on the kitchen floor where she had been knocked down by a tremendous blow on the back of her head, dealt by some unknown attacker when her face was turned towards the fire – destined never to be on the Rampage again.

Chapter 16

Joe had been at the Three Jolly Bargemen, smoking his pipe, from a quarter after eight o'clock to a quarter before ten. While he was there, my sister had been seen standing at the kitchen door, and had exchanged Good Night with a farm worker going home. The man was certain as to the time he saw her that it must have been before nine. When Joe came home an hour later, he found her struck down on the floor, and promptly got help.

Nothing had been stolen from any part of the house. Neither was there any sign of struggle in the kitchen. But, there was one remarkable piece of evidence found. She had been struck with something blunt and heavy, on the head and spine. After the blows were dealt, something heavy had been thrown down at her with considerable force, as she lay on her face. And on the ground beside her, when Joe picked her up, was a convict's leg-iron which had been filed off.

Joe, examining this iron with a smith's eye, declared it had not been filed off recently. The soldiers from the prison ship, who were there to help, claimed to know for certain that that particular manacle had not been worn by either of the two convicts who had escaped last night. Further, one of those two was already captured, and had not freed himself of his leg iron.

Knowing what I knew, I had a theory of my own. I believed the iron to be my convict's iron – the iron I had seen and heard him filing at a few years before – but I did not believe he had put it to its latest use. For, I believed somebody else had found it, and to have used it in this cruel case. Possibly Orlick, or maybe the strange man who had shown me the file at the Three Jolly Bargemen.

Now, as for Orlick; he had gone to town exactly as he told us when we met him up at the turnpike. He had been seen around town all evening in several public-houses, and he had come back with myself and Mr. Wopsle. There was no evidence against him, except for the argument that morning; and my sister had quarreled with him, and with everybody else around her, ten thousand times. As to the strange man; if he had come back for his two bank-notes, there could have been no argument about them because my sister was fully prepared to return them. Besides, there had been no struggle; the attacker had come in so silently and quickly that she had been knocked down before she could turn around. That left me out of ideas for who it could have been. But I was positive it was my convict's file, and that somebody had found it wherever he dropped it on the marshes those few years ago.

It was horrible to think that I had provided the weapon, however innocently, but I could hardly think otherwise. I struggled with my conscience, considering and reconsidering whether I should at last tell Joe all the story from that part of my childhood. Every day, for months afterwards, I would decide not to tell him, but then would re-argue the question the next morning. After all that, the decision came down to this: the secret was such an old one now, had become such a part of myself, that it would be now more likely than ever to alienate Joe from me if he believed it. And I had a further dread that he would not believe it, but would lump the secret together with the fabulous dogs and veal-cutlets as a horrible lie. However, I rationalized this decision with myself and decided to tell the full truth if I saw it had a chance of helping discover who the attacker was.

The constables were around the house for a week or two, and did pretty much what I have heard of similar authorities doing in other such cases. They arrested several obviously wrong people, they dreamed up fanciful theories, and kept trying to fit the circumstances to those theories instead of trying to figure out what happened based on the evidence. Also, they had a mysterious manner in how they drank at the Jolly Bargemen that was almost as good as catching the culprit. But not quite, for they never caught the person.

Long after the constables had left, my sister lay very ill in bed. Her sight was damaged, so that she saw objects multiplied and would reach for the wrong image; her hearing was greatly impaired; her memory also; and her speech was unintelligible. When, at last, she recovered enough that she could be helped down-stairs, it was still necessary to keep my slate always by her so she could indicate in writing what she could not indicate in speech. Since she was a bad speller with bad hand writing, and since Joe was a poor reader, complications arose between them which I was always called in to solve. Confusing mutton instead of medicine, the substitution of Tea for Joe, and the baker for bacon, were among the mildest of my own mistakes.

However, her temper was greatly improved, and she was patient. We were at a loss to find a suitable attendant for her until a circumstance happened conveniently to relieve us. Mr. Wopsle's great-aunt conquered a habit she had of being alive, and Biddy came to live with us.

It was about a month after my sister's reappearance in the kitchen when Biddy came to us with a small box containing all of her things, and became a blessing to our household. Above all, she was a blessing to Joe, for the dear old fellow was sadly torn up by the constant thought of the wreck of his wife. He'd turn to me every now and then and say, with tears in his blue eyes, "Such a fine figure of a woman as she once were, Pip!" Biddy took the cleverest charge of my sister, allowing Joe to get down to the Jolly Bargemen now and then for a change that did him good.

Biddy's first triumph in her new job was to solve a difficulty that had left me dumbfounded. I had tried hard at it, but had made nothing of it. Again and again and again, my sister had drawn on the slate a picture that looked like an unusual T, and then had eagerly called our attention to it as something she wanted. I had tried everything I could think of that began with a T, from tar, to toast, and tub. Eventually it dawned on me that the sign looked like a hammer, and when I yelled that word in her ear she began to hammer on the table in agreement. So, I brought in all our hammers, one after another, but they weren't what she wanted.

When my sister discovered that Biddy was very quick to understand her, she drew this mysterious sign again on the slate. Biddy looked thoughtfully at it, I shared with her my progress in deciphering it, she looked thoughtfully at my sister, and then exclaimed, "Why, of course! Don't you see? It's him!" and ran into the forge, followed by Joe and me.

It was Orlick, without a doubt! My sister had lost his name with her injuries, and could only identify him by his hammer. We told him why we wanted him to come into the kitchen, and, looking confused, he laid down his hammer, wiped his brow with his arm, and came slouching out of the forge.

I confess that I expected to see my sister accuse him, and that I was disappointed when she didn't. She was very pleased when he came into the kitchen and she seemed anxious to be on good terms with him. She motioned that she wanted him to be given something to drink. After that day, a day rarely passed without her drawing the hammer on her slate, and without Orlick's slouching in and standing patiently in front of her, as if he knew no more than I did what to make of it.

Chapter 17

I now fell into a regular routine of apprenticeship life, where the only eventful occurrence was the arrival of my birthday and my paying another visit to Miss Havisham. Sarah Pocket was still on duty at the gate, Miss Havisham was just as I had left her, and she spoke of Estella in the very same way, in practically the very same words. My visit lasted only a few minutes, and she gave me a one pound note when I was leaving, and told me to come again on my next birthday. I should mention that this became a yearly tradition. In politeness, I tried to decline taking the money the first time, but all that did was cause her to ask me very angrily if I expected more. From then on, I took it.

Despite time marching forward, nothing ever seemed to change in that house. Unfortunately, it served as a reminder to me, reinforcing my hate of being an apprentice blacksmith and the shame I felt of home.

One change I did gradually observe though, was a change in Biddy. Her hair grew bright and neat, and her hands were now always clean. She was not beautiful – she was common, and could not be like Estella – but she was pleasant and wholesome and sweet-tempered. She had not been with us more than a year when I observed to myself one evening that she had curiously thoughtful and attentive eyes; eyes that were very pretty and very good.

I noticed the change one night, when I was about sixteen. I lifted up my eyes from copying some passages from a book in my quest to improve myself, and saw Biddy watching what I was doing. I laid down my pen, and Biddy paused in her needlework without laying it down.

"Biddy," said I, "how do you manage it? Either I am very stupid, or you are very clever."

"I don't know, what is it that I manage?" returned Biddy, smiling.

She managed our whole household, and wonderfully too; but I didn't mean that, though that made what I did mean more surprising to her.

"How do you manage, Biddy," said I, "to learn everything that I learn, and always to keep up with me?" I was beginning to be very vain and proud of my knowledge, for I spent most of my money on it.

"I might as well ask you," said Biddy, "how you manage?"

"No; because when I come in from the forge at night, anyone can see me working hard at my learning. But you never have to work at it, Biddy."

"I suppose I must catch it – like a cough," said Biddy, quietly; and went on with her sewing.

I leaned back in my wooden chair and looked at Biddy sewing away, and I began to think she was a rather extraordinary girl. For, now that I thought of it, she was equally accomplished in the knowledge of my trade, and the names of the different sorts of tools and such. In short, whatever I knew, Biddy knew. Theoretically, she was already as good a blacksmith as I was, or better.

"You are one of those rare people, Biddy," said I, "who make the most of every chance. You were in an awful spot before you came here, and see how much better you are doing now!"

Biddy looked at me for an instant, and went on with her sewing. "I was your first teacher though; wasn't I?" said she, as she sewed.

"Biddy!" I exclaimed, in amazement. "Why, you are crying!"

"No I am not," said Biddy, looking up and laughing. "What put that thought in your head?"

What could have put it in my head, except the glistening of a tear as it dropped on her work? I sat silent, recalling what a plodding servant she had been until Mr. Wopsle's great-aunt died. I recalled the hopeless circumstances she was surrounded by in the miserable little shop and the miserable evening school, with that miserable old bundle of incompetence of a great-aunt always there. I remembered that even in those unfortunate times there must have been something remarkable about Biddy, for when I first felt my unhappiness in my life's situation, it felt natural reach out to her for help.

Biddy sat quietly sewing, shedding no more tears, and while I looked at her and thought about all this, it occurred to me that maybe I hadn't been grateful enough to Biddy. Maybe I was too restrained, and should have been more willing to share and bestow upon her my confidence and inner feelings.

"Yes, Biddy," I observed, when I finished thinking about it, "you were my first teacher, and we must talk together a little more, like we used to do. And I must consult you a little more, as I used to do. Let's have a quiet walk on the marshes next Sunday, Biddy, and a long chat."

My sister was never left alone now, and Joe was happy to take care of her on that Sunday afternoon, so Biddy and I went out together towards the church and marshes. It was summer-time, and lovely weather. When we had reached the marshes, I saw some sailing ships making their way on the river, and I began to combine Miss Havisham and Estella in my mind with that pretty view, in my usual way. When we came to the river bank and sat down, I decided that it was a good time and place to share with Biddy my inner turmoil, after swearing her to secrecy, first.

"Biddy," said I, "I want to be a gentleman."

"Oh, I wouldn't, if I was you!" she returned. "I don't think it would be good."

"Biddy," said I, with some severity, "I have particular reasons for wanting to be a gentleman."

"You know best, Pip; but don't you think you are happier as you are?"

"Biddy," I exclaimed, impatiently, "I am not at all happy as I am. I am disgusted with my job and with my life. I haven't been happy with either since I was bound apprentice. Don't be absurd."

"Was I absurd?" said Biddy, quietly raising her eyebrows; "I'm sorry; I didn't mean to be. I only want you to do well, and to be comfortable."

"Well then, understand once and for all that I can never be comfortable there; all I can be is miserable, Biddy! Unless I can lead a very different kind of life from the one I lead now."

"That's a pity!" said Biddy, shaking her head with a sorrowful air.

I told her she was right and it was a sad state for me to be in, but still, I couldn't help it.

"If I could have settled down," I said to Biddy, "and liked the forge even half as much as when I was little, I know it would have been much better for me. Joe and I might have become partners when I was finished with my apprenticeship. And I might have even grown up wanting to be with you, and we might have sat on this very bank on a fine Sunday, quite different people. I would have been good enough for you, wouldn't I, Biddy?"

Biddy sighed as she looked at the ships sailing on, and returned for answer, "Yes; I'm not very particular." It wasn't a flattering reply, but I knew she meant well.

"Instead of that," said I, plucking up some grass and chewing a blade or two, "see how I am going on. Dissatisfied, and uncomfortable, and – what would it matter to me, being coarse and common, if nobody had told me I was!"

Biddy turned her face suddenly towards mine, and looked far more intently at me than she had at the sailing ships.

"It was neither a very true nor a very polite thing to say to you," she remarked, "Who said it?"

I was caught off guard, for I had been rambling away without really seeing where I was going. I couldn't ignore it now, and I blurted out, "The beautiful young lady at Miss Havisham's, and she's more beautiful than anybody ever was, and I admire her dreadfully, and I want to be a gentleman because of her." Having made this lunatic confession, I began to throw my torn-up grass into the river, as if I had some thoughts of throwing myself in, too.

After a pause, Biddy quietly asked me, "Do you want to be a gentleman to spite her, or to win her over?"

"I don't know," I moodily answered.

"Because, if it's to spite her," Biddy pursued, "I should think that might be better accomplished by not caring about her words. And if it is to win her over, I should think she was not worth winning over."

Exactly what I had thought, many times, and even in that moment I agreed. But how could I, a poor bewildered village lad, avoid that self-imposed trap into which the best and wisest of men fall every day?

"It may be all quite true," said I to Biddy, "but I greatly admire her."

I turned over and lay on my face and got a good grab on my hair and twisted it hard. It would have been a fair punishment if I had lifted my face up by my hair and knocked it against the ground for belonging to such an idiot as myself.

Biddy was the wisest of girls, and she didn't try to reason with me anymore. She put her hand, which was a nice hand though roughened by work, on my hands, one after another, and gently took them out of my hair. Then she softly patted my shoulder in a soothing way, while I cried a little and felt vaguely convinced that I had been treated unfairly by somebody, or by everybody; I couldn't say which.

"I am glad of one thing," said Biddy, "and that is, that you felt you could give me your confidence, Pip. And I am glad of another thing, and that is, that of course you know you may depend upon my keeping it. If your first teacher had been your teacher now, she thinks she knows what lesson she would teach. But it would be a hard one to learn, and you have gone beyond her, and it's too late now." So, with a quiet sigh for me, Biddy rose from the bank, and said, with a fresh and pleasant change of voice, "Shall we walk a little further, or go home?"

"Biddy," I cried, getting up, putting my arm round her neck, and giving her a kiss on her cheek, "I shall always tell you everything."

"Till you're a gentleman," said Biddy.

"You know I never shall be, so that's always. Not that I have any need now to tell you anything, for you know everything I know – as I told you at home the other night."

"Ah." said Biddy, quite in a whisper, as she looked away at the ships. And then repeated, with her former pleasant change; "shall we walk a little further, or go home?"

I said to Biddy we would walk a little further, and the summer afternoon turned into the summer evening, and it was very beautiful. I began to consider whether I was better off, after all, in the life I had, rather than playing beggar my neighbor by candlelight in the room with the stopped clocks and being despised by Estella. I knew it would be best for me if I could get her out of my head and could go to work determined to like what I already had in life and make the best of it. I asked myself the question, didn't I realize that if Estella were beside me at that moment, instead of Biddy, that she would make me miserable? I had to admit that I knew it for certain, and I said to myself, "Pip, what a fool you are!"

Biddy was never insulting, or Biddy today and somebody else tomorrow; she would have felt only pain, and no pleasure, from giving me pain; she would much rather have wounded herself than me. How could it be then, that I did not like her much the better of the two?

"Biddy," said I, when we were walking homeward, "I wish you could put me right."

"I wish I could!" said Biddy.

"If I could only get myself to fall in love with you – you don't mind my speaking so openly to such an old friend?"

"Oh dear, not at all!" said Biddy. "Don't mind me."

"If I could only get myself to do it, that would be best for me."

"But you never will, you see," said Biddy, decisively.

In my heart I believed her to be right; and yet I felt just slightly offended, too, that she should be so sure about it.

On our way past the churchyard, who should pop up from slouching on the gate but Old Orlick.

"Halloa!" he growled, "where are you two going?"

"Where would we be going, but home?" said I.

"Well then," said he, "I'm jiggered if I don't see you home!"

This penalty of being jiggered was a favourite phrase of his. He attached no definite meaning to the word that I am aware of, but when I was younger I had a belief that if he had jiggered me, it would have been with a sharp and twisted hook.

Biddy was much against his going with us, and said to me in a whisper, "Don't let him come; I don't like him." Since I didn't like him either, I took the liberty of saying that we thanked him, but we didn't want seeing home. He laughed and dropped back, but came slouching after us at a little distance.

Curious to know whether Biddy suspected him of having had a part in that awful attack on my sister, I asked her why she did not like him.

"Oh!" she replied, glancing over her shoulder as he slouched after us, "because I – I am afraid he likes me."

"Did he ever tell you he liked you?" I asked, angrily.

"No," said Biddy, glancing over her shoulder again, "he never told me so; but he dances at me, whenever he can catch my eye."

I was very mad indeed upon Old Orlick's daring to admire her; as mad as if it were an attack against myself.

"But it makes no difference to you, you know," said Biddy, calmly.

"Right, Biddy, it makes no difference to me; only I don't like it; I don't approve of it."

"Neither do I," said Biddy. "Though, that makes no difference to you."

I kept an eye on Orlick after that night, and, whenever he tried to dance at Biddy, I got in front of him to obscure his demonstration. His job had been secured in Joe's forge because of my sister's sudden liking for him, or else I would have tried to get him fired.

My confused state of mind continued for the next year; trying to convince myself that I liked the forge and my trade; that Biddy was better than Estella; that I had nothing to be ashamed of in any of that, and I'd even begin to think that that was all true. But then a stray thought would take me back to the Havisham days, like a destructive missile, and scatter my wits again. Scattered wits take a long time picking up; and often, before I had got them well together, they would be scattered again in all directions, and I'd hope that perhaps after all Miss Havisham was going to make my fortune when my apprenticeship was done.

My apprenticeship never did finish, however, but was brought to a premature end, as I proceed to relate.

Chapter 18

I was now seventeen and in the fifth year of my apprenticeship to Joe, and it was a Saturday night. There was a group of us assembled around the fire at the Three Jolly Bargemen, listening to Mr. Wopsle as he read the newspaper aloud.

A famous murder had been committed, and Mr. Wopsle was reading it from the newspaper and acting it out in his theatrical way with his booming voice, pretending to be the victim, the attacker, and everybody involved with the case, and he portrayed the defendant quite grimly. We all enjoyed ourselves thoroughly and we came to the unanimous verdict of Wilful Murder.

Then, I became aware of a strange gentleman leaning over the back of the bench opposite me, watching the gathering. There was an expression of contempt on his face, and he bit the side of his great forefinger as he watched us.

"Well!" said the stranger to Mr. Wopsle, when he had finished, "you have settled it all to your own satisfaction, I have no doubt?"

Everybody was startled by him and looked up, as if the man were the murderer. He looked at everybody coldly and sarcastically.

"Guilty, of course?" said he. "Out with it!"

"Sir," returned Mr. Wopsle, "without having had the honour of meeting you, I do say Guilty." Upon this, we all took courage to unite in an agreed murmur.

"I know you do," said the stranger; "I knew you would. I told you so. But now I'll ask you a question. Do you know, or do you not know, that the law of England supposes every man to be innocent, until he is proved – proved! – to be guilty?"

"Sir," Mr. Wopsle began to reply, "as an Englishman myself, I--"

"Come!" said the stranger, biting his forefinger at him. "Don't evade the question. Either you know it, or you don't know it. Which is it to be?"

"Certainly I know it," replied Mr. Wopsle.

"Certainly you know it. Then why didn't you say so at first? Now, I'll ask you another question;" taking possession of Mr. Wopsle, as if he had a right to him. "Do you know that none of these witnesses have yet been cross-examined?"

Mr. Wopsle was beginning, "I can only say--" when the stranger stopped him.

"What? You won't answer the question, yes or no? Now, I'll try you again." Throwing his finger at him again. "Listen to me. Are you aware, or are you not aware, that none of these witnesses have yet been cross-examined? Come, I only want one word from you. Yes, or no?"

Mr. Wopsle hesitated, and we all began to have a rather poor opinion of him.

"Come!" said the stranger, "I'll help you. You don't deserve help, but I'll help you. Look at that paper you hold in your hand. What is it?"

"What is it?" repeated Mr. Wopsle, looking at it, much at a loss.

"Is it," pursued the stranger in his most sarcastic and suspicious manner, "the printed paper you have just been reading from?"

"Undoubtedly."

"Undoubtedly. Now, turn to that paper, and tell me whether it distinctly states that the prisoner expressly said that his legal advisers instructed him to refrain from defending himself yet?"

"I read that just now," Mr. Wopsle pleaded.

"Nevermind what you read just now, sir; I don't ask you what you read just now. Turn to the paper. No, no, no my friend; not to the top of the column; you know better than that; to the bottom, to the bottom." (We all began to think Mr. Wopsle was quite devious.) "Well? Have you found it?"

"Here it is," said Mr. Wopsle.

"Now, read that passage, and tell me whether it distinctly states that the prisoner expressly said that he was instructed by his legal advisers wholly to reserve his defence?"

Mr. Wopsle answered, "Those are not the exact words."

"Not the exact words!" repeated the gentleman, bitterly. "Is that the exact substance?"

"Yes," said Mr. Wopsle.

"Yes," repeated the stranger, addressing the rest of us with his right hand extended towards the witness, Wopsle. "And now I ask you men, what have you to say about the conscience of this man who, with those words before his eyes, can lay his head upon his pillow at night after having pronounced a fellow creature guilty, and that person not having been defended yet?"

We were all persuaded that Mr. Wopsle had gone too far, and he had better stop his recklessness while he still had time.

The strange gentleman, with an air of authority not to be disputed, left the back of the bench, and stepped into the space between the two benches, in front of the fire, where he remained standing facing us: his left hand in his pocket, and biting the forefinger of his right.

"From information I have received," said he, "I have reason to believe there is a blacksmith among you, by name Joseph – or Joe – Gargery. Which is the man?"

"Here is the man," said Joe.

The strange gentleman beckoned him, and Joe rose to join him.

"You have an apprentice," pursued the stranger, "commonly known as Pip? Is he here?"

"I am here!" I cried.

The stranger did not recognize me, but I recognized him. He was the gentleman I had met on the stairs, on my second visit to Miss Havisham. I had known him the moment I saw him looking over the bench, and now that I stood in front of him with his hand on my shoulder, I remembered again in detail, his large head, his dark complexion, his deep-set eyes, his bushy black eyebrows, his large watch-chain, his strong black dots of beard and whisker, and even the smell of scented soap on his large hands.

"I wish to have a private conference with you two," said he, "It will take a little time. Perhaps we had better go to your place of residence."

Amidst a wondering silence, we three walked out of the Jolly Bargemen and walked home. Our conference was held in the parlour, which was feebly lighted by one candle.

The strange gentleman sat down at the table by the candle and said, "My name is Jaggers, and I am a lawyer in London. I am pretty well known. I have unusual business to transact with you, and I start by explaining that it is not my business, but another's. If my advice had been asked, I would not be here. It was not asked, and so you see me here. What I have to do, I do as the confidential agent of another person. No more, no less."

He got up, and threw one of his legs over the back of the chair and leaned upon it; thus having one foot on the seat of the chair, and one foot on the ground.

"Now, Joseph Gargery, I am the bearer of an offer to relieve you of this young fellow, your apprentice. You would not object to cancel his apprentice indentures, at his request and for his good? You would want nothing for so doing?"

"Lord forbid that I should want anything for not standing in Pip's way," said Joe, staring.

"Lord forbidding is pious, but not to the purpose," returned Mr. Jaggers. "The question is, would you want anything? Do you want anything?"

"The answer is," returned Joe, sternly, "No."

I thought Mr. Jaggers glanced at Joe, as if he considered him a fool for his disinterestedness. But I was too bewildered between curiosity and surprise to be sure of it.

"Very well," said Mr. Jaggers. "Remember the admission you have made, and don't try to take it back."

"Who's going to try?" retorted Joe.

"Now, I return to this young fellow. And the communication I have got to make is, that he has great expectations."

Joe and I gasped, and looked at one another.

"I am instructed to communicate to him," said Mr. Jaggers, throwing his finger at me sideways, "that he will come into a handsome property. Further, that it is the desire of the present owner of that property that this young fellow be immediately removed from his present life and from this place, and be brought up as a gentleman – in a word, as a young fellow of great expectations."

My dream had come true, Miss Havisham was going to make my fortune on a grand scale!

"Now, Mr. Pip," pursued the lawyer, "I address the rest of what I have to say, to you. You are to understand, first, that it is the request of the person from whom I take my instructions that you always bear the name of Pip. You will have no objection, I dare say, to your expectations having that easy condition. But if you have any objection, this is the time to mention it."

My heart was beating so fast that I could scarcely stammer that I had no objection.

"I should think not! Secondly, Mr. Pip, the name of the person who is your benefactor is to remain a secret, until that person chooses to reveal themself. It is the intention of the person to reveal it first hand, by word of mouth, to yourself. When or where that may happen, I cannot say; no one can say. It may be years from now. You are to understand that you are most positively prohibited from asking me about this person in all the communications you may have with me. If you have a suspicion in your own heart, keep that suspicion there. You are also not to ask the reason for the secrecy; there may be important reasons, or it may be mere whim. Either way, the condition is made. Your acceptance of it is the only remaining condition from that person. The secret is solely held by that person and by me. Again, not a very difficult condition to accept for such a rise in fortune; but if you have any objection to it, this is the time to speak out."

Once more, I stammered with difficulty that I had no objection.

"I should think not! Now, Mr. Pip, I have done with stipulations. We come next to mere details of arrangement. You must know that, although I have used the term "expectations" more than once, you are not endowed with expectations only. There is already in my hands a sum of money more than sufficient for your suitable education and living expenses. You will please consider me your guardian. Oh!" for I was going to thank him, "I must tell you; I am paid for my services, or I wouldn't perform them. Now, it is considered that you must be better educated, in accordance with your new position in life, and that you will understand the importance and necessity of beginning at once."

I said I had always longed for it.

"Never mind what you have always longed for, Mr. Pip," he retorted; "keep to the record. If you long for it now, that's enough. Are you answering that you are ready to be placed immediately under a proper tutor? Is that it?"

I stammered yes, that was it.

"There is a certain tutor, of whom I have some knowledge, who I think might suit the purpose," said Mr. Jaggers. "I don't recommend him, mind you; because I never recommend anybody. The gentleman I speak of, is one Mr. Matthew Pocket."

Ah! I recognized the name directly. Miss Havisham's relation. The Matthew whom Mr. and Mrs. Camilla had spoken of, and whose place was to be at Miss Havisham's head, when she lay dead in her bride's dress on the banquet table.

"You know the name?" said Mr. Jaggers, looking shrewdly at me.

My answer was, that I had heard of the name.

"Oh!" said he. "You have heard of the name. But the question is, what do you say of it?"

I said, or tried to say, that I was much obliged to him for his recommendation--

"No, my young friend!" he interrupted, shaking his great head very slowly. "Remember!"

Not remembering, I began again that I was much obliged to him for his recommendation--

"No, my young friend," he interrupted, shaking his head and frowning and smiling both at once; "no, no, no; it's very well done, but it won't do; you are too young to stick me with it. Recommendation is not the word, Mr. Pip. Try another."

Correcting myself, I said that I was much obliged to him for his mention of Mr. Matthew Pocket--

"That's more like it!" cried Mr. Jaggers.

- And (I added), I would gladly try that gentleman.

"Good. You had better try him in his own house. The way shall be prepared for you, and you can see his son first, who is in London. When will you come to London?"

I said (glancing at Joe, who stood looking on, motionless), that I supposed I could come immediately.

"First," said Mr. Jaggers, "you should have some new clothes to come in, and they should not be working clothes. This day, next week. You'll want some money. Shall I leave you twenty pounds?"

He produced a long purse, with the greatest coolness, and counted them out on the table and pushed them over to me. This was the first time he had taken his leg from the chair. He sat astride of the chair when he had pushed the money over, and sat swinging the purse and eyeing Joe.

"Well, Joseph Gargery? You look dumbfounded."

"I am!" said Joe, in a very decided manner.

"It was understood that you wanted nothing for yourself, remember?"

"It were understood," said Joe. "And it are understood. And it ever will be similar according."

"But," said Mr. Jaggers, swinging his purse, "what if it was in my instructions to make you a present, as compensation?"

"As compensation for what?" Joe demanded.

"For the loss of his services."

Joe laid his hand upon my shoulder with the touch of a woman. I have often thought of him since, like the steam-hammer, that can crush a man or pat an egg-shell, in his combination of strength with gentleness. "Pip is that hearty welcome," said Joe, "to go free with his services, to honour and fortune. But if you think money can make compensation to me for the loss of the little child – what come to the forge – and ever the best of friends!--"

O dear good Joe, whom I was so ready to leave and so unthankful to, I see you again, with your muscular blacksmith's arm before your eyes, and your broad chest heaving, and your voice dying away.

But I encouraged Joe at the time. I begged him to be comforted, for (as he said) we had ever been the best of friends, and (as I said) we ever would be so. Joe scooped the tears from his eyes with his wrist, as if he were bent on gouging himself, but said not another word.

Mr. Jaggers had watched this, as if he thought Joe was the village idiot and I was his keeper. When it was over, he said, "Now, Joseph Gargery, I warn you this is your last chance. No half measures with me. If you mean to take a present that I have it in my charge to give you, speak out, and you shall have it. If on the contrary you mean to say--"

"Which I meantersay," cried Joe, still with tears in his eyes, but suddenly turning towards Mr. Jaggers with a fighting stance, shocking him into silence, "that if you come into my home bull-baiting and badgering me, then let's go! Which I meantersay, if you're a man, come on! Which I meantersay, that what I say I meantersay and I stand or fall by it!"

I pulled Joe away, and he immediately became calmed; merely stating to me in a polite manner, and as a notice to any one nearby whom it might happen to concern, that he were not a going to be bull-baited and badgered in his own home.

Mr. Jaggers had gotten up when Joe had assumed his stance, and had backed up near the door. Without showing any desire to come in again, he there delivered his final remarks, which were, "Well, Mr. Pip, I think the sooner you leave here – since you are to be a gentleman – the better. As mentioned, let our appointment be for this day next week, and you shall receive my printed address in the meantime. Come straight to my office in London. Understand now, in this matter of your expectations, I express no opinion, one way or the other. I am paid for my services. Now, understand that, finally. Understand that!"

He was throwing his finger at both of us, and I think he would have continued but for his thinking Joe was dangerous, and so he left.

Something came into my head a minute later which made me run after him, as he was going down to the Jolly Bargemen where he had left a hired carriage.

"I beg your pardon, Mr. Jaggers."

"Halloa!" said he, turning round, "what's the matter?"

"I wish to keep to your directions, Mr. Jaggers, so I thought I had better ask. Would there be any objection to my taking leave of anyone I know, before I go away?"

"No," said he, looking as if he hardly understood me. "No objection."

I thanked him and ran home again, and there I found that Joe had already locked the front door and was seated by the kitchen fire with a hand on each knee, gazing intently at the burning coals. Biddy sat next to him, and my sister was in the corner in her cushioned chair. I too sat down before the fire and gazed at the coals, and nothing was said by anybody for a long time.

The more I looked into the glowing coals, the more incapable I became of looking at Joe; the longer the silence lasted, the more unable I felt to speak. At length I got out, "Joe, have you told Biddy?"

"No, Pip," returned Joe, still looking at the fire, "which I left it to yourself to do, Pip."

"I would rather you told her, Joe."

"Pip's a gentleman of fortune then," said Joe, "and God bless him in it!"

Biddy dropped her work, and looked at me. Joe held his knees and looked at me. I looked at both of them. After a pause, they both heartily congratulated me; but there was a certain touch of sadness in their congratulations that I rather resented.

I took it upon myself to tell Biddy and Joe that my friends were under the same important obligation I was, to know nothing and say nothing about the maker of my fortune. It would all come out in good time, I observed, and in the meanwhile nothing was to be said, except that I had come into great expectations from a mysterious patron. Biddy nodded her head thoughtfully at the fire as she took up her work again, and said she would be very particular; and Joe, still holding his knees, said, "Ay, ay, I'll be partickler, Pip". Then they congratulated me again, and went on to express so much wonder at the idea of my being a gentleman that I didn't half like it.

Infinite pains were then taken by Biddy to convey to my sister some idea of what had happened. To the best of my belief, those efforts entirely failed. She laughed and nodded her head a great many times, and even repeated after Biddy, the words "Pip" and "Property." But I doubt if they had any meaning in them, and I could not paint a darker picture of her state of mind.

As Joe and Biddy became more at their cheerful ease again, I became quite gloomy. Of course, I was not dissatisfied with my fortune; but it is possible that I may have been, without quite realizing it, dissatisfied with myself. Anyhow, I sat with my elbow on my knee and my face upon my palm, looking into the fire, as those two talked about my going away, and about what they would do without me and all that.

"Saturday night," said I, when we had had our supper of bread-and-cheese and beer. "Five more days, and then the day before the day! They'll soon go."

"Yes, Pip," observed Joe, whose voice sounded hollow in his beer mug. "They'll soon go."

"Soon, soon go," said Biddy.

"I have been thinking, Joe, that when I go downtown on Monday and order my new clothes, I'll tell the tailor that I'll come and put them on there, or that I'll have them sent to Mr. Pumblechook's. It would be very disagreeable to be stared at by all the people here."

"Mr. and Mrs. Hubble might like to see you in your new genteel figure too, Pip," said Joe, cutting his bread with his cheese on it, and glancing at my untasted supper as if he thought of the time when we used to compare biting through our slices. "So might Wopsle. And the Jolly Bargemen might take it as a compliment."

"That's just what I don't want, Joe. They would make such a business of it – such a coarse and common business – that I couldn't bear myself."

“Ah, that indeed, Pip!" said Joe. "If you couldn't bear yourself--"

Biddy asked, as she sat holding my sister's plate, "Have you thought about when you'll show yourself to Mr. Gargery, and your sister, and me? You will show yourself to us, won't you?"

"Biddy," I returned with some resentment, "you are so exceedingly quick that it's difficult to keep up with you."

("She always were quick," observed Joe.)

I continued in a haughty tone, "If you had waited another moment, Biddy, you would have heard me say that I shall bring my clothes here in a bundle one evening – most likely on the evening before I go away."

Biddy said no more. After I had handsomely forgiven her, I exchanged an affectionate good-night with her and Joe, and went up to bed. When I got into my little room, I sat down and took a long look at it, as a common little room that I should soon be parted from and raised above, forever. However, it was furnished with pieces of my life, and at the same moment I fell into much the same confused division of mind between it and the better rooms to which I was going next week, as I had been so often torn in my mind between the forge and Miss Havisham's, and Biddy and Estella.

The sun had been shining brightly all day on the roof of my attic, and the room was warm. As I opened my window and looked out, I saw Joe come slowly outside below, and take a turn or two in the air. And then I saw Biddy join him, and bring him a pipe and light it for him. He never smoked so late, and it seemed to hint to me that he needed comforting, for some reason or other.

He stood smoking his pipe, and Biddy stood there too, quietly talking to him, and I knew that they talked of me, for I heard my name mentioned in an endearing tone by both of them more than once. I stopped listening and left the window, and sat down in my one chair by my bedside, feeling it very sorrowful and strange that this first night of my bright fortunes should be the loneliest I had ever known.

I put my light out, and crept into bed. It was an uneasy bed now, and I never slept the old sound sleep in it any more.

-

Chapter 19

Morning made a considerable difference in my general outlook on life. What was most on my mind was that I had to wait six days until I would leave.

Joe and Biddy were very sympathetic and pleasant when I spoke of our approaching separation; but they only referred to it when I did. After breakfast, Joe brought out my apprentice indentures from the parlour and we put them in the fire, and I felt that I was free. Feeling the freshness of my newly raised position in life, I went to church with Joe, and thought to myself during the sermon that perhaps the clergyman wouldn't be so sure about the rich man not being able to enter the kingdom of Heaven if he had thought it through a bit more.

After our early dinner, I went out for a walk alone, with the idea of it being a final time to visit the marshes. As I passed the church, if I had felt something before like shame regarding my companionship with the fugitive whom I had once seen limping among those graves with his leg iron, then just imagine my thoughts on this Sunday! My only comfort was that it had happened a long time ago, that he had doubtless been transported a long way off and that he was dead to me, and might be actually dead in the bargain.

No more low wet grounds, no more gates and mounds, no more of these cattle grazing. Henceforth, I was for London and greatness; not for blacksmith's work! I made my exultant way to the old cannon mound by the river, and, lying down there to consider the question of whether Miss Havisham intended for me to marry Estella or not, I fell asleep.

When I awoke, I was surprised to find Joe sitting beside me, smoking his pipe. He greeted me with a cheerful smile, and said:

"This being the last time, Pip, I thought I'd foller you."

"And Joe, I am very glad you did so."

"Thankee, Pip."

"You may be sure, dear Joe," I went on, after we had shaken hands, "that I shall never forget you."

"No, no, Pip!" said Joe, in a comfortable tone, "I'm sure of that. Ay, ay, old chap! Bless you, it just took a little time to wrap my head around the news, and it happened so quick, didn't it?"

Somehow, I was not very pleased with Joe's being so surprised at the news; I would have liked him to have said, "It does you credit, Pip," or something of that sort. Therefore, I merely said that the news had indeed come suddenly, but that I had always wanted to be a gentleman, and had often day dreamed about what I would do if I were one.

"Have you though?" said Joe. "Astonishing!"

"It's a pity now, Joe," said I, "that you did not get on a little more, when we had our lessons here, isn't it?"

"Well, I don't know," returned Joe. "I'm so awful dull. I'm only master of my own trade. "

What I had meant was, that when I came into my property and was able to do something for Joe, it would have been much more agreeable if he had been better qualified for a rise in his societal position. He was so perfectly oblivious to my meaning, however, that I thought I would mention it to Biddy instead.

So, when we had walked home and had had tea, I took Biddy into our little garden, and, after saying in an off-handed way that I would never forget her (to make her feel appreciated), said I had a favour to ask of her.

"And it is, Biddy," said I, "that you will take every opportunity of helping Joe on a little."

"How helping him on?" asked Biddy, with a steady sort of glance.

"Well! Joe is a dear good fellow – in fact, I think he is the dearest fellow that ever lived – but he is rather backward in some things. For instance, Biddy, in his learning and his manners."

Although I was looking at Biddy as I spoke, and although she opened her eyes very wide when I had spoken, she did not look at me.

"Oh, his manners! Aren't his manners good enough?" asked Biddy.

"My dear Biddy, they do very well here--"

"Oh! They do very well here?" interrupted Biddy.

"Hear me out – but if I were to move Joe into a higher sphere of society, as I shall hope to move him when I fully come into my property, they would hardly do him justice."

"And don't you think he knows that?" asked Biddy.

It was such a very thought-provoking question (for it had never remotely occurred to me), that I said, snappishly, "Biddy, what do you mean?"

Biddy said, "Have you never considered that he may be proud?"

"Proud?" I repeated, with disdainful emphasis.

"Oh! There are many kinds of pride," said Biddy, looking full at me and shaking her head; "pride is not all of one kind. He may be too proud to let anyone take him out of a place that he fills well, and with respect. I think he is proud, though it sounds bold of me to say so, for you must know him far better than I do."

"Now, Biddy," said I, "I am very sorry to see this in you. You are envious, Biddy, and grudging. You are dissatisfied on account of my rise in fortune, and you can't help showing it."

"If you have the heart to think so," returned Biddy, "say so. Say so over and over again, if you have the heart to think so."

"If you have the heart to be so, you mean, Biddy," said I, in a virtuous and superior tone; "don't put it off on me. I am very sorry to see it, and it's a – it's a bad side of human nature. I did intend to ask you to use any little opportunities you might have after I was gone of improving dear Joe. But after this, I ask you nothing. I am extremely sorry to see this in you, Biddy," I repeated. "It's a – it's a bad side of human nature."

"Whether you scold me or approve of me," returned poor Biddy, "you may equally count on me trying to do all that is in my power at all times. And whatever opinion you have of me shall make no difference in my remembrance of you. Yet, a gentleman should not be unjust, either," said Biddy, turning away her head.

I again warmly repeated that it was a bad side of human nature, and I walked down the little path away from her. She went into the house, and I went out at the garden gate and took a dejected stroll until supper-time; again, feeling it very sad and strange that this, the second night of my bright fortunes, should be as lonely and unsatisfactory as the first.

But, morning once again brightened my outlook. Putting on the best clothes I had, I went into town early to be there when the shops opened, and presented myself to Mr. Trabb, the tailor. He was having his breakfast in the parlour behind his shop, and did not think it worth his while to come out to me, but called me in to him.

"Well!" said Mr. Trabb, "How are you, and what can I do for you?"

Mr. Trabb was a prosperous old bachelor, and his open window looked into a prosperous little garden and orchard, and there was a prosperous iron safe in the wall beside his fireplace, and I did not doubt that heaps of his prosperity were stored in it in bags.

"Mr. Trabb," said I, "I'm sorry to have to mention, because it sounds like boasting, but I have come into a handsome property."

A change passed over Mr. Trabb. He forgot his breakfast, and got up from the table exclaiming, "Lord bless my soul!"

"I am going up to my guardian in London," said I, casually pulling some pound notes out of my pocket and looking at them; "and I want a fashionable suit of clothes to go in. I wish to pay for them, with cash."

"My dear sir," said Mr. Trabb, as he respectfully bowed, opened his arms, and took the liberty of touching me on the outside of each elbow, "don't hurt me by mentioning that. May I congratulate you? Would you do me the favour of stepping into the shop?"

Mr. Trabb's boy was the most arrogantly bold boy in all that countryside. When I had entered, he was sweeping the shop, and he had made his day more fun for himself by sweeping over me. He was still sweeping when I came out into the shop with Mr. Trabb, and he knocked the broom against all possible corners and obstacles, to express (as I understood it) that he was as good as any blacksmith, alive or dead.

"Hold that noise," said Mr. Trabb, with the greatest sternness, "or I'll knock your head off! Now sir, please do me the favour and be seated. Now, this," said Mr. Trabb, taking down a roll of cloth, and spreading it out over the counter, "is a very sweet article. I can recommend it for your purpose, sir, because it really is extra super. But you shall see some others. Give me Number Four, you!" (To the boy, and with a dreadfully severe stare, as if he could foresee the danger of that delinquent brushing me with it, or making some other sign of familiarity.)

Mr. Trabb never removed his stern eye from the boy until he had deposited number four on the counter and was at a safe distance again. Then, he commanded him to bring number five, and number eight. "And let me have none of your tricks here," said Mr. Trabb, "or you shall repent it, you young scoundrel, the longest day you have to live."

Mr. Trabb then bent over number four, and recommended it to me as a light cloth for summer wear, much in vogue among the nobility, and a material that it would be an honour for him to think of a distinguished fellow-townsman having worn. "Are you bringing numbers five and eight, you vagabond," said Mr. Trabb to the boy after that, "or shall I kick you out of the shop and bring them myself?"

I selected the materials for a suit, with the assistance of Mr. Trabb's judgment, and re-entered the parlour to be measured. For, although Mr. Trabb had my measurements already, and had previously been quite satisfied with them, he said apologetically that it "wouldn't do under existing circumstances, sir – wouldn't do at all." So, Mr. Trabb measured and calculated me as if I were an estate and he was the finest surveyor, and gave himself such a world of trouble that I felt that no suit of clothes could possibly compensate him for his trouble. When he had at last finished and had agreed to send the clothes to Mr. Pumblechook's that Thursday evening, he said, with his hand upon the parlour lock, "I know, sir, that London gentlemen aren't expected to patronize local work; but if you would give me a recommendation now and then in the quality work of a fellow townsman, I should greatly appreciate it. Good morning, sir, much obliged. - Door!"

The last word was flung at the boy, who had no idea what it meant. But I saw him collapse under his master's wrath, and my first undeniable experience of the tremendous power of money was that it had laid Trabb's boy on his back.

After this memorable event, I went to the hatter's, and the bootmaker's, and the hosier's. I also went to the coach-office and reserved my place for seven o'clock on Saturday morning. It wasn't necessary to explain everywhere that I had come into a handsome property; but whenever I said anything about it, it followed that the tradesman I was speaking to ceased to have his attention diverted elsewhere, and would concentrate his mind upon me. When I had ordered everything I wanted, I went to Pumblechook's, and, as I approached that gentleman's place of business, I saw him standing at his door.

He was waiting for me impatiently. He had been out early in his horse cart, and had stopped by the forge and heard the news. He then prepared a reception for me in his parlour, and he too ordered his shopman to "get out of the way" as my sacred self entered.

"My dear friend," said Mr. Pumblechook, taking me by both hands, when we were alone, "I give you joy of your good fortune. Well deserved, well deserved!"

This was coming to the point, and I thought it a sensible way of expressing himself.

"To think," said Mr. Pumblechook, "that I should have been the humble instrument of leading up to this, is a proud reward."

I begged Mr. Pumblechook to remember that nothing was to be ever said or hinted about the subject of my benefactor.

"My dear young friend," said Mr. Pumblechook, "if you will allow me to call you so--"

I murmured "Certainly," and Mr. Pumblechook took me by both hands again, "you must be hungry, you must be exhausted. Be seated. Here is a chicken and some tongue from the Blue Boar; one or two little things I had sent from there that I hope you may not despise. But, do I," said Mr. Pumblechook, getting up again the moment after he had sat down, "see before me, him that I played with in his time of happy childhood? And may I - may I - ?"

This "May I", meant might he shake hands? I consented, and he shook hands enthusiastically, and then sat down again.

"Here is wine," said Mr. Pumblechook. "Let us drink, Thanks to Fortune, and may she ever pick out her favourites justly! And yet I cannot," said Mr. Pumblechook, getting up again, "see before me the gentleman – and also drink to his honour – without again expressing - May I - May I - ?"

I said he might, and he shook hands with me again, and emptied his glass and turned it upside down. I did the same; and if I had turned myself upside down before drinking, the wine could not have gone more direct to my head.

Mr. Pumblechook helped me to the best cuts of the food, and took, comparatively speaking, no care of himself at all.

"And your sister," he resumed, "which had the honour of bringing you up by hand! It's a sad picture, to know that she's no longer able to fully understand the honour. May--"

I saw he was about to come at me again, and I stopped him.

"We'll drink her health," said I.

"Ah!" cried Mr. Pumblechook, leaning back in his chair, quite weakened with admiration, "that's the way you know 'em, sir!" (I don't know who "Sir" was, but it certainly wasn't me, and there was no third person present); "that's the way you know the noble-minded, sir! Ever forgiving and ever kind. It might," said the servile Pumblechook, putting down his glass in a hurry and getting up again, "seem to a common person, to have the appearance of repeating – but, may I - ?"

When he had done it, he resumed his seat and drank to my sister. "Let us never be blind," said Mr. Pumblechook, "to her faults of temper, but it is to be hoped she meant well."

I mentioned to Mr. Pumblechook that I wished to have my new clothes sent to his house, and he was ecstatic on my so honoring him. I mentioned my reason for not wanting a spectacle in the village, and he heartily agreed. There was nobody but himself, he hinted, worthy of my confidence, and – in short, might he? Then he asked me tenderly if I remembered our boyish games at math, and how we had gone together to have me bound apprentice, and, how he had ever been my favourite chosen friend as a child?

If I had drunk ten times as many glasses of wine as I had, I would have still known that he had never been at all like that towards me, and in my heart I should have rejected the idea. However, on that day, I remember feeling convinced that I had been much mistaken about him, and that he was a sensible practical good-hearted fellow.

Little by little, he began to even ask my advice about his own affairs. He mentioned that there was an opportunity to monopolize the local corn and seed trade; all that was lacking was More Capital. Those were the two little words, More Capital. Now, it appeared to him, that if that capital were invested into his business, perhaps through a silent partner, – who, by the way, would have nothing to do but walk in whenever he pleased and walk out twice a year with his fifty percent share of the profits – that it appeared to him that that might be an opening for a young enterprising gentleman with property. But he wanted to know what I thought of his idea? He had great confidence in my opinion, and what did I think? I gave it as my opinion that it seemed like a grand idea. The amazing genius of my opinion so struck him, that he no longer asked if he might shake hands with me, but said he really must – and did.

We drank all the wine, and Mr. Pumblechook pledged himself over and over again to keep Joseph up to the mark (I don't know what mark), and to provide me efficient and constant service (I don't know what service). He also made known to me for the first time in my life that he had always said of me, "That boy is no common boy, and mark me, his fortune will be no common fortune."

Finally, I went outside, with a dim perception that the sun was a little too bright, and I found that I had stumbled my way to the turnpike without having paid any attention to the road. Leaving the road, I turned into a field and had a long nap under a hedge to sleep the wine off before I went on my way home.

So, Tuesday, Wednesday, and Thursday, passed; and on Friday morning I went to Mr. Pumblechook's, to put on my new clothes and pay my visit to Miss Havisham. Mr. Pumblechook gave me his own room to dress in, and it was decorated with clean towels expressly for this event. My clothes were rather a disappointment, of course. Probably every new and eagerly expected garment ever put on since clothes were invented has fallen a bit short of the wearer's expectation. But, after I had had my new suit on about a half an hour, and had gone through a great deal of posing with Mr. Pumblechook's small dressing-mirror, it seemed to fit me better.

I went to Miss Havisham's and rang at the bell constrainedly, due to the stiff long fingers of my gloves. Sarah Pocket came to the gate, and positively reeled back when she saw me so changed; her face turned from brown to green and yellow.

"You?" said she. "You, good gracious! What do you want?"

"I am going to London, Miss Pocket," said I, "and want to say good-bye to Miss Havisham."

I was not expected, for she left me locked in the yard, while she went to ask if I were to be admitted. After a very short delay, she returned and took me up, staring at me all the way.

Miss Havisham was taking exercise in the room with the long spread table, leaning on her crutch. The room was dimly lighted by a few candles as before, and at the sound of our entrance, she stopped and turned. She was then just next to the rotted bride-cake.

"Don't go, Sarah," she said. "Well, Pip?"

"I start for London, Miss Havisham, tomorrow," I was exceedingly careful what I said, "and I thought you would kindly not mind my taking leave of you."

"This is quite a genteel outfit, Pip," said she, pointing her crutch around me, as if she, the fairy godmother who had changed me, were bestowing the finishing touch with her wand.

"I have come into such good fortune since I saw you last, Miss Havisham," I murmured. "And I am so grateful for it, Miss Havisham!"

"Ay, ay!" said she, looking at the flustered and envious Sarah, with delight. "I have seen Mr. Jaggers. I have heard about it, Pip. So, you go tomorrow?"

"Yes, Miss Havisham."

"And you are adopted by a rich person?"

"Yes, Miss Havisham."

"Not named?"

"No, Miss Havisham."

"And Mr. Jaggers is now your guardian?"

"Yes, Miss Havisham."

She quite gloated on these questions and answers, so keen was her enjoyment of Sarah Pocket's jealous dismay. "Well!" she went on, "you have a promising career before you. Be good – deserve it – and abide by Mr. Jaggers's instructions. Good-bye, Pip!"

She stretched out her hand, and I went down on my knee and put it to my lips. I had not considered how I should take leave of her; it came naturally to me at the moment, to do this. She looked at Sarah Pocket with triumph in her weird eyes, and so I left my fairy godmother, with both her hands on her crutch, standing in the midst of the dimly lighted room beside the rotten bride-cake that was hidden in cobwebs.

Sarah Pocket conducted me down, as if I were a ghost who must be seen out. She could not get over my appearance, and was completely bewildered. I said "Good-bye, Miss Pocket"; but she merely stared, and did not seem collected enough to know that I had spoken. Clear of the house, I made my way back to Pumblechook's, took off my new clothes, made them into a bundle, and went back home in my older clothes. I still did not feel very natural in my new suit, and I felt much more at ease carrying it than wearing it.

And now, those six days which were to have run out so slowly, had run out fast and were gone, and tomorrow looked me in the face more steadily than I could look back at it. As the six evenings had dwindled away, I had become more and more appreciative of being with Joe and Biddy. On this last evening, I dressed myself in my new clothes for their delight, and sat in my splendour until bedtime. But, we were all in very low spirits, and none the higher for pretending to be happier than we were.

I was to leave our village at five in the morning, carrying my little bag, and I had told Joe that I wished to walk away all alone. I am ashamed to admit that this idea originated in the contrast I felt there would be between how I looked and how Joe looked, and what people would think of it, if we went to the coach together. I had pretended with myself that that wasn't the reason; but when I went up to my little room on this last night, I felt compelled to admit that it was the reason, and I had an impulse to go back downstairs and beg Joe to walk with me in the morning. But, I did not.

All night there were coaches in my broken sleep, going to wrong places instead of to London – fantastic failures of journeys occupied my dreams until morning. Then, I got up and partly dressed, and sat at the window to take a last look out, and in so doing, fell asleep again.

Biddy was awake early to get my breakfast, and I awoke smelling the smoke of the kitchen fire, and I started up with a terrible idea that it must be late in the afternoon. But long after waking up again, and long after I had heard the clinking of the teacups and was quite ready to go downstairs, I couldn't bring myself to do it. I sat up there, repeatedly unlocking and locking my small bag, until Biddy called to me that I was late.

It was a hurried breakfast with no taste in it. I got up from the meal, saying with a sort of haste, as if it had only just occurred to me, "Well, I suppose I must be off!" and then I kissed my sister who was laughing to herself and nodding and shaking in her usual chair, and kissed Biddy, and threw my arms around Joe's neck. Then I took up my little bag and walked out. The last I saw of them was, when I soon heard a scuffle behind me, and looking back, saw Joe throwing an old shoe after me and Biddy throwing another old shoe. I stopped then, to wave my hat, and dear old Joe waved his strong right arm above his head, crying huskily "Hooroar!" and Biddy put her apron to her face.

I walked away at a good pace, thinking it was easier to go than I had supposed it would be, and that it would never have been proper to have had an old shoe thrown after the coach in sight of all the people in the market street. I whistled and tried to convince myself that leaving the village was easy. But, the village was very peaceful and quiet, and the morning mists were rising, as if to show me the world, and I had been so innocent and little there, and everything beyond was so unknown and big, that in a moment with a strong heave and sob I broke into tears. It happened by the finger-post at the end of the village, and I laid my hand upon it, and said, "Good-bye, O my dear, dear friend!"

Heaven knows we should never be ashamed of our tears, for they are rain upon the blinding dust covering our hard hearts, and can wash it clean. I was better after I had cried than before – more sorry, more aware of my own ingratitude, more gentle. If I had cried before, I would have had Joe walk with me.

I was so sobered by those tears, that when I was on the coach and it had left town, I debated with myself whether or not I should get out when we changed horses and walk back, and have another evening at home, and a better parting. We changed horses, and I had not made up my mind, and still figured that I could get out and walk back when we changed horses a second time.

We changed again, and yet again, and it was now too late and too far to go back, and I went on. And the mists had all solemnly risen now, and the world lay spread before me.

THIS IS THE END OF THE FIRST STAGE OF PIP'S EXPECTATIONS.

Chapter 20

The journey from our town to London took about five hours. It was a little past mid-day when our four-horse stage-coach got into the traffic of London.

We Britons had at that time decided that it was treasonable to doubt our having, and being, the best of everything. Otherwise, I think I might have thought that London was rather ugly, crooked, narrow, and dirty.

Mr. Jaggers had sent me his address; it was in Little Britain, and he had written after it on his card, "just out of Smithfield, and close by the coach-office." So, I took a coach there and we stopped in a gloomy street by an office door with MR. JAGGERS painted on it.

"How much?" I asked the coachman.

He answered, "A shilling – unless you wish to make it more."

I naturally said I had no wish to make it more.

"Then it must be a shilling," observed the coachman. "I don't want to get into trouble. I know him!" He darkly eyed Mr. Jaggers's name on the door, and shook his head.

When he had got his shilling and left (which appeared to relieve him), I went into the front office with my little bag in my hand and asked, Was Mr. Jaggers in?

"He is not," returned the clerk. "He is in Court right now. Am I addressing Mr. Pip?"

I let him know that he was addressing Mr. Pip.

"Mr. Jaggers left word for you to please wait in his office. He couldn't say how long he might be, since he's in court. But it stands to reason, his time being valuable, that he won't be longer than he can help."

With those words, the clerk opened a door, and ushered me into an inner room at the back, and left me alone in Mr. Jaggers' office. It was lighted by a skylight only, and was a most dismal place. The skylight was placed at an odd angle and the neighboring houses looked as if they had twisted themselves to peep down at me through it. There weren't as many papers lying around as I expected to see; but there were some odd objects that I did not expect to see – such as an old rusty pistol, a sword in a scabbard, and two dreadful casts on a shelf above his desk chair, each with a swollen face that looked itchy about the nose. Mr. Jaggers' own high-backed desk chair was of deadly black horse-hair, with rows of brass nails around it, like a coffin; and I fancied I could see how he leaned back in it, and bit his forefinger at the clients. The room was small, and the clients seemed to have had a habit of backing up against the wall, especially the one opposite to Mr. Jaggers' chair, since it was greasy from shoulders rubbing on it.

I sat down in the chair for his clients and became fascinated by the dismal atmosphere of the place. I remembered that the clerk had the same look of knowing something to everybody else's disadvantage that Mr. Jaggers had. I wondered about the history of all the odd objects in the room, and how they came to be there. I wondered whether the two swollen faces were from Mr. Jaggers' family, and, if he were so unlucky to have had a pair of such ill-looking family members, why he stuck them on that dusty perch instead of keeping them at home. I sat wondering and waiting in Mr. Jaggers' small room until I really could not bear the two casts any longer, and got up and went out.

I told the clerk that I would go for a walk while I waited, and I toured Little Britain. I became aware that other people were waiting about for Mr. Jaggers, too. There were two men of secret appearance lounging there, one of whom said to the other when they first passed me that "Jaggers would do it if it was to be done." There was a group of three men and two women standing at a corner, and one of the women was crying on her dirty shawl, and the other comforted her by saying, as she pulled her own shawl over her shoulders, "Jaggers is working for him Amelia, and what more could you have?" There was a red-eyed little man who came into the area while I was loitering there, who seemed highly excited, hopping around anxiously under a lamp-post and saying to himself in a kind of frenzy, "Oh Jaggers, Jaggers, Jaggers! The others all stagger, give me Jaggers!" These testimonies to the popularity of my guardian made a deep impression on me, and I admired and wondered about him more than ever.

Eventually, I saw Mr. Jaggers coming across the road towards me. All the others who were waiting saw him at the same time, and there was quite a rush at him. Mr. Jaggers, putting a hand on my shoulder and walking me on at his side without saying anything to me, spoke to his followers.

First, the two secret men.

"Now, I have nothing to say to you," said Mr. Jaggers, throwing his finger at them. "I want to know no more than I know. As to the result, it's a toss-up. I told you from the first it was a toss-up. Have you paid Wemmick?"

"We made the money up this morning, sir," said one of the men, submissively.

"I don't ask you when you made it up, or where, or whether you made it up at all. Has Wemmick got it?"

"Yes, sir," said both the men together.

"Very well; then you may go. Now, I won't have it!" said Mr Jaggers, waving his hand at them to put them behind him. "If you say a word to me, I'll quit the case."

"We thought, Mr. Jaggers--" one of the men began, pulling off his hat.

"That's what I told you not to do," said Mr. Jaggers. "You thought! I think for you; that's enough for you. If I want you, I know where to find you; I don't want you to find me. Now I won't have it. I won't hear a word."

The two men looked at one another as Mr. Jaggers waved them behind again, and humbly fell back and were heard no more.

"And now you!" said Mr. Jaggers, suddenly stopping, and turning on the two women with the shawls, "Amelia, is it?"

"Yes, Mr. Jaggers."

"And do you remember," retorted Mr. Jaggers, "that but for me you wouldn't be here, and couldn't be here?"

"Oh yes, sir!" exclaimed both women together. "Lord bless you, sir, well we knows that!"

"Then why," said Mr. Jaggers, "do you come here?"

"My William, sir!" the crying woman pleaded.

"Now, I tell you what!" said Mr. Jaggers. "Once and for all. If you don't know that your William's in good hands, I know it. And if you come here, bothering about him, I'll make an example of both him and you, and let him slip through my fingers. Have you paid Wemmick?"

"Oh yes, sir! Every last farden."

"Very well. Then you have done all you have got to do. Say another word – one single word – and Wemmick shall give you your money back and I'll be off the case."

This terrible threat caused the two women to stop immediately. No one remained now but the excitable little man, who had already raised the bottom of Mr. Jaggers's coat to his lips several times.

"I don't know this man!" said Mr. Jaggers, in the same devastating tone, "What does this fellow want?"

"My dear Mr. Jaggers. I'm brother to Abraham Lazarus."

"Who's he?" said Mr. Jaggers. "Let go of my coat."

The suitor, kissing the hem of the garment again before letting it go, replied, "Abraham Lazarus, arrested on suspicion of stealing gold-plated dishes."

"You're too late," said Mr. Jaggers. "I'm working for the other side."

"Holy father, Mr. Jaggers!" cried my excitable acquaintance, turning white, "don't say you're working against Abraham Lazarus!"

"I am," said Mr. Jaggers, "and that's the end of it. Get out of the way."

"Mr. Jaggers! Half a moment! My own cousin has gone to Mr. Wemmick in your office at this minute to offer him any price. Mister Jaggers! Half a quarter of a moment! If you're willing to be bought off from the other side – at any superior price! - money is no object! - Mister Jaggers - Mister -!"

My guardian turned away from this petitioner with supreme indifference, and left him dancing on the pavement as if it were red-hot. Without further interruption, we reached the front office where we found the clerk and a one-eyed man in a velveteen suit and fur cap.

"Here's Mike," said the clerk, getting down from his stool, and approaching Mr. Jaggers confidentially.

"Oh!" said Mr. Jaggers, turning to the man, "your man comes to trial this afternoon. Well?"

"Well, Master Jaggers," returned Mike, "after a deal o' trouble, I've found a witness, sir, as might do."

"What is he prepared to swear to on the stand?"

"Well, Master Jaggers," said Mike, "I suppose, anything."

Mr. Jaggers suddenly became most irate. "Now, I warned you before," said he, throwing his forefinger at the terrified client, "that if you ever presumed to talk that way here, I'd make an example of you. You infernal scoundrel, how dare you tell ME that?"

The client looked scared, but bewildered too, as if he didn't know what he had done wrong.

"Idiot!" said the clerk, in a low voice, giving him a stir with his elbow. "Do you need to say that face to face?"

"Now, I ask you, you blundering booby," said my guardian, very sternly, "once more and for the last time, what the man you have brought here is prepared to swear to in court?"

Mike looked hard at my guardian, as if he were trying to learn a lesson from his face, and slowly replied, "Either to character, or to having been in his company and never left him all the night in question."

"Now, be careful. In what position of life is this man?"

Mike looked at his cap, and looked at the floor, and looked at the ceiling, and looked at the clerk, and even looked at me, before beginning to reply in a nervous manner, "We've dressed him up like--" when my guardian blustered out:

"What? You WILL, will you?"

("Idiot!" added the clerk again, with another stir.)

After some helpless casting about, Mike brightened and began again:

"He is dressed like a respectable pie man. A sort of a pastry-cook."

"Is he here?" asked my guardian.

"I left him," said Mike, "sitting on some doorsteps around the corner."

"Take him past that window, and let me see him."

The window indicated, was the office window. We all three went to it, behind the wire blind, and presently saw Mike walk by in an accidental manner with a murderous-looking tall individual, wearing a short suit of white linen and a paper cap. This counterfeit baker was not remotely sober, and had a black eye in the green stage of recovery, which was covered in make-up.

"Tell him to take his witness away immediately," said my guardian to the clerk, in extreme disgust, "and ask him what he means by bringing such a fellow as that."

My guardian then took me into his own office, and while he ate lunch, standing, informed me what arrangements he had made for me. I was to go to "Barnard's Inn," where Matthew Pocket's son lived in an apartment, and where a bed had been sent in for me. I was to remain with young Mr. Pocket until Monday when I was to go with him to his father's house on a visit, that I might see how I liked him as my potential tutor. Also, I was told what my allowance was to be – it was a very large one – and he handed to me, from one of his drawers, the business cards of certain tradesmen with whom I was to make purchases for whatever I needed. "You will find your credit good with these tradesmen, Mr. Pip," said my guardian. "I shall by this means be able to check your bills, and to pull you up if I find you outrunning the constable. Of course, you'll go wrong somehow, but that's no fault of mine."

After I had pondered a little over this encouraging remark, I asked Mr. Jaggers if I could send for a coach? He said it was not worthwhile, I was so near my destination; Wemmick would walk there with me, if I pleased.

I then learned that Wemmick was the clerk in the next room. Another clerk was brought down from up-stairs to take his place while he was out, and I accompanied him into the street after shaking hands with my guardian. We found a new set of people lingering outside, but Wemmick made his way among them by saying coolly yet decisively, "I tell you it's no use; he won't have a word to say to any of you;" and we soon got clear of them, and went on side by side.

Chapter 21

Looking at Mr. Wemmick as we went along, I found him to be rather short in stature, with a square wooden face, whose expression seemed to have been imperfectly chipped out with a dull-edged chisel. I figured he was a bachelor from the frayed condition of his clothes, and it appeared that many of his friends had died, for, he wore at least four mourning rings and a brooch with the picture of a lady and a weeping willow at a tomb with an urn on it. I noticed, too, that several rings and seals hung at his watch chain, as if he were quite weighed down with remembrances of departed friends. He had glittering eyes – small, keen, and black – and thin wide lips; he appeared to have had them about forty to fifty years.

"So you were never in London before?" said Mr. Wemmick to me.

"No," said I.

"I was new here once," said Mr. Wemmick. "Wild to think of it now!"

"You are well acquainted with it then?"

"Why, yes," said Mr. Wemmick. "I know the moves of it."

"Is it a very wicked place?" I asked, more for the sake of saying something than for getting information.

"You may get cheated, robbed, and murdered in London. But there are plenty of people anywhere who'll do that for you."

"If there is bad blood between you and them," said I, to soften it off a little.

"Oh! I don't know about bad blood," returned Mr. Wemmick, "there's not much bad blood about. They'll do it, if there's anything to be gained by it."

"That makes it worse."

"You think so?" returned Mr. Wemmick. "Much about the same, I should say."

He wore his hat on the back of his head, and looked straight in front of him, walking in a self-contained way as if there were nothing in the streets that could get his attention. His mouth was such a post office of a mouth that he had a mechanical appearance of smiling. We had got to the top of Holborn Hill before I knew that it was merely a mechanical appearance, and that he was not smiling at all.

"Do you know where Mr. Matthew Pocket lives?" I asked Mr. Wemmick.

"Yes," said he, nodding in the direction. "At Hammersmith, west of London."

"Is that far?"

"Well! Say, five miles."

"Do you know him?"

"Why, you're a regular cross-examiner!" said Mr. Wemmick, looking at me with an approving air. "Yes, I know him; I know him."

There was an air of toleration in the way he said these words that rather depressed me; and I was still looking sideways at his block of a face in search of anything encouraging, when he announced that we had reached Barnard's Inn. My mood was not improved by the news, for, I had assumed it would be a nice hotel kept by somebody named Mr. Barnard, and be much fancier than the Blue Boar in my home town. However, it now seemed Mr. Barnard must have died, and his inn had become a dingy collection of shabby buildings squeezed together in a musty corner.

We entered through a gate into a melancholy little square of ground that looked as inviting as a foggy cemetery. I thought it had the most dismal trees in it, and about six of the most dismal houses that I had ever seen surrounded it. The windows of the houses were in every stage of falling apart and makeshift repair, with broken flower-pots, cracked glass, and dusty decay. Signs reading "To Let", "To Let", "To Let", glared at me from empty rooms of those houses, as if no new wretches ever came to live there. A dirty covering of soot and smoke lay on everything. As for the smell; dry rot, and wet rot, and all the silent rots that rot in neglected places, as well as the nearby horse coach stable, all churned themselves together in a ghostly concoction and moaned to me, "Try Barnard's Mixture."

Such a letdown was this realization of the first of my great expectations, that, I looked in dismay at Mr. Wemmick. "Ah!" said he, mistaking my look, "the lodging reminds you of the country. So it does me."

He led me into a corner of one of the houses and conducted me up a flight of stairs, which appeared to me to be slowly collapsing into sawdust, to an apartment on the top floor. MR. POCKET, JUN., was painted on the door, and there was a label on the letter-box, "Return shortly."

"He hardly thought you'd come so soon," Mr. Wemmick explained. "You don't need me anymore?"

"No, thank you," said I.

"As I hold the cash," Mr. Wemmick observed, "we shall most likely meet pretty often. Good day."

"Good day."

When we had shaken hands and he was gone, I opened the staircase window and nearly beheaded myself, for, the lines had rotted away, and it came down like a guillotine. Thankfully it was so quick that I had not stuck my head out. After this escape, I was content to take a foggy view of the other houses of the Inn and courtyard through the dirty window, and to stand gloomily looking out, saying to myself that London was definitely overrated.

Mr. Pocket, Junior's, idea of Shortly was not mine, for I had nearly maddened myself with looking out for half an hour, and had written my name with my finger several times in the dirt of every pane in the window, before I heard footsteps on the stairs below. Gradually, a gentleman of about my own age made his way up the stairs. He had a paper-bag under each arm and a container of strawberries in one hand, and was out of breath.

"Mr. Pip?" said he.

"Mr. Pocket?" said I.

"Dear me!" he exclaimed. "I am extremely sorry, but I knew there was a coach from your part of the country at midday, and I thought you would come by that one. The fact is, I have been out for your benefit – not that that is any excuse – but I thought, since you were coming from the country, that you might like a little fruit after dinner, and I went to Covent Garden Market to get it since theirs is good."

For a certain reason I had, I felt as if my eyes would pop out of my head in shock from recognition. I acknowledged his good intentions incoherently, and began to think this was a dream.

"Dear me!" said Mr. Pocket, Junior. "This door sticks so!"

As he was quickly making jam out of his fruit by wrestling with the door while the paper-bags were under his arms, I begged him to allow me to hold them. He gave them to me with an agreeable smile, and combated with the door as if it were a wild beast. It finally yielded so suddenly, that he staggered back upon me, and I staggered back upon the opposite door, and we both laughed. But, still I felt as if my eyes must start out of my head, and as if this must be a dream.

"Please come in," said Mr. Pocket, Junior. "Allow me to lead the way. It's rather sparse here, but I hope you'll be able to make out tolerably well till Monday. My father thought you would get on more agreeably through tomorrow with me than with him, and that you might like to take a walk about London. I am sure I shall be very happy to show London to you. As to our table, you won't find that bad, I hope, for its supplied from our coffee-house here, and (it is only right I should add) at your expense, such being Mr. Jaggers's directions. As to our lodging, it's not by any means splendid, because I have my own money to earn, and my father hasn't anything to give me, and I shouldn't be willing to take it even if he had. This is our sitting-room - just such chairs and tables and carpet and so forth that my parents could spare from home. You mustn't give me credit for the tablecloth and spoons and salt and pepper shakers, because they arrived for you from the coffee-house. This is my little bedroom; rather musty, but Barnard's is musty. This is your bed-room; the furniture's hired for you, but I trust it will work alright. If you should want anything, I'll go and fetch it. We shall be alone together here, but we shan't fight, I dare say. But, dear me, I beg your pardon, you're holding the fruit all this time. Please, let me take these bags from you. I am quite ashamed."

As I stood opposite to Mr. Pocket, Junior, delivering him the bags, One, Two, I saw the shocking appearance of recognition come into his own eyes that I knew were in mine, and he said, falling back:

"Lord bless me, you're the prowling boy!"

"And you," said I, "are the pale young gentleman!"

Chapter 22

The pale young gentleman and I stood looking at each other in Barnard's Inn, until we both burst out laughing. "The idea of its being you!" said he. "The idea of its being you!" said I. And then we looked at each other afresh, and laughed again. "Well!" said Mr. Herbert Pocket (for Herbert was the pale young gentleman's name), reaching out his hand good-humouredly, "it's all over now I hope, and it will be very noble of you if you'll forgive me for having beaten you up."

I made a modest reply, and we shook hands warmly.

"You hadn't come into your good fortune at that time?" said Herbert Pocket.

"No," said I.

"No," he agreed, "I heard it had happened very recently. I was rather on the look-out for good-fortune back then."

"Indeed?"

"Yes. Miss Havisham had sent for me, to see if she could take a fancy to me. But she couldn't – at all events, she didn't."

I thought it polite to remark that I was surprised to hear that.

"Bad taste," said Herbert, laughing, "but a fact. Yes, she had sent for me on a trial visit, and if I had come out of it successfully, I suppose I might have been provided for; perhaps I should have been what-you-may-called it to Estella."

"What's that?" I asked, with sudden gravity.

He was arranging his fruit in plates while we talked, which divided his attention, and was the cause of his having made this lapse of a word. "Affianced," he explained, still busy with the fruit. "Betrothed. Engaged. What's-his-named. Any word of that sort."

"How did you bear your disappointment?" I asked.

"Pooh!" said he, "I didn't care much for it. She's a Tartar."

"Miss Havisham?"

"I don't say No to that, but I meant Estella. That girl's hard and haughty and temperamental to the last degree, and has been brought up by Miss Havisham to wreak revenge on all the male sex."

"What relation is she to Miss Havisham?"

"None," said he. "Only adopted."

"Why should she wreak revenge on all the male sex? What revenge?"

"Lord, Mr. Pip!" said he. "Don't you know?"

"No," said I.

"Dear me! It's quite a story, and shall be saved till dinner-time. And now let me take the liberty of asking you a question. Why were you there, that day?"

I told him, and he listened until I had finished, and then burst out laughing again, and asked me if I was sore afterwards? I didn't ask him if he was, for that had been obvious.

"Mr. Jaggers is your guardian, I understand?" he went on.

"Yes."

"You know he is Miss Havisham's man of business and lawyer, and has her confidence when nobody else has?"

I felt this was bringing me towards dangerous ground. I answered with a constraint I made no attempt to hide, that I had seen Mr. Jaggers in Miss Havisham's house on the very day of our combat, but never at any other time, and that I believed he did not remember having ever seen me there.

"He was so obliging as to suggest my father to be your tutor. Of course, he knew about my father from his connection with Miss Havisham. My father is Miss Havisham's cousin; not that that means they are on good terms with each other, for he is a bad courtier and will not humor her."

Herbert Pocket had a frank and easy way with him that was very likable. I had never met anyone before or since who more strongly expressed to me, in every look and tone, a natural inability to do anything secret or mean. There was something wonderfully hopeful about his general attitude, and something that at the same time whispered to me that he would never be very successful or rich, though I wasn't sure why.

He was still a pale young gentleman, and had a certain conquered tiredness about him that did not seem to indicate natural strength. He wasn't handsome, but he was better than handsome, being extremely friendly and cheerful. His body was a little awkward, as in the days when my knuckles had pummeled it, but it looked as if it would always be light and young. Whether Mr. Trabb's local work would have sat more gracefully on him than on me may be a question; but I am sure that he carried off his rather old clothes much better than I carried off my new suit.

As he was so open about discussing things, I felt that holding back on my part would be impolite. So, I told him my small story, and stressed the part about my being forbidden to ask who my benefactor was. I further mentioned that as I had been brought up as a blacksmith in a country place, and knew very little of the ways of politeness, I would really appreciate it if he would give me a hint whenever he saw me unsure or going wrong.

"With pleasure," said he, "though I bet you'll need very few hints. We'll be together often, and I would like to banish any needless restraint between us. Will you do me the favour to call me by my first name, Herbert?"

I thanked him, and said I would. I informed him in exchange that my first name was Philip.

"I don't like Philip," said he, smiling, "for it sounds like a moral boy out of the spelling-book who was so lazy that he fell into a pond, or so fat that he couldn't see out of his eyes. I tell you what; we are so harmonious, and you have been a blacksmith – would you mind it?"

"I wouldn't mind anything you propose," I answered, "but I don't understand you."

"Would you mind Handel for a first name? There's a charming piece of music by Handel, called the Harmonious Blacksmith."

"I should like it very much."

"Then, my dear Handel," said he, turning round as the door opened, "here is the dinner, and I must beg of you to take the top of the table, because the dinner is of your providing."

This I would not hear of, so he took the top, and I faced him. It was a nice little dinner – seemed to me then, a very Lord Mayor's Feast – and I relished it all the more, being independent, with no old people by, and with London all around us.

We had made some progress in the dinner, when I reminded Herbert of his promise to tell me about Miss Havisham.

"True," he replied. "Let me introduce the topic, Handel, by mentioning that in London it is not the custom to put your knife in your mouth – for fear of accidents – and that while the fork is for that use, it is not put further in than necessary. It is scarcely worth mentioning, only it's as well to do as other people do. Also, the spoon is not generally used over-hand, but under. This has two advantages. You get at your mouth better (which after all is the object), and you save a good deal of the attitude of opening oysters, on the part of the right elbow."

He offered these friendly suggestions in such a lively way, that we both laughed and I scarcely blushed.

"Now," he pursued, "concerning Miss Havisham. Miss Havisham, you must know, was a spoiled child. Her mother died when she was a baby, and her father denied her nothing. Her father was a country gentleman down in your part of the world, and was a brewer. He was very rich and very proud. So was his daughter."

"Miss Havisham was an only child?" I guessed.

"Wait a moment, I am coming to that. No, she was not an only child; she had a half-brother. Her father privately married again – his cook, I think."

"I thought he was proud," said I.

"My good Handel, so he was. He married his second wife secretly, because he was proud, and in the course of time she died, but not before she had a son with him. After she was dead, I understand is when he first told his daughter about that marriage and the son, and then the son became a part of the family, living in the house you've visited. As the son grew into a young man, he became wild, extravagant, untrustworthy – altogether bad. Eventually his father disinherited him; but he softened when he was dying, and left his son well off, though not nearly so well off as Miss Havisham. She was now a rich heiress, and was sought after as a great match. Her half-brother had ample money from his inheritance, but, between debts and his extravagant habits, wasted it all quickly. There were strong differences between him and her, and it is suspected that he held a deep grudge against her, as having influenced their father's anger toward him. Now, I come to the cruel part of the story – merely breaking off, my dear Handel, to remark that a dinner-napkin will not go into a cocktail glass."

Why I was trying to pack mine into my glass, I have no idea. I only know that I found myself making the most strenuous exertions to compress it within that glass. Again, I thanked him and apologized, and he said in the cheerfullest manner, "Not at all, I am sure!" and resumed.

"There appeared upon the scene a certain man, who pursued and wooed Miss Havisham. I never saw him, for this happened around twenty-five years ago (long before you and I were born, Handel), but I have heard my father mention that he was a showy man. But he was not to be mistaken for a gentleman, my father most strongly maintains; because it is a principle of his that no man can be a true gentleman at heart, if he is not a true gentleman in manner. He says, no varnish can hide the grain of the wood; and that the more varnish you put on, the more the grain will show. Anyway, this man pursued Miss Havisham closely, and pretended to be devoted to her. I believe she had not shown much susceptibility up to that time with other men; but all the susceptibility she had certainly came out then, and she passionately loved him. There is no doubt that she perfectly idolized him. He used her affection systematically, and he got great sums of money from her, and he convinced her to buy her brother out of his share in the brewery (which had been left to him by his father) for more than it was worth, saying that when he was her husband he must manage it all for her."

"Miss Havisham was too haughty and too much in love to be warned by anyone. Her family members were poor and scheming, with the exception of my father; he was poor like them, but not scheming or jealous of her money. The only independent one among them, he warned her that she was doing too much for this man, and was placing herself too completely in his power. She angrily ordered my father out of the house, and my father has never seen her since."

I thought of her having said, 'Matthew will come and see me at last when I am laid dead upon that table'; and I asked Herbert why his father was so stubbornly against her?

"It's not that," said he, "but she accused him of being disappointed that he wasn't going to get money from her, and, if he were to go to her now, it would look true. So, the marriage day was set, the wedding dresses were bought, the wedding guests were invited. The day came, but not the Groom. He wrote her a letter--"

"Which she received," I struck in, "when she was dressing for her marriage? At twenty minutes to nine?"

"At the hour and minute," said Herbert, nodding, "at which time she afterwards stopped all the clocks. What was in the letter, more than that it most heartlessly broke the marriage off, I can't tell you, because I don't know. When she recovered from a bad illness that she had, she laid the whole place waste, as you have seen it, and she has never since looked upon the light of day."

"Is that all the story?" I asked, after considering it.

"All I know of it; and indeed, I only know so much through piecing it out for myself; for my father always avoids the topic, and even when Miss Havisham invited me to go there, told me no more of it than was absolutely necessary for me to understand. But I have forgotten one thing. It has been alleged that the man to whom she gave her misplaced love, was scheming the whole time with her half-brother; that it was a conspiracy between the two, and that they shared the profits."

"I wonder why he didn't marry her and get all the property," said I.

"He may have been married already, and shaming her cruelly may have been a part of her half-brother's scheme," said Herbert. "But, I don't know that."

"What became of the two men?" I asked, after again considering the subject.

"They fell into deeper shame and degradation – if there can be deeper – and ruin."

"Are they alive now?"

"I don't know."

"You said just now, that Estella was not related to Miss Havisham, but adopted. When adopted?"

Herbert shrugged his shoulders. "There has always been an Estella, since I have heard of a Miss Havisham. I know no more. And now, Handel," said he, finally throwing off the story as it were, "there is a perfectly open understanding between us. All that I know about Miss Havisham, you know."

"And all that I know," I retorted, "you know."

"I fully believe it. So, there can be no competition or ambiguity between you and me. And as to the condition of your expectations – namely, that you are not to inquire about or discuss to whom you owe them – you may be very sure that it will never be brought up by me or anyone belonging to me."

In truth, he said this with so much delicacy, that I felt the subject over, even though I should be under his father's roof for years and years to come. Yet he also said it with so much subtle meaning, too, that I felt he perfectly understood that Miss Havisham was my benefactress, just as I understood the fact myself.

It had not occurred to me before, that he had led up to that part for the purpose of clearing it out of our way; but we were so much the lighter and easier for having discussed it, that I now could tell this was the case. We had a great conversation, and I asked him what he did for a living? He replied, "I'm a capitalist – an Insurer of Ships." I suppose he saw me glancing about the room in search of some evidence of Shipping, or capital, for he added, "In the City."

I had grand ideas of the wealth and importance of Insurers of Ships in the City, and I began to think with awe, of having laid a young Insurer on his back, blackened his enterprising eye, and cut his responsible head open. But, again, there came upon me, for my relief, that odd impression that Herbert Pocket would never be very successful or rich.

"I won't be satisfied with merely using my capital in insuring ships. I shall buy up some good Life Assurance shares, and cut into that business. I shall also dabble a little in mining. None of these things will interfere with my chartering a few thousand tons on my own account. I think I shall trade," said he, leaning back in his chair, "to the East Indies, for silks, shawls, spices, dyes, drugs, and precious woods. It's an interesting trade."

"And the profits are large?" said I.

"Tremendous!" said he.

I wavered again, and began to think here were greater expectations than my own.

"I think I shall trade, also," said he, putting his thumbs in his waistcoat pockets, "to the West Indies, for sugar, tobacco, and rum. Also, to Ceylon, especially for elephants' tusks."

"You will want a good many ships," said I.

"A perfect fleet!" said he.

Quite overpowered by the magnificence of these transactions, I asked him where the ships he insured mostly traded to at present?

"I haven't begun insuring yet," he replied. "I am looking about me."

Somehow, 'looking about' seemed more in keeping with Barnard's Inn. I said (in a tone of conviction), "Ah-h!"

"Yes. I am in a counting-house, and looking about me."

"Is a counting-house profitable?" I asked.

"To – do you mean to the young fellow who's in it?" he asked, in reply.

"Yes; to you."

"Why, n-no; not to me." He said this with the air of one carefully calculating numbers in his head. "Not directly profitable. That is, it doesn't pay me anything, and I have to – keep myself."

This certainly did not seem profitable, and I shook my head as if implying that it would be difficult to get much capital from such a source of income.

"But the thing is," said Herbert Pocket, "that you look about you. That's the grand thing. You are in a counting-house, you know, and you look about you."

It struck me that you could also be outside of a counting-house, you know, and look about you; but I silently deferred to his experience.

"Then the time comes," said Herbert, "when you see your opportunity. And you take it, and you swoop in and you make your capital, and then there you are! When you have once made your capital, you have nothing to do but use it."

This was very like his way of conducting our encounter in Miss Havisham's garden. His manner of bearing his poverty, too, was exactly like his manner of bearing that defeat. It seemed to me that he took all blows and buffets now, with just the same attitude as he had taken mine then. It was evident that he had nothing around him but the simplest necessities, for just about everything that I commented on in his apartment turned out to have been sent in for me from the coffee-house or somewhere else.

Yet, having already made his fortune in his own mind, he was so modest with it that I felt quite grateful to him for not being puffed up. It was a pleasant addition to his naturally pleasant ways, and we got on famously. In the evening we went out for a walk in the streets, and went half-price to the Theatre; and next day we went to church at Westminster Abbey, and in the afternoon we walked in the Parks; and I wondered who made the shoes for all the horses there, and wished that Joe did.

The next day, Monday morning, at a quarter before nine, Herbert went to the counting-house to work – to look about him, too, I suppose – and I went with him for company. He was to leave in an hour or two to take me to Hammersmith to meet his father, and I was to wait around for him. It was a hot, dusty, grimy place, and I had doubts that it was the best place to look about ones-self.

I waited around until it was noon, and Herbert came for me. We went and had lunch at a famous restaurant which I then thought was wonderful, but now believe to have been the most over-rated place in Europe, and where I could not help noticing, even back then, that there was much more gravy on the tablecloths and waiters' clothes than on our steaks. After lunch we went back to Barnard's Inn and I got my little bag, and then we took a coach to Hammersmith. We arrived there at two or three o'clock in the afternoon, and had a short walk to Mr. Pocket's house. Lifting the latch of a gate, we passed directly into a little garden overlooking the river, where Mr. Pocket's children were playing about. And it appeared that Mr. and Mrs. Pocket's children were not growing up or being brought up, but were tumbling up.

Mrs. Pocket was sitting on a garden chair under a tree, reading, with her legs upon another garden chair; and Mrs. Pocket's two nursemaids were looking about while the children played. "Mamma," said Herbert, "this is young Mr. Pip." Upon which Mrs. Pocket received me with an appearance of friendly dignity.

"Master Alick and Miss Jane," cried one of the nurses to two of the children, "if you go a-bouncing up against them bushes you'll fall over into the river and be drownded, and what'll your pa say then?"

At the same time this nurse picked up Mrs. Pocket's handkerchief, and said, "If that don't make six times you've dropped it, Mum!" Upon which Mrs. Pocket laughed and said, "Thank you, Flopson," and settling herself in one chair only, resumed reading her book. Before she could have read half a dozen lines, she turned her eyes to me, and said, "I hope your mamma is quite well?" This unexpected question put me into such a difficulty that I began saying in the absurdest way that if there had been any such person I had no doubt she would have been quite well and would have been very much obliged and would have sent her compliments, when the nurse came to my rescue.

"Well!" she cried, picking up the dropped pocket handkerchief again, "if that don't make seven times! What ARE you a-doing of this afternoon, Mum!" Mrs. Pocket received her property, at first with a look of complete surprise as if she had never seen it before, and then with a laugh of recognition, and said, "Thank you, Flopson," and forgot me, and went on reading.

I found, now that I had time to count them, that there were at least six little Pockets there, in various stages of tumbling up. I had scarcely arrived at the total when a seventh was heard in the house, crying miserably.

"If there ain't Baby!" said Flopson, "Hurry up, Millers."

Millers, who was the other nurse, went into the house, and by degrees the child's crying was hushed and stopped. Mrs. Pocket was reading all this time, and I was curious to know what the book could be.

We were waiting, I guessed, for Mr. Pocket to come out to meet us; at any rate, we waited there, and so I had an opportunity of observing this remarkable family phenomenon that whenever any of the children got near Mrs. Pocket while playing, they always tripped themselves up and tumbled over her – always very much to her momentary astonishment. I couldn't figure out why this was happening, until eventually Millers came over with the baby, which baby was handed to Flopson, which Flopson was handing to Mrs. Pocket, when she too fell over Mrs. Pocket, baby and all, and was caught by Herbert and myself.

"Gracious me, Flopson!" said Mrs. Pocket, looking off her book for a moment, "everybody's tumbling!"

"Gracious you, indeed, Mum!" returned Flopson, very red in the face; "what have you got there?"

“What have I got here, Flopson?" asked Mrs. Pocket.

"Why, it's your footstool!" cried Flopson. "And if you keep it hidden under your skirts like that, then we can't help but keep tumbling over it. Here! Take the baby, Mum, and give me your book."

Mrs. Pocket acted on the advice, and awkwardly danced the infant a little in her lap, while the other children played around it. This had lasted only a very short time, then Mrs. Pocket issued an order that they were all to be taken into the house for a nap.

Given these circumstances, once Flopson and Millers had corralled the children into the house and Mr. Pocket came out of it to meet me, I wasn't very surprised to see that Mr. Pocket was a gentleman who looked rather confused and had tangled grey hair, as if he didn't quite seem able to put anything straight.

Chapter 23

Mr. Pocket said he was glad to see me, and he hoped I was not sorry to see him. "For, I'm not," he added, with a smile like his son's, "an intimidating looking person." He was a young-looking man, despite his grey hair and looking disheveled, and he seemed like a genuine, nice person. When he had talked with me a little, he said to Mrs. Pocket, "Belinda, I hope you have welcomed Mr. Pip?" And she looked up from her book, and said, "Yes." She then smiled at me absentmindedly and asked me if I liked the taste of orange-flower water? Since I had no idea where that question came from, I considered it to have been just sort of thrown out there, like her question about my mother, in a general conversational way.

I found out within a few hours that Mrs. Pocket was an only child, and that her father had been a knight and died sometime in the past. I think he had been knighted for handing some Royal Person either the trowel or the mortar on the occasion of laying the first stone of some building or other. Be that as it may, this Knight had convinced himself that his own deceased father (her grandfather) was supposed to have been a Baron, except that somebody had schemed to keep it from happening due to some unknown grudge. So, her father had counted himself as part of the Nobility based on this belief. Accordingly, he had directed that Mrs. Pocket be raised as somebody who must marry a person with a title, and who was to be kept from acquiring any domestic knowledge. So successfully was she guarded from learning anything productive that she had grown up highly ornamental, and perfectly helpless and useless.

Mr. Pocket had no title, but he had some money, and he needed all of it (and then some) to pay the servants and provide for his wife's required lifestyle of being pampered, which mostly made up for his lack of a title.

Both Mr. and Mrs. Pocket seemed so confused and out of touch with everything on the premises that I wondered who really owned the house and let them live there, until I found out it was the servants that seemed to run everything. It was a smooth way of life, for they took care of the family, but it was an expensive one. He therefore brought in young gentlemen to tutor to augment his income.

Mr. Pocket took me into the house and showed me my room, which was a pleasant one, and was furnished so that I could use it as my own private sitting-room. He then knocked at the doors of two other similar rooms, and introduced me to their occupants, by name Drummle and Startop, who were two other students like myself. Drummle was an old-looking young man of a heavy build. Startop was younger in years and appearance, and was reading and holding his head on both sides with his hands, as if he thought it might explode from gaining too much knowledge from the book.

We had lunch that first day, and while I was paying attention to my knife, fork, spoon, glass, and other instruments of self-destruction, Mrs. Pocket and Drummle were conversing. I learned that Drummle, whose first name was Bentley, was second in line to be a Baron, and that the book I had seen Mrs. Pocket reading in the garden was apparently all about titles, and that she knew the exact date at which her grandpapa was supposed to have been listed in the book, but of course wasn't. Drummle didn't say much (he seemed to be a sulky kind of fellow), but he appeared to recognize Mrs. Pocket as a peer of his and of noble birth.

No one but themselves showed any interest in this part of the conversation, and it appeared to me that it was painful to Herbert, and it seemed like it was going to last a long time, when a servant appeared with the bad news that the cook had misplaced the beef. To my absolute amazement I saw Mr. Pocket relieve the stress this news caused him by performing an extraordinary ritual, but nobody else paid attention to it because he apparently did this so often. He put his two hands into his messy hair, and appeared to make a great effort to lift himself up by it. When he had done this, and had failed to lift himself up, he quietly went back to what he was doing.

After lunch, the children were formally introduced. There were four little girls and two little boys, besides the baby who might have been either. They were brought in by Flopson and Millers, as if they had been out recruiting somewhere for children and had found these. Mrs. Pocket looked at the young Nobles-that-ought-to-have-been, as if she thought she might have seen them before, but didn't quite know what to make of them.

"Here! Give me your fork, Mum, and take the baby," said Flopson. "Don't hold it that way, or you'll get its head under the table."

Thus advised, Mrs. Pocket held it the wrong way anyway and hit its head on the table, which was announced to all of us by a loud thump and the baby crying.

"Dear, dear! Give it back to me, Mum," said Flopson; "and Miss Jane, come and dance for baby!"

One of the little girls, a tiny one who seemed to have volunteered to be in charge of the other children, stepped out of her place in line, and danced to and from the baby until it stopped crying, and laughed. Then, all the children laughed, and Mr. Pocket (who in the meantime had twice tried to lift himself up by his hair) laughed, and we all laughed and were glad.

Flopson then got the baby safely into Mrs. Pocket's lap and gave it a nutcracker to play with, at the same time advising Mrs. Pocket to notice that the handles of that tool would not agree with the baby's eyes, and sharply charged Miss Jane to look after the same. Then, the two nurses left the room.

I became quite nervous, as Mrs. Pocket fell into a discussion with Drummle and seemed to forget all about the baby on her lap, who was doing the most appalling things with the nutcracker. Eventually, little Jane saw that it was in danger of harming itself, and coaxed the dangerous weapon away. Mrs. Pocket did not approve of this, and said to her:

"You naughty child, how dare you? Go and sit down this instant!"

"Mamma dear," lisped the little girl, "baby would have put hith eyeth out."

"How dare you tell me that?" retorted Mrs. Pocket. "Go and sit down in your chair this moment!"

"Belinda," begged Mr. Pocket, from the other end of the table, "how can you be so unreasonable? Jane only interfered for the protection of baby."

"I will not allow anybody to interfere," said Mrs. Pocket, with hurt dignity. "I am surprised, Matthew, that you would expose me to this offense."

"Good God!" cried Mr. Pocket, in an outbreak of desolate desperation. "Are infants to be nutcrackered into their tombs, and is nobody to save them?"

"I will not be interfered with by Jane," said Mrs. Pocket, with a majestic glance at that innocent little offender. "I hope I know my poor grandpapa's noble position. Jane, indeed!"

Mr. Pocket got his hands in his hair again, and this time really did lift himself some inches out of his chair. "Hear this!" he helplessly exclaimed to the world. "Babies are to be nutcrackered dead, for people's poor grandpapa's noble positions!" Then he let himself down again, and became silent.

The rest of us looked awkwardly at the table-cloth while this was going on. A pause followed, during which the baby tried to reach for little Jane, who appeared to me to be the only member of the family (not including the servants) with whom it had any relationship.

"Mr. Drummle," said Mrs. Pocket, "will you ring for Flopson? Jane, you undutiful little thing, go and lie down. Now, baby darling, come with ma!"

The baby protested with all its might. It doubled itself up the wrong way over Mrs. Pocket's arm and was carried out while in full rebellion.

And it eventually got what it wanted anyway, for I saw it through the window after a few minutes, being cared for by little Jane.

The other five children were left behind, standing by the dinner-table. Mr. Pocket was well meaning, but wasn't much closer to his children than his wife was. He looked at them for a minute as if he couldn't figure out how they came to be living there, and why they hadn't been assigned by Nature to somebody else. Then, in a distant way, he asked them a few questions – like why little Joe had that hole in his shirt, who said, Pa, Flopson was going to mend it when she had time – and how little Fanny came by that sore on her finger, who said, Pa, Millers was going to tend to it when she didn't forget. Then, he melted into parental tenderness, and gave them each a shilling and told them to go and play; and then as they went out, he dismissed them from his mind with one very strong effort to lift himself up by his hair.

In the evening there was rowing on the river. As Drummle and Startop each had a boat, I decided I needed one. I was pretty good at most exercises in which country boys do well, but, as I wanted to have elegant technique for the Thames River, I hired a local skilled rower, to whom I was introduced by my new friends that evening. This expert almost lost me as a student when he complimented me, saying I had the arm strength of a blacksmith.

There was a dessert tray after we got home that night, and I think we would all have enjoyed ourselves, except a disagreeable domestic situation occurred. Mr. Pocket was in good spirits, when a housemaid came in, and said to him, "If you please, sir, I should wish to speak to you."

"Speak to your master?" said Mrs. Pocket, whose dignity was hurt again. "Sophia, how can you think of such a thing? Go and speak to Flopson. Or speak to me at some other time."

"Begging your pardon, ma'am," returned the housemaid, "I should wish to speak at once, and to speak to master."

So, Mr. Pocket followed her out of the room, and we made the best of ourselves until he came back.

"This is quite a sight, Belinda!" said Mr. Pocket, returning with grief and despair on his face. "The cook is lying passed out drunk on the kitchen floor, with a large bundle of our butter in the cupboard ready to sell!"

Mrs. Pocket instantly said, "This is that horrible Sophia's doing!"

"What do you mean, Belinda?" demanded Mr. Pocket.

"Sophia has told you," said Mrs. Pocket. "Did I not see her with my own eyes and hear her with my own ears, come into the room just now and ask to speak to you?"

"But, she just took me downstairs, Belinda," returned Mr. Pocket, "to show me the drunk cook, and the bundle."

"And do you defend her, Matthew," said Mrs. Pocket, "for making mischief?"

Mr. Pocket uttered a dismal groan.

"Am I, my grandpapa's granddaughter, to be nothing in the house?" said Mrs. Pocket. "Besides, the cook has always been a very nice and respectful woman, and has said she felt I was born to be a Duchess."

There was a sofa next to where Mr. Pocket stood, and he dropped into it like a dying gladiator, and said with a hollow voice, "Good night, Mr. Pip," and I thought it advisable to go to bed and leave him.

Chapter 24

After two or three days, when I had set myself up in my room there, Mr. Pocket and I had a long talk together. He knew more of my intended career than I knew myself, for he said he was told by Mr. Jaggers that I was not intended to learn any profession, but that I should be well enough educated for my destiny if I could "hold my own" with the average young prosperous man. I agreed, of course, not knowing any better.

He would be the teacher of all my studies. He was so straightforward, good-natured, and serious about teaching me, that he inspired me to be the same as a student. If he had shown indifference as a teacher, I have no doubt I would have done the same as a student; but he did not act that way, and each of us did the other justice.

When I had begun to settle down to my studies, it occurred to me that if I could keep my bedroom in Barnard's Inn, my life would be agreeably varied between living there and studying at Mr. Pocket's, while living with Herbert would also help improve my manners. Mr. Pocket did not object to this arrangement, but urged that before we could proceed with the plan that it must be approved by my guardian, so I went off to Little Britain and told my wish to Mr. Jaggers.

"If I could buy the furniture now hired for me," said I, "and one or two other little things, I should be quite at home there."

"Great!" said Mr. Jaggers, with a short laugh. "I told you you'd get on. Well! How much do you want?"

I said I didn't know how much.

"Come!" retorted Mr. Jaggers. "How much? Fifty pounds?"

"Oh, not nearly so much."

"Five pounds?" said Mr. Jaggers.

This was such a great fall, that I said, "Oh! More than that."

"More than that, eh!" retorted Mr. Jaggers, lying in wait for me, with his hands in his pockets, his head on one side, and his eyes on the wall behind me; "how much more?"

"It is so difficult to pick a number," said I, hesitating.

"Come!" said Mr. Jaggers. "Let's get at it. Twice five, will that do? Three times five, will that do? Four times five, will that do?"

I said I thought that would do handsomely.

"Four times five will do handsomely, will it?" said Mr. Jaggers, knitting his brows. "Now, what do you make of four times five?"

"What do I make of it?"

"Ah!" said Mr. Jaggers; "how much is that?"

"I suppose you make it twenty pounds," said I, smiling.

"Never mind what I make it, my friend," observed Mr. Jaggers, with a knowing and contradictory toss of his head. "I want to know what you make it."

"Twenty pounds, of course."

"Wemmick!" said Mr. Jaggers, opening his office door. "Take Mr. Pip's written order, and pay him twenty pounds."

This strongly marked way of doing business made a strongly marked impression on me, and not a good one. As Mr. Jaggers happened to leave the office now, and as Wemmick was talkative, I said to Wemmick that I hardly knew what to make of Mr. Jaggers's manner.

"Tell him that, and he'll take it as a compliment," answered Wemmick. "He don't mean that you should know what to make of it. - Oh!" for I looked surprised, "it's not personal; it's professional; only professional."

Wemmick was at his desk, lunching – and crunching – on a dry hard biscuit; pieces of which he threw from time to time into his slit of a mouth, as if he were putting them in a post office box to be mailed.

"Always seems to me," said Wemmick, "as if he had set a trap and was watching it. Suddenly – click – you're caught!"

I held back my internal remark that traps were not among the nicer things of life, and instead said that I supposed he was very skillful?

"The best." said Wemmick, "He's as deep as Australia." Pointing with his pen at the office floor, to mean that Australia was, for the purpose of his comment, to be on the opposite spot of the globe. "If there was anything deeper," added Wemmick, "he'd be it."

Then, I said I supposed he had a fine business, and Wemmick said, "Ca-pi-tal!" Then I asked if there were many clerks? to which he replied, "We don't need many clerks, because there's only one Jaggers, and people won't have him at second-hand. There are only four of us. Would you like to see 'em? You are one of us, as I may say."

I accepted the offer. When Mr. Wemmick had put all the biscuit into his post office mouth, and had paid me my money from a cash-box in a safe, we went up-stairs. The office was dark and shabby, and the greasy shoulders that had left their mark in Mr. Jaggers' room also seemed to have been shuffling up and down the staircase for years. There were three clerks upstairs, in three rooms, all engaged in talking with clients or making copies of papers. This, plus the first floor containing one clerk's office and Mr. Jaggers' office, was all the establishment.

When we went down-stairs again, Wemmick led me into my guardian's room and said, "This you've seen already."

"Please," said I, as the two revolting casts on the shelf with the twitchy faces caught my eye again, "whose likenesses are those?"

"These?" said Wemmick, getting up on a chair, and blowing the dust off the horrible heads before bringing them down. "These are two celebrated criminals. Famous clients of ours that got us a world of credit. This chap (why, you must have come down in the night and been peeping into the inkstand to get this blot on your eyebrow, you old rascal!) murdered his master, and, considering that he wasn't brought up to evidence, didn't plan it badly."

"Is it like him?" I asked, recoiling from the brute, as Wemmick spat upon his eyebrow and gave it a rub with his sleeve.

"Like him? It is him, you know. The cast was made in Newgate Prison, directly after he was taken down from the gallows. You liked me, didn't you, Old Artful?" said Wemmick to the cast. He then touched the brooch on his vest with the drawing of the lady and the weeping willow tree next to the tomb with the urn on it, and said to me, "He had it made for me!"

"Is the lady anybody?" said I.

"No," returned Wemmick. "Only his game. (You liked your bit of game, didn't you?) No, there was no lady in the court case except one – and she wasn't like this slender lady, and you wouldn't have caught her taking care of an urn like the one pictured here – unless there was liquor in it." Wemmick put down the cast and polished the brooch with his pocket-handkerchief.

"Did that other one come to the same end?" I asked. "He has the same look."

"You're right," said Wemmick; "it's the genuine look. Much as if one nostril was caught up with a fishhook. He forged wills, he also murdered the people that supposedly made the wills, too. You were a gentlemanly Cove, though" (Mr. Wemmick was again talking to the cast), "and you said you could write Greek. Ha! What a liar you were! I never met such a liar as you!" Before putting his late friend on his shelf again, Wemmick touched the largest of his mourning rings and said, "He sent out to buy it for me, only the day before."

While he was putting up the other cast and coming down from the chair, the thought crossed my mind that all of Wemmick's personal jewelry was received from similar sources. As he seemed to freely talk about such things, I ventured to ask him the question, after he had come back down and was dusting his hands.

"Oh yes," he answered, "these are all gifts of that kind. One brings another, you see; that's the way of it. I always take 'em. They're curiosities. And they're property. They may not be worth much, but, after all, they're property, and portable. It doesn't mean much to you with your brilliant future, but for myself, my guiding star always is, "Get hold of portable property"."

When I had voiced my support of that slogan, he went on to say, in a friendly manner, "If at any time when you have nothing better to do, if you wouldn't mind coming over to see me at my house in Walworth, I could offer you a place to sleep, and I should consider it an honour. I don't have much to show you; but such two or three curiosities that I have, you might like to see, and I am fond of a bit of gardening."

I said I should be delighted to accept his hospitality.

"Thankee," said he; "then we'll consider that it's to happen when convenient for you. Have you dined with Mr. Jaggers yet?"

"Not yet."

"Well," said Wemmick, "he'll give you wine, and good wine. I'll give you punch, and not bad punch. And now, I'll tell you something; when you go to dine with Mr. Jaggers, look at his housekeeper."

"Shall I see something very uncommon?"

"Well," said Wemmick, "you'll see a wild beast tamed. Not so very uncommon, you may tell me. I reply, that depends on the original wildness of the beast, and the amount of taming. It won't lower your opinion of Mr. Jaggers' powers. Keep your eye on it."

I told him I would, with all the interest and curiosity that his advice had awakened. As I was leaving, he asked me if I would like to spend five minutes to see Mr. Jaggers "at it?"

For several reasons, and not least because I didn't really know what Mr. Jaggers would be found to be "at," I answered Yes. We went into the city and arrived in a crowded police court, where my guardian had a woman under examination, or cross-examination – I don't know which – and was striking her, and the bench, and everybody present, with awe. If anybody said a word that he didn't approve of, he instantly required to have it "taken down." If anybody wouldn't make an admission, he said, "I'll have it out of you!" and if anybody made an admission, he said, "Now I've got you!" The judges shivered under a single bite of his finger. Thieves and the police hung in dread rapture on his words, and shrank when a hair of his eyebrows turned in their direction. Which side he was on, I couldn't tell, for he seemed to me to be grinding the whole place in a mill; I only know that when I snuck out on tiptoe, he was not on the judge's side; for, he was making the legs of that old gentleman shake under his table due to Mr. Jaggers' condemnation of his conduct as the representative of British law and justice in the chair that day.

Chapter 25

Bentley Drummle, who was so sulky a fellow that he even picked up a book as if its writer had hurt him, did not begin an acquaintance any better. He was heavy in body, movement, and comprehension, and his manner was lazy, proud, reserved, and suspicious. He came from a rich family down in Somersetshire. Thus, Bentley Drummle had come to Mr. Pocket when he was a head taller than that gentleman, and half a dozen heads thicker than most gentlemen.

Startop had been spoilt by a weak mother and kept at home when he ought to have been at school, but he was devotedly attached to her. He had a woman's delicacy of feature, and was, as Herbert said to me, exactly like his mother. I naturally took to him much more kindly than I did to Drummle, and even in the earliest evenings of our rowing he and I would travel homeward next to each other, talking from boat to boat, while Bentley Drummle came up behind us in our wake, alone, under the overhanging banks and among the shore plants, like some uncomfortable amphibious creature.

Herbert was my best companion and friend. I gave him a half-share in my boat, so he often came to his father's house with me; and my possession of a half-share in his apartment often brought me up to London with him. We used to walk between the two places at all hours.

When I had been in Mr. Pocket's family a month or two, Mr. and Mrs. Camilla showed up. Camilla was Mr. Pocket's sister. Georgiana, whom I had seen at Miss Havisham's on the same occasion, also showed up. She was a cousin of Mr. Pocket's. These people hated me with the hatred of jealousy and disappointment. In keeping with their character, they awkwardly flattered me and tried to gain my favor due to my prosperity and because of who was obviously funding it. Towards Mr. Pocket, they treated him as a grown-up infant that had no clue of his own best interests.

These were the surroundings among which I settled down, and applied myself to my education. I soon started expensive habits, and began to spend an amount of money that, only a few short months before, I would have thought was a fortune. But, through good and evil, I stuck to my books. Between Mr. Pocket and Herbert I learned fast; and, with one or the other always at my elbow to give me the help I wanted and clear obstructions out of my road, I would have been as great a dunce as Drummle if I had not done well.

I had not seen Mr. Wemmick for some weeks, when I thought I would write him a note and propose to accept his invitation and go home with him on a certain evening. He replied that it would give him much pleasure, and that he would expect me at the office at six o'clock. So I went, and there I found him, putting the key of his safe away.

"Did you think of walking down to Walworth?" said he.

"Certainly," said I, "if you approve."

"Very much," was Wemmick's reply, "for I have had my legs under the desk all day, and shall be glad to stretch them. Now, I'll tell you what I have got for supper, Mr. Pip. I have got a stewed steak – which is of home preparation – and a cold roasted fowl – which is from the cook's-shop. I think it's tender, because the master of the shop was a Juryman in some cases of ours the other day, and we let him down easy. I reminded him of it when I bought the bird, and I said, "Pick us out a good one, old Briton, because if we had chosen to keep you in the jury another day or two, we could easily have done it." He said to that, "Let me make you a present of the best fowl in the shop." I let him, of course. As far as it goes, it's property and portable. You don't object to an aged parent, I hope?"

I really thought he was still talking about the bird, until he added, "Because I have got an aged parent at my house." I then said what politeness required.

"So, you haven't dined with Mr. Jaggers yet?" he pursued, as we walked along.

"Not yet."

"He told me so this afternoon when he heard you were coming. I expect you'll have an invitation tomorrow. He's going to ask your pals, too. Three of 'em, ain't there?"

Although I was not in the habit of counting Drummle as one of my pals, I answered, "Yes."

"Well, he's going to ask the whole gang;" I hardly felt complimented by the word; "and whatever he gives you, he'll give you good. Don't look forward to variety, but you'll have excellence. And there's another interesting thing in his house," proceeded Wemmick after a moment's pause, as if his previous remark some weeks before about Mr. Jaggers' housekeeper was understood; "he never lets a door or window be fastened at night."

"Is he never robbed?"

"That's it!" returned Wemmick. "He says, and gives it out publicly, 'I want to see the man who'll rob me.' Lord bless you, I've heard him a hundred times if I have heard him once say to regular burglars in our front office, 'You know where I live; now, nothing is ever locked there; why don't you come try your craft at my house? Come; can't I tempt you?' Not a man of them, sir, would be bold enough to try it."

"They dread him so much?" said I.

"Dread him," said Wemmick. "I believe you they dread him. But he's also devious, even in his defiance of them. There's no silver, sir. Every spoon and tableware is cheap tin."

"So they wouldn't have much," I observed, "even if they--"

"Ah! But HE would have much," said Wemmick, cutting me short, "and they know it. He'd have their lives, and the lives of scores of 'em. He'd have all he could get. And it's impossible to say what he couldn't get, if he gave his mind to it. As to the absence of silver plate, that's only his natural depth, you know. A river is its natural depth, and he's his natural depth. Look at his watch-chain. That's real enough."

"It's very massive," said I.

"Massive?" repeated Wemmick. "I think so. And his watch is a gold repeater, and worth a hundred pounds if it's worth a penny. Mr. Pip, there are about seven hundred thieves in this town who know all about that watch; there's not a man, woman, or child among them who, if they identified the smallest link in that chain, wouldn't drop it as if it was red-hot once they knew what it was."

With such conversation we passed the time walking to the district of Walworth.

Once there, Walworth appeared to be a collection of back lanes, ditches, and little gardens, and to present the appearance of a rather quiet place. Wemmick's house was a little wooden cottage surrounded by gardens, and the top of it was cut out and painted like the top of a castle mounted with cannons.

"My own doing," said Wemmick. "Looks pretty; don't it?"

I highly commended it. I think it was the smallest house I ever saw, with the weirdest gothic windows (by far most of them fake, to keep up the appearance of the house being a castle), and a gothic door, almost too small to get in at.

"That's a real flagstaff, you see," said Wemmick, "and on Sundays I run up a real flag. Then look here. After I have crossed this bridge, I hoist it up – like so – and cut off the outside world."

This bridge was a plank, and it crossed a chasm about four feet wide and two feet deep. But it was very pleasant to see the pride with which he hoisted it up and secured it; smiling as he did so, with true joy and not merely mechanically.

"At nine o'clock every night, Greenwich time," said Wemmick, "I fire the cannon. There it is, you see! And when you hear it go, I think you'll say it's a Stinger."

The piece of ordnance referred to was mounted in a separate fortress, constructed of lattice-work. It was protected from the weather by an ingenious little tarp set up like an umbrella.

"Then, at the back," said Wemmick, "out of sight, so as not to impede the theme of fortifications – for it's a principle with me, if you have an idea, carry it out and keep it up – I don't know whether that's your opinion--"

I said, Yes, decidedly.

" - At the back, there's a pig, and there are chickens and rabbits; then, I knock together my own little frame, you see, and grow cucumbers; and you'll judge at supper what sort of a salad I can raise. So, sir," said Wemmick, smiling again, but seriously too, as he shook his head, "if my little place was ever besieged, it would hold out a devil of a time due to my provisions."

Then, he led me to a pleasant little garden arbour about a dozen yards away, but the path had such ingenious twists in it that it took quite a long time to get there; and in this place our glasses were already set for us.

"I am my own engineer, and my own carpenter, and my own plumber, and my own gardener, and my own Jack of all Trades," said Wemmick, in acknowledging my compliments. "Well; it's a good thing, you know. It brushes the Newgate Prison cobwebs away from my mind, and pleases the Aged. You wouldn't mind being at once introduced to the Aged, would you?"

I expressed the readiness I felt, and we went into the castle. There, sitting by a fire, was a very old man in a flannel coat; clean, cheerful, comfortable, and well cared for, but intensely deaf.

"Well, aged parent," said Wemmick, shaking hands with him in a merry way, "how am you?"

"All right, John; all right!" replied the old man.

"Here's Mr. Pip, aged parent," said Wemmick, "and I wish you could hear his name. Nod away at him, Mr. Pip; that's what he likes. Nod away at him, if you please, like winking!"

"This is a fine place of my son's, sir," cried the old man, while I nodded as hard as I possibly could. "This spot and these beautiful works upon it ought to be kept together by the Nation, after my son passes on, for the people's enjoyment."

"You're as proud of it as Punch, ain't you, Aged?" said Wemmick, looking at the old man with his hard face really softened; "there's a nod for you;" giving him a tremendous one; "there's another for you;" giving him a still more tremendous one; "you like that, don't you? If you're not tired, Mr. Pip – though I know it's tiring to strangers – will you tip him one more? You can't think how it pleases him."

I tipped him several more, and he was in great spirits. He got up to go feed the chickens, and Wemmick and I went back outside to have our punch in the arbour. He told me, as he smoked a pipe, that it had taken him a good many years to bring the property up to its present state of perfection.

"Is it your own, Mr. Wemmick?"

"O yes," said Wemmick, "I have got hold of it, a bit at a time. It's all mine, by George!"

"Is it, indeed? I hope Mr. Jaggers admires it?"

"Never seen it," said Wemmick. "Never heard of it. Never seen the Aged. Never heard of him. No; the office is one thing, and private life is another. When I go into the office, I leave the Castle behind me, and when I come into the Castle, I leave the office behind me. If it's not in any way disagreeable to you, you'll oblige me by doing the same. I don't wish it professionally spoken about."

Of course I agreed to his request. The punch being very nice, we sat there drinking it and talking until it was almost nine o'clock. "Getting near gun-fire," said Wemmick then, as he laid down his pipe; "it's the Aged's treat."

Entering the Castle again, we found the Aged heating the fire poker, with expectant eyes, as a prelude to this great nightly ceremony. Wemmick stood with his watch in his hand, until the moment arrived for him to take the red-hot poker from the Aged, and go to the cannon fortress outside under its umbrella tarp. He took the poker, went outside, and presently the cannon went off with a Bang that shook the crazy little box of a cottage as if it must fall to pieces, and made every glass and teacup in it ring. Upon this, the Aged – who I believe would have been blown out of his arm-chair except for holding on with his elbows – cried out exultingly, "He's fired! I heerd him!" and I nodded my head at the old gentleman until it is no figure of speech to say that I absolutely could not see him.

During the time between then and supper, Wemmick showed me his collection of curiosities. They had mostly criminal origins; the pen with which a famous forgery had been committed, a distinguished razor or two, some locks of hair, and several written confessions – upon which Mr. Wemmick set particular value as being, to use his own words, "every one of 'em Lies, sir." Mixed in were other curiosities he acquired, some he made, and some tobacco-stoppers carved by the Aged. They were all displayed in that chamber of the Castle into which I had first entered, and which served not only as the general sitting-room, but as the kitchen too.

There was a neat little girl in attendance who looked after the Aged during the day. When her work was done, the bridge was lowered to let her exit, and she left for the night. The supper was excellent; and though I wished the pig and his pen might have been a little farther away, I was heartily pleased with my whole entertainment. Nor was there any drawback on my little turret bedroom, beyond there being such a very thin ceiling between me and the flagstaff that when I lay down on my back in bed it seemed as if I had to balance that pole on my forehead all night.

Wemmick was up early in the morning, and I am afraid I heard him cleaning my boots. After that, he fell to gardening, and I saw him from my gothic window pretending to employ the Aged, and nodding at him in a most devoted manner. Our breakfast was as good as the supper, and at half-past eight precisely we left for Little Britain. By degrees, Wemmick got dryer and harder as we went along, and his mouth tightened into a post-office again. At last, when we got to his place of business and he pulled out his key from his coat-collar, he looked as unconscious of his Walworth property as if the Castle and the drawbridge and Aged had all been a forgotten memory, blown into space by the last firing of his cannon.

Chapter 26

It happened as Wemmick had told me it would, that I had an early chance of comparing my guardian's house with that of Wemmick's. My guardian was in his office, washing his hands with his scented soap, when I came in with Wemmick. Mr. Jaggers called me to him, and gave me the invitation for myself and friends which Wemmick had prepared me to receive. "No ceremony," he stipulated, "and no formal dinner dress, and say tomorrow." I asked him where we should go (for I had no idea where he lived), and I believe it was in his general nature not to make anything like an admission, so he instead replied, "Come here, and I'll take you home with me."

I'll take this opportunity of mentioning that he washed his clients off of himself as if he were a surgeon or a dentist. He had a closet in his room, fitted up for the purpose, which smelt of scented soap. It had an unusually large towel on a roller inside the door, and he would wash his hands, and wipe them and dry them all over this towel, whenever he came in from a police-court or dismissed a client from his room. When I and my friends arrived there at six o'clock the next day, he seemed to have been busy on a darker case than usual, for, we found him in this closet, not only washing his hands, but washing his face and gargling his throat. And even when he had done all that, and had wiped himself off with his towel, he took out his penknife and scraped the case out of his fingernails before he put his coat on.

There were some people slinking about as usual when we went out into the street, who were evidently anxious to speak with him; but there was something so conclusive in the halo of scented soap which encircled his presence that they gave it up for that day. As we walked along, he was recognized every so often by some face in the crowd of the streets, and whenever that happened he talked louder to me; but he never otherwise recognized anybody, or took notice that anybody recognized him.

He led us to Gerrard-street, Soho, to a house on the south side of that street. Rather a stately house of its kind, but badly in need of painting, and with dirty windows. He took out his key and opened the door, and we all went into a stone hall, bare, gloomy, and little used. So, up a dark brown staircase into a series of three dark brown rooms on the first floor.

Dinner was in the best of these rooms; the second was his dressing-room; the third, his bedroom. He told us that he had the whole house, but rarely used more of it than we saw. The table was comfortably set – no silver in the tableware, of course – and at the side of his chair were the accessories for the evening. I noticed throughout the dinner that he kept everything under his own hand, and distributed everything himself.

There was a bookcase in the room; from the backs of the books I saw that they were about evidence, criminal law, criminal biography, trials, acts of parliament, and such things. The furniture was all very solid and good, like his watch-chain. It had an official look, however, and there was nothing merely decorative to be seen. In a corner was a little table of papers with a shaded lamp, so that he seemed to bring the office home with him.

He hadn't met my three companions before, and to my surprise he seemed at once to be mainly, if not only, interested in Drummle.

"Pip," said he, putting his large hand on my shoulder and moving me to the window, "I don't know one from the other. Who's the Spider?"

"The spider?" said I.

"The blotchy, sprawly, sulky fellow."

"That's Bentley Drummle," I replied; "the one with the delicate face is Startop."

Not acknowledging "the one with the delicate face", he replied, "Bentley Drummle is his name, is it? I like the look of that fellow."

He immediately began to talk to Drummle. He was not at all deterred by Drummle's replying in his heavy uncommunicative way, but apparently was inspired by it to try and get him to talk. I was looking at the two, when the housekeeper entered, with the first dish for the table.

She was a woman of about forty, I guessed – but I may have thought her younger than she really was. She was rather tall, of a thin and nimble figure, extremely pale, with large faded eyes, and long thick hair.

She set the dish on the table, touched my guardian quietly on the arm with a finger to notify that dinner was ready, and vanished. We took our seats at the round table, and my guardian kept Drummle on one side of him, while Startop sat on the other. It was a nice dish of fish that the housekeeper had put on the table, and we had equally nice lamb afterwards, and then an equally choice bird. Sauces, wines, all the accessories we wanted, and all of the best, were given out by our host from the collection by his side; and when they had been passed around the table, he always put them back again. Similarly, he dealt us clean plates and knives and forks for each course, and put those just used into two baskets on the ground by his chair. No other attendant than the housekeeper appeared, and she brought every dish.

Since I had been advised to take particular notice of the housekeeper by Wemmick, I observed that whenever she was in the room she kept her eyes attentively on my guardian, and that she would remove her hands from any dish she put before him, hesitatingly, as if she dreaded his calling her back, and wanted him to speak when she was near, if he had anything to say. I thought I detected by his manner that he knew this, and held her in suspense on purpose.

Dinner started off happily, and, although my guardian seemed to follow conversation subjects rather than start them, I knew that he managed to wrench the weakest parts of our character out of our mouths. For myself, I found that I was talking about my tendency to spend too much money and to boast of my great prospects before I quite knew that I had opened my lips. It was so with all of us, but with no one more than Drummle.

Our conversation turned upon our rowing feats, and Drummle was made fun of for always coming up behind us in that slow amphibious way of his. Drummle, upon hearing this, informed our host that he much preferred the dinner room to our company, and that as to skill he was more than our master, and that as to strength he could scatter us like leaves. By some method, my guardian wound him up to being a little short of ferocious about his strength; and he rolled up his shirt and flexed his arm to show how muscular it was, and we all did the same in a ridiculous competitive manner.

By now, the housekeeper was clearing the table. My guardian, ignoring her, was leaning back in his chair biting the side of his forefinger and showing an interest in Drummle, that, to me, was quite inexplicable. Suddenly, he clapped his large hand on the housekeeper's, like a trap, as she stretched it across the table. So suddenly did he do this that we all stopped in our foolish arm competition.

"If you talk of strength," said Mr. Jaggers, "I'll show you a wrist. Molly, let them see your wrist."

Her trapped hand was on the table, but she had already put her other hand behind her waist. "Master," she said, in a low voice, with her eyes attentively and entreatingly fixed upon him. "Don't."

"I'll show you a wrist," repeated Mr. Jaggers, with an immovable determination. "Molly, let them see your wrist."

"Master," she again murmured. "Please!"

"Molly," said Mr. Jaggers, not looking at her, but obstinately looking at the opposite side of the room, "let them see both your wrists. Show them. Come!"

He took his hand from hers, and turned that wrist up on the table. She brought her other hand from behind her, and held the two out side by side. The last wrist was much disfigured – deeply scarred across and across. When she held her hands out, she took her eyes from Mr. Jaggers, and turned them watchfully on every one of the rest of us, one after the other.

"There's power here," said Mr. Jaggers, coolly tracing out the sinews with his forefinger. "Very few men have the power of wrist that this woman has. It's remarkable what mere force of grip there is in these hands. I have had occasion to notice many hands; but I never saw a stronger grip, man's or woman's, than these."

While he said these words in a leisurely critical style, she continued to look at every one of us in regular succession as we sat. The moment he ceased, she looked at him again. "That'll do, Molly," said Mr. Jaggers, giving her a slight nod; "you have been admired, and can go." She withdrew her hands and went out of the room, and Mr. Jaggers filled his glass and passed around the wine.

"At half-past nine, gentlemen," said he, "we must break up. Pray make the best use of your time. I am glad to see you all. Mr. Drummle, I drink to you."

If his object in singling out Drummle were to bring him out of his shell still more, it perfectly succeeded. In a sulky triumph, Drummle showed his ill-tempered disapproval of the rest of us, becoming more and more offensive until he became downright intolerable. Through all his stages, Mr. Jaggers followed him with the same strange interest.

In our boyish lack of discretion, I dare say we drank too much, and I know we talked too much. We became particularly mad at some sneer of Drummle's, to the effect that we were too free with our money. It led to my remarking, with more zeal than discretion, that he wasn't one to talk, since Startop had lent him money right in front of me just the week or so before.

"Well," retorted Drummle; "he'll be paid."

"I don't mean to imply that he won't," said I, "but it might make you hold your tongue about us and our money, I should think."

"You should think!" retorted Drummle. "Oh Lord!"

I went on, meaning to be very severe, "I bet that you wouldn't lend money to any of us, if we needed it."

"You're right," said Drummle. "I wouldn't lend one of you a sixpence. I wouldn't lend anybody a sixpence."

"Rather mean to borrow under those circumstances, I should say."

"You should say," repeated Drummle. "Oh Lord!"

His lack of any intelligent reply was so very aggravating that I said, disregarding Herbert's efforts to stop me, "Come, Mr. Drummle, since we are on the subject, I'll tell you what Herbert here and I discussed, when you borrowed that money."

"I don't want to know what Herbert there and you discussed," growled Drummle. And I think he added in a lower growl that we might both go to the devil and shake ourselves.

"I'll tell you anyway," said I, "whether you want to know or not. We said that as you put it in your pocket, so very glad to get it, that you seemed to be immensely amused at his being so weak to lend it to you."

Drummle laughed outright, and sat laughing in our faces, with his hands in his pockets, plainly signifying that it was quite true, and that he despised us, as asses all.

Startop, with a much better grace than I had shown, encouraged him to be a little more agreeable. Startop was a lively bright young fellow, and Drummle was the exact opposite, and he tended to resent Startop's existence as a direct personal offense. Drummle retorted in a coarse lumpish way, and Startop tried to turn the discussion aside with some small pleasantry that made the rest of us laugh. Resenting this little success more than anything, Drummle, without any threat or warning, pulled his hands out of his pockets, swore, picked up a large glass, and would have flung it at Startop's head, but for our host's dexterously seizing it at the instant when it was raised to be thrown.

"Gentlemen," said Mr. Jaggers, deliberately putting down the glass, and hauling out his gold watch by its massive chain, "I am exceedingly sorry to announce that it's half-past nine."

On this hint we all rose to depart. Before we got to the street door, Startop was cheerily calling Drummle "old boy," as if nothing had happened. But the old boy was so far from responding, that he would not even walk back to Mr. Pocket's on the same side of the street as Startop; so, Herbert and I, who remained in town and went to Barnard's Inn, saw them going down the street on opposite sides; Startop leading, and Drummle lagging behind in the shadow of the houses, much as he followed in his boat.

As Mr. Jaggers' door was not yet shut, I thought I would leave Herbert outside for just a moment, and run up-stairs again to say a word to my guardian. I found him in his dressing-room already washing his hands of us.

I told him I had come up again to say how sorry I was that anything disagreeable should have occurred during dinner, and that I hoped he would not blame me much.

"Pooh!" said he, washing his face, and speaking through the water-drops; "it's nothing, Pip. I like that Spider though."

He had turned towards me now, and was toweling himself dry.

"I am glad you like him, sir," said I - "but I don't."

"No, no," my guardian agreed; "don't have too much to do with him. Keep as clear of him as you can. But I like the fellow, Pip; he is one of the true sort. Why, if I was a fortune-teller--"

Looking out of the towel, he caught my eye.

"But I am not a fortune-teller," he said, "You know what I am, don't you? Good-night, Pip."

"Good-night, sir."

In about a month after that, the Spider's time with Mr. Pocket was up for good, and, to the great relief of all the house except Mrs. Pocket, he went home to the family hole.

Chapter 27

"MY DEAR MR PIP,

"I write this by request of Mr. Gargery, to let you know that he is going to London with Mr. Wopsle and would be glad if allowed to see you. He would arrive at Barnard's Hotel Tuesday morning 9 o'clock, when if not agreeable please leave word. Your poor sister is much the same as when you left. We talk of you in the kitchen every night, and wonder what you are saying and doing. If you consider it childish, then please excuse it for the love of poor old days. No more, dear Mr. Pip, from

Your ever obliged, and affectionate servant,

BIDDY.

P.S. He wishes me most particular to write "what larks". He says you will understand. I hope and do not doubt it will be agreeable to see him even though you are a gentleman, for you had ever a good heart, and he is a worthy worthy man. I have read him all except only the last little sentence, and he wishes me most particular to write again "what larks."

I received this letter on Monday morning, and therefore its appointment was for the next day. Let me confess how I looked forward to Joe's coming.

Not with pleasure, though I was bound to him by so many ties and hadn't seen him since I left our village, some six months ago. No; I looked forward to it with considerable disturbance, some dread, and a keen sense of being out of place; that he just wouldn't fit in and would embarrass me. If I could have kept him away by paying money, I certainly would have done it. My greatest comfort was that he was coming to Barnard's Inn, and not to Mr. Pocket's, and therefore would not be seen by Bentley Drummle. I had little objection to his being seen by Herbert or his father, for both of whom I had respect; but I was sharply sensitive to his being seen by Drummle, whom I held in contempt. So, throughout life, our worst weaknesses and meannesses are usually committed for the sake of the people whom we most despise.

Recently, I had begun decorating our apartment in Barnard's Inn in a quite unnecessary, expensive, and inappropriate way. By this time, the rooms were vastly different from how I had found them. I had got on so fast recently that I had even hired a servant boy from my washerwoman's family, in bondage and slavery to whom I might have been said to spend my days. For, after I had made the monster and had clothed him with a blue coat, canary waistcoat, white tie, creamy breeches, and boots, I had to find him something to do and a great deal to eat; and with both of those horrible requirements he haunted my existence.

This servant was ordered to be on duty at eight on Tuesday morning out in the hall, and Herbert suggested certain things for breakfast that he thought Joe would like. I came into town on the Monday night to be ready for Joe, and I got up early in the morning, and arranged the sitting room and breakfast-table to look as splendid and impressive as possible. Unfortunately, the morning was drizzly, and an angel could not have concealed the fact that Barnard's Inn was shedding sooty tears outside the window.

As the time approached, I wanted to run away, but the servant was in the hall as ordered, and presently I heard Joe on the staircase. I knew it was Joe, by his clumsy manner of coming up-stairs – his boots being always too big for him – and by the time it took him to read the names on the other floors on his way up. When at last he stopped outside our door, I could hear his finger tracing over the painted letters of my name, and I afterwards distinctly heard him breathing in at the keyhole. Finally, he gave a faint single rap, and Pepper – such was the embarrassing name of the servant boy – announced "Mr. Gargery!" I thought he would never finish wiping his feet, and that I must go out to lift him off the mat, but at last he came in.

"Joe, how are you, Joe?"

"Pip, how AIR you, Pip?"

With his good honest face all glowing and shining, and his hat put down on the floor between us, he caught both my hands and worked them straight up and down, as if I had been a water pump.

"I am glad to see you, Joe. Give me your hat."

But Joe, picking it up carefully with both hands, like a bird's-nest with eggs in it, wouldn't hear of parting with that piece of property, and persisted in standing there, holding it, and talking over it in a most uncomfortable way.

"Which you have that growed," said Joe, "and that swelled, and that gentle-folked;" Joe considered a little before he discovered this word; "as to be sure you are an honour to your king and country."

"And you, Joe, look wonderfully well."

"Thank God," said Joe, "I'm about the same. And your sister, she's no worse than she were. And Biddy, she's ever right and ready. And all friends is no backwarder, if not no forwarder. 'Ceptin Wopsle; he's had a drop."

All this time (still with both hands taking great care of his bird's-nest), Joe was rolling his eyes round and round the room, and round and round the flowered pattern of my clothes.

"Had a drop, Joe?"

"Why yes," said Joe, lowering his voice, "he's left the Church, and went into the playacting. Which the playacting have likeways brought him to London along with me. And his wish were," said Joe, getting the bird's-nest under his left arm for the moment and groping in it for an egg with his right; "if no offence, as I would hand you this."

I took what Joe gave me, and found it to be the crumpled playbill of a small theatre, announcing the first appearance, in that very week, of "the celebrated amateur actor, whose unique performance in Hamlet has lately created a great sensation in local dramatic circles."

"Were you at his performance, Joe?" I inquired.

"I were," said Joe, with emphasis and solemnity.

"Was there a great sensation?"

"Well, it was quite lively..."

A change in Joe's face informed me that Herbert had entered the room. So, I presented Joe to Herbert, who held out his hand; but Joe backed from it, and held on to his bird's-nest of a hat instead.

"I'm your servant, Sir" said Joe in greeting to Herbert, with an awkward sort of bow. Here Joe's gaze fell on the servant boy, who was putting some toast on the table, and Joe plainly had an intention to make that young gentleman one of the family, and I frowned it down and confused Joe more. "I hope you and Pip, which I meantersay, you two gentlemen – I hope you get your health in this small house? For it may be a very good inn, according to London opinions," said Joe, confidentially, "and I believe its character do stand; but I wouldn't keep a pig in it myself."

Having given this flattering testimony to the merits of our apartment, and having incidentally shown this tendency to call me "sir," Joe, was invited to sit down at the table. He looked all around the room for a suitable spot on which to put his hat – as if it could only rest on a few very rare substances in nature – and ultimately stood it on an extreme corner of the chimney-piece, from which it ever afterwards fell off at intervals.

"Do you take tea, or coffee, Mr. Gargery?" asked Herbert.

"Thankee, Sir," said Joe, stiff from head to foot, "I'll take whichever is most agreeable to yourself."

"What do you say to coffee?"

"Thankee, Sir," returned Joe, evidently dispirited by the proposal, "since you are so kind as make choice of coffee, I will not run contrary to your own opinions. But don't you never find it a little 'eating?"

"Say tea then," said Herbert, pouring it out.

Here Joe's hat tumbled off the mantel-piece, and he started out of his chair and picked it up, and fitted it to the same exact spot, as if it were an absolute point of good manners that it should tumble off again soon.

"When did you come to town, Mr. Gargery?"

"Were it yesterday afternoon?" said Joe, after coughing behind his hand, as if he had had time to catch the whooping-cough since he came. "No it were not. Yes it were. Yes. It were yesterday afternoon."

"Have you seen anything of London, yet?"

"Why, yes, Sir," said Joe, "me and Wopsle went off straight to look at the theater. But we didn't find that it come up to its likeness in the play bills on the shop doors; which I meantersay," added Joe, in an explanatory manner, "as it is drawn on the flyers too architectooralooral."

I really believe Joe would have prolonged this word into a perfect Chorus, but for his attention being attracted by his hat, which was falling off the mantle again. Indeed, it demanded from him a constant attention, and a quickness of eye and hand.

As to his shirt-collar, and his coat-collar, they were perplexing to think about. Why should a man scrape himself to that extent, before he could consider himself fully dressed? Why should he think it necessary to be purified by suffering to wear his holiday clothes? Then he fell into such inexplicable pauses of meditation, with his fork midway between his plate and his mouth; had his eyes attracted in such strange directions; was afflicted with such remarkable coughs; sat so far from the table, and dropped so much more than he ate, and pretended that he hadn't dropped it, and I meanwhile sat in quiet embarrassment and restraint; that I was heartily glad when Herbert left us for the city.

I had neither the good sense nor the good feeling to know that this was all my fault, and that if I had been easier with Joe, Joe would have been easier with me. I felt impatient and out of temper with him, which made him all the more out-of-sorts with me.

"Us two being now alone, Sir," began Joe.

"Joe," I interrupted, pettishly, "how can you call me, Sir?"

Joe looked at me for a single instant with something faintly like disapproval. Utterly preposterous as his tie was, and as his collars were, I was conscious of a sort of dignity in the look.

"Us two being now alone," resumed Joe, "and me having the intentions and abilities to stay not many minutes more, I will now mention what have led to my being here. Well, Sir, this is how it were. I were at the Bargemen t'other night, Pip;" whenever he subsided into affection, he called me Pip, and whenever he relapsed into politeness he called me Sir; "when there come up in his horse cart, Pumblechook. Which he do comb my hair the wrong way sometimes, by telling people up and down town as it were him which ever was your childhood companion and playfellow."

"Nonsense. It was you, Joe."

"Which I fully believed it were, Pip," said Joe, slightly tossing his head, "though it matters little now, Sir. Well, Pip, Pumblechook come to me at the Bargemen, and his word were, 'Joseph, Miss Havisham she wish to speak to you.'"

"Miss Havisham, Joe?"

"'She wish,' were Pumblechook's word, 'to speak to you.'" Joe sat and rolled his eyes at the ceiling.

"Yes, Joe? Go on, please."

"Next day, Sir," said Joe, looking at me as if I were a long way off, "having cleaned myself, I go and I see Miss A."

"Miss A., Joe? Miss Havisham?"

"Which I say, Sir," replied Joe, with an air of legal formality, as if he were making his will, "Miss A., or otherways Havisham. She then told me, 'Mr. Gargery. You are in correspondence with Mr. Pip?' Having had a letter from you, I were able to say 'I am.' 'Would you tell him, then,' said she, 'that which Estella has come home and would be glad to see him.'"

I felt my face fire up as I looked at Joe. I hope one remote cause of its firing may have been my consciousness that if I had known his errand, I should have given him more encouragement.

"Biddy," pursued Joe, "when I got home and asked her to write the message to you, a little hung back. Biddy says, "I know he will be very glad to have it by word of mouth, it is holiday time, you want to see him, go!" I have now concluded, Sir," said Joe, rising from his chair, "and, Pip, I wish you ever well and ever prospering to a greater and greater height."

"But you are not going now, Joe?"

"Yes I am," said Joe.

"But you are coming back to dinner, Joe?"

"No I am not," said Joe.

Our eyes met, and all the "Sir" melted out of that manly heart as he gave me his hand.

"Pip, dear old chap, life is made of ever so many partings welded together, and one man's a blacksmith, and one's a whitesmith, and one's a goldsmith, and one's a coppersmith. Divisions among such must come, and must be met as they come. If there's been any fault at all today, it's mine. You and me is not two figures to be together in London; nor yet anywheres else but what is private and understood among friends. It ain't that I am proud, but that I want to be right, as you shall never see me no more in these clothes. I'm wrong in these clothes. I'm wrong out of the forge, the kitchen, or off the marshes. You won't find half so much fault in me if you think of me in my forge clothes, with my hammer in my hand, or even my pipe. You won't find half so much fault in me if, supposing as you should ever wish to see me, you come and put your head in at the forge window and see Joe the blacksmith, there, at the old anvil, in the old burnt apron, sticking to the old work. I'm awful dull, but I hope I've beat out something nigh the rights of this at last. And so GOD bless you, dear old Pip, old chap, GOD bless you!"

I had not been mistaken in my belief that there was a simple dignity in him. His ill-fitting clothes could no more get in its way when he spoke these words than it could get in its way in Heaven. He touched me gently on the forehead, and went out. As soon as I could recover myself, I hurried out after him and looked for him in the nearby streets, but he was gone.

Chapter 28

It was clear that I must head to my old town the next day, and in my guilt it was equally clear that I must stay at Joe's. But, by the time I had reserved my seat for the next day's coach, I was having second thoughts about staying at Joe's, and began to invent reasons and make excuses for staying at the Blue Boar instead. I'd be an inconvenience at Joe's; I wasn't expected, and my bed wouldn't be ready; I'd be too far from Miss Havisham's, and she might not like it. All other swindlers on earth are nothing compared to the self-swindlers, and with such make-believe issues did I cheat myself.

Having settled that I must go to the Blue Boar, I couldn't make up my mind if I should bring my servant or not. It was tempting to think of showing off that expensive Mercenary at the Blue Boar; it was almost wonderful to imagine going to the tailor and casually producing him in front of Trabb's boy to show him up. On the other hand, Trabb's boy might worm himself into my servant's confidence and tell him things; or, reckless and desperate wretch as I knew he could be, might hoot at him in the street. My patroness, too, might hear of him, and not approve. On the whole, I decided to leave that expensive accessory behind.

At that time it was customary to carry convicts down to the dockyards by stage-coach. As I had often heard of this and had more than once seen them on the road dangling their ironed legs over the coach roof, I wasn't surprised when Herbert, meeting me in the coach yard before I left, came up and told me there were two convicts going down with me. But I had a reason that was an old reason now, for faltering and turning pale whenever I heard the word 'convict'.

"You don't mind them, Handel?" said Herbert.

"Oh, no!"

"I thought you seemed as if you didn't like them?"

"I can't pretend that I do like them, and I suppose you don't particularly, either. But I don't mind them."

"See! There they are," said Herbert, "What a degraded and vile sight it is!"

There were two of them, with a jailor guard. The two convicts were handcuffed together, and had irons on their legs - irons of a pattern that I knew well. They wore the grey clothes that I also knew well. Their keeper had a pistol and carried a thick-knobbed club under his arm, but he was on good terms with them, and stood beside them, with an air about him as if the convicts were an interesting exhibition not open at the moment, and he was the curator. One convict was taller and stouter than the other, but his clothes couldn't disguise him; I knew his half-closed eye at one glance.

There stood the man whom I had seen on the bench at the Three Jolly Bargemen years ago, and who had given me the two one-pound notes!

It was easy to tell that so far he hadn't recognized me. He looked at me, and his eye appraised my watch-chain, and then he spat and said something to the other convict, and they laughed and turned to look at something else.

The situation got worse. It turned out that there were no places for the two prisoners but on the seat in front, behind the coachman. When this was announced, a gentleman with a bad cough, who had taken the fourth place on that seat, flew into a most violent protest, and said that it was a breach of contract to mix him up with such villainous company, and that it was poisonous and shameful, and I don't know what else.

"Don't take it so much amiss, sir," pleaded the jailor to the angry passenger; "I'll sit next to you myself. I'll put 'em on the outside of the row. They won't interfere with you, sir. You needn't know they're even there."

"And don't blame me," growled the convict I had recognized. "I don't want to go. I am quite ready to stay behind. As far as I am concerned anyone's welcome to my place."

"Or mine," said the other, gruffly. "I wouldn't have inconvenienced none of you, if I'd had my way." Then, they both laughed, and began cracking nuts, and spitting the shells on the ground, as I really think I should have liked to do myself if I had been in their place and been so despised by everybody.

At length, it was voted that there was no help for the angry gentleman, and that he must either ride alongside the convicts or remain behind. So, he got into his seat, still making complaints, and the jailor got into the seat next to him, and the convicts hauled themselves up as well as they could, and the convict I had recognized sat behind me with his breath on the hair of my head.

"Good-bye, Handel!" Herbert called out as we started. I thought what a blessed fortune it was that he had found another name for me than Pip.

It is impossible to express with what sharpness I felt the convict's breathing, not only on the back of my head, but all along my spine. He seemed to have more breathing business to do than other men, and to make more noise in doing it; and I was conscious of growing high-shouldered on one side, in my efforts to quietly fend him off.

The weather was miserable, and the two convicts cursed the cold. It made us all lethargic before we had gone far, and we all slept off and on, and shivered and were silent. I dozed off, considering the question whether I ought to give the man his two pounds back before losing sight of him, and how it could best be done.

I almost fell forward, and awoke with a fright. I must have slept longer than I thought, since it was now dark and I could make out that we were in marsh country. Cowering forward for warmth and to use me as a screen against the wind, the convicts were closer to me than before. The very first words I heard them say as I woke up were the words in my own mind, "Two One Pound notes."

"How'd he get 'em?" said the convict I had never seen.

"How should I know?" returned the one-eyed man. "He had 'em stowed away somehows. Give to him by friends, I expect."

"I wish," said the other, with a bitter curse at the cold, "that I had 'em here."

"Two one pound notes, or friends?"

"Two one pound notes. I'd sell all the friends I ever had for one, and think it a blessed good bargain. Well? So he says - ?"

"So he says," resumed the convict I had recognized - "it was all said and done in half a minute, behind a pile of timber in the Dockyard - 'You're going to be discharged?' he asked me. Yes, I was. Would I find out that boy that had fed him and kept his secret, and give him them two one pound notes? Yes, I would. And I did."

"More fool you," growled the other. "I'd have spent 'em, on food and drink. He must have been a newcomer. Mean to say he knowed nothing of you?"

"Not a bit. Different prison gangs and different ships. He was tried again for prison breaking, and got made a Lifer and sent to Australia."

"And was that the only time you worked in this part of the country?"

"The only time."

"What was your opinion of the place?"

"A most beastly place. Mudbank, mist, swamp, and work; work, swamp, mist, and mudbank."

They both condemned my home marsh country in very strong language, and gradually growled themselves out, and had nothing left to say.

After overhearing this discussion, I would definitely have gotten down off the coach and been left in the middle of the dark highway, except I was certain that the man still had no suspicion of my identity. Indeed, I was not only so changed physically in growing up, but I was so differently dressed and in such different circumstances that it was not at all likely he could have known me without accidental help. Still, the coincidence of our being together on the coach was strange enough to fill me with a dread that some other coincidence might at any moment connect me with my name, and he'd know me.

For this reason, I got off the coach as soon as we entered town. As for the convicts, they went on with the coach, and I knew they were going to be taken to the river and the black prison ship.

I could not have said what I was afraid of, for my fear was undefined and vague, but there was great fear upon me. As I walked to the Blue Boar, I felt that a dread, much more than just the mere nervousness of a convict potentially recognizing me, made me tremble. It took no distinctness of shape, and I'm sure it was the revival for a few minutes of the terror of childhood.

The coffee-room at the Blue Boar was empty, and I had sat down to my dinner there, when the waiter recognized me. He asked me if he should send a messenger to get Mr. Pumblechook?

"No," said I, "certainly not."

The waiter appeared surprised, and took the earliest opportunity of putting a dirty old copy of a local newspaper so directly in my way that I picked it up and read this paragraph:

"Our readers will learn, in reference to the recent romantic rise in fortune of a young artificer in iron of this neighbourhood, that the youth's earliest patron, companion, and friend was a highly-respected individual, not entirely unconnected with the corn and seed trade. We record HIM as the Mentor of this young man, for it is good to know that our town produced the founder of the latter's fortunes."

I'm positive that if I had gone even as far away as the North Pole, I still would have met somebody there that would have told me that Pumblechook was my earliest patron and the founder of my fortunes.

Chapter 29

In the morning I was up and out of the Blue Boar. It was too early yet to go to Miss Havisham's, so I loitered into the country on Miss Havisham's side of town – which was not Joe's side, I could always go there tomorrow – thinking about my patroness, and painting brilliant pictures of her plans for me in my mind.

She had adopted Estella, she had as good as adopted me, and it had to be her intention to bring us together. She left it for me to restore the desolate house, to admit the sunshine into the dark rooms, to set the clocks a-going and the cold hearths a-blazing, to tear down the cobwebs – in short, do all the shining deeds of the young Knight of romance, and marry the Princess.

I planned out my walk as to arrive at the gate at my old time. When I had rung at the bell with an unsteady hand, I turned my back to the gate while I tried to get my breath and keep the beating of my heart moderately quiet. I heard the side door open, and steps come across the court-yard, but I pretended not to hear, even when the gate swung on its rusty hinges.

Being at last touched on the shoulder, I started and turned. I was surprised for real then, to find myself confronted by the last man I should have expected to see as the porter of Miss Havisham's door.

"Orlick!"

"Ah, young master, there's more changes than yours. But come in, come in. It's opposed to my orders to hold the gate open."

I entered and he swung it shut, locked it, and took the key out. "Yes!" said he, turning around to face me, after he had taken a few steps towards the house. "Here I am!"

"How did you come here?"

"I come here on my legs," he retorted.

"Are you here for good?"

"I ain't here for harm, young master, I suppose?"

I was not so sure of that. I had time to ponder his response in my mind, while he slowly lifted his heavy glance from the pavement, up my legs and arms, to my face.

"Then you have left the forge?" I said.

"Do this look like a forge?" replied Orlick, sending his glance all round him with an air of injury. "Now, do it look like it?"

I asked him how long since he had left Gargery's forge?

"One day is so like another here," he replied, "that I don't know without casting it up. However, I come here some time after you left."

"I could have told you that, Orlick."

"Ah!" said he, drily. "But then you've got to be a scholar."

By this time we had come to the house, where I found his room to be one just within the side door, with a little window in it looking on the court-yard. Certain keys were hanging on the wall, to which he now added the gate-key; and his patchwork-covered bed was in a little inner recess.

"I never saw this room before," I remarked; "but there used to be no Porter here."

"No," said he; "not till it got about that there was no protection on the premises, and it come to be considered dangerous, with convicts going up and down. And then I was recommended to the place as a man who could give another man as good as he brought, and I took it. It's easier than bellowsing and hammering. - That's loaded, that is."

My eye had been caught by a gun with a brass bound stock over the chimney-piece, and his eye had followed mine.

"Well," said I, not desirous of more conversation, "shall I go up to Miss Havisham?"

"Burn me, if I know!" he retorted, first stretching himself and then shaking himself; "my orders ends here, young master. I give this here bell a rap with this here hammer, and you go on along the passage till you meet somebody."

"I am expected, I believe?"

"Burn me twice over, if I can say!" said he.

Upon that, I turned down the long passage which I had first walked in my thick boots, and he made his bell sound. At the end of the passage, while the bell was still reverberating, I found Sarah Pocket, who appeared to have now become green and yellow by reason of me.

"Oh!" said she. "You, is it, Mr. Pip?"

"It is, Miss Pocket. I am glad to tell you that Mr. Pocket and family are all well."

"Are they any wiser?" said Sarah, with a dismal shake of the head; "they had better be wiser, than well. Ah, Matthew, Matthew! You know your way, sir?"

Tolerably, for I had gone up the staircase in the dark many a time. I ascended it now, in lighter boots than before, and tapped in my old way at the door of Miss Havisham's room. "Pip's knock," I heard her say, immediately; "come in, Pip."

She was in her chair near the old table, in the old dress, with her two hands crossed on her stick, her chin resting on them, and her eyes on the fire. Sitting near her, with the white shoe that had never been worn, in her hand, and her head bent as she looked at it, was an elegant lady whom I had never seen.

"Come in, Pip," Miss Havisham continued to mutter, without looking around or up; "come in, Pip, how do you do, Pip? So, you kiss my hand as if I were a queen, eh? - Well?"

She looked up at me suddenly, only moving her eyes, and repeated in a grimly playful manner,

"Well?"

"I heard, Miss Havisham," said I, rather at a loss, "that you were so kind as to wish me to come and see you, and I came directly."

"Well?"

The lady whom I had never seen before, lifted up her eyes and looked archly at me, and then I saw that the eyes were Estella's eyes. But she was so much changed, was so much more beautiful, so much more womanly, so much advanced, that I seemed to have made none. I felt, as I looked at her, that I slipped hopelessly back into the coarse and common boy again. O the sense of distance and inequality that came over me, and the inaccessibility that hovered about her!

She gave me her hand. I stammered something about the pleasure I felt in seeing her again, and about my having looked forward to it for a long, long time.

"Do you find her much changed, Pip?" asked Miss Havisham, with her greedy look, and striking her stick upon a chair that stood between them, as a sign to me to sit down there.

"When I came in, Miss Havisham, I thought there was nothing of Estella in the face or figure; but now it all settles down so curiously into the old--"

"What? You are not going to say into the old Estella?" Miss Havisham interrupted. "She was proud and insulting, and you wanted to go away from her. Don't you remember?"

I said confusedly that that was long ago, and that I knew no better then, and the like. Estella smiled with perfect composure, and said she had no doubt of my having been quite right, and of her having been very disagreeable.

"Is he changed?" Miss Havisham asked her.

"Very much," said Estella, looking at me.

"Less coarse and common?" said Miss Havisham, playing with Estella's hair.

Estella laughed, and looked at the shoe in her hand, and laughed again, and looked at me, and put the shoe down. She treated me as a boy still, but she lured me on.

We sat in the room among the old strange influences which had so worked themselves upon me as a child, and I learnt that she had just come home from France, and that she was going to London. It was settled that I should stay there all the rest of the day, return to the Blue Boar at night, and head back home to London tomorrow. When we had conversed for a while, Miss Havisham sent us two out to walk in the neglected garden. She said that after our walk that she would like me to wheel her about a little as in our old times.

So, Estella and I went out into the garden and soon found ourselves near the area where I had my encounter with the pale young gentleman, now Herbert. I was trembling in spirit and worshipping the very hem of her dress; she was quite composed, and most decidedly not worshipping the hem of mine. As we drew near to the place of the altercation, she stopped and said:

"I must have been a peculiar little girl to hide and see that fight that day, but I did, and I enjoyed it very much."

"You rewarded me very much."

"Did I?" she replied, in a forgetful way. "I remember I had a great objection to your adversary, because I was upset that he should be brought here to pester me with his company."

"He and I are great friends now."

"Are you? I think I remember now, that you study with his father?"

"Y-Yes."

I made the admission with reluctance, for it seemed to paint a boyish image, and she already treated me more than enough like a boy.

"Since your change of fortune and prospects, you have changed your friends," said Estella.

"Naturally," said I.

"And necessarily," she added, in a haughty tone; "what was fit company for you once, would be quite unfit company for you now."

In my conscience, I doubt very much whether I had any lingering intention left of going to see Joe; but if I had, her observation squashed it.

"You had no idea of your approaching good fortune, in those times?" said Estella.

"Not the least."

The air of completeness and superiority with which she walked at my side, and the air of youthfulness and submission with which I walked at hers, made a contrast that I strongly felt. It would have tormented me even more than it did if I had not believed that I was set apart by Miss Havisham and assigned to her.

The garden was too overgrown for easily walking in, and after we had gone around it two or three times, we came out again into the brewery yard. I reminded her where she had come out of the house and given me my meat and drink, and she said, "I don't remember."

"Not remember that you made me cry?" said I. "No," said she, and shook her head and looked about her. I truly believe that her not remembering and not minding in the least, made me cry again, inwardly – and that is the sharpest crying of all.

"You must know," said Estella, condescending to me as a brilliant and beautiful woman might, "that I have no heart – if that has anything to do with my memory."

I stumbled through some words to the effect that I took the liberty of doubting that it could be true. That I knew better. That there could be no such beauty without a heart.

"Oh! I have a heart to be stabbed in or shot in, I have no doubt," said Estella, "and, of course, if it ceased to beat, I should cease to be. But you know what I mean. I have no softness there, no – sympathy – sentiment – nonsense."

As she stood there, looking steadily at me while she talked, I had the strangest feeling of some sort of familiar recognition that I hadn't had before. Was it anything that I had seen in Miss Havisham? No. In some of Estella's looks and gestures there was that tinge of resemblance to Miss Havisham, having grown up with her. And yet, I could not trace this feeling to Miss Havisham. I looked again, and though she was still looking at me, the suggestion was gone.

What was it?

"I am serious," said Estella, not so much with a frown (for her brow was smooth) as with a darkening of her face; "if we are to spend much time together, you had better believe it at once. No!" imperiously stopping me as I opened my lips. "I have not given my tenderness anywhere. I have never had any such thing to give. Let us make one more round of the garden, and then go in. Come! You shall not shed tears for my cruelty today; you shall be my Page, and give me your shoulder."

Her beautiful dress had trailed upon the ground. She held it in one hand now, and with the other lightly touched my shoulder as we walked. We walked around the ruined garden two or three more times, and at last we went back into the house. There I heard, with surprise, that my guardian had come down to see Miss Havisham on business, and would come back for dinner. While we were out, the chandeliers had been lighted in the room with the rotting bridal cake, and Miss Havisham was in her wheeled chair waiting for me.

It was like pushing the chair itself back into the past, when we began the old slow circuit around the ashes of the bridal feast. But, in that gloomy room Estella looked more bright and beautiful than before, and I was under stronger enchantment.

The time so melted away, that our early dinner-hour drew close at hand, and Estella was going to leave to prepare herself. Before she left, we stopped near the center of the long table, and Miss Havisham, with one of her withered arms stretched out of the chair, brought Estella's hand to her and kissed it, with a ravenous intensity that was quite dreadful.

Then, Estella being gone and we two left alone, she turned to me, and said in a whisper:

"Is she beautiful, graceful, well-grown? Do you admire her?"

"Everybody must who sees her, Miss Havisham."

She drew an arm round my neck, and drew my head close down to hers as she sat in the chair. "Love her, love her, love her! How does she use you?"

Before I could answer (if I could have even answered so difficult a question at all), she repeated, "Love her, love her, love her! If she favours you, love her. If she wounds you, love her. If she tears your heart to pieces – and as it gets older and stronger, it will tear deeper – love her, love her, love her!"

Never had I seen such passionate eagerness in a person's speech. I could feel the muscles of her thin arm round my neck, swell with the fierceness that possessed her.

"Hear me, Pip! I adopted her to be loved. I bred her and educated her to be loved. I developed her into what she is, that she might be loved. Love her!"

She said the word often enough that there was no doubt that she meant to say it. But if the often repeated word had been hate instead of love – despair – revenge – death – it could not have sounded more like a curse.

"I'll tell you," said she, in the same hurried passionate whisper, "what real love is. It is blind devotion, unquestioning self-humiliation, utter submission, trust and belief against yourself and against the whole world, giving up your whole heart and soul to the slayer – as I did!"

Not knowing what to say to her, I became conscious of a scent that I knew, and turning, saw my guardian in the room.

Miss Havisham had seen him as soon as I, and was (like everybody else) afraid of him. She made a strong attempt to compose herself, and stammered that he was as punctual as ever.

"As punctual as ever," he repeated, coming up to us. "How do you do, Pip? Shall I give you a ride, Miss Havisham? Once round? And so, you are here, Pip?"

I told him when I had arrived, and how Miss Havisham had wished me to come and see Estella. To which he replied, "Ah! Very fine young lady!" Then he pushed Miss Havisham in her chair before him, with one of his large hands, and put the other in his trousers-pocket as if the pocket were full of secrets.

"Well, Pip! How often have you seen Miss Estella before?" said he, when he came to a stop.

"How often?"

"Ah! How many times? Ten thousand times?"

"Oh! Certainly not so many."

"Twice?"

"Jaggers," interposed Miss Havisham, much to my relief; "leave my Pip alone, and go with him to your dinner."

He complied, and we groped our way down the dark stairs together. While we were still on our way to those detached apartment houses across the paved courtyard at the back, he asked me how often I had seen Miss Havisham eat and drink, offering me a range of choice, as usual, between a hundred times and once.

I thought about it, and said, "Never."

"And never will, Pip," he retorted, with a frowning smile. "She has never allowed herself to be seen doing either, since she lived this present life of hers. She wanders about in the night, and then lays hands on such food as she takes."

"Please, sir," said I, "may I ask you a question?"

"You may," said he, "and I may decline to answer it. Put your question."

"Estella's name. Is it Havisham or - ?" I had nothing to add.

"Or what?" said he.

"Is it Havisham?"

"It is Havisham."

This brought us to the dinner-table, where Estella and Sarah Pocket awaited us. Mr. Jaggers presided, Estella sat opposite to him, I faced my green and yellow friend. We dined very well, and were waited on by a maid-servant whom I had never seen in all my comings and goings, but who, for anything I knew, had been in that mysterious house the whole time.

After dinner, a bottle of choice old port was placed before my guardian (he was evidently well acquainted with the vintage), and the two ladies left us. When he and I were left alone together, he sat with an air upon him of having information that he alone possessed, and it was really too much for me to bear. He cross-examined his very wine when he had nothing else in hand. He held it between himself and the candle, tasted the wine, rolled it in his mouth, swallowed it, looked at his glass again, smelt the wine, tried it, drank it, filled again, and cross-examined the glass again, until I was as nervous as if I had known the wine to be telling him something to my disadvantage. Three or four times I feebly thought I would start conversation; but whenever he saw me going to ask him anything, he looked at me with his glass in his hand, and swishing his wine in his mouth, as if requesting me to take notice that it was of no use to talk to him, for he couldn't answer.

Afterwards, Mr. Jaggers and I went up to Miss Havisham's room, where we found Estella in her usual place, and we four played cards. Before my guardian and I had arrived in the room, Miss Havisham had put some of the most beautiful jewels from her dressing-table into Estella's hair, and about her bosom and arms. I even saw Mr. Jaggers look at her from under his thick eyebrows, and raise them a little, when her loveliness was in front of him.

We played until nine o'clock, and then it was arranged that when Estella came to London I would be informed of her coming and would meet her at the coach; and then I took leave of her for the night, and left for the Blue Boar.

My guardian lay in the next room to mine at the inn. Far into the night, Miss Havisham's words, "Love her, love her, love her!" sounded in my ears. I adapted them for my own repetition, and said to my pillow, "I love her, I love her, I love her!" hundreds of times. Then, a burst of gratitude came upon me, that she should be destined for me, once the blacksmith's boy. Then, I thought if she were, as I feared, by no means as grateful as I was for that destiny yet, when would she begin to be interested in me? When should I awaken the heart within her that was sleeping now?

Ah me! I thought those were high and great emotions. But it never crossed my mind that there was anything low and small in my keeping away from Joe, because I knew she would despise him. It had only been a day since Joe's love, honesty, and forthrightness had made me feel ashamed of my conduct towards him and brought tears into my eyes. But, they had soon dried, God forgive me! soon dried.

Chapter 30

After thinking the matter over while I was getting dressed at the Blue Boar the next morning, I decided to tell my guardian that I doubted that Orlick was the right sort of man to fill a post of trust at Miss Havisham's. "Why, of course he is not the right sort of man, Pip," said my guardian, comfortably satisfied beforehand on the general principle, "because the man who fills the post of trust never is the right sort of man." It seemed to please him to find that this particular job was not held by the right sort of man, and he listened in a satisfied manner while I told him what I knew of Orlick. "Very good, Pip," he observed, when I had finished, "I'll go there soon, and fire our friend." Rather alarmed by this hasty action, I was in favor of delaying a little, and even hinted that Orlick might be difficult to deal with. "Oh no he won't," said my guardian, "I should like to see him argue the question with me."

Since we were going back together to London by the mid-day coach, and as I was terrified of running into Pumblechook and having to deal with his groveling praise, this gave me an opportunity of saying that I wanted a walk. I said that I would walk along the road to London while Mr. Jaggers was busy, if he would let the coachman know that I would get into my seat when they caught up to me. I was thus freed to leave the Blue Boar immediately after breakfast. I made a wide loop around Pumblechook's premises and felt I was safe from running into him.

It was interesting to be in the quiet old town once more, and it was agreeable to be suddenly recognized every so often and stared after. I was enjoying the attention, until Fate threw me in the way of that miscreant, Trabb's boy.

I saw Trabb's boy approaching me, lashing himself with an empty blue bag. Deciding that having a serene face and ignoring him would be the best course of action, and would be most likely to stifle his evil mind, I kept walking with that expression on my face. I was rather congratulating myself on my success, when suddenly the knees of Trabb's boy shook together, his cap fell off, his arms and legs trembled violently, he staggered out into the road, and cried to the nearby people, "Hold me! I'm so frightened!" pretending to be in terror by seeing the majesty of my appearance.

This was hard to put up with, but this was nothing compared to what he had planned. I kept walking, pretending not to see him, and he got up and ran off down a side alley after I was well past him. I had not got much further down the street, when I again saw Trabb's boy approaching me. This time, he wore the blue bag like my great-coat, and was strutting along the sidewalk towards me on the opposite side of the street, with several delighted young friends to whom he from time to time pompously exclaimed, with a wave of his hand, "Don't know yah! Sorry, don't know yah!" Words cannot state how mad I was at Trabb's boy, when, passing each other on opposite sides of the street, he pulled up his shirt-collar, smirked condescendingly, and said to his attendants, "Don't know yah! Upon my soul, I don't know yah!" He followed this up by cat calling and hooting at me as I left town over the bridge, thoroughly disgracing me.

Unless I had taken the life of Trabb's boy, I really do not even now see what I could have done except put up with his insults. To have fought with him in the street would have been futile and degrading. I wrote, however, to Mr. Trabb by next day's mail, to say that Mr. Pip must decline to deal further with a business such as his that employed a boy who was so revolting.

The coach, with Mr. Jaggers inside, eventually caught up to me, and I took my seat, and arrived in London safe – but not sound, for my heart hurt. As soon as I arrived, I sent an apologetic barrel of oysters and codfish to Joe, which I thought at the time made up for not having visited him, and then went on to Barnard's Inn.

I found Herbert dining on cold meat, and was delighted to welcome me back. Having sent my servant to the coffee-house to get something for dinner, I felt that I must confide that evening to my friend. As I didn't want to discuss what I had to say in front of Pepper, I sent him to the theater. A better proof of my bondage to that servant could scarcely be found; it was ridiculous the lengths I went through to find him something to do. It got so bad that I sometimes sent him to Hyde Park Corner just to see what time it was.

Our dinner finished, I said to Herbert, "My dear Herbert, I have something important to tell you."

"My dear Handel," he returned, "I shall esteem and respect your confidence."

"It concerns myself, Herbert," said I, "and one other person."

Herbert crossed his feet, looked at the fire with his head on one side, then looked at me because I hadn't continued.

"Herbert," said I, "I love – I adore – Estella."

Instead of being surprised, Herbert replied in an easy matter-of-course way, "Exactly. Well?"

"Well, Herbert? Is that all you can say? Well?"

"What next, I mean?" said Herbert. "Of course I know that."

"How could you know it?" said I.

"How could I know it, Handel? Why, from you."

"I never told you."

"Told me! You've never told me when you get your hair cut, but I have eyes to see it. You have always adored her, ever since I have known you. You brought your adoration along with your bag here, together. When you told me your own story, you told me plainly that you began adoring her the first time you saw her, when you were very young indeed."

"Very well, then," said I, "I have never stopped adoring her. And she's come back from France, a most beautiful and most elegant creature. And I saw her yesterday. And if I adored her before, I now doubly adore her."

"Lucky for you then, Handel," said Herbert, "that you are picked out and chosen for her. Without stepping on forbidden ground, we may venture to say that there can be no doubt between ourselves of that fact. Have you any idea yet, of Estella's views on the adoration question?"

I shook my head gloomily. "Oh! She definitely does not adore me," said I.

"Patience, my dear Handel; time enough, time enough. But you seem to have something more to say?"

"I am ashamed to say it," I returned, "and yet it's no worse to say it than to think it. You call me a lucky fellow. Of course, I am. I was a blacksmith's boy practically yesterday. I know I have done nothing to raise myself in life, and that Fortune alone has raised my position; that is being very lucky. And yet, when I think of Estella--"

("And when don't you, you know?" Herbert threw in, with his eyes on the fire; which I thought kind and sympathetic of him.)

" - Then, my dear Herbert, I cannot tell you how dependent and uncertain I feel, and how exposed to luck I am. Avoiding forbidden ground, as you did just now, I may still say that on the dedication of one person (without saying who it is) all my expectations depend. And at best, it's so unsatisfactory to only know so vaguely what those promised expectations even are!" In saying this, I relieved my mind of what had always been there, more or less, though no doubt more so since yesterday.

"Now, Handel," Herbert replied, in his happy hopeful way, "it seems to me that in you are looking into your gift-horse's mouth with a magnifying-glass. Likewise, it seems to me that you're overlooking one of the best points of the animal: didn't you tell me that Mr. Jaggers told you in the beginning, that you were not endowed with expectations only? And even if he had not told you so, could you believe that of all men in London, Mr. Jaggers would be the one to be your guardian unless he was sure of the outcome? As to the rest, you must bide your guardian's time, and he must bide his client's time. You'll be twenty-one before you know it, and then perhaps you'll get some further enlightenment."

"What a hopeful disposition you have!" said I, gratefully admiring his cheery ways.

"I ought to have," said Herbert, "for I don't have much else. I must admit, by-the-way, that the good sense of what I have just said is not my own, but my father's. The only remark I ever heard him make on your story was this final one: "The thing is settled and done, or Mr. Jaggers wouldn't be involved." And now before I say anything more about my father or me, and repay your trust with my own, I want to make myself seriously disagreeable to you for a moment – positively repulsive."

"You won't succeed," said I.

"Oh yes I will!" said he. "One, two, three, and now I'm in for it. Handel, my good fellow;" though he spoke in this light tone, he was very serious: "I have been thinking since we have been talking here, that Estella surely cannot be a condition of your inheritance, if she was never referred to by your guardian. Am I right in understanding what you've told me, that he never referred to her, directly or indirectly, in any way? Never even hinted that your patron might have views as to your marriage?"

"Never."

"Now, Handel, you know I'm not jealous, upon my soul and honour! Not being bound to her, can you not detach yourself from her? - I told you I would be disagreeable."

I turned my head aside, for, with a rush and a sweep, a feeling like that which had come over me on the morning when I left the forge and cried by the village finger-post now struck my heart again. There was silence between us for a little while.

"Yes; but my dear Handel," Herbert went on, as if we had been talking instead of silent, "you've had this dream for years, since you were a boy, I know this is serious for you. Think of her upbringing, and think of Miss Havisham. Think of what she is herself (now I am repulsive and you hate me). This may lead to miserable things."

"I know it, Herbert," said I, with my head still turned away, "but I can't help it."

"You can't detach yourself?"

"No. Impossible!"

"You can't try, Handel?"

"No. Impossible!"

"Well!" said Herbert, getting up with a lively shake as if he had been asleep, and stirring the fire; "now I'll try to make myself agreeable again!"

So he went around the room and shook the curtains out, put the chairs in their places, tidied the books and so forth that were lying about, looked into the hall, peeped into the mailbox, shut the door, and came back to his chair by the fire, where he sat down, nursing his left leg in both arms.

"I was going to say something about my family. May I ask you if you have ever noticed, down in your part of the country, that the children of not exactly suitable marriages are always most anxious to be married?"

This was such an odd question, that I asked him in return, "Is it so?"

"I don't know," said Herbert, "that's what I want to know. Because it is definitely the case with us. My poor sister Charlotte who was just younger than me and died before she was fourteen, was a perfect example. Little Jane is the same. Little Alick has already made arrangements for his union with a suitable young person. And indeed, I think we are all engaged, except the baby."

"Then you are?" said I.

"I am," said Herbert; "but it's a secret."

I assured him of my keeping the secret, and begged him to tell me the details. He had spoken so sensibly and feelingly of my weakness that I wanted to know something about his strength.

"May I ask the name?" I said.

"Name of Clara," said Herbert.

"Live in London?"

"Yes. Perhaps I ought to mention," said Herbert, who had become curiously dejected since we entered on this topic, "that she is rather below my mother's nonsensical family notions of titles. Her father had something to do with food on passenger-ships. I think he was a type of purser."

"What is he now?" said I.

"He's an invalid now," replied Herbert.

"Living on - ?"

"On the second floor," said Herbert. Which was not at all what I meant, for I had intended my question to apply to how he made his income now. "I have never seen him, for he has always kept his room overhead, since I have known Clara. But I have heard him constantly. He makes tremendous rows – roars, and pegs at the floor with some frightful instrument." In looking at me and then laughing heartily, Herbert for the time recovered his usual lively manner.

"Don't you expect to see him?" said I.

"Oh yes, I constantly expect to see him come tumbling through the ceiling. But I don't know how long the rafters may hold."

When he had once more laughed heartily, he became meek again, and told me that the moment he began to get his Capital together, it was his intention to marry this young lady. "But," he added as a disappointing footnote, "you can't get married, you know, while you're looking about you."

As we sat looking at the fire, lost in thought, I put my hands in my pockets. A folded piece of paper in one of them attracted my attention. I opened it and found it to be the playbill I had received from Joe, about Mr. Wopsle's play. "And bless my heart," I involuntarily added aloud, "it's tonight!"

This changed the subject in an instant, and made us hurriedly decide to go to the play. So, I pledged myself to comfort and aid Herbert in his marital quest, and Herbert told me that his fiance already knew of me and that he would introduce us, and we warmly shook hands upon our mutual confidence and trust. We then blew out our candles, made up the fire, locked our door, and went forth in quest of Mr. Wopsle and the Theater.

Chapter 31

Once we had taken our seats and Hamlet was underway, we had made some small effort in the beginning to applaud Mr. Wopsle and the cast; but it was hopeless to keep trying. The whole cast, including Mr. Wopsle, was dressed laughably and performed terribly; the large woman playing the queen had several metal bands around her body as part of her costume, and the audience began to call her "the kettle drum". The dead king lying on stage seemed to have a cough that he carried with him into the afterlife. This led the audience to chant out to him to "turn over!" which he did not appreciate. The audience was obnoxious during the whole tragedy, constantly heckling Mr. Wopsle's lines much to their enjoyment and laughter.

Therefore, we had sat, feeling badly for him, but also laughing from ear to ear. I laughed in spite of myself all the time, the whole thing was so absurd. When the tragedy was over, and he had been called for and hooted by the audience, I said to Herbert, "Let's leave at once, or we might run into him."

We tried to get out as fast as we could, but we were not quick enough. Standing at the door was a man with an unnatural heavy smear of eyebrow, who caught my eyes as we advanced, and said, when we came up to him:

"Mr. Pip and friend?"

Identity of Mr. Pip and friend confessed.

"Mr. Wopsle," said the man, "would be glad to have the honour."

"Yes," said I. "Shall we follow you?"

"Just a few steps, please." When we were in a side alley, he turned and asked, "How did you think he looked? - I dressed him."

I don't know what he was supposed to look like, but I said he had looked very nice.

We all squeezed through a little dirty door into a tiny closet of a room. Here Mr. Wopsle was taking his costume off, and there was just enough room for us to look at him over one another's shoulders by keeping the door wide open.

"Gentlemen," said Mr. Wopsle, "I am proud to see you. I hope, Mr. Pip, you will excuse my sending round. I had the happiness to know you in former times, and the Drama has ever had an appreciation by the noble and the affluent."

Meanwhile, Mr. Wopsle, sweating profusely, was trying to get himself out of his princely robes.

"Skin the stockings off, Mr. Wopsle," said the owner of that property, "or you'll bust 'em. Bust 'em, and you'll bust five-and-thirty shillings.

Shakspeare never was complimented with a finer pair. Keep quiet in your chair now, and leave 'em to me."

With that, he went upon his knees to get Mr. Wopsle's stocking off; who, when the first stocking came off, would certainly have fallen over backward with his chair, except there was no room to fall anyhow.

I had been afraid until then to say a word about the play. But then, Mr. Wopsle looked up at us smugly, and said, "Gentlemen, how did it seem to go?"

Herbert said from behind (at the same time poking me), "Capitally." So I said "Capitally."

"How did you like my reading of the character, gentlemen?" said Mr. Wopsle, almost with patronage.

Herbert said from behind (again poking me), "Massive and concrete." So I said boldly, as if I had thought of it, and must had to insist upon it, "Massive and concrete."

"I am glad to have your support, gentlemen," said Mr. Wopsle, with an air of dignity, in spite of his being pushed against the wall at the time, and holding on by the seat of his chair.

"But I'll tell you one thing," said the man who was on his knees pulling on Mr. Wopsle's stocking, "which you need to improve. I don't care who says contrary; I tell you so. You're not supposed to have your legs in profile. The last Hamlet as I dressed made the same mistake in his reading at rehearsal, until I got him to put a large red wafer on each of his shins, and then at that rehearsal whenever his acting brought him into profile, I called out "I don't see no wafers!" And at night his acting was lovely."

Mr. Wopsle smiled at me, as much as to say "a faithful servant – I overlook his folly"; and then said aloud, "My view is a little classic and thoughtful for them here; but they will improve, they will improve."

Herbert and I said together, Oh, no doubt they would improve.

I felt so sorry for him that I took the opportunity of his turning around to have his suspenders put on him – which pushed us out of the doorway – to ask Herbert what he thought of having him home to supper? Herbert said he thought it would be kind to do so; therefore, I invited him, and he went to Barnard's with us, and he sat until two o'clock in the morning, reviewing his success and developing his plans. I forget in detail what they were, but I have a general recollection that he was to begin with reviving the Drama, and to end with destroying it; inasmuch as his eventual death would leave the theater and acting profession utterly without a chance or hope without him.

Miserably I went to bed after all, and miserably thought of Estella, and miserably dreamed that my expectations were all cancelled.

Chapter 32

One day when I was busy with my books and Mr. Pocket, I received a note in the mail, the mere outside of which threw my heart into a great flutter; for, though I had never seen the handwriting on it before, I could guess whose hand had written it. It had no normal beginning, such as Dear Mr. Pip, or Dear Pip, or Dear Sir, or Dear Anything, but said this:

"I'm coming to London the day after tomorrow by the mid-day coach. I believe it was settled you should meet me? Miss Havisham has that impression, and I write in obedience to it. She sends you her regard.

Yours, ESTELLA."

If there had been time, I probably would have ordered several suits of clothes for this occasion; but as there was not, I had to make due with those that I had. My appetite vanished instantly, and I knew no peace or rest until the day arrived. Not that its arrival brought me either of those things, for, then I was worse than ever, and began hanging around the coach-office before the coach had even left the Blue Boar back in our town. Even though I knew this perfectly well, I still felt as if it were not safe to let the coach-office be out of my sight longer than five minutes at a time. In this state of unreasonable mind I had performed the first half-hour of a watch of four or five hours, when Wemmick happened to walk by.

"Halloa, Mr. Pip," said he; "how do you do? I should hardly have thought you'd be hanging around here."

I explained that I was waiting to meet somebody who was coming up by coach, and I asked him how the Castle and the Aged were doing.

"Both flourishing, thank you," said Wemmick, "and particularly the Aged. He's in wonderful spirits. He'll be eighty-two next birthday. I have a notion of firing the cannon eighty-two times, if the neighbourhood shouldn't complain, and if that cannon of mine can handle it. However, this is not London talk. Where do you think I am going to?"

"To the office?" said I, for he was tending in that direction.

"Closest thing to it," returned Wemmick, "I am going to Newgate Prison. We are working on a banker's-parcel case right now, and I must have a word or two with our client."

"Did your client commit the robbery?" I asked.

"Bless your soul and body, no," answered Wemmick, very drily. "But he is accused of it. So might you or I be. Either of us might be accused of it, you know."

"Only neither of us is," I remarked.

"Yah!" said Wemmick, touching me on the chest with his forefinger; "you're a deep one, Mr. Pip! Would you like to have a look at Newgate? Have you time to spare?"

I had so much time to spare that the proposal came as a relief, even though I felt compelled to keep my eye on the coach-office. Muttering to Wemmick that I would ask the coach office clerk whether I had time to walk with him, I went into the office and asked the clerk (much to his frustration) the earliest time that the coach could arrive – which I already knew, quite as well as he. I then rejoined Mr. Wemmick, I looked at my watch and, pretending to be surprised by the information I had received from it, accepted his offer.

We were at Newgate Prison in a few minutes, and we entered the interior of the jail. It struck me that Wemmick walked among the prisoners much as a gardener might walk among his plants. This idea was first put into my head by his seeing one of these prisoners, and reacting as if he had been a plant that had sprung up overnight, saying to the man, "What, Captain Tom? Are you there? Ah, indeed!" and also, "Is that Black Bill behind the water tank? Why, I didn't look for you these past two months, how are you doing?"

He was very popular, though something of the atmosphere of Mr. Jaggers hung about him too, forbidding approach beyond certain limits. His recognition of each client consisted of a nod, tightening his post office mouth a little more, and putting his hands in his pockets. In one or two instances there was a problem in the prisoner having enough money for Mr. Jaggers' services, and then Mr. Wemmick, backing as far as possible from the insufficient money produced, said, "it's no use, my boy, I'm not in charge, I can't take it. If you don't have enough then you had better try another lawyer. There are plenty of them in the profession, and what is not worth the time of one, may be worth the time of another. That's my recommendation to you. Now, who's next?"

Thus, we walked through Wemmick's prison greenhouse, until he turned to me and said, "Notice the man I shall shake hands with." I would have done so anyway, without his advice, since he hadn't shaken hands with anyone yet.

Almost as soon as he had spoken, a portly man in a worn out olive-coloured coat and a face with an unhealthy colored complexion came up to the bars of his cell. He had eyes that went wandering about when he tried to concentrate them, and he put his hand up to his hat with a half-serious and half-comedic military salute.

"Colonel, to you!" said Wemmick, saluting back; "how are you, Colonel?"

"All right, Mr. Wemmick."

"Everything was done that could be done, but the evidence was too strong for us, Colonel."

"Yes, it was too strong. I think I shall be out of this on Monday, sir," he said to Wemmick.

"Perhaps," returned my friend, "but there's no knowing."

"I am glad to have the chance of bidding you good-bye, Mr. Wemmick," said the man, stretching out his hand between two bars.

"Thankye," said Wemmick, shaking hands with him. "Same to you, Colonel."

"If what was on me when I was arrested had been real, Mr. Wemmick," said the man, unwilling to let his hand go, "I should have asked the favour of your wearing another ring – in acknowledgment of your work on my case."

"I'll accept the thought in place of the deed," said Wemmick. "By-the-way, you were quite a fan of pigeons." The man looked up at the sky. "I am told you had a remarkable breed of them. Could you get any friend of yours to bring me a pair, if you've no further use for 'em?"

"It shall be done, sir."

"All right," said Wemmick, "they shall be taken care of. Good afternoon, Colonel. Good-bye!" They shook hands again, and as we walked away Wemmick said to me in a hushed voice, "A counterfeiter, a very good one. The Recorder's report will be made today, and he is sure to be executed on Monday. Still you see, a pair of pigeons are portable property, all the same." With that, he looked back, and nodded at this soon-to-be-dead plant, and then cast his eyes about him in walking out of his garden, as if he were considering what other pot would go best in the Colonel's place.

Mr. Wemmick and I left Newgate Prison and parted ways at his office in Little Britain, where seekers of Mr. Jaggers's services were lingering about as usual, and I returned to my watch in the street of the coach-office, with some three hours left to go.

I spent the whole time thinking how strange it was that I should be surrounded by all this taint of prison and crime; that, in my childhood out on our lonely marshes on a winter evening I should have first encountered it. That it had reappeared on two occasions, like a stain that was faded but not gone, and that it should even now infuse itself into my fortune and advancement. My thoughts drifted to the beautiful young Estella, proud and refined, and I thought with absolute disgust of the contrast between the jail and her. I wished that Wemmick had not met me that day, or that I had not gone with him to Newgate, so that, of all the days in the year, I might not have had the prison on my breath and on my clothes on the day I was seeing Estella. I beat the prison dust off my feet as best as I could, and I shook it out of my clothes, and I exhaled its air from my lungs. So contaminated did I feel, that the time waiting for the coach passed quickly, and I didn't feel quite clean yet when I saw her face at the coach window and her hand waving to me.

In seeing the motion of her hand waving, I had that same vague shadow of recognition, as if I had seen her mannerisms somewhere else before. The feeling appeared and was gone again in an instant; what was it?

Chapter 33

In her furred travelling-dress, Estella seemed more delicately beautiful than she had ever seemed yet, even in my eyes. Her manner was more charming toward me than before, and I thought I saw Miss Havisham's influence in the change.

After I had collected her luggage I remembered – having forgotten everything but her in the meantime – that I had no idea where she was going.

"I am going to Richmond," she told me. "I am to have a carriage, and you are to take me. This is my purse, and you are to pay my charges out of it. Oh, you must take the purse! We have no choice, you and I, but to obey our instructions. We are not free to do what we want to do, you and I."

As she looked at me in giving me the purse, I hoped there was an inner meaning in her words. She said them casually, but not with displeasure.

"A carriage will have to be sent for, Estella. Will you rest here a little?"

"Yes, I am to rest here a little, and I am to drink some tea, and you are to take care of me the while."

She drew her arm through mine, as if it must be done, and I requested a waiter, who had been staring at the coach like a man who had never seen one in his life, to take us to a private sitting-room. With that, he led us to the worst room of the establishment; a tiny room with an anchovy sauce serving dish and somebody's shoes. On my objecting to this room, he took us into a large room with a dinner-table for thirty. He took my order, which was merely "Some tea for the lady," and went out of the room in a very low state of mind.

The smell in the room, with its strong combination of horse stable mixed with soup-stock, might have led a person to conclude that the coaching part of the business was not doing well, and that the resourceful owner was boiling down the horses for the restaurant portion of the business. Yet, the room was the world to me, since Estella was in it. I thought that with her I could have been happy there for life. (I was not at all happy there at the time, however, and I knew it well.)

"Where are you going to, at Richmond?" I asked Estella.

"I am going to live," said she, "at a great expense, with a lady there, who has the power – or says she has – of taking me around and introducing me to people, and introducing people to me."

"I suppose you will be glad to have variety and admiration?"

"Yes, I suppose so."

She answered so carelessly, that I said, "You speak about yourself as if you were someone else."

"Where did you learn how I speak of others? Come, come," said Estella, smiling delightfully, "I must talk in my own way. How are you doing with Mr. Pocket?"

"I live quite pleasantly there; at least--" It appeared to me that I was losing a chance.

"At least?" repeated Estella.

"At least as pleasantly as I could anywhere, away from you."

"You silly boy," said Estella, quite composedly, "how can you talk such nonsense? Your friend Mr. Matthew, I believe, is superior to the rest of his family?"

"Very superior indeed. He is nobody's enemy--"

"Don't add 'but his own'," interposed Estella, "for I hate that sort of man. But he really is disinterested, and above small jealousy and spite, I have heard?"

"I have every reason to say so, yes."

"You have not every reason to say so of the rest of his family," said Estella, nodding at me with an expression of face that was at once grave and rallying, "for they give Miss Havisham reports and insinuations to your disadvantage. They watch you, tell lies about you, write letters about you (anonymous, sometimes), and you are the torment and the focus of their lives. You can scarcely realize to yourself the hatred those people feel for you."

"They do me no harm, I hope?"

Instead of answering, Estella burst out laughing. This was very odd to me, and I looked at her in confusion. When she stopped – and she had not laughed in her typical careless way, but with real enjoyment – I said, in my hesitant way with her, "I hope I may suppose that you would not be amused if they did me any harm."

"No, no you may be sure of that," said Estella. "I laugh because they fail. Oh, those people with Miss Havisham, and the tortures they undergo!" She laughed again, and even now when she had told me why, her laughter was very odd to me, for I could not doubt its being genuine, and yet it seemed too much for the occasion, and out of place. I thought there must really be something more here than I knew; she saw the thought in my mind, and answered it.

"It's not easy, even for you." said Estella, "to know what satisfaction it gives me to see those people thwarted, or what an enjoyable sense of the ridiculous I have when they are made to look ridiculous. For, you were not brought up in that strange house from a mere baby – I was. You didn't have your little wits sharpened by their conspiring against you under their mask of sympathy and pity that appears soft and soothing, but is not – I had."

It was no laughing matter with Estella now, nor was she summoning these remembrances from any shallow place in her mind. I would not have wanted to be the cause of that look of hers for all my expectations in a heap.

"Two things I can tell you," said Estella. "First, you may set your mind at ease that these people never will – never would, in hundred years – hurt your standing with Miss Havisham, in any way, great or small. Second, I am grateful to you as the cause of their being so busy with themselves and so futile, and there is my opinion upon it."

As she gave me her hand playfully – for her darker mood had been just momentary – I held it and put it to my lips. "You ridiculous boy," said Estella, "will you never take warning? Or do you kiss my hand in the same spirit in which I once let you kiss my cheek?"

"What spirit was that?" said I.

"I must think a moment. A spirit of contempt for the fawners and plotters."

"If I say yes, may I kiss the cheek again?"

"You should have asked before you touched the hand. But, yes, if you like."

I leaned down, and her calm face was like a statue's. "Now," said Estella, gliding away the instant I touched her cheek, "you are to take care that I have some tea, and you are to take me to Richmond."

Her reverting to this tone, as if our association were forced upon us and we were mere puppets, gave me pain; but everything in our relationship gave me pain. Whatever her tone with me happened to be, I could put no trust in it, and build no hope on it; and yet I went on against trust and against hope. Why repeat it a thousand times? So it always was.

I rang for the tea, and the waiter brought in by degrees some fifty accessories to that drink, but of tea there wasn't a glimpse. A teaboard, cups and saucers, plates, knives and forks (including meat carvers), spoons (various), salt containers, a small little muffin confined with the utmost security under a strong iron lid, a soft bit of butter sitting in a quantity of parsley, a loaf of bread, two pieces of toast, and finally a fat family urn, which the waiter staggered in with, expressing on his face burden and suffering. After a long absence at this stage of the entertainment, he eventually came back with a precious looking casket containing twigs. These I soaked in hot water, and so, out of all of that, I extracted one cup of I-don't-know-what, for Estella.

With the bill paid, and the waiter tipped, and the stable boy not forgotten, and the chambermaid taken into consideration – in a word, the whole business bribed and Estella's purse much lightened – we got into our coach and drove away.

Turning into Cheapside and rattling up Newgate street, we were soon under the prison walls of which I was so ashamed. "What place is that?" Estella asked me, leaning her head out the window.

I made a foolish charade of not at first recognizing it, and then told her. She looked at it, and drew in her head again from out the window, and murmured "Wretches!" I would not have confessed to my visiting it for anything.

"Mr. Jaggers," said I, by way of putting it neatly on somebody else, "has the reputation of being more in the secrets of that dismal place than any man in London."

"He is more in the secrets of every place, I think," said Estella, in a low voice.

"You have been accustomed to see him often, I suppose?"

"I have been accustomed to see him sporadically, ever since I can remember. But I know him no better now than I did before I could speak. What is your own experience of him? Do you advance with him?"

"Once you get used to his distrustful manner," said I, "I have done very well."

"Are you close?"

"I have dined with him at his private house."

"I fancy," said Estella, shrinking "that must be a curious place."

"It is a curious place."

We fell into other talk, and it was mainly about the way we were travelling, and about what parts of London lay on this side of it, and what on that. The great city was almost new to her, she told me, for she had never left Miss Havisham's neighbourhood until she had gone to France, and she had merely passed through London then in going and returning. I asked her if my guardian had any charge of her while she remained here? To that she emphatically said "God forbid!" and no more.

It was impossible for me to avoid seeing that she wanted to attract me; that she made herself charming; and would have won me even if the task had needed work. Yet this didn't make me any happier, because, even if she had not taken that tone of our relationship being forced on her by others, I would have felt that she held my heart in her hand because she happened to choose to do it, and not because it would have caused her any remorse to crush it and throw it away.

When we passed through Hammersmith, I showed her where Mr. Matthew Pocket lived, and said it wasn't too far away from Richmond, and that I hoped I should see her sometimes.

"Oh yes, you are to see me; you are to come when you think proper; you are to be mentioned to the family; indeed, you are already mentioned."

I asked if it was a large household she was going to be a member of?

"No; there are only two; mother and daughter. The mother is a lady of some importance, though not averse to increasing her income."

"I wonder Miss Havisham could part with you again so soon."

"It is a part of Miss Havisham's plans for me, Pip," said Estella, with a sigh, as if she were tired; "I am to write to her constantly and see her regularly and report how I go on – I and the jewels – for they are nearly all mine now."

It was the first time she had ever called me by my name. Of course, she did so on purpose, and she knew that I would treasure it.

We came to Richmond all too soon, though it was now evening, and our destination there was a house by the Green. It was a solemn, dignified old house, whose glory days of being royal court favorites were well behind it.

A bell was rung, and two maids came fluttering out to receive Estella. Her luggage now taken inside, she gave me her hand and a smile, and said good night, and disappeared inside as the door closed. And still I stood there, looking at the house, thinking how happy I would be if I lived there with her; but also knowing that I was never happy when I was with her, but always miserable.

I got into the carriage to be taken back to Mr. Pocket's, and I got in with a bad heart-ache, and I got out with a worse heart-ache. Mr. Pocket was out lecturing; for, he was a most delightful lecturer on how to run households, and his essays on the management of children and servants were considered the very best text-books about those themes. But, Mrs. Pocket was at home, and was in a little difficulty on account of the baby's having been given a sewing needle case to keep him busy and quiet during an unexplained absence of Millers. And more needles were missing than could be regarded as safe for such a young baby either to have been applied externally or to have swallowed.

Mr. Pocket gave excellent advice, and had a clear perception of things and a fair and impartial mind. As such, I had an idea in my heartache of begging him to accept my confidence as I had with Herbert and getting his advice. But, I happened to look up at Mrs. Pocket as she sat reading her book of dignities and titles after she prescribed Bed as the correct remedy for baby and the missing needles, and I thought – Well – No, I better not bother him.

Chapter 34

As I had grown used to having my expectations, I had begun to notice their effect on myself and those around me. I tried to hide their influence on my own character as much as possible, but I knew very well that it was not all good. I lived in a state of constant anxiety regarding my behaviour to Joe. My conscience was not at all comfortable about how I had treated Biddy. I'd wake up in the middle of the night, thinking that I would've been happier and better off if I had never seen Miss Havisham's face, and had grown to manhood happy to be partners with Joe in the honest old forge. Many evenings, when I sat alone looking at the fire, I thought that after all, there was no fire like the forge fire and the kitchen fire back at home.

Yet, Estella was so inseparable from all my restlessness of mind that I couldn't tell how much of my change in character was due to myself, with or without my expectations. In other words, if I never had my expectations, but still had Estella to dwell on, I think I'd still be miserable.

Now, concerning the influence of my expectations on others, it was much clearer to me to see that it was not beneficial to anybody, and especially not to Herbert. My lavish habits led his easy-going nature into expenses that he could not afford, corrupted the simplicity of his life, and disturbed his peace with anxieties and regrets.

So now, as naturally happens when you turn a little luxury into a great luxury, I began to gather a large debt. As soon as I started, Herbert couldn't help but start, too. At Startop's suggestion, we joined a club called The Finches of the Grove. I have never figured out the point of this institution, unless if it was that the members should dine expensively once every two weeks, to argue among themselves as much as possible, and to cause six waiters to get drunk on the stairs. This happened every time, despite the opening toast: "Gentlemen, may the present promotion of good feeling ever reign predominant among the Finches of the Grove."

The Finches spent their money foolishly, and the first Finch I saw, when I had the honour of joining the Grove, was Bentley Drummle. At that time he was floundering about town in a horse cart of his own, and doing a great deal of damage to the posts on the street corners. Occasionally, he shot himself out of his cart head-first over the front, and I saw him on one occasion deliver himself at the door of the Grove in this unintentional way. But I'm getting a bit ahead of myself, for I was not a Finch yet, and could not be, according to the sacred laws of their club, until I turned twenty-one.

During this period of my life we spent as much money as we could, and got as little for it as people would give us. We were always more or less miserable, and most of our friends were, as well. There was a happy falsehood among us that we were constantly enjoying ourselves, but in truth we weren't. To the best of my belief, this last condition is a pretty common one.

I was at Mr. Pocket's about half the week, and when I was there, I hung around Richmond, hoping to see Estella. Mr. Pocket grew greyer, and tried oftener to lift himself out of his perplexed life by his hair, while Mrs. Pocket continued to trip up the family with her footstool, read her book of titles, and tell us about her grandpapa.

Trusting in my own income and expectations, I would willingly have taken Herbert's expenses on myself; but Herbert was proud, and I could not make that offer to him. So, he got into difficulties in every direction, and continued to look about him without making any progress in acquiring his Capital. But, he persevered and would say, "I find the truth to be, Handel, that an opening won't come to one, but one must go to it – so I have been."

If we hadn't been best friends, I would think that we hated each other every morning. I detested our apartment at Barnard's beyond expression, and could not endure the sight of my servant's clothes, which looked more expensive and less worth it in the morning than at any other time of the day. As we got more and more into debt, breakfast became smaller and smaller. On one occasion at breakfast, threatened by letter with legal action, "not entirely unconnected", as my local newspaper might have put it, "with jewelry," I went so far as to grab my servant by his collar and shake him off his feet, up in the air, for presuming to suppose that we wanted a pastry roll.

Every so often I would say to Herbert, as if it were a remarkable discovery, "My dear Herbert, we are getting on badly."

"My dear Handel," Herbert would say to me, in all sincerity, "if you will believe me, those very words were on my lips, by a strange coincidence."

"Then, Herbert," I would respond, "let us look into our affairs."

We always felt profoundly satisfied from making an appointment for this purpose. I always thought this was how you conducted business; this was the way to confront the thing, to take the foe by the throat. And I know Herbert thought so too.

We'd order something special for dinner, along with a bottle of something similarly special, in order that our minds might be fortified for the work ahead of us. Dinner over, we produced a bundle of pens, a large supply of ink, and a good amount of paper. For, there was something very comforting in having plenty of stationary on hand.

I would then take a sheet of paper and write across the top of it, "Memorandum of Pip's debts", with Barnard's Inn and the date very carefully added. Herbert would also take a sheet of paper, and write across it with similar formalities, "Memorandum of Herbert's debts."

Each of us would then refer to a confused heap of receipts and bills at our side that we had collected, which had been previously thrown into drawers, worn into holes in pockets, half-burnt in lighting candles, stuck for weeks in the mirror frame, and otherwise damaged. The sound of our pens going greatly inspired us, so much so that I sometimes found it difficult to distinguish between writing the bill information down in my list, and actually paying the money; both gave me a similar feeling of accomplishment.

When we had written a little while, I would ask Herbert how he was doing? Herbert was usually scratching his head in a most regretful manner at the sight of his growing numbers.

"They are mounting up, Handel," Herbert would say; "upon my life, they are mounting up."

"Be firm, Herbert," I would retort, "Confront the debts; look them in the face; stare them down."

"So I would, Handel, only they are staring me down."

However, my determination would have its effect, and Herbert would go back to work again. After a while he would give up once more, on the plea that he had not got the bill from Cobbs's, or Lobbs's, or Nobbs's, or whoever.

"Then, Herbert, estimate; estimate it in round numbers, and mark it down."

"What a fellow of resource you are!" my friend would reply, with admiration. "Really your business powers are very remarkable."

I thought so too. I established with myself the reputation of a first-rate man of business – prompt, decisive, energetic, clear, cool-headed. When I had got all my bills written down on my list, I compared each entry with the bill, and ticked it off. My self-approval when I ticked an entry was quite a luxurious sensation. When I had no more ticks to make, I folded all my bills up uniformly and tied the whole thing into a nice even bundle. Then I did the same for Herbert (who modestly said he did not have my administrative genius), and he felt that I had brought his debts into a focus for him.

My business habits had one other bright feature, which I called "leaving a Margin." For example, supposing Herbert's debts to be one hundred and sixty-four pounds, I would say, "Leave a margin, and put them down at two hundred." Or, supposing my own to be four times as much, I would leave a margin, and put them down at seven hundred. I had the highest opinion of the wisdom of leaving this Margin, but I have to admit that on looking back, it was an expensive idea. For, we always ran into new debt immediately, to the full extent of the margin, and sometimes got pretty far into another margin.

But there was a peaceful calm after these examinations of our debts that gave me, at least for a while, an admirable opinion of myself. Soothed by my work, my methods, and Herbert's compliments, I would sit with our two bundles and feel like a Bank of some sort, rather than a regular person.

We were conducting this financial wizardry one evening, when we heard a letter drop through the slit of our door, and fall to the rug. "It's for you, Handel," said Herbert, going out and coming back with it, "and I hope there is nothing the matter." This was in reference to its heavy black seal and border.

The letter was signed TRABB & CO., and its contents were simply that I was an honoured sir, and that they needed to inform me that Mrs. J. Gargery had departed this life last Monday, at six twenty in the evening, and that my attendance was requested at the funeral on next Monday at three o'clock in the afternoon.

Chapter 35

It was the first time that a grave had opened in the road of my life, and the gap it made in the smooth ground was large. After this news, the image of my sister in her chair by the kitchen fire haunted me night and day. That my old home could exist, without her in it, was something I was unable to wrap my mind around.

Whatever my fortunes might have been, there was no way I could have thought of my sister with much tenderness. But I suppose there is a shock of regret which may exist without much tenderness. Under its influence (and perhaps to make up for the lack of any affection I had felt for her) I was seized with a violent anger against the attacker who had caused her so much suffering. I felt that with sufficient proof I could have revengefully pursued whoever it was to the last degree.

Having written to Joe to offer consolation, and to assure him that I would come to the funeral, I passed the days in between in the curious state of mind I have described. I went to town early that Monday morning, and arrived at the Blue Boar with plenty of time to walk over to the forge.

When I came within sight of it, I saw that Trabb and Co. had taken over the house and installed a circus of funeral trimmings. Two dismally absurd looking teenage boys, each dressed in black and proudly displaying a crutch decorated in a black bandage – as if that could possibly provide any comfort to anybody – were guarding the front door. All the children of the village, and most of the women, were admiring these sentries and the closed windows of the house and forge. As I came up to the house, one of the two boys knocked at the door for me – implying that I was far too exhausted by grief to have strength left to knock for myself.

Another employee of Trabb dressed up in black (a carpenter I recognized, who had once eaten two geese on a bet) opened the door, and showed me into the best parlour. Here, Mr. Trabb had taken for himself the best table and had covered it all in black cloth and pins. At the moment of my arrival, he had just finished covering somebody's hat with black cloth, so he held out his hand for my hat. But I, misled by his hand, and confused by the occasion, shook hands with him instead.

Poor dear Joe, tangled up in a little black cloak tied in a large bow under his chin, was seated apart at the upper end of the room, where, as chief mourner, he had evidently been assigned to sit by Mr. Trabb. When I bent down and said to him, "Dear Joe, how are you?" he said, "Pip, old chap, you knowed her when she were a fine figure of a--" and clasped my hand and said no more.

Biddy, looking very neat and modest in her black dress, went quietly here and there, and was very helpful. When I had greeted Biddy, as I thought it not a time for talking, I went and sat down near Joe, and began to wonder in what part of the house it – she – my sister – was. The smell of sweet cake was in the parlour, and I looked about for the table of refreshments. It was hardly visible until one had got accustomed to the gloom, but there was a cut-up plum-cake upon it, along with cut-up oranges, sandwiches, biscuits, and two flasks that I recognized as ornaments, but had never seen used in all my life; one full of wine, and the other with sherry. Standing at this table, I became aware of the toady Pumblechook in a black cloak and several yards of black cloth wrapped around his hat, who was alternately stuffing himself and making obvious servile movements to catch my attention. The moment he succeeded, he came over to me (breathing sherry and crumbs), and said in a subdued voice, "May I, dear sir?" and did. I then saw Mr. and Mrs. Hubble. We were all going to "follow", and were all in the process of being tied up separately by Trabb into ridiculous black bundles of cloth.

"Which I meantersay, Pip," Joe whispered me, as we were being what Mr. Trabb called "formed" in the parlour, covering us with his black cloth, "which I meantersay, sir, as I would rather have carried her to the church myself, along with three or four friends with willing hearts, but it was considered that the neighbours would look down on that as lacking proper respect."

"Pocket-handkerchiefs out, all," said Mr. Trabb, in a depressed business-like voice. "Pocket-handkerchiefs out. We are ready!"

So, we all put our pocket-handkerchiefs to our faces, as if our noses were bleeding, and filed out two by two; Joe and I, then Biddy and Pumblechook, and lastly Mr. and Mrs. Hubble. The remains of my poor sister had been brought round to the kitchen door by six coffin bearers, and, it appeared to be a point of the Undertaking ceremony that the six coffin bearers must be covered and blinded under a horrible black velvet drape with a white border. The thing looked like a blind monster with twelve human legs, shuffling and blundering along, under the guidance of two keepers – the two boys from the front door, followed by the six of us.

The neighbourhood, however, highly approved of these arrangements, and we were much admired as we went through the village. The more youthful and vigorous part of the community would make dashes now and then to cut us off, and lie in wait to intercept us while they were hidden. At such times the more excited among them would call out on seeing us, "Here they come! Here they are!" and we were all but cheered.

As we slowly trudged along behind the coffin bearers, I was much annoyed by the fawning Pumblechook, who, since he was behind me, persisted all the way in arranging my streaming black hatband and smoothing my cloak. My thoughts were further distracted by the excessive pride of Mr. and Mrs. Hubble, who were incredibly conceited to be members of so distinguished a procession.

Finally leaving the village, we got out into the marsh land and went into the churchyard, close to the graves of my parents. And there my sister was laid quietly in the earth while birds sang high above it, and the light wind strewed it with beautiful shadows of clouds and trees.

Pumblechook's behavior had no bounds of shame. While we were at the grave-side, and the priest was reading noble passages about how fleeting life is and how we can't take anything with us when we die, I heard him cough the exception of the case of a young gentleman who had unexpectedly come into a large property. When we had returned to the forge, he told me that he wished my sister could have known that I had done her so much honour, and he had the gall to hint that she would have considered it a reasonable trade for her death. After that, he drank all the rest of the sherry, and Mr. Hubble drank the wine. Finally, he went away with Mr. and Mrs. Hubble – to have a festive evening of it, I was positive, and to tell the Jolly Bargemen that he was the founder of my fortunes and my earliest benefactor.

When they were all gone, and when Trabb and his men – but not his boy, he hadn't been there – had crammed their black cloth and funerary accessories into bags and had left, the house felt more wholesome. Soon afterwards, Biddy, Joe, and I, had a cold dinner together. We dined in the best parlour, not in the old kitchen, and Joe was so exceedingly careful with what he did with his knife and fork and the salt bowl and what not, that it was all very uptight and uncomfortable. But, after dinner, when I made him smoke his pipe, and when I had loitered with him about the forge, and when we sat down together on the great block of stone outside it, we got on better. I noticed that after the funeral Joe changed his clothes so far as to make a compromise between his Sunday dress and working clothes, in which the dear fellow looked natural, and like the Man he was.

He was very much pleased by my asking if I might sleep in my own little room, and I was pleased too, for, I felt that I had done rather a great thing in making the request. When evening was closing in, I took an opportunity of getting into the garden with Biddy for a little talk.

"Biddy," said I, "I think you should have written to me about these sad matters."

"Do you, Mr. Pip?" said Biddy. "I would have written if I had thought that."

"I don't mean to be unkind, Biddy, when I say I think you should have thought that."

"Do you, Mr. Pip?"

She was so quiet, and had such an orderly, good, and pretty way with her, that I did not like the thought of making her cry again. After looking a little at her downcast eyes as she walked beside me, I gave up pressing that point and switched subjects.

"I suppose it will be difficult for you to remain here now, Biddy dear?"

"Oh! I can't do so, Mr. Pip," said Biddy, in a tone of regret, but still of quiet conviction. "I have been speaking to Mrs. Hubble, and I am going to live with her tomorrow. I hope we shall be able to take some care of Mr. Gargery, together, until he settles down."

"How are you going to live, Biddy? If you want any mo--"

"How am I going to live?" repeated Biddy, interrupting, with a momentary flush upon her face. "I'll tell you, Mr. Pip. I am going to try to get the job of teacher in the new school nearly finished here. I can be well recommended by all the neighbours, and I hope I can be industrious and patient, and teach myself while I teach others. You know, Mr. Pip," pursued Biddy, with a smile, as she raised her eyes to my face, "the new schools are not like the old, but I learnt a good deal from you after that time, and have had time since then to improve."

"I think you would always improve, Biddy, under any circumstances."

I walked a little further with Biddy, looking silently at her downcast eyes.

"I have not heard the particulars of my sister's death, Biddy."

"They are very slight, poor thing. She had been in one of her bad states – though they had got better recently, rather than worse – for four days, when she came out of it in the evening, and said quite plainly, 'Joe.' As she had never said any word for a long time, I ran and got Mr. Gargery from the forge. She made signs to me that she wanted him to sit down close to her, and wanted me to put her arms around his neck. So I put them around his neck, and she laid her head down on his shoulder quite content and satisfied. And so she soon said 'Joe' again, and once 'Pardon,' and once 'Pip.' She never lifted her head up any more, and it was just an hour later when we laid it down on her own bed, because we found she was gone."

Biddy cried; the darkening garden and the stars that were coming out were blurred in my own eyesight as well.

"Nothing was ever discovered, Biddy?"

"Nothing."

"Do you know what became of Orlick?"

"I think he is working in the quarries."

"You've seen him then? - Why are you looking at that dark tree in the lane?"

"I saw him there, on the night she died."

"That was not the last time either, Biddy?"

"No; I have seen him there, since you and I have been walking here. - It is of no use," said Biddy, laying her hand on my arm, as I was for running over there, "you know I would not deceive you; he was not there a minute, and he is gone now."

It revived my intense anger to find that she was still pursued by this fellow, and I felt deeply ingrained against him. I told her so, and told her that I would spend any money or take any pains to drive him out of that country. By degrees she led me into more temperate talk, and she told me how Joe loved me, and how Joe never complained of anything – she didn't say of me; she had no need, I knew what she meant – but ever did his duty in his life, with a strong hand, a quiet tongue, and a gentle heart.

"Indeed, it would be hard to say too much for him," said I; "and Biddy, we must often speak of these things, for of course I shall be down here often now. I am not going to leave poor Joe alone."

Biddy didn't say a single word.

"Biddy, don't you hear me?"

"Yes, Mr. Pip."

"Not to mention you calling me Mr. Pip, which appears to me to be in bad taste Biddy, what do you mean by it?"

"What do I mean?" asked Biddy, timidly.

"Biddy," said I, in a virtuously self-asserting manner, "I must request to know what you mean by this?"

"By this?" said Biddy.

"Now, don't echo," I retorted. "You didn't used to do that, Biddy."

"Didn't used to!" said Biddy. "O Mr. Pip! Didn't used to!"

Well! I rather thought I would give up pushing why she called me Sir now, too. After another silent turn in the garden, I went back to my main question.

"Biddy," said I, "I made a remark saying I was going to be coming down here often, to see Joe, which you received with a meaningful silence. Have the goodness, Biddy, to tell me why."

"Are you quite sure, then," asked Biddy, stopping in the narrow garden walk, and looking at me with a clear and honest eye, "that you WILL come to see him often?"

"Oh dear me!" said I, as if I found myself compelled to give up Biddy in despair. "This really is a very bad side of human nature! Don't say any more, if you please, Biddy. This shocks me very much."

I kept Biddy at a distance during supper, and, when I went up to my own old little room, bid her goodnight as formally as I could. As often as I was restless in the night, I lay there thinking what an unkind, unfair thing Biddy had said to me in doubting my intentions to spend more time with Joe.

Early in the morning I was to go back to London. So, early in the morning I was out, and looking in, unseen, at one of the wooden windows of the forge. There I stood for several minutes, looking at Joe, already at work with a glow of health and strength upon his face that made it look as if the bright sun of the life in store for him were shining on it.

"Good-bye, dear Joe! - No, don't wipe it off - for God's sake, give me your blackened hand! - I shall be down soon, and often."

"Never too soon, sir," said Joe, "and never too often, Pip!"

Biddy was waiting for me at the kitchen door, with a mug of new milk and a crust of bread. "Biddy," said I, when I gave her my hand at parting, "I am not angry, but I am hurt."

"No, don't be hurt," she pleaded quite pathetically, "let only me be hurt, if I have been unfair."

Once again, as when I first left that town, the mists were rising as I walked away from the forge. If the mists had told me, as I suspect they did, that Biddy was right and that I wouldn't come back despite my pledge, then all I can say is – the mists would have been right, too.

Chapter 36

Herbert and I went on from bad to worse, increasing our debts, looking into our affairs, leaving Margins and other similar bad ideas. Time went on and I came of age, just like Herbert predicted, before I quite knew where I was.

Herbert himself had come of age eight months before me. As he had no expectations, the event did not make a big sensation in Barnard's Inn. But we had looked forward to my twenty-first birthday with much speculation and anticipation, for we had both figured that my guardian could hardly help saying something of importance on that occasion.

I had taken care to have it well understood at Mr. Jaggers' office when my birthday was. On the day before it, I received an official note from Wemmick, informing me that Mr. Jaggers would be glad if I would pay a visit to his office at five in the afternoon of my birthday. This convinced us that something great was going to happen, and I arrived at Mr. Jaggers' right on time, and full of nervous anticipation.

In the outer office, Wemmick offered me his congratulations and motioned me with a nod into my guardian's office. It was November, and my guardian was standing in front of his fire leaning his back against the chimney-piece, with his hands clasped behind his back, under his coattails.

"Well, Pip," said he, "I must call you Mr. Pip to-day. Congratulations, Mr. Pip."

We shook hands – he was always a remarkably short hand shaker – and I thanked him.

"Take a chair, Mr. Pip," said my guardian.

As I sat down, and he remained standing, I felt at a disadvantage, which reminded me of that old time when I had been put upon a tombstone.

"Now my young friend," my guardian began, as if I were a witness in the box, "I am going to have a word or two with you."

"If you please, sir."

"What do you suppose," said Mr. Jaggers, bending forward to look at the ground, and then throwing his head back to look at the ceiling, "what do you suppose you are living at the rate of?"

"At the rate of, sir?"

"At," repeated Mr. Jaggers, still looking at the ceiling, "the - rate - of?" And then looked all around the room, and paused with his pocket-handkerchief in his hand, half-way to his nose.

I had looked into my debts so often that I had thoroughly destroyed any idea I might ever have had of what they were. Reluctantly, I confessed I was unable to answer the question. This reply seemed agreeable to Mr.

Jaggers, who said, "I thought so!" and blew his nose with an air of satisfaction.

"Now, I have asked you a question, my friend," said Mr. Jaggers. "Have you anything to ask me?"

"Of course, it would be a great relief to me to ask you several questions, sir; but I remember the rules of my expectations."

"Ask one," said Mr. Jaggers.

"Is my benefactor to be made known to me today?"

"No. Ask another."

"Is that information to be made known to me soon?"

"Hold off on that subject a moment," said Mr. Jaggers, "and ask about something else."

I looked around me, but there appeared to be now no possible escape from the question, "Have – I – anything to receive, sir?" On that, Mr. Jaggers said triumphantly, "I thought we should come to it!" and called to Wemmick to give him a piece of paper. Wemmick appeared, handed it to him, and disappeared.

"Now, Mr. Pip," said Mr. Jaggers, holding the piece of paper, "listen, if you please. You have been drawing money pretty freely here. Your name occurs pretty often in Wemmick's cash-book. But, you are in debt, of course?"

"I am afraid I must say yes, sir."

"You know you must say yes, don't you?" said Mr. Jaggers.

"Yes, sir."

"I don't ask you what you owe, because you don't know; and if you did know, you wouldn't tell me, you would say less. Yes, yes, my friend," cried Mr. Jaggers, waving his forefinger to stop me, as I made a show of protesting, "it's likely enough that you think you wouldn't, but you would. You'll excuse me, but I know better than you. Now, take this piece of paper in your hand. You've got it? Very good. Now, unfold it and tell me what it is."

"This is a bank-note," said I, "for five hundred pounds."

"That is a bank-note," repeated Mr. Jaggers, "for five hundred pounds. And a very handsome sum of money too, I think. You consider it so?"

"How could I do otherwise!"

"Ah! But answer the question," said Mr. Jaggers.

"Undoubtedly."

"You consider it, undoubtedly, a handsome sum of money. Now, that handsome sum of money, Pip, is your own. It is a present to you on this day, in earnest of your expectations. And at the rate of that handsome sum of money per year, and at no higher rate, you are to live until the donor of the whole appears. That is to say, you will now take your money affairs entirely into your own hands, and you will draw from Wemmick one hundred and twenty-five pounds per quarter, until you are in communication with your benefactor, and no longer with the mere agent. As I have told you before, I am the mere agent. I follow my instructions, and I am paid for doing so. I think them unfair, but I am not paid for giving any opinion on their merits."

I was beginning to express my gratitude to my benefactor for the great liberality with which I was treated, when Mr. Jaggers stopped me. "I am not paid, Pip," said he, coolly, "to carry your words to anyone." He then gathered up his coat-tails, as he had gathered up the subject, and stood frowning at his boots as if he suspected them of plotting against him.

After a pause, I hinted:

"There was a question just now, Mr. Jaggers, which you desired me to put off for a moment. I hope I am doing nothing wrong in asking it again?"

"What is it?" said he.

I might have known that he would never help me out, but it took me some effort to have to re-phrase the question again, as if it were new. "Is it likely," I said, after hesitating, "that my patron, the benefactor you have spoken of, Mr. Jaggers, will soon--" there I delicately stopped.

"Will soon what?" asked Mr. Jaggers. "That's no question as it stands, you know."

"Will soon come to London," said I, after casting about for a precise form of words, "or summon me anywhere else?"

"Now here," replied Mr. Jaggers, fixing me for the first time with his dark deep-set eyes, "we must revert to the evening when we first encountered one another in your village. What did I tell you then, Pip?"

"You told me that it might be years from now when that person appeared."

"Just so," said Mr. Jaggers, "that's my answer."

As we looked at one another, I felt my breath come quicker in my strong desire to get something out of him. And as I felt that it came quicker, and as I could tell he saw that eagerness in me, I felt that I had less chance than ever of getting anything out of him.

"Do you suppose it will still be years from now, Mr. Jaggers?"

Mr. Jaggers shook his head – not in answering the question, but in altogether negating any idea that he could possibly be made to answer it.

"Listen," said Mr. Jaggers, warming the backs of his legs with the backs of his warmed hands, "I'll be plain with you, my friend Pip. That's a question I must not be asked. You'll understand that better when I tell you it's a question that might cause trouble for me. Come! I'll go a little further with you, I'll say something more."

He bent down so low to frown at his boots, that he was able to rub the calves of his legs in the pause he made.

"When that person comes forward," said Mr. Jaggers, straightening himself up, "you and that person will settle your own affairs. When that person comes forward, my part in this business will end. When that person comes forward, it will not be necessary for me to know anything about it. And that's all I have got to say."

We looked at one another until I withdrew my eyes, and I looked thoughtfully at the floor. From this last speech I concluded that Miss Havisham, for some reason or no reason, had not let him know her plans for Estella and me; that maybe he resented not being included in knowing her full plan. Or, that maybe he really did know about that part of her plan, and objected to it and would have nothing to do with it. When I raised my eyes again, I found that he had been shrewdly looking at me all the time, and was doing so still.

"If that is all you have to say, sir," I remarked, "then there can be nothing left for me to say."

He nodded in agreement, pulled out his large watch, and asked me where I was going to dine? I replied at my own chambers, with Herbert. As a necessary act of politeness, I asked him if he would join us, and he promptly accepted the invitation. But he insisted on walking home with me, in order that I might make no extra preparation for him, and first he had a letter or two to write, and (of course) had his hands to wash. So, I said I would go into the outer office and talk to Wemmick.

The fact was, that when the five hundred pounds had come into my pocket, a thought had come into my head which had been often there before, and it occurred to me that I should discuss this idea with Wemmick.

He had already locked up his safe, and made preparations for going home.

"Mr. Wemmick," said I, "I want to ask your opinion. I am very desirous to serve a friend."

Wemmick tightened his post-office mouth and shook his head, as if his opinion were dead against any fatal weakness of that sort.

"This friend," I pursued, "is trying to get started in business, but has no money, and finds it difficult and disheartening to make a beginning. Now, I want somehow to help him to a beginning."

"With money down?" said Wemmick, in a tone drier than any sawdust.

"With some money down," I replied, for an uneasy remembrance shot across me of that symmetrical bundle of bills waiting for me at home; "and perhaps some anticipation of my expectations."

"Mr. Pip," said Wemmick, "I should like to list off for you on my fingers, if you please, the names of the various bridges nearby. Let's see; there's London, Southwark, Blackfriars, Waterloo, Westminster, and Vauxhall. There's as many as six bridges, you see, to choose from."

"I don't understand you," said I.

"Choose your bridge, Mr. Pip," returned Wemmick, "walk out onto it, and throw your money into the river, and you know the end of it. Give it to a friend, and you may know the end of it too – but it's a less pleasant end."

I could have posted a newspaper in his mouth, his closed lips were so wide and flat after saying this.

"This is very discouraging," said I.

"Meant to be so," said Wemmick.

"Then is it your opinion," I inquired, with a little displeasure, "that a man should never--"

" - Invest portable property in a friend?" said Wemmick. "Certainly he should not. Unless he wants to get rid of the friend – and then it becomes a question of how much portable property it may be worth to get rid of him."

"And that," said I, "is your deliberate opinion, Mr. Wemmick?"

"That," he returned, "is my deliberate opinion in this office."

"Ah!" said I, pressing him, for I thought I saw a loophole here, "but would that be your opinion at Walworth?"

"Mr. Pip," he replied, with gravity, "Walworth is one place, and this office is another. Much like the Aged is one person, and Mr. Jaggers is another. They must not be mixed together. My Walworth opinion must be taken at Walworth; none but my official opinion can be taken in this office."

"Very well," said I, much relieved, "then I shall look you up at Walworth, you may depend on it."

"Mr. Pip," he returned, "you will be welcome there, in a private and personal capacity."

We had held this conversation in a low voice, well knowing my guardian's ears to be the sharpest of the sharp. As he now appeared in his doorway, toweling his hands off, Wemmick put on his greatcoat and stood by to snuff out the candles. We all three went into the street together, and from the door-step Wemmick turned his way, and Mr. Jaggers and I turned ours, towards Barnard's Inn.

That evening, I couldn't help wishing more than once that Mr. Jaggers had had an Aged at his house, or a Cannon, or a Something, or a Somebody, to unbend his brows a little. It was an uncomfortable thought on a twenty-first birthday, that coming of age seemed hardly worthwhile in such a guarded and suspicious world as he made out of it. He was a thousand times better informed and cleverer than Wemmick, and yet I would a thousand times rather have had Wemmick to dinner. And Mr. Jaggers didn't just make me gloomy, because after he left, Herbert said he felt that he must have committed a felony and forgotten the details of it, he felt so dejected and guilty.

Chapter 37

Deciding that Sunday was the best day for getting Mr. Wemmick's Walworth opinion, I made a pilgrimage to his Castle. On my arrival, I found the Union Jack flying and the drawbridge pulled up. Not discouraged by this show of defiance to the world, I rang at the gate, and was admitted in a most peaceful manner by the Aged.

"My son, sir," said the old man, after securing the drawbridge, "had it in his mind that you might happen to drop in, and he left word that he would soon be home from his afternoon's walk. He is very regular in his walks; very regular in everything."

I nodded at the old gentleman as Wemmick himself might have nodded, and we went in and sat down by the fireside.

Curious to know what the old gentleman knew about Mr. Jaggers, I roared that name at him. He confused me greatly by laughing heartily and replying in a very sprightly manner, "No, to be sure, you're right!" And to this hour I have not the faintest notion what he meant or what joke he thought I had made.

I was wondering whether I could come up with anything on purpose to say that would have amused him half as much as this imaginary joke, when I was startled by a sudden click in the wall on one side of the chimney, and the tumbling open of a little wooden flap with "JOHN" written on it. The old man, following my eyes, cried with great triumph, "My son's come home!" and we both went out to the drawbridge.

It was worth any amount of money to see Wemmick waving a salute to me from the other side of the moat, when we could have shaken hands across it with the greatest ease. The Aged was so delighted to work the drawbridge that I made no offer to assist him, but stood quiet until Wemmick had come across and had presented me to Miss Skiffins, a lady accompanying him.

Miss Skiffins was of a wooden appearance, and her mouth, like Mr. Wemmick's, was in the post-office branch of the service. She might have been some two or three years younger than Wemmick, and I judged her to possess portable property. She seemed to be a nice lady, and showed a high regard for the Aged. It didn't take long to discover that she was a frequent visitor at the Castle, for, on our going inside, and my complimenting Wemmick on his ingenious invention for announcing himself to the Aged, he begged me to give my attention for a moment to the chimney, and he left the room. Very soon the "JOHN" door closed up, and another click came, and another little door tumbled open on the other side of the chimney with "MISS SKIFFINS" on it. Then that door closed up. Then both little doors tumbled open together, and shut up together. On

Wemmick's return from working these mechanical devices, I expressed my great admiration for them, and he said, "Well, you know, they're both pleasant and useful to the Aged. And by George, sir, it's a thing worth mentioning that of all the people who come to this gate, the secret of those pulls is only known to the Aged, Miss Skiffins, and me!"

"And Mr. Wemmick made them," added Miss Skiffins, "with his own hands, and out of his own head."

While Miss Skiffins was taking off her bonnet (she retained her green gloves during the evening as a visible sign that there was company), Wemmick invited me to take a walk with him around the property, and see how his island looked in wintertime. Thinking that he did this to give me an opportunity of getting his Walworth opinion, I seized the opportunity as soon as we were out of the Castle.

Having thought of the matter with care, I approached my subject as if I had never hinted at it before. I informed Wemmick that I was anxious on behalf of Herbert Pocket, and I told him how we had first met and fought in Miss Havisham's garden as children. I described Herbert's home, and his character, and his having no income but such as he was dependent on his father for, and that was uncertain and unreliable.

I described the advantages I had gained from knowing him and having his help with showing me genteel manners and such, and I confessed that I feared I hadn't repaid him very well; that he might have done better without me and my expectations in his life. Keeping Miss Havisham in the background at a great distance, I still hinted at the possibility of my having competed with him in his prospects at a young age, and shared my certainty of his possessing a generous soul and being far above any mean distrusts, retaliations, or vile plans.

I told Wemmick that for all these reasons, and because he was my best friend, I wished my own good fortune to reflect some rays upon him, and therefore I sought advice from Wemmick's experience and knowledge of men and affairs. I asked how I could best try with my resources to help Herbert to an income – say a hundred pounds per year, to keep him in good hope and heart – and gradually to buy him onto some small partnership. In conclusion, I begged Wemmick to understand that my help must always be given without Herbert's knowledge or suspicion, and that there was no one else in the world with whom I could get this advice. I wound up by laying my hand on his shoulder, and saying, "I can't help confiding in you, though I know it must be troublesome to you; but that is your fault, for having ever brought me here."

Wemmick was silent for a little while, and then said with a kind of start, "Well you know, Mr. Pip, I must tell you one thing. This is devilish good of you."

"Say you'll help me to be good then," said I.

"Good God," replied Wemmick, shaking his head, "that's not my trade."

"But then, this is not the office of your trade," said I.

"You are right," he returned. "You hit the nail on the head. Mr. Pip, I'll put on my considering-cap, and I think all you want to do may be done in steps. Skiffins (that's her brother) is an accountant and agent. I'll look him up and go to work for you."

"I thank you ten thousand times."

"On the contrary," said he, "I thank you, for though we are strictly in our private and personal capacity, still I have to confess that there are Newgate cobwebs about me, and this type of kindness brushes them away."

After a little further conversation, we returned to the Castle where we found Miss Skiffins preparing tea. The duty of making the toast was delegated to the Aged, and that excellent old gentleman was so intent upon it that he seemed to me in some danger of melting his eyes. It was no small meal that we were going to make, but a vigorous feast. The Aged prepared such a stack of buttered toast that I could scarcely see him over it; while Miss Skiffins brewed such a large quantity of tea that the pig in the back yard became strongly excited and repeatedly expressed his desire to participate with us.

The flag had been taken in for the night, and the cannon had been fired at the right moment of time, and I felt as snugly cut off from the rest of London as if the moat were thirty feet wide by as many deep. I inferred from the methodical nature of Miss Skiffins's arrangements that she made tea there every Sunday night, and I rather suspected that a brooch she wore was a piece of portable property that had been given to her by Wemmick.

After the feast, we drew close to the fire, and Wemmick said, "Now Aged Parent, read us the paper."

Wemmick explained to me while the Aged got his glasses out, that this was their usual custom, and that it gave the old gentleman infinite satisfaction to read the news aloud. "I won't offer an apology," said Wemmick, "for he isn't capable of many pleasures – are you, Aged P.?"

"All right, John, all right," returned the old man, seeing himself spoken to.

"Only tip him a nod every now and then when he looks off his paper," said Wemmick, "and he'll be as happy as a king. We're all paying attention, Aged One."

"All right John, all right!" returned the cheerful old man, so busy and so pleased that it really was quite charming.

As he wanted the candles close to him, and as he was always on the verge of putting either his head or the newspaper into them, he required as much watching as a gunpowder mill. But Wemmick was equally untiring and gentle in his vigilance, and the Aged read on, quite oblivious to his many rescues. Whenever he looked at us, we all expressed the greatest interest and amazement, and nodded until he resumed again.

As Wemmick and Miss Skiffins sat side by side, I observed a slow and gradual lengthening of Mr. Wemmick's mouth into a smile, seemingly tied to his slowly and gradually stealing his arm around Miss Skiffins's waist. Eventually, I saw his hand appear on the other side of Miss Skiffins; but at that same moment Miss Skiffins neatly stopped him with her green glove, unwound his arm again as if it were simply a scarf or belt, and laid it on the table in front of her, almost as if she wasn't even thinking about it.

I soon noticed Wemmick's arm beginning to disappear again, and gradually fading out of view. Shortly afterwards, his mouth began to widen again into a smile. After a good deal of suspense, I saw his hand appear on the other side of Miss Skiffins. Instantly, Miss Skiffins stopped it as before and laid it on the table in the same casual, nonchalant way. The table seemed to represent the path of virtue, and I can safely say that during the whole time of the Aged's reading, Wemmick's arm was straying from that path and being brought back to it by Miss Skiffins.

At last, the Aged read himself into a light sleep. Wemmick brought out a little bottle and some glasses, and we all had something warm to drink, including the Aged, who was soon awake again. I observed that Miss Skiffins and Wemmick drank out of the same glass. Of course I knew better than to offer to see Miss Skiffins home, and under the circumstances I thought I had better go first, which I did, taking a cordial leave of the Aged, and having spent a pleasant evening.

Before a week was over, I received a note from Wemmick, sent from Walworth, stating that he hoped he had made some progress in that matter pertaining to our private and personal capacities, and that he would be glad if I could come and see him about it. So, I went out to Walworth again, and yet again, and yet again, and I saw him by appointment in the City several times, but never held any communication with him on the subject in or near his work office.

We found a worthy young merchant, just starting out, who wanted intelligent help, and who wanted capital, and who eventually would want a partner. Between him and me, secret documents were signed of which Herbert was the subject, and I paid him half of my five hundred pounds down and set up various other payments, some to fall due at certain dates out of my income, some contingent on my coming into my full property. Miss Skiffins's brother conducted the negotiation. Wemmick helped guide it throughout, but never appeared in it.

The whole business was so cleverly managed that Herbert had no suspicion of me being in it. I'll never forget the radiant face with which he came home one afternoon and told me, as a great piece of news, of his having met a man named Clarriker (the young merchant's name), and of Clarriker's having taken an extraordinary liking to him, and of Herbert's belief that his opening had come at last. Day by day as his hopes grew stronger and his face brighter, he must have thought me a more and more affectionate friend, for I had the greatest difficulty in restraining my tears of triumph when I saw him so happy. Eventually, the thing being done, and he having that day become part of Clarriker's House, and he having talked to me for a whole evening in a flush of pleasure and success, I did really cry for real with joy when I went to bed, to think that my expectations had done some good to somebody.

The turning point of my life now opens on my view. But, before I proceed to narrate it, and before I pass on to all the changes it involved, I must give one chapter to Estella. It is not too much to give to the theme that so long filled my heart.

Chapter 38

If that solemn old house in Richmond should ever come to be haunted when I am dead, it would surely be by my ghost. O the many, many nights and days through which the uneasy spirit within me haunted that house when Estella lived there! Let my body be where it would, my spirit was always wandering around that house.

A widow named Mrs. Brandley owned the house and had been a friend of Miss Havisham before her seclusion. Mrs. Brandley had one daughter several years older than Estella, and they were in what is called "a good position", and visited, and were visited by, many people. Little, if any, feeling of warmth existed between them and Estella, but the understanding was established that they were necessary to her and she was necessary to them.

Inside Mrs. Brandley's house, and outside Mrs. Brandley's house, I suffered every kind of torture that Estella could cause me. The nature of my relationship with her, being on terms of familiarity but not being on terms of favour, just made it worse. If I had been her secretary, or half-brother, or poor relation, I could not have felt further from my hopes when I was nearest to her. The privilege of calling her by her name, and hearing her call me by mine, I'm pretty sure almost maddened her other admirers; I know for sure that it almost maddened me.

She had admirers without end, and used me to tease them. No doubt my jealousy made an admirer of every one who went near her, but there were more than enough of them without needing that.

There were picnics, plays, operas, concerts, parties, all sorts of pleasures through which I pursued her – and they were all miseries to me. I never had one hour's happiness in her company, and yet my mind was constantly dwelling on the happiness of having her with me unto death.

Throughout this part of our relationship she routinely went back to that tone of voice which sounded like our association was forced on us. There were other times when she would suddenly check herself and speak genuinely, and would seem to pity me.

"Pip, Pip," she said one evening, coming to such a check, "will you never take warning?"

"Of what?"

"Of me."

"Warning not to be attracted by you, do you mean, Estella?"

"Do I mean! If you don't know what I mean, you're blind."

I should have replied that Love was commonly said to be blind, but for the reason that I always was restrained – and this was not the least of my miseries – by a feeling that it was unfair to press myself on her, when she knew that she could not choose but to obey Miss Havisham. My dread always was, that this knowledge she had that I was to be her future husband and that it was all planned out for her, put me at odds with her pride, and made me the subject of a rebellious struggle in her heart.

"At any rate," said I, "I have no warning given to me just now, for you wrote to me to come to you, this time."

"That's true," said Estella, with a cold careless smile that always chilled me. She went on to say, “Miss Havisham wishes to have me visit for a day at Satis House. You are to take me there, and bring me back, if you will. She would rather I did not travel alone, and objects to having my maid accompany me, for she has a sensitive horror of being talked about by such people. Can you take me?"

"Can I take you, Estella!"

"You can then? The day after tomorrow, if you please. You are to pay all charges out of my purse. You hear the condition of your going?"

"And must obey," said I.

This was all the preparation I received for that visit, or for others like it. Miss Havisham never wrote to me, nor had I ever so much as seen her handwriting. We went down on the day after the next, and we found her in the room where I first saw her, and it is needless to add that there was no change in Satis House.

She was even more dreadfully fond of Estella than she had been when I last saw them together. I repeat the word “fond” advisedly, for there was something positively dreadful in the energy of her looks and embraces. She hung upon Estella's beauty, hung upon her words, and hung upon her gestures, as though she were devouring the beautiful creature she had raised.

From Estella she looked at me, with a searching glance that seemed to pry into my heart and probe its wounds. "How does she use you, Pip; how does she use you?" she asked me again, with her witch-like eagerness, even within Estella's hearing. But, when we sat by her flickering fire at night, she was most weird. For then, keeping Estella's hand drawn through her arm and clutched in her own hand, she extracted from Estella the names and conditions of the men whom she had enchanted. As Miss Havisham dwelt upon this list with the intensity of somebody with a mortally hurt and diseased mind, she sat with her other hand on her crutch stick with her chin resting on it, and her bright eyes glaring at me, looking like a specter.

I saw in this exchange between the two of them that Herbert was right; that Estella really was sent by Miss Havisham to wreak her revenge on all men. At least, I deduced, for a certain length of time until her vengeance was gratified. It made me wretched, with a bitter sense of dependence on Miss Havisham, and it awakened a feeling of degradation as well. I understood why Estella was assigned to me in the interim to be her courier; that while the prize may be reserved for me in the end, I still had to endure seeing her being sent out to attract and torment and do mischief, so I was to be tormented by a version of this vengeance, like the other admirers. It also made sense why Mr. Jaggers wouldn't commit to, or even mention, knowing anything about this type of twisted plan.

It happened on this particular visit that some sharp words arose between Estella and Miss Havisham. It was the first time I had ever seen them opposed.

We were seated by the fire, as just now described, and Miss Havisham still had Estella's arm drawn through her own, and still clutched Estella's hand in hers, when Estella gradually began to detach herself. She had shown a proud impatience more than once before, and had seemed to endure that fierce affection, rather than accept or return it.

"What!" said Miss Havisham, flashing her eyes at her, "are you tired of me?"

"Only a little tired of myself," replied Estella, disengaging her arm, and moving to the great chimney-piece, where she stood looking down at the fire.

"Speak the truth, you ingrate!" cried Miss Havisham, passionately striking her stick upon the floor; "you are tired of me."

Estella looked at her with perfect composure, and again looked down at the fire. Her graceful figure and her beautiful face showed a detached indifference to the wild heat of Miss Havisham that was almost cruel.

"You stock and stone!" exclaimed Miss Havisham. "You cold, cold heart!"

"What?" said Estella, preserving her attitude of indifference as she leaned against the great chimney-piece and only moving her eyes; "do you scold me for being cold? You, of all people?"

"Are you not?" was the fierce retort.

"You should know," said Estella, calmly. "I am what you have made me. Take all the praise, take all the blame; take all the success, take all the failure; in short, take me."

"O, look at her, look at her!" cried Miss Havisham, bitterly, "So hard and thankless, on the hearth where she was reared! Where I took her into this wretched breast when it was first bleeding from its stabs, and where I have lavished years of tenderness upon her!"

"I had no say in the agreement," said Estella, "for I could barely walk and speak when it was made. But what would you have? You have been very good to me, and I owe everything to you. What would you have?"

"Love," replied the other.

"You have it."

"I have not," said Miss Havisham.

"Mother by adoption," retorted Estella, but never raising her voice as the other did, never yielding either to anger or tenderness, "I have said that I owe everything to you. All I possess is freely yours. All that you have given me is at your command to have again. Beyond that, I have nothing. And if you ask me to give you what you never gave me, my gratitude and duty cannot do impossibilities."

"Did I never give her love!" cried Miss Havisham, turning wildly to me. "Did I never give her a burning love, inseparable from jealousy at all times, and from sharp pain, while she speaks this way to me! Let her call me mad, let her call me mad!"

"Why should I call you mad," returned Estella, "I, of all people? Does anyone live who knows what set plans you have, half as well as I do? Does anyone live who knows what a steady memory you have, half as well as I do? I who have sat on this same hearth on the little stool that is even now beside you there, learning your lessons and looking up into your face, when your face was strange and frightened me."

"Soon forgotten!" moaned Miss Havisham. "Times soon forgotten!"

"No, not forgotten," retorted Estella. "but treasured up in my memory. When have you found me not following your teaching and your lessons? When have you found me giving admission here," she touched her bosom with her hand, "to anything that you taught me to exclude? Be fair with me."

"So proud, so proud!" moaned Miss Havisham.

"Who taught me to be proud?" returned Estella. "Who praised me when I learnt my lesson?"

"So hard, so hard!" moaned Miss Havisham.

"Who taught me to be hard?" returned Estella. "Who praised me when I learnt my lesson?"

"But to be proud and hard to ME!" Miss Havisham quite shrieked, as she stretched out her arms. "Estella, you're not supposed to be proud and hard to ME!"

Estella looked at her for a moment with a kind of calm wonder, but was not otherwise disturbed. When the moment was past, she looked down at the fire again.

"I cannot think," said Estella, raising her eyes after a silence "why you should be so unreasonable when I come to see you after a separation. I have never forgotten what happened to you and what caused it. I have never been unfaithful to you or your schooling. I have never shown any weakness that I can charge myself with."

"Would it be weakness to return my love?" exclaimed Miss Havisham. "But yes, yes, she would see it that way!"

"I begin to think," said Estella, in a musing way, after another moment of calm wonder, "that I almost understand how this happened. Imagine, if you had brought up an adopted daughter completely in the dark confinement of these rooms, and had let her know that there was such a thing as "love", but taught her that it was an enemy and a destroyer, and had destroyed you and would destroy this daughter too, but at the same time you wanted her to naturally feel and embrace it. If she couldn't do it, would you be disappointed and angry with her?"

Miss Havisham, with her head in her hands, sat making a low moaning sound, but gave no answer.

"So," said Estella, "I must be taken as I have been made. The success is not mine, the failure is not mine, but the two together make me."

Miss Havisham had sat down on the floor, among the faded bridal relics with which it was strewn. I took advantage of the moment – I had been looking for one since they started this exchange – to leave the room. When I left, Estella was standing by the great chimney-piece, just as she had stood throughout. Miss Havisham's grey hair was all adrift upon the ground, among the other bridal wrecks, and was a miserable sight to see.

I walked with a heavy heart in the starlight outside for an hour or so, about the court-yard, the brewery, and the ruined garden. When I decided I should check back in with them, I found Estella sitting at Miss Havisham's knee, taking up some stitches in one of those old articles of dress that were dropping to pieces. Afterwards, Estella and I played at cards, like we used to – only we were skillful now, and played French games – and so the evening wore away, and I went to bed.

I slept in the separate building across the court-yard. It was the first time I had ever gone to bed in Satis House, and sleep refused to come near me. A thousand Miss Havishams haunted me. She was on this side of my pillow, on that, at the head of the bed, at the foot, behind the half-opened door of the dressing-room, in the room overhead, in the room beneath – everywhere.

Before we left next day, there was no revival of the disagreement between her and Estella, nor was it ever revived on any similar trip; and there were four similar trips, to the best of my remembrance. Nor, did

Miss Havisham's manner towards Estella change, except that I believed it to have something like fear mixed in with its former characteristics.

It is impossible to turn this page of my life without putting Bentley Drummle's name upon it, or else I would, very gladly.

On a certain occasion when the Finches were assembled at the Grove, and when good feeling was being promoted in the usual way by nobody's agreeing with anybody about anything, the presiding Finch called the Grove to order. Mr. Drummle had not yet toasted a lady, which, according to the solemn rules of the group, it was the brute's turn to do that day. I thought I saw him leer in an ugly way at me while the glasses were being passed around, but as there was no love lost between us, that might easily be. Imagine my surprise and anger when he called upon the Finches to pledge him to "Estella!"

"Estella who?" said I.

"Never you mind," retorted Drummle.

"Estella of where?" said I. "You are bound to say of where." Which he was, as a Finch.

"Of Richmond, gentlemen," said Drummle, putting me out of the question, "and a peerless beauty."

Much he knew about peerless beauties, a mean miserable idiot! I whispered to Herbert.

"I know that lady," said Herbert, across the table, when the toast had been honoured.

"Do you?" said Drummle.

"And so do I," I added, with a scarlet face.

"Do you?" said Drummle. "Oh, Lord!"

This was the only retort – except throwing glasses or pottery – that the heavy creature was capable of making; but, I became as highly enraged by it as if it had been a witty reply, and I immediately rose from my seat and asked how he had the nerve to come down to that Grove – we always talked about coming down to that Grove, as a neat Parliamentary turn of expression – come down to that Grove, toasting a lady of whom he knew nothing. Mr. Drummle upon this, started up out of his seat, and demanded what I meant by that? At which point, I made him the extreme reply that I believed he knew where I was to be found if he wanted to back his words up.

Whether it was possible to proceed without blood after this exchange of words, was a question on which the Finches were divided. The debate about it grew so lively, that at least six more honourable Finches told six more that they believed they knew where they were to be found. However, it was decided at last (the Grove being a Court of Honour) that if

Mr. Drummle would bring a certificate from the lady, proving that he had the honour of her acquaintance, Mr. Pip must express his regret as a gentleman and a Finch, for "becoming a little hot under the collar." It was decided that the evidence must be produced the next day, and Drummle appeared with a polite little note in Estella's hand writing, that she had had the honour of dancing with him several times. This left me no option but to regret that I had "become a little hot under the collar," and to reject the idea that I was to be found anywhere. Drummle and I then sat snorting at one another for an hour, while the Grove went back to disagreeing about anything and everything, and finally the promotion of good feeling was declared to have gone ahead at an amazing rate.

I tell this lightly, but it was no light thing to me. For, there's no way to express what pain it gave me to think that Estella should show any favour to such a contemptible, clumsy, sulky blockhead as him, so very far below average. No doubt I would have been miserable no matter who she favored; but a worthier man would have caused me a different kind of distress.

It was easy for me to find out, and I did soon find out, that Drummle had begun to follow her closely, and that she allowed him to do it. He held on, in a dull persistent way, and Estella held him on; now with encouragement, now with discouragement, now almost flattering him, now openly despising him, now knowing him very well, now scarcely remembering who he was.

The Spider, as Mr. Jaggers had called him, was used to lying in wait, however, and had the patience of his type of animal. Added to that, he had a blind confidence in his money and in his family greatness. So, the Spider, stubbornly watching Estella, out-watched many brighter insects, and would often uncoil himself and drop at the right nick of time.

At a certain Assembly Ball at Richmond, where Estella had outshone all other beauties, this blundering Drummle so hung about her, and with so much toleration on her part, that I decided to speak to her about him. I took the next opportunity, which was when she was waiting for Mrs. Brandley to take her home, and was sitting apart among some flowers, ready to go. I was with her, for I almost always accompanied them to and from such places.

"Are you tired, Estella?"

"Rather, Pip."

"You should be."

"Say rather, I should not be; for I have my letter to Satis House to write, before I go to sleep."

"Describing tonight's triumph?" said I. "Surely a very poor one, Estella."

"What do you mean? I didn't know there had been any."

"Estella," said I, "look at that fellow in the corner yonder, who is looking over here at us."

"Why should I look at him?" returned Estella, with her eyes on me instead. "What is there in that fellow in the corner yonder – to use your words – that I need look at?"

"Indeed, that is the very question I want to ask you," said I. "For he has been hovering about you all night."

"Moths, and all sorts of ugly creatures," replied Estella, with a glance towards him, "hover about a lighted candle. Can the candle help it?"

"No," I returned; "but cannot the Estella help it?"

"Well!" said she, laughing, after a moment, "Perhaps. Yes. Anything you like."

"But, Estella, please listen. It makes me wretched that you should encourage a man so generally despised as Drummle. You know he is despised."

"Well?" said she.

"You know he is as awkward within, as without. An ill-tempered, stupid fellow."

"Well?" said she.

"You know he has nothing going for him but money, don't you?"

"Well?" said she again; and each time she said it, she opened her lovely eyes the wider.

To overcome the difficulty of getting past that one word reply of hers, I used it myself, and said, "Well! Then, that is why it makes me wretched."

"Pip," said Estella, casting her glance over the room, "don't be foolish about its effect on you. It may have its effect on others, and may be meant to have. It's not worth discussing."

"Yes it is," said I, "because I cannot bear that people should say, 'she throws away her graces and attractions on a mere boor, the lowest in the crowd.'"

"I can bear it," said Estella.

"Oh! don't be so proud, Estella, and so inflexible."

"He calls me proud and inflexible!" said Estella, opening her hands. "And in his next breath scolds me for stooping to a boor!"

"There is no doubt you do," said I, a bit hurriedly, "for I have seen you give him looks and smiles this very night, such as you never give to – me."

"Do you want me then," said Estella, turning suddenly with a fixed and serious, if not angry, look, "to deceive and entrap you?"

"Do you deceive and entrap him, Estella?"

"Yes, and many others – all of them but you. Here is Mrs. Brandley. I'll say no more."

And now that I have given the one chapter to the theme that so filled my heart, and so often made it ache and ache again, I move on to the event that had been brewing over me longer yet; the event that had begun to be prepared for when I was still a child.

Chapter 39

I was now twenty-three years old. Not another word had I heard to enlighten me about my expectations. Herbert and I had left Barnard's Inn more than a year before and we now lived in a more upscale area of London, in the Garden Court section of the Temple neighborhood, down by the river.

I no longer studied or lived part-time with Herbert's father, though we were still on the best of terms. I had an inability to settle to any calling or profession, which I hope was because my expectations were uncertain. I had a taste for reading though, and I read regularly many hours a day. My plan for Herbert's career was still progressing, and everything else with me was as it had been at the close of the previous chapter.

Business had taken Herbert on a journey to Marseilles, France. I was alone, and not liking it. Depressed and anxious, always hoping that tomorrow or the next week would show me a clear path, and always disappointed that it never came, I sadly missed the cheerful face and ready response of my friend.

It was wretched weather; stormy and wet, and mud, mud, mud, deep in all the streets. We lived at the top of the last house in the Temple, and the wind rushing up the river shook the house that night, like a cannon firing. When the rain came with it and dashed against the windows, I felt as if I was in a storm-beaten lighthouse. Occasionally, the smoke came rolling back down the chimney as though it could not bear to go out into such a night; and when I set the doors open and looked down the staircase, the staircase lamps were blown out; and when I shaded my face with my hands and looked through the black windows I saw that the lamps in the courtyard were blown out, and that the lamps on the bridges and the shore were shuddering with the storm.

I read with my watch upon the table, intending to close my book at eleven o'clock and go to bed. As I shut it, I heard a footstep on the stair. Remembering then, that the staircase-lights were blown out, I took up my reading-lamp and went out to the stair-head. Whoever was below had stopped on seeing my lamp, for all was quiet.

"There is someone down there, is there not?" I called out, looking down.

"Yes," said a man's voice from the darkness beneath.

"What floor do you want?"

"The top. Mr. Pip."

"That is my name. There is nothing the matter?"

"Nothing the matter," returned the man, and he came on up.

I stood with my lamp held out over the stair-rail, and he came slowly within its light. It was a shaded lamp, to shine upon a book, and its circle of light was very small; so that he was in it for a mere instant, and then out of it. In the instant, I had seen a face that was strange to me, looking up at me as if pleased by the sight of me for some reason.

Moving the lamp as the man moved, I made out that he was substantially dressed, but roughly; like a voyager by sea. That he had long iron-grey hair. That his age was about sixty. That he was a muscular man, strong on his legs, and that he was browned and hardened by exposure to weather. As he ascended the last stair or two, and the light of my lamp included us both, I saw, with a stupid kind of amazement, that he was holding out both his hands to me.

"Please, what is your business?" I asked him, recoiling a bit and not taking his hands.

"My business?" he repeated, pausing and dropping his hands. "Ah! Yes. I will explain my business, shortly."

"Do you wish to come in?"

"Yes," he replied; "I wish to come in, Master."

I had asked him the question rudely, for I resented the sort of bright and gratified recognition that still shone in his face. I resented it, because it seemed to imply that he expected me to respond to it. But, I took him into the room I had just left, and, having set the lamp on the table, asked him as civilly as I could, to explain himself.

He looked around at my apartment in the strangest manner – one of wondering pleasure, as if the things he saw were his – and he pulled off a rough outer coat, and his hat. Then, I saw that his head was furrowed and bald, and that the long iron-grey hair grew only on its sides. But, I saw nothing at all that explained him or who he was.

He slowly rubbed his right hand over his head. "It's disappointing to a man," he said, in a coarse broken voice, "after having looked forward so distant, and come so far. But you're not to blame for that – neither of us is to blame for that. I'll speak in half a minute. Give me half a minute, please."

He sat down on a chair before the fire, and covered his forehead with his large brown veinous hands. I looked at him attentively then, and shrank a little from him; but I did not know him.

"There's no one here," said he, looking over his shoulder, "is there?"

"Why do you, a stranger coming into my rooms at this time of the night, ask that question?" said I.

"You're a game one," he returned, shaking his head at me with a deliberate affection, at once most unintelligible and most exasperating;

"I'm glad you've grow'd up a game one! But don't try to catch hold of me. You'd be sorry afterwards to have done it."

I gave up the intention he had detected, for suddenly I knew him! I couldn't recall a single feature of him, but I knew him! If the wind and the rain had driven away all the years in between and had swept us back to the churchyard where we first stood face to face, I could not have known my convict more clearly than I knew him now as he sat in the chair before the fire.

Seeing my face change in recognizing him, he came back to where I stood, and held out both his hands to me. Not knowing what to do – for, in my astonishment I had lost my wits – I mechanically gave him my hands. He grasped them heartily, raised them to his lips, kissed them, and still held them.

"You acted noble, my boy," said he. "Noble, Pip! And I have never forgot it!"

He looked as if he were even going to hug me, and I laid a hand upon his chest to stop him.

"Stay!" said I. "Keep off! If you are grateful to me for what I did when I was a little child, I hope you have shown your gratitude by mending your way of life. If you have come here to thank me, it was not necessary. Still, however you have found me, goodness must have brought you here, and I will not repulse you; but surely you must understand that - I--"

My attention was so distracted by the unusual look he was giving me that the words died away on my tongue.

"You was saying," he observed, "that surely I must understand. What, surely must I understand?"

"That, I cannot wish to renew that chance meeting with you from long ago, under these different circumstances. I am glad to believe you have repented and recovered yourself. I am glad that, thinking I deserve to be thanked, you have come to thank me. But, despite that, our ways are different ways. You are wet, and you look weary. Will you drink something before you go?"

He stood, keenly observant of me, and said, "Yes, I think that I will drink (I thank you) afore I go."

There was a tray ready on a side-table. I brought it to the table near the fire, and asked him what he would have? He touched one of the bottles without looking at it or speaking, and I made him some hot rum-and-water. I tried to keep my hand steady while I did so, but his look at me as he leaned back in his chair made my hand very difficult to master. When at last I gave the glass to him, I saw with amazement that his eyes were full of tears.

Up to this time I had remained standing, not to disguise that I wished him gone. But I was softened by his tears, and felt disappointment coming from him. "I hope," said I, hurriedly putting something into a glass for myself, and pulling a chair up to the table, "that you will not think I spoke harshly to you just now. I had no intention of doing it, and I am sorry for it if I did. I wish you well, and happy!"

As I put my glass to my lips, he stretched out his hand to me. I gave him mine, and then he drank, and drew his sleeve across his eyes and forehead.

"How are you living?" I asked him.

"I've been a sheep-farmer, stock-breeder, other trades besides, away in Australia," said he, "many a thousand mile of stormy water off from here."

"I hope you have done well?"

"I've done wonderfully well. There's others went out with me as has done well too, but no man has done nigh as well as me. I'm famous for it."

"I am glad to hear it."

"I hope to hear you say so, my dear boy."

Not paying much attention to his comment, I asked him something that had just come into my mind.

"Have you ever seen a messenger you once sent to me," I inquired, "since he undertook that trust?"

"Never set eyes upon him. I wasn't likely to."

"He came faithfully, and he brought me the two one-pound notes. I was a poor boy then, as you know, and to a poor boy they were a little fortune. But, like you, I have done well since, and you must let me pay them back. You can put them to some other poor boy's use." I took out my purse.

He watched me as I laid my purse upon the table and opened it, and he watched me as I separated two one-pound notes from its contents. They were clean and new, and I spread them out and handed them over to him. Still watching me, he laid them one upon the other, folded them long-wise, gave them a twist, set fire to them at the lamp, and dropped the ashes into the tray.

"May I make so bold," he said then, with a smile that was like a frown, and with a frown that was like a smile, "as to ask you how you have done well, since you and me was out on them marshes?"

"How?"

"Yes."

He emptied his glass, got up, and stood at the side of the fire, with his heavy brown hand on the mantelshelf. He put a foot up to the bars, to dry and warm it, and the wet boot began to steam; but, he neither looked at it, nor at the fire, but steadily looked at me. It was only now that I began to tremble.

When my lips had parted, and had shaped some words that were without sound, I forced myself to tell him that I had been chosen to succeed to some property.

"Might a mere varmint ask what property?" said he.

I faltered, "I don't know."

"Might a mere varmint ask whose property?" said he.

I faltered again, "I don't know."

"Could I make a guess, I wonder," said the Convict, "at your income since you come of age. As to the first figure now... five?"

With my heart beating like a heavy hammer, I rose out of my chair, and stood with my hand upon the back of it, looking wildly at him.

"Concerning a guardian," he went on. "There ought to have been some guardian, or such-like, whiles you was a minor. Some lawyer, maybe. As to the first letter of that lawyer's name now... would it be J?"

All the truth of my position came flashing on me in a flood; its disappointments, dangers, disgraces, consequences of all kinds, rushed in in such a multitude that I was borne down by them and had to struggle for every breath I drew.

"Suppose that," he resumed, "the employer of that lawyer whose name begun with a J, and might be Jaggers – suppose that employer had come over the sea here, to Portsmouth, and had wanted to find you. 'However, you have found me,' you says just now. Well! However, did I find you? Why, I wrote from Portsmouth to a person in London, for your address. That person's name? Why, Wemmick."

I could not have spoken one word, even to save my life. I stood, with a hand on the chair-back and a hand on my heart, where I seemed to be suffocating – I stood like that, looking wildly at him, until I grasped at the chair, when the room began to surge and turn. He caught me, led me to the sofa, propped me up against the cushions, and bent on one knee before me, bringing the face that I now well remembered, and that I shuddered at, very near to mine.

"Yes, Pip, dear boy, I've made a gentleman out of you! It's me what has done it! I swore that time, sure as ever I earned a pound, that pound should go to you. I swore afterwards, sure as ever I speculated and got rich, you should get rich. I lived rough, that you should live smooth; I worked hard, that you should be above work. What odds, dear boy? Am I telling you, for you to feel a obligation to me? Not a bit. I tell you, for you to know that this hunted dog that you kept alive, was able to make a gentleman – and, Pip, you're him!"

The revulsion I felt for the man, the disgust with which I shrank from him, couldn't have been more if he had been some terrible beast.

"Look'ee here, Pip. I'm your second father. You're my son. I've put away money, only for you to spend. When I was a shepherd in a solitary hut, not seeing any faces but those of sheep till I half forgot what men's and women's faces was like, I see yours. I see you there many times, as plain as ever I see you on them misty marshes. 'Lord strike me dead!' I says each time, 'But if I gets liberty and money, I'll make that boy a gentleman!' And I done it. Why, look at you, dear boy! Look at this here lodging of yours, fit for a lord! A lord? Ah! You shall show money with lords for wagers, and beat 'em!"

In his heat and triumph, and in his knowledge that I had been nearly fainting, he did not mention how badly I was receiving all of this. It was the one grain of relief I had.

"Look'ee here!" he went on, taking my watch out of my pocket, and turning towards him a ring on my finger, while I recoiled from his touch as if he had been a snake, "a gold one and a beauty; that's a gentleman's, I hope! A diamond all set round with rubies; that's a gentleman's, I hope! Look at your linen; fine and beautiful! Look at your clothes; better ain't to be got! And your books too," turning his eyes round the room, "mounting up, on their shelves, by hundreds! And you read 'em, don't you? I see you'd been reading 'em when I come in. Ha, ha, ha! You shall read 'em to me, dear boy! And if they're in foreign languages what I don't understand, I shall be just as proud as if I did."

Again he took both my hands and put them to his lips, while my blood ran cold within me.

"Don't you mind talking, Pip," said he, after again drawing his sleeve over his eyes and forehead, and he was all the more horrible to me that he was so sincere, "you can't help but keep quiet, dear boy. You ain't looked slowly forward to this as I have; you wasn't prepared for this, as I was. But didn't you ever think it might be me?"

"O no, no, no," I returned, "Never, never!"

"Well, you see it was me, and single-handed. Never a soul in it but my own self and Mr. Jaggers."

"Was there no one else?" I asked.

"No," said he, with a glance of surprise: "who else should there be? And, dear boy, how good looking you have grow'd! There's bright eyes somewheres - eh? Isn't there bright eyes somewheres, that you love?"

O Estella, Estella!

"They shall be yours, dear boy, if money can buy 'em. Not that a gentleman so well set up as you can't win 'em of his own game; but money shall back you! Let me finish what I was a-telling you, dear boy. From that there hut and that there hiring-out, I got money left me by my master (which died, and had been a convict, same as me), and I got my liberty and went into business for myself. In every single thing I went for, I went for you. I says to myself, 'Lord strike a blight upon it if it ain't for him!' It all prospered wonderful. It was the money left me, and the gains of the first few years what I sent home to Mr. Jaggers – all for you – when he first come after you, agreeable to my letter."

O, that he had never come! That he had left me at the forge – far from contented, but yet, by comparison happy!

"And then, dear boy, it was a compensation to me, to know in secret that I was making a gentleman. The horses of them colonists might fling up dust over me as I was walking. What do I say? I says to myself, 'I'm making a better gentleman than you'll ever be!' When one of 'em says to another, 'He was a convict, a few year ago, and is a ignorant common fellow, he's just lucky'; what do I say? I says to myself, 'If I ain't a gentleman, and ain't got no learning, I'm at least the owner of one. All of you owns animals and land; which of you owns a brought-up London gentleman?' This way I kept myself a-going. And this way I held steady in my mind that I would for certain come one day and see my boy, and make myself known to him, on his own ground."

He laid his hand on my shoulder. I shuddered at the thought that for anything I knew, his hand might be stained with blood.

"It wasn't easy, Pip, or safe, for me to leave where I was. But I was determined, and my mind was made up. At last I done it. Dear boy, I done it!"

I tried to collect my thoughts, but I was stunned. Throughout this torrent of words from him, I was dazed and couldn't concentrate well on what he was saying.

"Where will you put me?" he asked, presently. "I must be put somewheres, dear boy."

"To sleep?" said I.

"Yes. And to sleep long and sound," he answered, "for I've been sea-tossed and sea-washed, months and months."

"My friend and companion," said I, rising from the sofa, "is absent; you must have his room."

"He won't come back tomorrow, will he?"

"No," said I, answering almost mechanically, in spite of my utmost efforts, "not tomorrow."

"Because, look'ee here, dear boy," he said, dropping his voice, and laying a long finger on my breast in an impressive manner, "caution is necessary."

"How do you mean? Caution?"

"By G - , it's Death!"

"What's death?"

"I was sent for life. It's death to come back. I'll be hanged if I'm discovered and arrested."

That was all I needed; the wretched man, after loading me with his gold and silver chains for years, had risked his life to come to me, and I held it there in my keeping!

My first care was to close the shutters, so that no light might be seen from outside, and then to close and lock the doors. While I did so, he stood at the table drinking rum and eating biscuits; and when I saw him doing this, I saw my convict on the marshes at his meal again. It almost seemed to me as if he would stoop down soon to file at his leg.

I got Herbert's room prepared and asked him if he wanted to go to bed? He said yes, but asked me for some of my "gentleman's linen" to put on in the morning. I brought it out, and laid it ready for him, and my blood again ran cold when he again took me by both hands to bid me good night.

I got away from him, without knowing how I did it, and stoked the fire in the room where we had been together, and sat down by it, afraid to go to bed. For an hour or more, I remained too stunned to think; and it was not until I began to think, that I began to fully know how wrecked I was, and how the ship in which I had sailed had fallen apart.

Miss Havisham's intentions towards me were all a mere dream; purely my own invented fantasy. Estella was not meant for me, I only suffered in Satis House as a convenience; as a sting for Miss Havisham's greedy family, and as a dummy for Estella to practice on when nobody else was available. Those were the first sharp pains I had. But, the sharpest and deepest pain of all, was that it was for the convict and his money that I had deserted Joe.

I would not have gone back to Joe or Biddy now for any incentive; simply, I suppose, because my sense of my own worthless conduct to them was bigger than every incentive. I could never, never, undo what I had done in abandoning them.

Bubbling up with these reflections came the memory that, as a child, I had seen the convict to be a desperately violent man; that I had heard that other convict say that he had tried to murder him; that I had seen him down in the ditch tearing and fighting like a wild beast. Based on that, I half-formed a fear that it might not be safe to be in the same apartment with him in the night. The fear grew strong enough that it made me take a candle and go in and look at him in Herbert's room.

He was asleep, and quietly too, though he had a pistol lying on the pillow. Assured of this, I softly removed the key to the outside of his door, and turned it on him before I sat down again by the fire. Gradually I slipped from the chair and lay asleep on the floor. When I awoke, the clocks of the churches were striking five, the candles were burned out, the fire was dead, and the wind and rain intensified the thick black darkness.

THIS IS THE END OF THE SECOND STAGE OF PIP'S EXPECTATIONS.

Chapter 40

It was fortunate for me that I had to take precautions to ensure (as much as I could) the safety of my dreaded visitor; for, this task kept me busy and not dwelling on all the other thoughts of my situation.

The impossibility of keeping him concealed in the apartment was obvious. It could not be done, and the attempt to do it would inevitably create suspicion. I had no servant anymore, but I was looked after by an explosive old female who was assisted by an animated rag-bag whom she called her niece, and to try to keep a room secret from them would be to invite their curiosity. They both had weak eyes, which I had blamed on their chronically spying in at keyholes, and they were always around when not wanted. Indeed, that was their only reliable quality besides stealing. Not to create an enticing mystery for these people, I decided to announce in the morning to them and to the gate watchman that my uncle had unexpectedly come from the country for a visit.

I lighted my fire and fell into a doze before it, waking several times before finally falling off into a deep sleep from which the daylight woke me with a start.

All this time I had never been able to consider my own situation, nor could I do so yet. I didn't have the will to think about it. I was greatly dejected and distressed, but in an incoherent sort of way. As to forming any plan for the future, I could no more do that than I could form an elephant.

At last, the old woman and the niece came in and were surprised at the sight of me and the fire. I informed them that my uncle had arrived in the night and was then asleep, and that the breakfast preparations were to be modified accordingly. Then, I washed and dressed while they knocked the furniture about and made a dust; and so, in a sort of dream or sleep-waking, I found myself sitting by the fire again, waiting for - Him - to come to breakfast.

By-and-by, the two mercenaries left, and his door opened and he came out. I could not bring myself to bear the sight of him, and I thought he had a worse look by daylight.

"I do not even know," said I, speaking low as he took his seat at the table, "by what name to call you. I have given out that you are my uncle."

"That's it, dear boy! Call me uncle."

"You assumed some name, I suppose, on board ship?"

"Yes, dear boy. I took the name of Provis."

"Do you mean to keep that name?"

"Why, yes, dear boy, it's as good as another - unless you'd like another."

"What is your real name?" I asked him in a whisper.

"Magwitch," he answered, in the same tone; "first name, Abel."

"What were you brought up to be?"

"A Varmint, dear boy."

He answered quite seriously, and used the word as if it meant some profession.

"Are you known in London?"

"I hope not!" said he, giving his neck a jerk with his forefinger that made me turn hot and sick.

"Were you known in London, once?"

"Not really, dear boy. I was in the provinces mostly."

"Were you - tried - in London?"

"Which time?" said he, with a sharp look.

"The last time."

He nodded. "First knowed Mr. Jaggers that way, he was my lawyer."

It was on my lips to ask him what he was tried for, but he took up a knife, gave it a flourish and said, "And what I done is worked out and paid for!" and dug in at his breakfast.

He ate in a ravenous way that was very disagreeable, and all his actions were crude, noisy, and greedy. Some of his teeth had fallen out since I saw him eat on the marshes, and as he turned his food in his mouth, and turned his head sideways to bring his strongest fangs to work on it, he looked terribly like a hungry old dog. If I had begun with any appetite, he would have taken it away, and I would have sat much as I did – disgusted by everything about him, and gloomily staring at the table cloth.

"I'm a heavy grubber, dear boy," he said, as a polite kind of apology when he made an end of his meal, "but I always was. If it had been in my constitution to be a lighter grubber, I might have got into lighter trouble. Similarly, I must have my smoke. When I was first hired out as shepherd t'other side the world, it's my belief I would have turned into a crazy sheep myself, if I hadn't had my smoke."

As he said so, he got up from the table, and putting his hand into the breast of the pea-coat he wore, brought out a short black pipe, and a handful of loose tobacco. Having filled his pipe, he put the surplus tobacco back again, as if his pocket were a drawer. Then, he took a live coal from the fire with the tongs, and lighted his pipe at it, and then turned round on the hearth-rug with his back to the fire, and went through his favourite action of holding out both his hands for mine.

"And this," said he, dandling my hands up and down in his, as he puffed at his pipe; "and this is the gentleman what I made! The real genuine One! It does me good fur to look at you, Pip. All I ask, is, to stand by and look at you, dear boy!"

I released my hands as soon as I could, and found that I was beginning slowly to settle down to the contemplation of my condition. What I was chained to, and how heavily, became understandable to me, as I heard his hoarse voice, and sat looking up at his furrowed bald head with its iron grey hair at the sides.

"I mustn't see my gentleman a footing it in the mire of the streets; there mustn't be no mud on his boots. My gentleman must have horses, Pip! Horses to ride, and horses to drive, and horses for his servant to ride and drive as well. Shall colonists have their horses, and not my London gentleman? No, no. We'll show 'em another pair of shoes than that, Pip, won't us?"

He took out of his pocket a great thick pocket-book, bursting with money, and tossed it on the table.

"There's something worth spending in that there book, dear boy. It's yours. All I've got ain't mine; it's yours. Don't you be afeerd of it. There's more where that come from. I've come to the old country for to see my gentleman spend his money like a gentleman. That'll be my pleasure. And blast you all!" he wound up, looking round the room and snapping his fingers once with a loud snap, "blast you every one, from the judge in his wig, to the colonist a stirring up the dust, I'll show a better gentleman than the whole lot of you put together!"

"Stop!" said I, almost in a frenzy of fear and dislike, "I want to speak to you. I want to know what is to be done. I want to know how you are to be kept out of danger, how long you are going to stay, what plans you have."

"Look'ee here, Pip," said he, laying his hand on my arm in a suddenly altered and subdued manner; "first of all, look'ee here. I forgot myself half a minute ago. What I said was low; that's what it was; low. Look over it, Pip. I ain't a-going to be low."

"First," I resumed, half-groaning, "what precautions can be taken against your being recognized and seized?"

"No, dear boy," he said, in the same tone as before, "that don't go first. Lowness goes first. I ain't took so many years to make a gentleman, not without knowing what's due to him. Look'ee here, Pip. I was low; that's what I was; low. Please look over it, dear boy."

Some sense of how grimly ludicrous this all was made me give a fretful laugh, as I replied, "I have looked over it. In Heaven's name, don't harp on it!"

"Yes, but look'ee here," he persisted. "Dear boy, I ain't come so far, not to be low. Now, go on, dear boy. You was a-saying--"

"How are you to be guarded from the danger you have got yourself into?"

"Well, dear boy, the danger ain't so great. There's Jaggers, and there's Wemmick, and there's you. Who else would know?"

"Is there no chance person who might identify you in the street?" said I.

"Well," he returned, "there ain't many. I don't intend to advertise myself in the newspapers by the name of Abel Magwitch come back from Botany Bay, Australia. Years have rolled away, and who's to gain by it? Still, look'ee here, Pip. If the danger had been fifty times as great, I would have come to see you anyway, just the same."

"And how long do you remain?"

"How long?" said he, taking his black pipe from his mouth, and dropping his jaw as he stared at me. "I'm not a-going back. I've come for good."

"Where are you to live?" said I. "What is to be done with you? Where will you be safe?"

"Dear boy," he returned, "there's disguising wigs can be bought for money, and there's hair powder, and spectacles, and black clothes - shorts and what not. Others has done it safe before, and what others has done before, others can do again. As to the where and how of living, dear boy, give me your own opinions on it."

"You take it smoothly now," said I, "but you were very serious last night, when you swore it was Death."

"And so I swear it is Death," said he, putting his pipe back in his mouth, "and Death by the rope, in the open street not far from here, and it's serious that you should fully understand it to be so. What then, when that's once done? Here I am. To go back now, would be as bad as to stay – worse, even. Besides, Pip, I'm here, because I've meant it by you, years and years. As to what I dare, I'm an old bird now, as has dared all manner of traps since first I was fledged, and I'm not afraid to perch upon a scarecrow. If there's Death hid inside of it, then let him come out, and I'll face him, and then I'll believe in him, and not before then. And now, let me have a look at my gentleman again."

Once more, he took me by both hands and surveyed me with an air of admiring proprietorship, smoking with great satisfaction all the while.

It appeared to me that I could do no better than get him some quiet lodging nearby, which he could move to when Herbert returned, whom I expected in two or three days. That the secret must be confided to

Herbert as a matter of unavoidable necessity was plain to me. But it was by no means so plain to Mr. Provis (I decided to call him by that name), who reserved his consent to Herbert's knowing who Provis really was until he should have seen him and formed a favourable judgment himself. "And even then, dear boy," said he, pulling a greasy little clasped black Testament out of his pocket, "we'll have him on his oath."

I can't say for certain that my terrible patron carried this little black Bible about the world with him solely to swear people on in cases of emergency, but I can say that I never knew him to put it to any other use. The book itself had the appearance of having been stolen from some court of justice. Perhaps his knowledge of similar bibles, combined with his own experience of them in court, gave him a reliance on its powers as a sort of legal spell or talisman.

As he was at present dressed in seafaring clothes, I next discussed with him what he should wear. He cherished an extraordinary belief in the virtues of "shorts" as a disguise, and had in his own mind sketched a dress for himself that would have made him something between a dean and a dentist. It was with considerable difficulty that I won him over to the assumption of a look more like a prosperous farmer's; and we arranged that he should cut his hair close, and wear a little powder. Lastly, as he had not yet been seen by the laundress or her niece, he was to keep himself out of their view until his change of clothes was made.

It would seem a simple matter to decide on these precautions, but in my dazed and distracted state it took so long that I did not get outside to start making them reality until two or three in the afternoon. He was to remain shut up in the apartment while I was gone, and was on no account to open the door.

I knew of a respectable lodging-house in Essex-street, the back of which looked into the Temple where my apartment was, and was almost within shouting distance of my windows. I went there first and was lucky enough to secure the second floor for my uncle, Mr. Provis. I then went from shop to shop, making such purchases as were necessary to the change in his appearance. This business finished, I headed to Little Britain. Mr. Jaggers was at his desk, but, seeing me enter, got up immediately and stood before his fire.

"Now, Pip," said he, "be careful."

"I will, sir," I returned. For, I had well thought out what I was going to say.

"Don't commit yourself," said Mr. Jaggers, "and don't commit anyone. You understand - anyone. Don't tell me anything; I don't want to know anything, I am not curious."

Of course, I could tell that he knew my benefactor had arrived.

"I merely want, Mr. Jaggers," said I, "to assure myself that what I have been told is true. I have no hope of its being untrue, but at least I may verify it."

Mr. Jaggers nodded. "Did you say 'told' or 'informed'?" he asked me. "Told would seem to imply verbal communication. You can't have verbal communication with a man in Australia, you know."

"I will say, informed, Mr. Jaggers."

"Good."

"I have been informed by a person named Abel Magwitch, that he is the benefactor so long unknown to me."

"That is the man," said Mr. Jaggers, "- in Australia."

"And only he?" said I.

"And only he," said Mr. Jaggers.

"I am not so unreasonable, sir, as to think you are responsible for my mistakes and wrong conclusions; but I always supposed it was Miss Havisham."

"As you say, Pip," returned Mr. Jaggers, turning his eyes upon me coolly, and taking a bite at his forefinger, "I am not responsible for that."

"And yet it looked so like it, sir," I pleaded with a downcast heart.

"Not a particle of evidence, Pip," said Mr. Jaggers, shaking his head. "Take nothing on its looks; take everything on evidence. There's no better rule."

After standing silent for a little while, I sighed and said, "I have no more to say. I have verified my information, and there's an end."

"And Magwitch - in Australia - having at last disclosed himself," said Mr. Jaggers, "you will understand, Pip, how rigidly throughout my communication with you, I have always adhered to the strict line of fact. There has never been the least departure from the strict line of fact. You are quite aware of that?"

"Quite, sir."

"I communicated to Magwitch – in Australia – when he first wrote to me – from Australia – the warning that he must not expect me ever to deviate from the strict line of fact. I also communicated to him another warning. He appeared to me to have obscurely hinted in his letter at some distant idea he had of seeing you in England here. I cautioned him that I must hear no more of that; that he was not at all likely to obtain a pardon; that he was banished for the rest of his natural life, and that his presenting himself in this country would be an act of felony, rendering him liable to the extreme penalty of the law. I gave Magwitch that warning," said Mr.

Jaggers, looking hard at me; "I sent it to Australia. He guided himself by it, no doubt."

"No doubt," said I.

"I have been informed by Wemmick," pursued Mr. Jaggers, still looking hard at me, "that he has received a letter, sent from Portsmouth, from a colonist of the name of Purvis, or--"

"Or Provis," I suggested.

"Or Provis – thank you, Pip. Perhaps it is Provis? Perhaps you know it's Provis?"

"Yes," said I.

"You know it's Provis. A letter, sent from Portsmouth, from a colonist by the name of Provis, asking for your address, on behalf of Magwitch. Wemmick sent him the address, I understand, by return of post. Probably it is through Provis that you have received the explanation of Magwitch – in Australia?"

"It came through Provis," I replied.

"Good day, Pip," said Mr. Jaggers, offering his hand, "glad to have seen you. In writing to Magwitch – in Australia – or in communicating with him through Provis, have the goodness to mention that the particulars and vouchers of our long account shall be sent to you, together with the balance; for there is still a balance remaining. Good day, Pip!"

We shook hands, and he looked hard at me as long as he could see me. I turned at the door, and he was still looking hard at me, while the two vile casts on the shelf seemed to be trying to get their eyelids open, and to force out of their swollen throats, "O, what a man he is!"

Wemmick was out, and even if he had been at his desk he could have done nothing for me. I went straight back to my apartment, where I found the terrible Provis drinking rum-and-water and smoking tobacco, in safety.

Next day the clothes I had ordered all came home, and he put them on. Whatever he put on looked less fitting for him than what he had worn before. There was something in him that made it hopeless to attempt to disguise him. The more I dressed him and the better I dressed him, the more he looked like the fugitive on the marshes. The influences of his solitary life away in Australia were showing, and gave him a savage air that no clothes could tame. In all his ways of sitting and standing, and eating and drinking, of taking out his great horn-handled jack-knife and wiping it on his legs and cutting his food, of chopping a wedge off his bread and using it to soak up the last bits of gravy round and round his plate, as if to make the most of an allowance; in these ways and a thousand other small nameless instances every minute in the day, there was Prisoner and Felon branded on him, plain as plain could be.

I had convinced him not to wear shorts, but he was bound and determined to try to wear a bit of powder in his hair against my advice. He tried it, but on him it worked about as well as rouge does on the dead; it simply magnified his state of awfulness. It was abandoned as soon as tried, and he wore his grizzled hair cut short.

Words cannot describe the dreadful mystery that he was to me. When he fell asleep in the evening, sitting in the easy-chair, I would sit and look at him, wondering what he had done, and would imagine all sorts of possible crimes, until I had a powerful impulse to jump up and run away from him. I might have actually done just that, too, despite all he had done and given up for me, except that I knew Herbert was coming home soon. Once, I actually did start out of bed in the night and begin to dress myself in my worst clothes, hurriedly intending to leave him there with everything else I possessed, and enlist for India as a soldier.

I doubt if a ghost could have been more terrible to me, up in those lonely rooms in the long evenings and long nights, with the wind and the rain. A ghost couldn't have been taken and hanged because of me, and the thought that he could be was one more addition to my troubles. When he was not asleep, or playing a complicated kind of solitaire game with a ragged pack of cards - a game that I never saw before or since, and in which he recorded his winnings by sticking his jack-knife into the table - when he was not engaged in either of these activities, he would ask me to read to him - "Foreign language, dear boy!" While I complied, he, not understanding a single word, would stand before the fire surveying me with the air of an Exhibitor.

I write this as if it lasted a year, and it felt like it, but it was about five days. Expecting Herbert all the time, I dared not go out, except when I took Provis for a walk after dark. Eventually, one evening when dinner was over and I had fallen asleep, I was awakened by the welcome footstep on the staircase. Provis, who had been asleep too, staggered up at the noise I made, and in an instant I saw his jack-knife shining in his hand.

"Quiet! It's Herbert!" I said; and Herbert came bursting in, with the airy freshness of six hundred miles of France upon him.

"Handel, my dear fellow, how are you, and again how are you? I seem to have been gone a year! Why, so I must have been, for you have grown quite thin and pale! Handel, my – Halloa! I beg your pardon."

He was stopped in his running on and in his shaking hands with me, by seeing Provis. Provis, regarding him with a fixed attention, was slowly putting away his jack-knife, and groping in another pocket for something else.

"Herbert, my dear friend," said I, shutting the double doors, while Herbert stood staring and wondering, "something very strange has happened. This is – a visitor of mine."

"It's all right, dear boy!" said Provis coming forward, with his little clasped black Bible, and then addressing himself to Herbert. "Take it in your right hand. Lord strike you dead on the spot, if ever you split in any way sumever! Kiss it!"

"Do as he wishes," I said to Herbert. So, Herbert, looking at me with a friendly uneasiness and amazement, complied, and Provis immediately shaking hands with him, said, "Now you're on your oath, you know. And never believe me on mine, if Pip shan't make a gentleman out of you!"

Chapter 41

I can't describe how astonished Herbert was, when he and I and Provis sat down before the fire and I recounted the whole of the secret. Enough, that I saw my own feelings reflected in Herbert's face, and, not least among them, my disgust towards the man who had done so much for me.

What would alone have made a division between that man and us, even if there had been nothing else, was his triumph in my story. He had no perception of the possibility of my finding any fault with my good fortune. His boast that he had made me a gentleman, and that he had come to see me support that character on his ample resources, was a boast he made on my behalf quite as much as for himself. That it was a highly agreeable boast to both of us was a conclusion quite established in his own mind.

We were anxious for the time when he would go to his apartment and leave us together, but he was evidently jealous of leaving us alone, and sat late. It was midnight before I took him round to Essex-street to his new lodging, and saw him safely in at his own dark door. When it closed upon him, I experienced the first moment of relief I had known since the night of his arrival.

I was becoming paranoid about who might know him and notice us, and I began to look about me in taking my guest out after dark, and in bringing him back; and I looked about me now. Difficult as it is in a large city to avoid the suspicion of being watched when the mind is conscious of that danger, it didn't seem that any of the people within sight cared about my movements. As I crossed by the fountain, I saw his lighted back windows looking bright and quiet, and, when I stood for a few moments in the doorway of the building where I lived, before going up the stairs, Garden-court was as still and lifeless as the staircase was when I ascended it.

Herbert received me with open arms, and I had never felt before, so blessedly, what it is to have a friend. When he had spoken some sound words of sympathy and encouragement, we sat down to consider the question, What was to be done?

"What," said I to Herbert, "what is to be done?"

"My poor dear Handel," he replied, holding his head, "I am too stunned to think."

"So was I, Herbert, when the blow first fell. Still, something must be done. He is intent upon various new expenses - horses, and carriages, and lavish appearances of all kinds. He must be stopped somehow."

"You mean that you can't accept--"

"How can I?" I interposed, as Herbert paused. "Think of him! Look at him!"

An involuntary shudder passed over both of us.

"Yet I am afraid the dreadful truth is, Herbert, that he is attached to me, strongly attached to me. Was there ever such a fate!"

"My poor dear Handel," Herbert repeated.

"Then," said I, "after all, stopping short here, never taking another penny from him, think what I owe him already! Then again, I am heavily in debt – very heavily for me, who have now no expectations – and I have been bred to no calling, and I am fit for nothing."

"Well!" Herbert protested. "Don't say fit for nothing."

"What am I fit for? I know only one thing that I am fit for, and that is to go enlist as a soldier. And I might have gone, my dear Herbert, except I needed to see you and get advice from my best friend."

Of course, I broke down crying there, and of course Herbert, beyond seizing a warm grip of my hand, pretended not to know it.

"Anyhow, my dear Handel," said he presently, "soldiering won't do. If you were to renounce this patronage and these favours, I suppose you would do so with some faint hope of one day repaying what you have already been given. Not very strong, that hope, if you went soldiering! Besides, it's absurd. You would be infinitely better in Clarriker's house, small as it is. I am working up towards a partnership, you know."

Poor fellow! He little suspected with whose money.

"But there is another question," said Herbert. "This is a determined man, who has long had one fixed idea. More than that, he seems to me (I may misjudge him) to be a man of a desperate and fierce character."

"I know he is," I returned, and I told him what I had not mentioned in my story; of that fight he had with the other convict in the ditch.

"See, then," said Herbert; "think of this! He comes here at the peril of his life to see his dream come true. In the moment of its happening, after all his toil and waiting, you pull the rug from under his feet, destroy his dream, and make his gains worthless to him. Do you see nothing that he might do, under the disappointment?"

"I have seen it, Herbert, and had nightmares about it, ever since the fatal night of his arrival. Nothing has been in my thoughts so distinctly, as his getting himself arrested and hung."

"Then you may rely upon it," said Herbert, "that there would be great danger of his doing it. That is his unintentional power over you as long as he remains in England, and that could be his reckless course of action if you abandon him."

The idea of his being arrested and hung because of me was awful, and I knew I'd regard myself in some ways as his murderer. I said to Herbert that even if Provis were recognized and taken by accident, that I would still blame myself, however innocent I was.

But there was no putting off the question, What was to be done?

"The first and the main thing to be done," said Herbert, "is to get him out of England. You will have to go with him, and then he may be convinced to go."

"But get him where I will, could I prevent his coming back?"

"My good Handel, is it not obvious that with Newgate Prison in the next street, it's more hazardous here to reject him than elsewhere. You need a reason to get him out of England; perhaps that other convict or something else in his life can be used as a convincing case."

"There, again!" said I, with my open hands held out, as if they contained the desperation of the case. "I know nothing of his life. It has almost made me mad to sit here each night and look at him; a man so wrapped up with my fortunes and misfortunes, and yet so unknown to me, except as the miserable wretch who terrified me two days in my childhood!"

"Handel," said Herbert, "you feel convinced that you can take no further benefits from him, do you?"

"Fully. Surely you would, too, if you were in my place?"

"And you feel convinced that you must break your ties with him?"

"Herbert, can you ask me?"

"And you feel compassion for his life that he has risked on your account, and that you must save him, if possible, from throwing it away. Well, then you must get him out of England before you stir a finger to disentangle yourself from him. Once you are both out of England, then separate yourself, in Heaven's name, and we'll see it out together, dear old boy."

It was a comfort to shake hands on it, even with only that done.

"Now, Herbert," said I, "with reference to gaining some knowledge of his history. There is but one way that I know of. I must ask him point-blank."

"Yes. Ask him," said Herbert, "when we sit at breakfast in the morning." For, he had said when he left that he would come have breakfast with us.

With this plan formed, we went to bed. I had the wildest dreams concerning him, and woke unrefreshed; I woke, too, only to recover the fear which I had gotten rid of in the night, of his being found out as a returned convict. Waking, I never lost that fear.

He came over at the appointed time, took out his jack-knife, and sat down to his meal. He was full of plans "for his gentleman's coming out strong, and like a gentleman," and urged me to begin speedily upon the pocket-book, which he had left in my possession. He considered the chambers and his own lodging as temporary residences, and advised me to look out at once for a "fashionable crib" near Hyde Park, in which he could have "a shake-down".

When he had made an end of his breakfast, and was wiping his knife on his leg, I said to him, "After you were gone last night, I told my friend of the man you were fighting when the soldiers found you on the marshes. You remember?"

"Remember!" said he. "I think so!"

"We want to know something about that man – and about you. It is strange to know no more about either, and particularly you, than I was able to tell him last night. Is not this as good a time as another for our knowing more?"

"Well!" he said, after consideration. "You're on your oath, you know, Pip's comrade?"

"Definitely," replied Herbert.

"As to anything I say, you know," he insisted. "The oath applies to all."

"I understand it to do so."

"And look'ee here! Whatever I done is worked out and paid for," he insisted again.

"So be it."

He spread a hand on each knee, and, after turning an angry eye on the fire for a few silent moments, looked round at us and said what follows.

Chapter 42

"Dear boy and Pip's comrade. I am not going to tell you my life like a song or a story-book, but will give it you short and handy. In jail and out of jail, in jail and out of jail, in jail and out of jail. There, you got it. That's my life pretty much, down to such times as I got shipped off, after Pip stood up as my friend.

"Pretty much everything's been done to me, except hanged. I've been locked up as much as a silver tea-kettle. I've been carted here and carted there, and put out of this town and put out of that town, and stuck in the stocks, and whipped and worried and drove. I've no more notion where I was born than you have - if even that much. The earliest I can remember is I was living in Essex as a child, stealing turnips for my living. Someone had run away from me - a man - a tinker - and he'd took the fire with him, and left me very cold.

"I know'd my name to be Abel Magwitch. How did I know it? Much as I know'd the birds' names in the trees to be chaffinch, sparrow, and thrush. I might have thought it was all lies together, only since the birds' names turned out true, I supposed mine was, too.

"So far as I could find, there wasn't a soul that see young Abel Magwitch, but what caught fright at me, and either drove me off, or arrested me. I was arrested so often that I regularly grow'd up arrested.

"This is the way it was, that I got the reputation of being hardened. 'This is a terrible hardened one,' they says to prison visitors, picking me out. 'May be said to live in jails, this boy.' Then they looked at me, and I looked at them, and they measured my head, some of them – I wish they'd a-measured my empty stomach - and others of 'em give me pamphlets that I couldn't read, and made speeches to me that I couldn't understand. They always went on with me about the Devil. But what the Devil was I to do? I must put something into my stomach, mustn't I? - Sorry, I'm acting low again. Dear boy and Pip's comrade, don't you be afeerd of me being low.

"Tramping, begging, thieving, working sometimes when I could – though that wasn't as often as you may think, till you put the question to yourselves whether you would have been eager to give me work, if we had just met. By being a bit of a poacher, a bit of a labourer, a bit of most things that don't pay and lead to trouble, I got to be a man. A deserting soldier in a Traveller's Rest learnt me to read; and a travelling Giant that gave his autograph at a penny a time learnt me to write. I wasn't locked up as often as before, but I wore out my good share of jail keys still.

"Over twenty years ago I met a man whose skull I'd crack with this poker, like the claw of a lobster, if he was here now. His name was

Compeyson; and that's the man, dear boy, that you saw me a-pounding in the ditch, according to what you truly told your comrade after I left last night.

"He was a gentleman, this Compeyson, and he had learning. He was a smooth one to talk, and good at the ways of gentlefolks. He was good-looking, too. I met him at a horse race; him and some others were sitting among the tables when I went in, and the landlord (which had some knowledge of me) called him over and said to him, 'I think this is a man that might suit you' - meaning I was.

"Compeyson looks at me very noticing, and I look at him. He has a watch and a chain and a ring and a breast-pin and a handsome suit of clothes.

"'To judge from appearances, you're out of luck,' says Compeyson to me.

"'Yes, master, and I've never been in it much.'

"'Luck changes,' says Compeyson, 'perhaps yours is going to change.'

"I says, 'I hope it may be so. There's room.'

"'What can you do?' says Compeyson.

"'Eat and drink,' I says, 'if you'll find the materials.'

"Compeyson laughed, looked at me again very noticing, gave me five shillings, and told me to meet the next night, same place.

"So I went to Compeyson next night, same place, and Compeyson took me on to be his man and partner. And what was Compeyson's business in which we was to go partners? Compeyson's business was swindling, handwriting forging, stolen bank-note passing, and such-like. All sorts of traps as Compeyson could set with his head, and keep his own legs out of and get the profits from and let another man do the work, was Compeyson's business. He had no more heart than an iron file; he was as cold as death, and he had the head of the Devil.

"There was another in league with Compeyson, named Arthur. He was in a decline, and was a shadow to look at. Him and Compeyson had swindled a rich lady some years before I met them, and they'd made a pot of money from it; but Compeyson betted and gamed, and he'd have run through the king's taxes. So, Arthur was a-dying, and a-dying poor and delirious, and Compeyson's wife (which Compeyson kicked, mostly) was a-having pity on him when she could, and Compeyson was a-having pity on nothing and nobody.

"I should have taken a warning from Arthur's fate with Compeyson, but I didn't; and I won't pretend I was particular – for what would be the good of it, dear boy and comrade? So, I begun with Compeyson, and a poor tool I was in his hands. Arthur lived at the top of Compeyson's house, and Compeyson kept a careful account against him for board and lodging, in case he should ever get better to pay it off. But Arthur soon settled the account. The second or third time as ever I see him, he died in a fit of hallucinations, raving in fear about some woman all in white who was coming to get him. Compeyson's wife and I (Compeyson never lifted a finger to do anything himself) had to hold him down in his bed, he was so delirious. While we held him down, he made one last unholy shriek of fear, convulsed, and died.

"Compeyson took it easy as a good riddance for both sides. Him and me was soon busy, and first he swore me (being ever artful) on my own book - this here little black book, dear boy, what I swore your comrade on.

"Not to go into the things that Compeyson planned, and I done – which would take a week - I'll simply say to you, dear boy, and Pip's comrade, that that man got me into such nets as made me his slave. I was always in debt to him, always under his thumb, always a-working, always a-getting into danger. He was younger than me, but he was crafty, and he'd got learning, and he overmatched me five hundred times told with no mercy. My Missis as I had the hard time with – Stop though! I haven't mentioned her yet--"

He looked about him in a confused way, as if he had lost his place in the book of his remembrance; he turned his face to the fire, and spread his hands broader on his knees, and lifted them off and put them on again.

"There ain't no need to go into it," he said, looking round once more. "The time with Compeyson was almost as hard a time as ever I had; that said, all's said. Did I tell you as I was tried, alone, for misdemeanour, while with Compeyson?"

I answered, No.

"Well!" he said, "I was, and got convicted. As to arrested on suspicion, that was twice or three times in the four or five year that it lasted with Compeyson; but evidence was lacking. At last, me and Compeyson was both committed for felony – on a charge of putting stolen notes in circulation – and there was other charges, too. Compeyson says to me, 'Separate defenses, no communication,' and that was all. And I was so miserable poor that I sold all the clothes I had, except what hung on my back, before I could get Jaggers.

"When we was in court, I noticed first of all what a gentleman Compeyson looked, with his curly hair and his black clothes and his white pocket-handkerchief, and what a common sort of a wretch I looked. When the prosecution opened and the evidence was presented, I noticed how heavy it all bore on me, and how light on him. When the evidence was given in the box, I noticed how it was always me that had come forward, and could be swore to, how it was always me that the money had been paid to, how it was always me that had seemed to work the thing and get the profit. But, when the defense come on, then I see the plan plainer; for, says Compeyson's lawyer, 'My lord and gentlemen, here you have before you, side by side, two persons as your eyes can separate easily; one, the younger, well brought up, who will be spoke to as such; one, the elder, ill brought up, who will be spoke to as such. One, the younger, seldom if ever seen in these here transactions, and only suspected; the other, the elder, always seen in them and always with his guilt brought home. Can you doubt, if there is but one guilty person, which is the one; and, if there are two guilty, which is much the worse one?' and such-like. And when it come to character, wasn't it Compeyson as had been to school, and wasn't it his schoolfellows as was in this position and in that, and wasn't it him as had been know'd by witnesses in such fine clubs and societies? And wasn't it me as had been tried before, and as had been know'd to be in and out of jail my whole life? And when it come to speech-making and play-acting, wasn't it Compeyson that could speak to the jury with his face dropping every now and then into his white pocket-handkerchief with false tears, and with Bible verses in his speech, too – and wasn't it me as could only say, 'Gentlemen, this man at my side is a most precious rascal'? And when the verdict come, wasn't it Compeyson as was recommended to mercy on account of good character and bad company, and giving up all the information he could against me, and wasn't it me as got never a word but Guilty? And when I says to Compeyson, 'Once out of this court, I'll smash that face of yours!' ain't it Compeyson as prays the Judge to be protected, and gets two jailors to stand between us? And when we're sentenced, ain't it him as gets seven years, and me fourteen, and ain't it him as the Judge is sorry for, because he might a done so well, and ain't it me as the Judge perceives to be an old offender of violent passion, likely to come to worse?"

He had worked himself into a frenzy, but he checked it, took two or three short breaths, swallowed, and stretching out his hand towards me said, in a reassuring manner, "I ain't a-going to be low, dear boy!"

He had so heated himself that he took out his handkerchief and wiped his face and head and neck and hands, before he could go on.

"I had said to Compeyson that I'd smash that face of his, and I swore Lord smash mine! to do it. We was in the same prison-ship, but I couldn't get at him, though I tried. At last I come behind him and hit him on the cheek to turn him round and get a smashing one at him, when I was seen and seized. The black-hole of that ship wasn't a strong one, to a judge of black-holes that could swim and dive, like me. I escaped to the shore, and

I was hiding among the graves there, envying them that were in them, with all their troubles over with, when I first see my boy!"

He gave me a look of affection that made him almost repulsive to me again, though I felt great pity for him.

"Through my boy, I understood that Compeyson was out on them marshes, too. Upon my soul, I half believe he escaped the ship in his terror to get away from me, not knowing it was me as had got ashore before him. I hunted him down. I smashed his face. 'And now,' says I 'as the worst thing I can do, caring nothing for myself, I'll drag you back.' And I'd have swum off, towing him by the hair, if it had come to that, and I'd a got him aboard without the soldiers.

"Of course, he had much the best of it to the last – his character was so good. He said he had escaped when he was made half-wild by me and my murderous intentions, and his punishment for escaping was light. I was put in irons, brought to trial again, and sent for life. But I didn't stop for life, dear boy and Pip's comrade, now being here."

He wiped himself again, as he had done before, and then slowly took his tobacco from his pocket, and plucked his pipe from his button-hole, and slowly filled it, and began to smoke.

"Is he dead?" I asked, after a silence.

"Is who dead, dear boy?"

"Compeyson."

"He hopes I am, if he's alive, you may be sure," with a fierce look. "I never heard no more of him."

Herbert had been writing with his pencil in the cover of a book. He softly pushed the book over to me, as Provis stood smoking with his eyes on the fire, and I read in it:

"Miss Havisham's half-brother's name was Arthur. Compeyson is the man who was to marry Miss Havisham."

I shut the book and nodded slightly to Herbert, and put the book down. Neither of us said anything, and we both looked at Provis as he stood smoking by the fire.

Chapter 43

If Compeyson were alive and discovered that Provis had returned, it wasn't hard to guess what would happen next. Compeyson was mortally afraid of Provis, and he wouldn't hesitate for a moment to inform the police to ensure Provis was gotten rid of for good.

Never had I mentioned anything about Estella to Provis. But, I said to Herbert that before I could go abroad with Provis, I must see both Estella and Miss Havisham. This was when we were left alone after Provis told us his story. I decided to go out to Richmond next day, and I went.

On my presenting myself at Mrs. Brandley's house, Estella's maid was called over to tell me that Estella had gone to see Miss Havisham, as usual. Not as usual, I said, for she had never yet gone back there without me; when was she coming back? The maid was reluctant to answer, but she said that she believed that when Estella came back, it would only be for a short time. I couldn't understand this answer, and it seemed I was not supposed to understand it, so I went home again in complete confusion.

Another night-consultation with Herbert after Provis had gone home (I always took him home, and always looked well about me), led us to the conclusion that nothing should be said to Provis about going abroad until I came back from Miss Havisham's. In the meantime, Herbert and I were to think up ideas about what would be best to say to Provis; whether we should make up a reason of being afraid that he was being watched; or whether I, who had never been abroad, should propose an exciting trip. Either way, we both felt that we needed to get him out of England as soon as possible.

Next day, I had the meanness to lie to Provis that I had promised Joe I'd go see him that day, but by this point I was capable of almost any meanness towards Joe or his name. Provis was to be strictly careful while I was gone, and Herbert was to look out for him. I told him I was to be gone only one night, and, when I returned, we'd begin work on his plans for making me a gentleman on a grander scale.

Having now cleared the way for my trip to Miss Havisham's, I set off by the early morning coach before dawn. When we drove up to the Blue Boar after a drizzly ride, whom should I see come out under the gateway to look at the coach, but Bentley Drummle!

Since he pretended not to see me, I pretended not to see him. It was a poor performance on both sides; all the poorer because we both went into the coffee-room, where he had just finished his breakfast, and where I ordered mine. I hated seeing him in my home town, for I knew very well why he had come there.

Pretending to read a smeary newspaper long out of date, I sat at my table while he stood before the fire. As I sat there and stewed, it became an enormous injury to me that he stood in front of the fire, and I got up, determined to have my share of it. I had to put my hand behind his legs for the poker when I went up to the fire-place to stir the fire, but I still pretended not to know him.

"Is this a cut?" said Mr. Drummle.

"Oh!" said I, poker in hand; "it's you, is it? How do you do? I was wondering who was hogging the fire."

With that, I poked tremendously, and having done so, planted myself side by side with Mr. Drummle, my shoulders squared and my back to the fire.

"You have just come down?" said Mr. Drummle, edging me a little away with his shoulder.

"Yes," said I, edging him a little away with my shoulder.

"Beastly place," said Drummle. "Your part of the country, I think?"

"Yes," I assented. "I'm told it's very like your Shropshire."

"Not in the least like it," said Drummle.

Here Mr. Drummle looked at his boots, and I looked at mine, and then Mr. Drummle looked at my boots, and I looked at his.

"Have you been here long?" I asked, determined not to yield an inch of the fire.

"Long enough to be tired of it," returned Drummle, pretending to yawn, but equally determined.

"Do you stay here long?"

"Can't say," answered Mr. Drummle. "Do you?"

"Can't say," said I.

I felt here, through a tingling in my blood, that if Mr. Drummle's shoulder had claimed another hair's breadth of room, I would have jerked him into the window; equally, that if my own shoulder had urged a similar claim, Mr. Drummle would have jerked me into the nearest box. He whistled a little. So did I.

"Large tract of marshes about here, I believe?" said Drummle.

"Yes. What about them?" said I.

Mr. Drummle looked at me, and then at my boots, and then said, "Oh!" and laughed.

"Are you amused, Mr. Drummle?"

"No," said he, "not particularly. I am going out for a ride in the saddle. I mean to explore those marshes for amusement. Out-of-the-way villages there, they tell me. Curious little public-houses – and forges. Waiter!"

"Yes, sir."

"Is that horse of mine ready?"

"Brought round to the door, sir."

"I say. Look here, you sir. The lady won't ride to-day; the weather won't do."

"Very good, sir."

"And I don't dine, because I'm going to dine at the lady's."

"Very good, sir."

Then, Drummle glanced at me, with an arrogant triumph on his heavy face that cut me to the heart, dull as he was, and so exasperated me that I had to keep myself from throwing him on the fire.

One thing was plainly clear to both of us, and it was that neither of us could give up our spot by the fire. There we stood, well squared up in front of it, shoulder to shoulder and foot to foot, with our hands behind us, not budging an inch. The horse was visible outside in the drizzle at the door, my breakfast was put on the table, Drummle's was cleared away, the waiter invited me to begin, I nodded to the waiter, and Drummle and I both stood our ground.

"Have you been to the Grove since?" said Drummle.

“No," said I, "I had quite enough of the Finches the last time I was there."

"Was that when we had a difference of opinion?"

"Yes," I replied, very shortly.

"Come, come! They let you off easily enough," sneered Drummle. "You shouldn't have lost your temper."

"Mr. Drummle," said I, "you are not qualified to give advice on that subject. When I lose my temper (not that I admit having done so on that occasion), I don't throw glasses."

"I do," said Drummle.

After glancing at him once or twice, in an increased state of smouldering ferocity, I said:

"Mr. Drummle, I did not seek this conversation, and I don't think it an agreeable one."

"I’m sure it's not," said he, arrogantly over his shoulder, "I don't think anything about it."

"And therefore," I went on, "if you agree, I will suggest that we hold no kind of communication in the future."

"Quite my opinion," said Drummle, "and what I should have suggested myself, or done, more likely – without suggesting. But don't lose your temper. Haven't you lost enough without that?"

"What do you mean, sir?"

"Wai-ter!" said Drummle, by way of answering me.

The waiter reappeared.

"Look here, you sir. You quite understand that the young lady don't ride to-day, and that I dine at the young lady's?"

"Quite so, sir!"

When the waiter had felt my fast cooling tea-pot with the palm of his hand, and had looked imploringly at me and had left, Drummle, careful not to move the shoulder next me, took a cigar from his pocket and bit the end off, but showed no sign of stirring. Choking and boiling as I was, I felt that we could not go a word further, without saying Estella's name, which I could not endure to hear him utter. Therefore, I looked stonily at the opposite wall, as if there were no one else present, and forced myself to silence. How long we might have stayed in this ridiculous position is impossible to say, but for the intrusion of three farmers – led by the waiter, I think – who came into the coffee-room unbuttoning their great-coats and rubbing their hands, and as they charged at the fire, we were obliged to give way to them. Drummle went outside; I went to my table and my now lukewarm breakfast.

I saw him through the window, grabbing his horse's mane, and mounting in his blundering brutal manner, and sidling and backing away. Too heavily out of sorts to eat my breakfast, I washed the weather and the journey from my face and hands, and went out to the memorable old house that it would have been so much the better for me never to have entered, never to have seen.

Chapter 44

In the room where the dressing-table stood, and where the wax candles burnt on the wall, I found Miss Havisham and Estella. Miss Havisham was seated on a small loveseat near the fire, and Estella on a cushion at her feet. Estella was knitting, and Miss Havisham was watching her. They both raised their eyes as I went in, and both saw a change in me. I concluded that from the look they exchanged.

"And what wind," said Miss Havisham, "blows you here, Pip?"

Though she looked steadily at me, I saw that she was rather confused. As for Estella, pausing a moment in her knitting with her eyes upon me and then going on, I fancied that I read in the action of her fingers, as plainly as if she had spoken to me, that she perceived I had discovered my real benefactor.

"Miss Havisham," said I, "I went to Richmond yesterday, to speak to Estella; and finding that some wind had blown her here, I followed."

Miss Havisham motioned to me for the third or fourth time to sit down, so I took the chair by the dressing-table, which I had often seen her occupy. With all that ruin at my feet and about me, it seemed a natural place for me that day.

"What I had to say to Estella, Miss Havisham, I will say in front of you, soon – in a few moments. It will not surprise you, it will not displease you. I am as unhappy as you can ever have meant me to be."

Miss Havisham continued to look steadily at me. I could see in the action of Estella's fingers as they worked that she listened to what I said, but she did not look up.

"I have found out who my patron is. It is not a fortunate discovery, and is not likely ever to enrich me in reputation, social status, fortune, or anything. There are reasons why I must say no more of that. It is not my secret, but another's."

As I was silent for a while, looking at Estella and considering how best to go on, Miss Havisham repeated, "It's not your secret, but another's. Well?"

"When you first caused me to brought here, Miss Havisham; when I belonged to the village over yonder that I wish I had never left; I suppose I really did come here, as any other random boy might have been brought – as a kind of servant, to gratify a want or whim, and to be paid for it?"

"Ay, Pip," replied Miss Havisham, steadily nodding her head, "you did."

"And that Mr. Jaggers--"

"Mr. Jaggers," said Miss Havisham, taking me up in a firm tone, "had nothing to do with it, and knew nothing of it. His being my lawyer, and his being the lawyer of your patron, is a coincidence. He's the lawyer for many people, so it might easily happen. Be that as it may, it did happen, and was not caused or planned by anyone."

"But when I fell into the mistake I have so long remained in, of believing you were my patron, at least you led me on?" said I.

"Yes," she returned, again nodding, steadily, "I let you go on."

"Was that kind?"

"Who am I," cried Miss Havisham, striking her stick upon the floor and flashing into wrath so suddenly that Estella glanced up at her in surprise, "who am I, for God's sake, that I should be kind?"

It was a weak complaint to have made, and I had not meant to make it. I told her so, as she sat brooding after this outburst.

"Well, well!" she said. "What else?"

"I was liberally paid for my old attendance here," I said, to soothe her, "in being apprenticed, and I have asked these questions only for my own information. What follows has another, I hope more impartial and practical purpose. In humouring my mistake, Miss Havisham, you punished – practiced on – you can supply whatever term expresses your intention – your selfish family?"

"I did. It's their own fault! You know my history, why should I be at the pains of helping either them, or you? You all made your own snares, I never made them!"

Waiting until she was quiet again – for this, too, flashed out of her in a wild and sudden way – I went on.

"I have been constantly among one family of your relations, Miss Havisham, since I went to London. I know they thought you were my patron, just as I did. It would be false and low of me if I did not tell you, whether you believe it or not, that you deeply wrong both Mr. Matthew Pocket and his son Herbert, if you suppose them to be anything other than generous, honest, and incapable of anything designing or mean."

"They are your friends," said Miss Havisham.

"They made themselves my friends," said I, "even when they believed that I, and not them, had your favor; and when Sarah Pocket, Miss Georgiana, and Mistress Camilla were definitely not my friends."

This contrasting of them with the rest seemed, I was glad to see, to do them good with her. She looked at me keenly for a little while, and then said quietly:

"What do you want for them?"

"Only," said I, "that you would not mix them in with the others. They may be of the same blood, but, believe me, they are not of the same nature."

Still looking at me keenly, Miss Havisham repeated:

"What do you want for them?"

"I am not so cunning, you see," I said, in answer, conscious that I reddened a little, "as that I could hide from you that I do want something. Miss Havisham, if you would spare the money to do my friend Herbert a lasting service in life, but, because of the nature of the case, must be done without his knowledge, I could show you how."

"Why must it be done without his knowledge?" she asked, settling her hands upon her stick, that she might listen to me more attentively.

"Because," said I, "I began the service myself, more than two years ago, without his knowledge, and I don't want to be betrayed. Why I can't finish it, I cannot explain; it's a part of the secret which is another person's and not mine."

She gradually turned her eyes from me over to the fire. After watching it for what appeared to be a long time, she was roused by the collapse of some of the red coals, and looked towards me again – at first, vacantly – then, with a gradually concentrating attention. All this time, Estella knitted on. When Miss Havisham had fixed her attention on me, she said, speaking as if there had been no lapse in our dialogue:

"What else?"

"Estella," said I, turning to her now, and trying to command my trembling voice, "you know I love you. You know that I have loved you long and dearly."

She raised her eyes to my face, on being thus addressed, and her fingers plied their work, and she looked at me with an unmoved face. I saw that Miss Havisham glanced from me to her, and from her to me.

"I would have said this sooner, except for my long mistake. In thinking Miss Havisham was my benefactor, I believed that she meant us for one another. While I thought you could not help yourself because of that plan, I refrained from saying it. But I must say it now."

Preserving her unmoved face, and with her fingers still going, Estella shook her head.

"I know," said I, in answer to that action; "I know. I have no hope that I shall ever call you mine, Estella. I don't know what will become of me very soon, how poor I may be, or where I may go. Still, I love you. I have loved you ever since I first saw you in this house."

Looking at me perfectly unmoved and with her fingers busy, she shook her head again.

"It would have been cruel in Miss Havisham, horribly cruel, to practice on the susceptibility of a poor boy, and to torture me through all these years with a false hope, if she had thought about the gravity of what she did. But I don't think she did; I think that in dealing with her own trial, she forgot the one she made for me, Estella."

I saw Miss Havisham put her hand to her heart and hold it there, as she sat looking by turns at Estella and at me.

"It seems," said Estella, very calmly, "that there are sentiments, fancies – I don't know what to call them – which I am not able to comprehend. When you say you love me, I know what you mean, as a form of words, but nothing more. You address nothing in my breast; you touch nothing there. I don't have feelings for what you are saying at all. I have tried to warn you of this, now, haven't I?"

I said in a miserable manner, "Yes."

"Yes. But you wouldn't be warned, for you thought I didn't mean it."

"I thought and hoped you could not mean it. You, so young, untried, and beautiful, Estella! Surely it is not in Nature."

"It is in my nature," she returned. And then she added, with a stress upon the words, "It is in the nature that was formed within me. I make a great difference between you and all other people when I say that much. I can do no more."

"Is it not true," said I, "that Bentley Drummle is in town here, and pursuing you?"

"It is quite true," she replied, referring to him with the indifference of utter contempt.

"That you encourage him, and ride out with him, and that he dines with you this very day?"

She seemed a little surprised that I should know it, but again replied, "Quite true."

"You cannot love him, Estella!"

Her fingers stopped for the first time, as she retorted rather angrily, "What have I told you? Do you still think, in spite of it, that I do not mean what I say? I told you I don't love anybody!"

"You would never marry him, Estella?"

She looked towards Miss Havisham, and considered for a moment with her work in her hands. Then she said, "Why not tell you the truth? Yes, I am going to be married to him."

I dropped my face into my hands, but was able to control myself better than I could have expected, considering what agony it gave me to hear her say those words. When I raised my face again, there was a ghastly look upon Miss Havisham's face.

"Estella, dearest dearest Estella, do not let Miss Havisham lead you into this fatal step. Put me aside for ever – you have done so, I well know – but give yourself to some worthier person than Drummle. Miss

Havisham gives you to him as the greatest injury that could be done to the many far better men who admire you, and to the few who truly love you. Among those few, there may be one who loves you even as dearly, though not so long, as I. Take him, and I can bear it better, for your sake!"

"I am going," she said again, in a gentler voice, "to be married to him. The preparations for my marriage are in work, and I shall be married soon. Why do you unfairly mention the name of my mother by adoption? It is my own idea, not hers."

"Your own act, Estella, to fling yourself away upon a brute?"

"On whom should I fling myself away?" she retorted, with a smile. "Should I fling myself away upon the man who would the soonest feel (if people do feel such things) that I took nothing to him? There! It is done. I shall do well enough, and so will my husband. As to leading me into what you call this fatal step, Miss Havisham would have had me wait, and not marry yet; but I am tired of the life I have led, which has very few charms for me, and I am willing enough to change it. Say no more. We shall never understand each other."

"Such a mean brute, such a stupid brute!" I urged in despair.

"Don't be afraid of my being a blessing to him," said Estella, "I shall not be that. Come! Here is my hand. Do we part on this, you idealistic boy – or man?"

"O Estella!" I answered, as my bitter tears fell fast on her hand, despite my trying to stop them, "even if I remained in England and could hold my head up with the rest, how could I see you Drummle's wife?"

"Nonsense," she returned, "This will pass in no time."

"Never, Estella!"

"You will get me out of your thoughts in a week."

"Out of my thoughts! You are part of my existence; part of myself. You have been in every line I have ever read since I first came here, the rough common boy whose poor heart you wounded even then. You have been the embodiment of every graceful fancy that my mind has ever known since then – part of the river, the clouds, the light, the darkness, the wind, the sea, the streets. Estella, to the last hour of my life, you cannot choose but remain part of my character, part of the little good in me, part of the evil. But, in this separation, I will think of you only with the good, and I will faithfully think of you like that, always, for you must have done me far more good than harm, let me feel now what sharp sadness I may. O God bless you, God forgive you!"

In what ecstasy of unhappiness I got these broken words out of myself, I don't know. The rhapsody welled up within me, like blood from an inner wound, and gushed out. I held her hand to my lips some lingering moments, and so I left her. But ever afterwards, I remembered that while Estella looked at me merely with doubting wonder, Miss Havisham, her hand still covering her heart, had a ghastly stare of pity and remorse.

All done, all gone! So much was done and gone, that when I went out at the gate, the light of the day seemed of a darker colour than when I went in. For a while, I hid myself among some lanes and by-paths, and then struck off to walk all the way to London. For, I had by that time calmed down enough as to realize that I could not go back to the inn and see Drummle there; that I could not bear to sit in the coach and be spoken to; that I could do nothing half so good for myself as tire myself out walking to London.

It was past midnight when I crossed London Bridge. I was not expected till tomorrow, but I had my keys, and, if Herbert had gone to bed, could get to bed myself without disturbing him.

I came in at a different gate to the Temple than I usually did, and as I was very muddy and weary, I did not take offense that the night watchman examined me with much attention as he held the gate a little way open for me to pass in. To help his memory I mentioned my name.

"I was not quite sure, sir, but I thought so. Here's a note, sir. The messenger that brought it asked if you would be so good as to read it by my lantern?"

Much surprised by the request, I took the note. It was directed to Philip Pip, Esquire, and above that were the words, "PLEASE READ THIS, HERE." I opened it and read inside, in Wemmick's hand-writing:
"DON'T GO HOME."

Chapter 45

Turning away from the Temple gate as soon as I had read the warning, I got a coach to take me to an inn in Covent Garden. In those times a bed was always to be got there at any hour of the night, and the night clerk on duty lighted the candle next in order on his shelf, and showed me straight into the bedroom next in order on his list. It was a small sort of vault on the ground floor at the back, with an awful huge monster of a four-post bed in it, filling the room, seemingly having to put one of its legs into the fire-place and another into the doorway in order to fit in the room, and squeezing the room's wretched little washing-stand in the process.

As I had asked for a night-light, the front desk clerk had brought me in a little candle, placed in a tin cylinder with holes in it that created a frightful, staringly wide-awake pattern on the walls. When I had got into bed, despite feeling weary and wretched, I found that I could no more close my own eyes than I could close the eyes of the foolish tin candle cover. And so, in the gloom and death of the night, we stared at each other.

What an awful night! How anxious, how dismal, how long! All night, the vision of DON'T GO HOME danced before my eyes. Why I was not to go home, and what had happened at home, and when I should go home, and whether Provis was safe at home, were all questions occupying my mind so busily that one might have supposed there could be no more room in it for anything else. Even when I thought of Estella and how we had parted that day forever, this vague caution DON'T GO HOME pursued me and pushed all else aside. I at last dozed for a bit, in sheer exhaustion of mind and body.

I had left instructions that I was to be awakened at seven, for it was plain that I must see Wemmick before seeing anyone else, and equally plain that this was a case in which I could only have his private and personal capacity sentiments. It was a relief to get out of the room where the night had been so miserable, and I needed no second knocking at the door to startle me from my uneasy bed.

Wemmick's Castle battlements came into my view at eight o'clock. The little servant happened to be entering the fortress with two hot rolls, so I crossed the drawbridge in her company, and therefore came without announcement into the presence of Wemmick as he was making tea for himself and the Aged. An open door to a side room provided a view of the Aged in bed.

"Halloa, Mr. Pip!" said Wemmick. "You did come home, then?"

"Yes," I returned, "but I didn't go home."

"That's all right," said he, rubbing his hands. "I left a note for you at each of the Temple gates, on the chance. Which gate did you come to?"

I told him.

"I'll go round to the others later today and destroy the notes," said Wemmick. "It's a good rule never to leave documentary evidence if you can help it, because you don't know that it may be used. I'm going to take a liberty with you, would you mind toasting this sausage for the Aged P.?"

I said I should be delighted to do it.

"Then you can go about your work, Mary Anne," said Wemmick to the little servant, "which leaves us to ourselves, don't you see, Mr. Pip?" he added, winking, as she disappeared.

I thanked him for his friendship and caution, and proceeded to talk in a low tone, while I toasted the Aged's sausage and he buttered the Aged's roll.

"Now, Mr. Pip, you know," said Wemmick, "you and I understand one another. We are in our private and personal capacities, and we have been engaged in a confidential transaction before today. Official sentiments are one thing. This is beyond official."

I cordially agreed. I was so very nervous, that I had accidentally lighted the Aged's sausage on fire like a torch, and had to blow it out.

"I accidentally heard, yesterday morning," said Wemmick, "being in a certain place where I once took you - even between you and me, it's as well not to mention names when avoidable--"

"Much better not, I understand you," knowing he meant Newgate prison.

"I heard there, by chance, yesterday morning," said Wemmick, "that a certain person from overseas, possessing portable property – I don't know who it may really be – we won't name this person--"

"Not necessary," said I, knowing he meant Provis.

" – had made quite a stir in a certain part of the world where certain people go to live for the rest of their life, and not of their own choice, and paid for by the government. This person disappeared from that place, suddenly. From which," said Wemmick, "conjectures and theories had been formed. I also heard that you at your apartment had been watched, and might be watched again."

"By whom?" said I.

"I wouldn't go into that," said Wemmick, evasively, "it might clash with official responsibilities. I heard it, as I have in my time heard other curious things in that same place. I don't tell it you based on information I received; I overheard it."

He took the toasting-fork and sausage from me as he spoke, and set forth the Aged's breakfast neatly on a little tray. He placed his breakfast before him with great care, and said, "All right, ain't you, Aged P.?" To which the cheerful Aged replied, "All right, John, my boy, all right!" As there seemed to be an unspoken understanding that the Aged was not in a presentable state, and was therefore to be considered invisible, I pretended not to notice any of this exchange.

"This business of someone watching me at my apartment," I said to Wemmick when he came back, "is related to the person of portable property you mentioned, correct?"

Wemmick looked very serious. "I can't say for sure that it is. But it either is, or it will be, or it's in great danger of being."

As I saw that he was restrained by loyalty to his office in Little Britain from saying as much as he could, and as I knew with thankfulness to him how far out of his way he went to say what he did, I could not press him. But I told him, after a little thinking over the fire, that I would like to ask him a question, subject to his answering or not answering as he deemed right, and I had faith in him that his course would be right. He paused in his breakfast, and, crossing his arms, nodded to me once to ask my question.

"You have heard of a man of bad character, whose true name is Compeyson?"

He answered with a nod.

"Is he living?"

One other nod.

"Is he in London?"

He gave me one other nod, compressed the post-office exceedingly, gave me one last nod, and went on with his breakfast.

"Now," said Wemmick, "questioning being over," which he emphasized and repeated for my guidance; "I came to the realization I did, after hearing what I heard. I went to your apartment to find you; not finding you, I went to Clarriker's to find Mr. Herbert."

"And him you found?" said I, with great anxiety.

"And him I found. Without mentioning any names or going into any details, I let him understand that if he was aware of a certain person being in the apartment or in the immediate neighbourhood, then he had better get that person out of the way while you were out of town."

"He would be greatly puzzled what to do?"

"He was puzzled what to do; more so, because I gave him my opinion that it was not safe to try to get that person too far out of the way currently. Mr. Pip, I'll tell you something. Under existing circumstances there is no place like a large city to get lost in when once you are in it. Don't break cover too soon. Lie close. Wait till things slacken before you try to leave London, even for foreign shores."

I thanked him for his valuable advice, and asked him what Herbert had done?

"Mr. Herbert," said Wemmick, "after being a mess for half an hour, struck out a plan. He mentioned to me as a secret, that he is courting a young lady who has, as no doubt you are aware, a bedridden father. Which father, having been in the Purser line of life, lies in bed near a big window where he can see the ships sail up and down the river. You are acquainted with the young lady, most probably?"

"Not personally," said I. The truth was, that she had objected to me at first as an expensive companion who did Herbert no good. Also, when Herbert had first suggested that I meet her, she had received the proposal with such low enthusiasm that Herbert had felt obliged to confide how she felt about me, with his suggestion that some time should pass and circumstances get better before I met her. When I had begun to advance Herbert's prospects in secret, I was assured that I had risen in Clara's opinion as his prospects had risen, though I still had not met her yet. However, I didn't trouble Wemmick with these details.

"The house by the river, with the big window," said Wemmick, "is owned by a respectable widow who has a furnished upper floor to rent out. Mr. Herbert asked me, what did I think of that as a temporary residence for a certain person? Now, I thought very well of it, for three reasons. Firstly, it's well out of your normal routine and places you visit. Secondly, without going near it yourself, you could always hear of the safety of this certain person through Mr. Herbert. Thirdly, after a while and when it might be smart, if you should want to get that person on board a foreign boat, there he is, ready by the river."

Much comforted by this arrangement, I thanked Wemmick again and again, and begged him to proceed.

"Well, sir! Mr. Herbert threw himself into the business eagerly, and by nine o'clock last night he had moved this certain person quite successfully to his new apartment. At his previous residence it was made to be understood that he was summoned to Dover, and in fact he was taken down the Dover road on his way out. Now, another great advantage of all this is, that it was done without you, and when, if anyone was concerning himself about your movements, then you were ever so many miles off and quite otherwise busy. This diverts suspicion and confuses it; and for that same reason I recommended that even if you came back last night, you should not go home. It creates more confusion, and you want confusion."

Wemmick, having finished his breakfast, here looked at his watch, and began to get his coat on.

"And now, Mr. Pip," said he, "I have probably done the most I can do; but if I can ever do more – from a Walworth point of view, and in a strictly private and personal capacity – I shall be glad to do it. Here's the address. There can be no harm in your going there tonight and seeing for yourself that all is well before you go home – which is another reason for your not going home last night. But after you have gone home, don't go back there. You are very welcome, I am sure, Mr. Pip, and let me finally stress one important point to you." He laid his hands upon my shoulders, and added in a solemn whisper, "Take this evening's chance to get hold of his portable property. You don't know what may happen to him; don't let anything happen to the portable property."

There was no way to make Wemmick understand my opposite feelings about that, so I didn't bother to try.

"Time's up," said Wemmick, "and I must be off. If you had nothing more pressing to do than to stay here till dark, that's what I would advise. You look very much worried, and it would do you good to have a perfectly quiet day with the Aged – he'll be up presently – and a little bit of – you remember the pig?"

"Of course," said I.

"Well, and a little bit of him. That sausage you toasted was his, and he was in all respects a first-rater. Do try him, if its only for old acquaintance sake. Good-bye, Aged Parent!" in a cheery shout.

"All right, John; all right, my boy!" piped the old man from within.

I soon fell asleep before Wemmick's fire, and the Aged and I enjoyed one another's company by falling asleep in front of it more or less all day. We had pork loin for dinner, and greens from his garden, and I nodded at the Aged with a good intention whenever I failed to do it drowsily. When it was quite dark, I left the Aged preparing the fire for toast, and I inferred from the number of teacups, as well as from his glances at the two little doors in the wall, that Miss Skiffins was expected.

Chapter 46

I left Wemmick's at eight o'clock that evening and headed towards the house where Herbert had hidden Provis away. It was an area of London I'd never been to before called Mill Pond Bank, along the river. This was down near the ship-builders and ship-breakers area, and I got lost several times along the way, but I eventually came round a corner and found myself in Mill Pond Bank. It was a fresh kind of place, all things considered, where the wind from the river had room to turn itself around, and there were two or three trees in it.

There were a few houses in Mill Pond Bank, and the one I wanted was three stories tall and the name plate on the door read 'Mrs. Whimple'. I knocked, and a pleasant looking elderly woman answered. Herbert was immediately by her side and he silently led me into the parlour and shut the door. It was an odd sensation to see his very familiar face looking quite at home in that very unfamiliar room and place.

"All is well, Handel," said Herbert, "and he is quite satisfied, though eager to see you. My dear girl is with her father, and if you'll wait till she comes down, I'll introduce you, and then we'll go up-stairs. - That's her father."

I had become aware of an alarming growling overhead, and my face had probably expressed that.

"I am afraid he is a sad old rascal," said Herbert, smiling, "but I have never seen him. Don't you smell rum? He is always at it."

"At rum?" said I.

"Yes," returned Herbert, "and you may suppose it helps with his gout. He insists, too, in keeping all the food upstairs in his room, and serving it out. He keeps it on shelves over his head, and will weigh it all out before serving. His room must be like a general store."

While he spoke, the growling noise became a prolonged roar, and then died away.

"What else can be the consequence," said Herbert, in explanation, "if he will cut the cheese? A man with the gout in his right hand – and everywhere else – can't expect to saw with a knife through a thick Double Gloucester cheese without hurting himself."

He seemed to have hurt himself very much, for he gave another furious roar.

"To have Provis for an upper lodger is quite a godsend to Mrs. Whimple," said Herbert, "for of course, most people in general won't stand that noise. A curious place, Handel, isn't it?"

It was a curious place, indeed; but remarkably well kept and clean, and I said so.

"Mrs. Whimple," said Herbert, "is the best of housewives, and I really do not know what my Clara would do without her motherly help. For, Clara has no mother of her own, Handel, and no family in the world but old Gruffandgrim."

"Surely that's not his name, Herbert?"

"No, no," said Herbert, laughing, "that's my name for him. His name is Mr. Barley. But what a blessing it is for me to love a girl who has no other family, and who can never bother herself, or anybody else, about family relations!"

Herbert had told me on former occasions, and now reminded me, that he first knew Miss Clara Barley when she was completing her education at a school in Hammersmith, and that on her being recalled home to nurse her father, he and she had confided their affection to the motherly Mrs. Whimple, and she had helped protect it with equal kindness and discretion, ever since. It was understood that nothing of a romantic nature could possibly be confided to her father, due to his being totally unable to consider any subject more emotional than Gout, Rum, and Purser's stores.

As we were talking in a low tone while Old Barley's growl vibrated in the beam that crossed the ceiling, the room door opened, and a very pretty and small dark-eyed girl of twenty or so came in with a basket in her hand. Herbert tenderly took the basket from her, and presented "Clara." She really was a most charming girl and might have passed for a captive fairy whom that ferocious Ogre, Old Barley, had pressed into his service.

"Look here," said Herbert, showing me the basket, with a compassionate and tender smile after we had talked a little. "Here's poor Clara's supper, served out every night. Here's her allowance of bread, a slice of cheese, and some rum – which I drink. This is Mr. Barley's breakfast for tomorrow, served out to be cooked. Two lamb chops, three potatoes, some split peas, a little flour, two ounces of butter, a pinch of salt, and all this black pepper. It's stewed up together and taken hot, and it's a nice thing for the gout, I should think!"

There was something so loving and innocent in how Herbert and Clara interacted that I would not have undone the engagement between them for all the money in Provis's wallet I had never opened.

I was looking at her with admiration, when suddenly the growl swelled into a roar again, and a frightful bumping noise was heard above, as if a giant with a wooden leg were trying to pound it through the ceiling to get to us. Upon this Clara said to Herbert, "Papa wants me, darling!" and ran away.

"There is an unconscionable old shark for you!" said Herbert. "What do you suppose he wants now, Handel?"

"I don't know," said I. "Something to drink?"

"That's it!" cried Herbert, as if I had made an extraordinary guess. "He keeps his grog ready-mixed in a little tub on the table. Wait a moment, and you'll hear Clara lift him up to drink some. - There he goes!" We heard another roar, with a prolonged shake at the end. "Now," said Herbert, as it was silent upstairs now, "he's drinking. Now," said Herbert, as the growl resumed in the ceiling beam once more, "he's down on his back again!"

Clara returned soon afterwards, and Herbert accompanied me upstairs to see Provis, leaving Clara downstairs. As we passed Mr. Barley's door, he was heard hoarsely muttering the following sea shanty inside; I'm substituting words of good wishes in place of some of his words, which were quite the opposite:

"Ahoy! Bless your eyes, here's old Bill Barley. Here's old Bill Barley, bless your eyes. Here's old Bill Barley on the flat of his back, by the Lord. Lying on the flat of his back, like a drifting old dead flounder, here's your old Bill Barley, bless your eyes. Ahoy! Bless you."

Herbert informed me that old Barley would talk to himself day and night, muttering this chant of self-pity. During the day, he would console himself this way, while also having one eye at a telescope which was fitted on his bed for the convenience of viewing the river.

In his two cabin rooms at the top of the house, in which Mr. Barley was less audible than below, I found Provis comfortably settled. He expressed no alarm, and seemed to feel none that was worth mentioning; but it struck me that he was softened - indefinably, for I could not have said how, and could never afterwards recall how when I tried; but certainly, he was.

While resting at Wemmick's, I had decided to say nothing to Provis about Compeyson. For anything I knew, his hatred towards the man might lead to him seeking Compeyson out and bringing about his own destruction in the process. Therefore, when Herbert and I sat down with him by his fire, I asked him first of all whether he relied on Wemmick's judgment and sources of information?

"Ay, ay, dear boy!" he answered, with a grave nod, "Jaggers knows."

"Then, I have talked with Wemmick," said I, "and have come to tell you what caution he gave me and what advice."

This I did accurately, only with-holding what I just mentioned about Compeyson; and I told him how Wemmick had heard, in Newgate prison (whether from officers or prisoners I could not say), that he was under some suspicion, and that my apartment had been watched; how Wemmick had recommended his keeping a low profile for a time, and my keeping away from him since I was being watched; and what Wemmick had said about getting him abroad. I added that, of course, when the time came, I would go with him, or would follow close after him, as might be safest in Wemmick's judgment. What was to happen after that, I did not discuss, mainly because it wasn't at all clear in my own mind what I would do, now that I saw him in that softer condition, and in danger for my sake. As to his plan of altering my way of living by enlarging my expenses from his pocket book, I stressed that in our present circumstances that it would be simply ridiculous at least, and more likely very dangerous.

He could not deny this, and indeed was very reasonable throughout. His coming back was a gamble, he said, and he had always known it would be a gamble. He said he would do nothing to make the situation worse, and he had very little fear of his safety with such good help.

Herbert, who had been looking at the fire and pondering, said that an idea had come into his thoughts arising out of Wemmick's suggestion, "We are both good rowers, Handel, and could take him down the river ourselves when the right time comes. No boat would then be hired for the purpose, and no boatmen; that would save at least a chance of suspicion, and any chance is worth saving. Never mind that it's cold out; don't you think it might be a good thing if you began at once to keep a boat at the stairs of our apartment, and were in the habit of rowing up and down the river? You fall into that habit, and then who notices or minds? Do it twenty or fifty times, and there is nothing special in your doing it the twenty-first or fifty-first."

I liked this scheme, and Provis was quite elated by it. We agreed to begin as soon as possible, and that Provis should never hail us if we rowed past Mill Pond Bank. Instead, we agreed that he should pull down one of the blinds in a window of his room as a signal whenever he saw us and all was right.

Our conference now over and everything arranged, I rose to go. I remarked to Herbert that he and I had better not go home together, that he should wait a half an hour after me. "I don't like to leave you here," I said to Provis, "though I cannot doubt your being safer here than near me. Good-bye!"

"Dear boy," he answered, clasping my hands, "I don't know when we may meet again, and I don't like Good-bye. Say Good Night!"

"Good night! Herbert will go regularly between us, and when the time comes you may be certain I shall be ready. Good night, Good night!"

We thought it best that he should stay in his own rooms, and we left him on the landing outside his door, holding a light over the stair-rail to light us down stairs. Looking back at him, I thought of the first night of his return when our positions were reversed, and I was up above at my landing and he was on the stairs below coming up. I never would have guessed that night that my heart could ever be as heavy and anxious at parting from him as it was now.

Old Barley was growling and swearing when we repassed his door, with no appearance of having stopped or of intending to. When we got to the foot of the stairs, I asked Herbert whether he had kept the name of Provis as the lodger upstairs. He replied, certainly not, and that the lodger was now known as Mr. Campbell. He also explained that all that was known about Mr. Campbell, as far as Mrs. Whimple and Clara were concerned, was that he (Herbert) had Mr. Campbell consigned to him, and felt a strong personal interest in his being well cared for and living a secluded life. So, when we went into the parlour where Mrs. Whimple and Clara were seated at work, I said nothing of my own interest in Mr. Campbell, but kept it to myself.

When I had taken leave of the pretty gentle dark-eyed girl, and of the motherly woman, I felt as if Mill Pond Bank had grown into quite a different place. Old Barley might be as old as the hills, and might swear like a whole field of troopers, but there were redeeming youth and trust and hope enough in Mill Pond Bank to fill it to overflowing. And then I thought of Estella, and of our parting, and went home very sadly.

All things were as quiet around our apartment as I had ever seen them. I walked past the fountain two or three times before I descended the steps that were between me and my apartment, but I was quite alone. Herbert coming to my bedside when he came in – for I went straight to bed, depressed and exhausted – made the same report. Opening one of the windows after that, he looked out into the moonlight, and told me that the pavement was solemnly empty.

The next day, I set myself to get the boat. It was soon done, and the boat was brought round to the stairs near the river and lay where I could reach her within a minute or two. Then, I began to go out as for training and practice; sometimes alone, sometimes with Herbert. I was often out in the cold, rain, and sleet, but nobody took much notice of me after I had been out a few times. At first, I kept above Blackfriars Bridge; but as the hours of the tide changed, I headed towards London Bridge. It was Old London Bridge in those days, and at certain states of the tide there was a rush and fall of water there which gave it a dangerous reputation. But I knew well enough how to "shoot" the bridge after seeing it done, and so I began to row about among the shipping down there. The first time I passed Mill Pond Bank, Herbert and I were pulling a pair of oars; and, both in going and returning, we saw a blind in his window come down, signaling all was okay. Herbert was usually there three or more times in a week, and he never brought me a single word of news that was at all alarming. Still, I knew that there was cause for alarm, and I could not get rid of the notion of being watched. Once you have that feeling, it is a haunting idea; how many innocent people I suspected of watching me, it would be hard to add up.

In short, I was always full of fears for Magwitch, previously also known as Provis, now also known as Mr. Campbell, who was in hiding down at Mill Pond Bank. Herbert had sometimes said to me that he found it pleasant to stand at one of our windows after dark, when the tide was running down river, and to think that it was flowing towards Clara. But I thought with dread that it was flowing towards Magwitch, and that any boat on its surface might be his pursuers, going swiftly, silently, and surely, to subdue him.

Chapter 47

Some weeks passed without bringing any change. I waited for any news from Wemmick, but nothing came. If I didn't know him as well as I did, I might have doubted him; but I knew he had our best interests at heart, so I had to tell myself to be patient.

My financial situation began to look gloomy, and I was pressed for money by more than one creditor and had to sell some easily spared jewelry for cash. But I had made up my mind that it would be a heartless fraud to take more money from my patron in the current state of my uncertain thoughts and plans. Therefore, I had sent him the unopened wallet to hold in his own keeping, and I felt a kind of satisfaction in not having profited by his generosity since he revealed himself to me. Whether that feeling of satisfaction was a false kind or a true kind, I hardly know, but I felt better either way in not taking any more of his money.

As time wore on, a belief settled heavily upon me that Estella had gotten married. Afraid of having it confirmed, though it was all but assured, I avoided the newspapers and begged Herbert (to whom I had confided how I had parted from her) never to speak of her to me. Why I clung to this last little crumb of hope, how should I know? Why did you, who read this, commit a similar irrational hope of your own last year, or last month, or last week?

It was an unhappy life that I lived, and my one dominant anxiety (making its home at Mill Pond Bank) towered over all my other anxieties like a high mountain above a range of mountains. I would wake up in my bed with fresh terror that he was discovered; I would sit listening at night with dread for Herbert's returning steps on the stairs, worried they would be quicker than usual and bringing evil news. Despite all that, and many other similar self-imposed trials, time marched on and no new actual causes for fear arose. I was condemned to inaction and a state of constant suspense, and I rowed about in my boat, and waited, waited, waited, as best I could.

There were certain times when I rowed down river that, when the tide turned, I could not fight the current to get back home. At those times, I left my boat at a wharf near the Customs House, to be brought up afterwards to the stairs by my apartment. It had a happy side effect of serving to make me and my boat a common sight among the waterside people there. From this type of occasion sprang two meetings that I have now to tell of.

One afternoon, late in the month of February, I came ashore at the wharf at dusk. I had pulled down as far as Greenwich with the ebb tide, and had turned back with the tide. It had been a fine bright day, but had become foggy as the sun dropped, and I had had to carefully feel my way back among the shipping. Both in going and returning, I had seen the signal in Provis' window, All Well.

As it was a raw evening and I was cold, I thought I would comfort myself with dinner; and as I had nothing but hours of dejection and solitude before me if I went home, I thought I would go to the play after I ate. The theatre where Mr. Wopsle had achieved his questionable triumph was in that same waterside neighborhood, and to that theatre I decided to go. I was aware that Mr. Wopsle had not succeeded in reviving the Drama, but, quite the contrary, had rather contributed to its decline.

I dined on this occasion at what Herbert and I used to call a "geographical chop-house", where there were maps of the world stained into every tablecloth, and charts of gravy crusted onto every one of the knives. I ate a listless dinner there, and by-and-by I roused myself and went to the play.

This play was no better than the last one I had seen Mr. Wopsle in, and the audience received it similarly. Mr. Wopsle's character apparently had plenty of time on his hands, and I observed with great surprise that he spent most of it staring in my direction, as if he were lost in amazement.

There was something so remarkable in the way Mr. Wopsle was looking toward me, and he seemed to be turning so many things over in his mind and to grow so confused, that I could not understand it. I sat thinking about it the rest of the play, and was still thinking of it when I came out of the theatre an hour afterwards, and found him waiting for me near the door.

"How do you do?" said I, shaking hands with him as we turned down the street together. "I saw that you saw me."

"Saw you, Mr. Pip!" he returned. "Yes, of course I saw you. But who else was there?"

"Who else?"

"It's the strangest thing," said Mr. Wopsle, drifting into his lost look again, "and yet, I could swear to him."

Becoming alarmed, I asked Mr. Wopsle to explain his meaning.

"Whether I would have noticed him if you hadn't been there, I can't be positive," said Mr. Wopsle, going on in the same lost way, "yet, I think I still would have."

These words gave me a chill, and I involuntarily looked at the city streets around me.

"Oh! He's not around now," said Mr. Wopsle. "He left, before I went off stage, I saw him go."

Having the reason that I had for being suspicious, I even suspected this poor actor of plotting against me; to entrap me into some admission about Provis. Therefore, I glanced at him as we walked on together, but said nothing.

"I had a strange idea that he must be with you, Mr. Pip, till I saw that you were quite unaware of him, sitting behind you there, like a ghost."

My former chill crept over me again, but I was determined not to speak yet, for his words could be consistent with my paranoid suspicion of his motives, or he could have been genuine; I couldn't tell which yet. Of course, I was perfectly sure that Provis had not been there.

"I dare say you wonder at me, Mr. Pip; indeed, I see you do. But it is so very strange! You'll hardly believe what I am going to tell you. I could hardly believe it myself, if you told me."

"Indeed?" said I.

"No, indeed. Mr. Pip, do you remember in old times on a certain Christmas Day when you were a child, and I dined at Gargery's, and some soldiers came to the door to get a pair of handcuffs mended?"

"I remember it very well."

"And you remember that there was a chase after two convicts, and that we joined in it, and that Gargery took you on his back, and that I took the lead and you kept up with me as well as you could?"

"I remember it all very well." Better than he thought, especially the last part.

"And you remember that we caught up with the two convicts in a ditch, and that there was a fight between them, and that one of them had a face severely beaten by the other?"

"Yes," said I, "I remember all that."

"Then, Mr. Pip, one of those two prisoners sat behind you tonight. I saw him over your shoulder."

"Steady!" I thought. I asked him then, "Which of the two do you suppose you saw?"

"The one who had been beaten," he answered readily, "and I'll swear I saw him! The more I think of him, the more certain I am of him."

"This is very curious!" said I, with the best act I could put on of its being nothing important to me. "Very curious indeed!"

I cannot exaggerate the agitation into which this conversation threw me, or the exposed terror I felt at Compeyson's having been behind me "like a ghost." For, if he had ever been out of my thoughts for a few moments since the hiding had begun, it seemed to be in those very moments when he was closest to me. To think that I should be so unconscious and off my guard after all my care, was as if I had shut a hundred doors to keep him out and then had found him standing by my elbow. I could not doubt two things; that he was there because I was there, and that however invisible the appearance of danger might be, danger was nonetheless always near and active.

I put such questions to Mr. Wopsle as, When did the man come in? He could not tell me that; he saw me, and over my shoulder he saw the man. It was not until he had seen him for some time that he began to identify him; but he had from the first vaguely associated him with me, and known him as somehow connected to me in the old village days. How was he dressed? Prosperously, but not noticeably otherwise; he thought, in black. Was his face at all disfigured? No, he believed not. I believed not, too, for, although I had not taken any special notice of the people behind me, I thought it likely that a disfigured face would have attracted my attention.

When Mr. Wopsle had shared with me all that he could remember, and when I had treated him to a little appropriate refreshment, we parted. It was between twelve and one o'clock in the morning when I reached my apartment, and the gates were shut. No one was near me when I went in and went home.

Herbert had come in, and we held a very serious meeting by the fire. But there was nothing to be done, except to communicate to Wemmick what I had learned, and to remind him that we waited for his guidance. As I thought that I might compromise him if I went too often to his Castle in Walworth, I made this communication by letter. I wrote it before I went to bed, and went out and posted it; and again, no one was near me. Herbert and I agreed that we could do nothing else but be very cautious. And we were very cautious, indeed – more cautious than before, if that were possible – and I for my part never went near Mill Pond Bank except when I rowed by, and then I only looked at it as I looked at anything else.

Chapter 48

The second of the two meetings referred to in the last chapter occurred about a week after the first. I had again left my boat at the wharf below Bridge; the time was an hour earlier in the afternoon; and, undecided where to dine, I had strolled up into Cheapside. I was strolling along it, surely the most unsettled person in all the busy street, when a large hand was laid upon my shoulder by someone overtaking me. It was Mr. Jaggers' hand, and he passed it through my arm.

"As we are going in the same direction, Pip, we may walk together. Where are you bound for?"

"For my apartment, I think," said I.

"Don't you know?" said Mr. Jaggers.

"Well," I returned, glad for once to get the better of him in cross-examination, "I do not know, for I have not made up my mind."

"You are going to dine?" said Mr. Jaggers. "You don't mind admitting that, I suppose?"

"No," I returned, "I don't mind admitting that."

"And you have no plans?"

"I don't mind admitting also, that I have no plans."

"Then," said Mr. Jaggers, "come and dine with me."

I was going to excuse myself, when he added, "Wemmick's coming." So, I changed my excuse into an acceptance – the few words I had uttered served as the beginning of either – and we went along Cheapside and slanted off towards his office in Little Britain.

At the office there was the usual letter-writing, hand-washing, candle-snuffing, and safe-locking that closed the business of the day. As I stood waiting by Mr. Jaggers' fire, its rising and falling flames made the two casts on the shelf look as if they were playing a diabolical game of peek-a-boo with me.

We went to Gerrard-street, all three together, in a hackney coach. As soon as we got there, dinner was served. Although I knew I would never get any hint of Wemmick's Walworth sentiments while he was at Mr. Jaggers' home, I at least was hoping to catch his eye now and then in a friendly way. But it was not to be done. He turned his eyes on Mr. Jaggers whenever he raised them from the table, and was as dry and distant to me as if there were twin Wemmicks and this was the wrong one.

"Did you send that note of Miss Havisham's to Mr. Pip, Wemmick?" Mr. Jaggers asked, soon after we began dinner.

"No, sir," returned Wemmick, "it was going by post, when you brought Mr. Pip into the office. Here it is." He handed it to Mr. Jaggers, instead of to me.

"It's a note of two lines, Pip," said Mr. Jaggers, handing it on to me, "sent up to me by Miss Havisham, on account of her not being sure of your address. She tells me that she wants to see you on a little matter of business you mentioned to her. You'll go down to see her?"

"Yes," said I, casting my eyes over the note, which was exactly in those terms.

"When do you think you'll go?"

"I have an impending engagement," said I, glancing at Wemmick, who was putting fish into his post-office, "that makes me rather uncertain of my time. At once, I think."

"If Mr. Pip has the intention of going at once," said Wemmick to Mr. Jaggers, "he needn't write an answer, you know."

Receiving this as a hint that it was best not to delay, I settled that I would go to-morrow, and said so. Wemmick drank a glass of wine and looked with a grimly satisfied air at Mr. Jaggers, but not at me.

"So, Pip! Our friend the Spider," said Mr. Jaggers, "has played his cards. He has won the pool."

It was as much as I could do to agree.

"Hah! He is a promising fellow – in his way – but he may not have it all his own way. The stronger will win in the end, but the stronger has to be found out first. If he should turn to, and beat her--"

"Surely," I interrupted, with a burning face and heart, "you do not seriously think that he is scoundrel enough for that, Mr. Jaggers?"

"I didn't say so, Pip. I am putting a case. If he should turn to and beat her, he may possibly get the strength on his side; if it should be a question of intellect, he certainly will not. It would be only a guess to give an opinion how a fellow of that sort will turn out in such circumstances, because it's a toss-up between two results."

"May I ask what they are?"

"A fellow like our friend the Spider," answered Mr. Jaggers, "either beats, or cringes. Ask Wemmick his opinion."

"Either beats or cringes," said Wemmick, not at all addressing himself to me.

"So, here's to Mrs. Bentley Drummle," said Mr. Jaggers, taking a pitcher of nice wine from his cart, and filling glasses for each of us and for himself, "and may the question of supremacy be settled to the lady's satisfaction! To the satisfaction of both the lady and the gentleman, it never will be. Now, Molly, Molly, Molly, Molly, how slow you are today!"

She was at his elbow when he addressed her, putting a dish upon the table. As she withdrew her hands from it, she fell back a step or two, nervously muttering some excuse. And a certain action of her fingers as she spoke got my attention.

"What's the matter?" said Mr. Jaggers.

"Nothing. Only the subject we were speaking of," said I, "was rather painful to me."

She stood looking at her master, not understanding whether she was free to go, or whether he had more to say to her and would call her back if she did go. Her look was very intent. Surely, I had seen exactly such eyes and such hands on a memorable occasion very lately!

He dismissed her, and she glided out of the room. But her image remained before me in my mind, as plainly as if she were still there. I looked at those hands, I looked at those eyes, I looked at that flowing hair, and I compared them with other hands, other eyes, and other hair that I knew of, and with what those might look like after twenty years and a stormy life. I thought how the same feeling had come back when I saw a face looking at me and a hand waving to me from a stage-coach window. And I felt absolutely certain that this woman was Estella's mother.

Mr. Jaggers had seen me with Estella, and was not likely to have missed the feelings for her I had not tried to hide. He nodded when I said the subject was painful to me, clapped me on the back, served round the wine again, and went on with his dinner.

Only twice more did the housekeeper reappear, and then her stay in the room was very short, and Mr. Jaggers was sharp with her. But her hands were Estella's hands, and her eyes were Estella's eyes, and if she had reappeared a hundred times I couldn't have been any surer that my conviction was the truth.

It was a dull evening, for Wemmick drew his wine when it came round, quite as a matter of business – just as he might have drawn his pay check when that came round – and with his eyes on his employer, sat in a state of perpetual readiness for cross-examination. From my point of view, he was the wrong twin all the time, and only externally like the Wemmick of Walworth.

We took our leave early, and left together. Even when we were groping among Mr. Jaggers's stock of boots for our hats, I felt that the right twin was on his way back; and we had not gone half a dozen yards down Gerrard-street in the Walworth direction before I found that I was walking arm-in-arm with the right twin, and that the wrong twin had evaporated into the evening air.

"Well!" said Wemmick, "That's over! He's a wonderful man, in his way; but I feel that I have to screw myself up when I dine with him – and I dine more comfortably unscrewed."

I felt that this was a good statement of the case, and told him so.

"Wouldn't say it to anybody but yourself," he answered. "I know that what is said between you and me goes no further."

I asked him if he had ever seen Miss Havisham's adopted daughter, Mrs. Bentley Drummle? He said no. To avoid being too abrupt, I then spoke of the Aged, and of Miss Skiffins. He looked rather sly when I mentioned Miss Skiffins, and stopped in the street to blow his nose, with a roll of the head and a flourish not quite free from a bit of boastfulness.

"Wemmick," said I, "do you remember telling me before I first went to Mr. Jaggers' private house, to notice that housekeeper?"

"Did I?" he replied. "Ah, I dare say I did. Deuce take me," he added, suddenly, "I know I did. I find I am not quite unscrewed yet."

"A wild beast tamed, you called her."

"And what do you call her?"

"The same. How did Mr. Jaggers tame her, Wemmick?"

"That's his secret. She has been with him many years."

"I wish you would tell me her story. I feel a particular interest knowing it. You know that what is said between you and me goes no further."

"Well!" Wemmick replied, "I don't know her story – that is, I don't know all of it. But what I do know, I'll tell you. We are in our private and personal capacities, of course."

"Of course."

"Twenty or so years ago, that woman was tried for murder and was acquitted. She was a very beautiful young woman, and I believe had some gipsy blood in her. Anyhow, her blood was hot enough when it was riled up, as you may suppose."

"But she was acquitted."

"Mr. Jaggers was for her," pursued Wemmick, with a look full of meaning, "and worked the case in a way quite astonishing. It was a desperate case, and it was comparatively early days with him then, and he worked it to general admiration. In fact, it may almost be said to have made his reputation. He worked it himself at the police-office, day after day for many days, contending against even a committal, putting everything he had into working it. The murdered person was a woman; a woman a good ten years older than her, and very much larger, and very much stronger. It was a case of jealousy. They both led vagabond lives, and the accused woman had been married very young, though illegitimately, to a vagabond man, and she was a perfect fury in terms of jealousy. The murdered woman – more a match for the man based on age – was found dead in a barn near Hounslow Heath. There had been a violent struggle, perhaps a fight. She was bruised and scratched and torn, and had been held by the throat at last and choked to death. Now, there was no reasonable evidence to implicate anybody but this young woman, and, on the improbability of her having been able to do it, Mr. Jaggers chiefly rested his case. You may be sure," said Wemmick, touching me on the sleeve, "that he never dwelt upon the strength of her hands then, though he sometimes does now."

I had told Wemmick of his showing us her wrists, that day of the dinner party.

"Well, sir!" Wemmick went on, "it happened that this woman was so very cleverly dressed from the time of her arrest, that she looked much smaller than she really was. In particular, the sleeves of her dress were so skillfully put together that her arms had quite a delicate look to them. She had only a bruise or two on her – nothing unusual for a vagabond – but the backs of her hands were all torn, and the question was, was it with fingernails? Now, Mr. Jaggers showed that she had struggled through a great lot of brambles which were not as high as her face, but which she could not have got through and kept her hands out of. And bits of those brambles were actually found in her skin and put in as evidence, as well as the fact that the brambles in question were found on examination to have been broken through, and to have little shreds of her dress and little spots of blood upon them here and there. But the boldest point he made, was this. It was attempted to be set up by the prosecution as the proof of her jealousy, that she was under strong suspicion of having, at about the time of the murder, frantically killed her child by this vagabond man – a child some three years old – to revenge herself upon him. Mr. Jaggers worked that, in this way. "We say these are not marks of finger-nails, but marks of brambles, and we show you the brambles. You say they are marks of finger-nails, and you set up the hypothesis that she destroyed her child. You must accept all consequences of that hypothesis. For anything we know, she may have destroyed her child, and the child in clinging to her may have scratched her hands. What then? You are not trying her for the murder of her child, why don't you? As to this case, if you will have scratches, we say that, for anything we know, you may have accounted for them, assuming for the sake of argument that you have not invented them!" To sum up, sir," said Wemmick, "Mr. Jaggers was altogether too much for the Jury, and they gave in and acquitted her."

"Has she been in his service ever since?"

"Yes; but not only that," said Wemmick. "She went into his service immediately after her acquittal, tamed as she is now. She has since been taught how to do her duties, but she was tamed from the beginning."

"Do you remember the sex of the child?"

"Said to have been a girl."

"You have nothing more to say to me tonight?"

"Nothing. I got your letter and destroyed it. Nothing."

We exchanged a cordial Good Night, and I went home, with new matter for my thoughts, though with no relief from the old.

Chapter 49

Putting Miss Havisham's note in my pocket, that it might serve as my credentials for appearing at Satis House in case she was surprised to see me, I went down again by coach the next day. But I got off the coach early and walked the rest of the distance; I wanted to get into the town quietly by streets seldom taken, and to leave it in the same way.

The best light of the day was gone when I arrived at the house. The birds, as they flew about the bare high trees of the estate, seemed to call out to me that the place was changed, and that Estella was gone out of it forever.

An elderly woman, whom I had seen before as one of the servants who lived in the house across the back courtyard, opened the gate. The lighted candle stood in the dark passage within, as it always had, and I picked it up and ascended the staircase alone. Miss Havisham was not in her own room, but was in the larger room across the landing. Looking in at the door, after knocking with no answer, I saw her sitting on the hearth in a ragged chair, close to, and lost in the contemplation of, the ashy fire.

Doing as I had often done, I went in, and stood, touching the old chimney-piece, where she could see me when she raised her eyes. There was an air of utter loneliness upon her that moved me to feel pity for her, even though she had purposefully done me the deepest of injuries throughout most of my life by letting me think she was my benefactor. As I stood feeling bad for her, and thinking how my life had also become part of the wrecked fortunes of that house, she raised her eyes to me. She stared, and said in a low voice, "Is it real?"

"It is I, Pip. Mr. Jaggers gave me your note yesterday, and I have lost no time."

"Thank you. Thank you."

As I brought another of the ragged chairs to the hearth and sat down, I noticed a new expression on her face, as if she were afraid of me.

"I want," she said, "to pursue that subject you mentioned to me when you were last here, and to show you that I am not all stone. But perhaps you can never believe, now, that there is anything human in my heart?"

When I said some reassuring words, she stretched out her tremulous right hand, as though she was going to touch me; but she recalled it again before I understood the action, or knew how to receive it.

"You said, speaking for your friend, that you could tell me how to do something useful and good. Something that you would like done, is it not?"

"Something that I would like done very much."

"What is it?"

She set her hand upon her stick and looked at the fire with a strong expression of forcing herself to listen. I began explaining to her that secret history of the partnership with Clarriker, and told her how I had hoped to complete the transaction out of my means, but how I was no longer able to. That part of the subject (I reminded her) involved matters which I could not share, for they were the weighty secrets of another.

"So!" said she, nodding her head in understanding, but not looking at me. "And how much money is still needed?"

I was rather afraid of stating it, for it sounded a large sum. "Nine hundred pounds."

"If I give you the money for this purpose, will you keep my secret as you have kept your own?"

"Quite as faithfully."

"And your mind will be more at rest?"

"Much more at rest."

"Are you very unhappy now?"

She asked this question, still without looking at me, but in an unusual tone of sympathy. I could not reply at the moment, for my voice failed me. She put her left arm across the head of her stick, and softly laid her forehead on it.

"I am far from happy, Miss Havisham; but I have other causes of unease than any you know of. They are the secrets I have mentioned."

After a little while, she raised her head and looked at the fire again.

"It is noble in you to tell me that you have other causes of unhappiness. Is it true?"

"Too true."

"Can I only serve you, Pip, by serving your friend? Regarding that as done, is there nothing I can do for you yourself?"

"Nothing. I thank you for the question. I thank you even more for the tone of the question. But, there is nothing."

She presently rose from her seat, and looked about the blighted room for the means of writing. There were none there, and she took from her pocket a yellow set of ivory tablets, mounted in tarnished gold, and wrote upon them with a pencil in a case of tarnished gold that hung from her neck.

"You are still on friendly terms with Mr. Jaggers?"

"Quite. I dined with him yesterday."

"This is an authority to him to pay you that money, to lay out at your irresponsible discretion for your friend. I keep no money here; but if you would rather Mr. Jaggers knew nothing of the matter, I will send it to you."

"Thank you, Miss Havisham; I have not the least objection to receiving it from him."

She read me what she had written, and it was direct and clear, and evidently intended to absolve me from any suspicion of profiting by the receipt of the money. I took the tablets from her hand, and it trembled again, and it trembled more as she took off the chain to which the pencil was attached, and put it in mine. All this she did, without looking at me.

"My name is on the first leaf. If you can ever write under my name, "I forgive her," though ever so long after my broken heart is dust – please do it!"

"O Miss Havisham," said I, "I can do it now. There have been sore mistakes; and my life has been a blind and thankless one; and I want forgiveness and direction myself far too much to be bitter with you."

She turned her face to me for the first time since she had averted it, and, to my amazement, I may even add to my terror and shock, dropped on her knees at my feet; with her folded hands raised to me as if she were praying or begging.

I begged her to rise, and got my arms about her to help her up; but she only grabbed my hand which was nearest to her grasp, and hung her head over it and wept. I had never seen her shed a tear before, and, in the hope that the relief might do her good, I stood bending over her without speaking. She was not kneeling now, but was down upon the ground.

"O!" she cried, despairingly. "What have I done! What have I done!"

"If you mean, Miss Havisham, what have you done to injure me, let me answer. Very little. I would have loved her under any circumstances. - Is she married?"

"Yes."

It was a needless question, for a new feeling of desolation in the house had told me so.

"What have I done! What have I done!" She wrung her hands, and crushed her white hair, and returned to this cry over and over again. "What have I done!"

I didn't know how to answer her, or how to comfort her. That she had done an awful thing in taking an impressionable little girl to mold into the form that her spurned affection and wounded pride had found vengeance in, I knew full well. But, in shutting out the light of day, I knew equally well that she had also shut out infinitely more; that she had secluded herself from a thousand natural and healing influences; that her mind, brooding and solitary, had grown diseased.

"Until you spoke to her the other day, and until I saw in you a mirror that showed me what I once felt myself, I did not know what I had done.

What have I done! What have I done!" And so again, twenty, fifty times over, What had she done!

"Miss Havisham," I said, when her cry had died away, "you may dismiss me from your mind and conscience. But Estella is a different case, and if you can ever undo any scrap of what you have done wrong in keeping a part of her right nature away from her, it will be better to do that than to mourn the past the rest of your life."

"Yes, yes, I know it. But, Pip – my Dear!" There was an earnest womanly compassion for me in her new affection. "Believe this: when she first came to me, I meant to save her from misery like my own. At first, I meant no more."

"Well!" said I. "I hope so."

"But as she grew, and promised to be very beautiful, I gradually did worse, and with my praises, and with my jewels, and with my teachings, and with this figure of myself always before her a warning to back and point my lessons, I stole her heart away and put ice in its place."

"Better," I could not help saying, "to have left her a natural heart, even to be bruised or broken."

With that, Miss Havisham looked distractedly at me, and then burst out again, What had she done!

"If you knew all my story," she pleaded, "you would have some compassion for me and a better understanding of me."

"Miss Havisham," I answered, as delicately as I could, "I believe I may say that I do know your story, and have known it ever since I first left this neighbourhood. It has inspired me to feel great compassion for you, and I hope I understand it and its influences. Does our history between us give me any excuse for asking you a question about Estella? Not as she is, but as she was when she first came here?"

She was seated on the ground, with her arms on the ragged chair, and her head leaning on them. She looked full at me when I said this, and replied, "Go on."

"Whose child was Estella?"

She shook her head.

"You don't know?"

She shook her head again.

"But Mr. Jaggers brought her here, or sent her here?"

"Brought her here."

"Will you tell me how that came about?"

She answered in a low whisper and with caution; "I had been shut up in these rooms a long time (I don't know how long; you know what time the clocks keep here), when I told him that I wanted a little girl to raise and love, and save from my fate. I had first seen him when I sent for him to lay this place waste for me; having read of him in the newspapers, before I and the world parted. He told me that he would look about him for such an orphan child. One night he brought her here asleep, and I called her Estella."

"Might I ask her age then?"

"Two or three. She herself knows nothing, but that she was left an orphan and I adopted her."

So convinced I was of Mr. Jaggers' housekeeper being Estella's mother that I needed no further evidence to establish the fact in my own mind. But, to any mind, I thought, the connection here was clear and straight.

What more could I hope to do by prolonging the interview? I had succeeded on behalf of Herbert, Miss Havisham had told me all she knew of Estella, and I had said and done what I could to ease her mind. No matter with what other words we parted, we parted.

Twilight was closing in when I went down stairs into the natural air. I called to the woman who had opened the gate when I entered, that I would not trouble her just yet, but would walk around the place before leaving. For, I had a hunch that I would never be there again, and I felt that the dying light was suited to my last view of it.

I made my way to the ruined garden. I went all around it; by the corner where Herbert and I had fought our battle; by the paths where Estella and I had walked. So cold, so lonely, so dreary all!

Passing on into the front courtyard, I hesitated whether to call the woman to let me out at the locked gate, or first to go up-stairs and assure myself that Miss Havisham was as safe and well as I had left her. I choose the latter and went up to see her.

I looked into the room where I had left her, and I saw her seated in the ragged chair upon the hearth close to the fire, with her back towards me. In the moment when I was withdrawing my head to go quietly away, I saw a great flaming light spring up. In the same moment, I saw her running at me, shrieking, with a whirl of fire blazing all about her, and soaring at least as many feet above her head as she was tall.

I had a double-caped great-coat on, and over my arm another thick coat. I got them off, threw her down, and got them over her to put the flames out. I dragged the great cloth from the table for the same purpose, and with it dragged down the heap of rottenness on it and it all crashed to the floor, along with all the ugly things that had lived there. We were on the ground struggling like desperate enemies; the closer I covered her, the more wildly she shrieked and tried to free herself. I acted on instinct and wasn't aware of anything until I knew that we were on the floor by the great table, and that patches of tinder, still alight, which a moment ago had been her faded bridal dress, were floating in the smoky air.

Then, I looked around and saw the disturbed beetles and spiders running away over the floor, and saw the servants coming in with breathless cries at the door. I still held her forcibly down with all my strength, like a prisoner who might escape.

She was insensible, and I was afraid to have her moved, or even touched. Assistance was sent for and I held her down until it came, as if I unreasonably fancied (I think I did) that if I let her go, the fire would break out again and consume her. When I got up, on the surgeon's coming to her with other aid, I was astonished to see that both my hands were burnt; for, I had no knowledge of it through the sense of feeling.

On examination it was pronounced that she had received serious burns, but that they weren't hopeless; the danger lay mainly in the nervous shock she had received. The surgeon directed that her bed be carried into that room and laid upon the great table, which happened to be well suited to the dressing of her injuries. When I saw her again, an hour afterwards, she lay indeed where I had seen her strike her stick so many years before, and had heard her say that she would lie one day.

Though every vestige of her dress was burnt, as they told me, she still had something of her old ghastly bridal appearance; for, they had covered her to the throat with white cotton-wool, and as she lay with a white sheet loosely overlying that.

I found, on questioning the servants, that Estella was in Paris, and I got a promise from the surgeon that he would write to her before the next mail pick up. I took it upon myself to inform Miss Havisham's family; I intended to communicate with Mr. Matthew Pocket only, and leave him to do as he liked about informing the rest. This I did next day, through Herbert, as soon as I returned to town.

There was a time, that evening, when Miss Havisham spoke calmly of what had happened, though with a certain terrible energy. Towards midnight she began to wander in her speech, and after that it gradually set in that she said innumerable times in a low solemn voice, "What have I done!" And then, "When she first came, I meant to save her from misery like mine." And then, "Take the pencil and write under my name, 'I forgive her!'" She never changed the order of these three sentences, but she sometimes left out a word in one or other of them; never putting in another word, but always leaving a blank and going on to the next word.

As I could not help her anymore there, and as I had my own pressing anxieties and fears living at Mill Pond Bank, I decided that evening that I would return to London by the early morning coach. At about six o'clock in the morning, therefore, I leaned over her and touched her lips with mine, just as they said, not stopping even though being touched, "Take the pencil and write under my name, 'I forgive her.'"

Chapter 50

My burned hands had been dressed two or three times in the night, and again in the morning. My left arm was a good deal burned to the elbow, and, less severely, as high as the shoulder. It was very painful, but I felt thankful it was no worse. My right hand was not so badly burnt, and I could still move my fingers. It was bandaged, of course, but much less inconveniently than my left hand and arm; those I carried in a sling, and I could only wear my coat like a cloak, loose over my shoulders and fastened at the neck. My hair had been caught by the fire, but not my head or face.

When Herbert had been down to Hammersmith and seen his father, he came back to me at our apartment, and devoted the day to nursing me. He was the kindest of care-givers, and at regular times took off the bandages and soaked them in the cooling liquid that was kept ready, and put them on again with a patient tenderness that I was deeply grateful for.

At first, as I lay quiet on the sofa, I found it painfully difficult to get rid of the memory of the flames; their hurry and noise, and the fierce burning smell. If I dozed for a minute, I was awakened by Miss Havisham's cries, and by her running at me with all that height of fire above her head. This pain of the mind was much harder to fight against than the bodily pain I suffered; and Herbert, seeing that, did his best to divert my attention.

Neither of us spoke of the boat, but we both thought of it. That was made apparent by our avoidance of the subject, and by our agreeing – without agreement – to make the recovery of the use of my hands a question of hours, not of weeks. At any time Wemmick could signal us that it was time to get Provis out of England, and I was needed to row with Herbert, and I clearly could not do so with my injuries.

My first question when I saw Herbert had been whether all was well down at Mill Pond Bank? As he said Yes with perfect confidence and cheerfulness, we did not resume the subject until the day was wearing away to night. But then, as Herbert changed the bandages, more by the light of the fire than by the outer light, he went back to it spontaneously.

"I sat with Provis last night, Handel, two solid hours. Do you know he improves?"

"Yes, I said to you I thought he was softened when I last saw him."

"So you did. And so he is. He was very talkative last night, and told me more of his life. You remember in his life's story he told us where he broke off about some woman that he called "his Missus" that he had had great trouble with?"

"I had forgotten that, Herbert, but I remember it now you speak of it."

"Well! He went into that part of his life, and a dark, wild part it is. It seems - there's a bandage off most charmingly, and now comes the cool one – it seems that the woman was a young woman, and a jealous woman, and a revengeful woman; revengeful, Handel, to the last degree."

"To what last degree?"

"Murder. - Does it strike too cold on that sensitive place?"

I flinched at his words, not at the pain. "I don't feel it. How did she murder? Whom did she murder?"

"Why, the deed may not have deserved quite so terrible a name," said Herbert, "but, she was tried for it, and Mr. Jaggers defended her, and the reputation of that defense first made his name known to Provis. It was another and a stronger woman who was the victim, and there had been a struggle, in a barn. Who began it, or how fair or unfair it was, may be doubtful; but how it ended is certainly not doubtful, for the victim was found throttled."

"Was the accused woman found guilty?"

"No; she was acquitted. - My poor Handel, I hurt you!"

"It is impossible to be gentler, Herbert. Yes? What else?"

"This acquitted young woman and Provis had a little child before this trouble started; a little child that Provis loved very much. On the evening of the very night when the larger woman was strangled, his young wife presented herself before him for one moment, and swore that she would destroy the child (which was in her possession), and he would never see it again; then, she vanished. - You don't think your breathing is affected, my dear boy? You seem to breathe quickly."

"Perhaps I do, Herbert. Did the woman keep her oath and destroy the child?"

"There comes the darkest part of Provis's life. She did."

"That is, he says she did."

"Why, of course, my dear boy," returned Herbert, in a tone of surprise, and again bending forward to get a closer look at me. "He says it all. I have no other information."

"No, to be sure."

"Now," pursued Herbert, "whether he had been unfaithful to the child's mother, Provis doesn't say; but, she had shared some four or five years with him of the wretched life he described to us, and he seems to have felt pity for her. Therefore, fearing he should be called upon by the court to provide evidence about this destroyed child, and in so doing contribute to her receiving a death sentence, he hid himself (despite grieving for the child), and kept himself “dark”, as he says, out of the way and out of the trial, and was only vaguely talked of as a certain man called

Abel, out of whom the jealousy arose. After the acquittal, she disappeared, and thus he lost the child and the child's mother."

"I want to ask--"

"A moment, my dear boy, and I have done. That evil genius, Compeyson, the worst of scoundrels among many scoundrels, knowing of Provis' keeping out of the way during her trial and of the reasons he had for doing so, of course afterwards held the knowledge over his head as a way of keeping him poorer and working him harder. It was clear last night that this barbed the point of Provis's hatred towards him."

"I want to know, Herbert" said I, "whether he told you when this happened?"

"Let me remember then. He said, 'about twenty years ago, and almost directly after I took up with Compeyson.' How old were you when you came upon him in the little churchyard?"

"I think I was seven."

"Ay. It had happened some three or four years before then, he said, and you reminded him of the little girl so tragically lost, who would have been about your age."

"Herbert," said I, in a hurried way, "Do I seem to be in any fever, or that my head is much disordered by the accident of last night?"

"N-no, my dear boy," said Herbert, after taking a moment to examine me. "You are rather excited, but you are quite yourself."

"I know I am quite myself. And the man we have in hiding down the river, is Estella's Father."

Chapter 51

What purpose I had in mind when I was determined to trace out and prove Estella's parentage, I cannot say. It will shortly be seen that the question was not in my mind in a distinct shape until it was defined clearly by a wiser head than my own.

But, when Herbert and I had held our momentous conversation, I was seized with a feverish conviction that I had to hunt the matter down – that I couldn't let it rest, but that I had to see Mr. Jaggers and come at the bare truth. I really do not know whether I felt that I did this for Estella's sake, or whether I wanted to let Provis know some rays of the romantic interest I had so long felt for her. Perhaps the second option may be nearer to the truth.

Anyway, I could scarcely be held back from going over to his house that night. Herbert's advice, that if I did go over that I would probably be stricken useless when our fugitive's safety would depend upon me, alone restrained my impatience. On the understanding, again and again repeated, that no matter what I was going to see Mr. Jaggers tomorrow, I at length agreed to keep quiet and to have my injuries looked after and to stay at home. Early the next morning we went out together, and at the corner of Giltspur-street by Smithfield, I left Herbert to go his way into the City, and took my way to Mr. Jaggers' office.

There were routine occasions when Mr. Jaggers and Wemmick went over the office accounts, checked off the vouchers, and put all things straight. On these occasions Wemmick took his books and papers into Mr. Jaggers' office, and one of the upstairs clerks came down into the outer office to take Wemmick's place. Finding such a clerk at Wemmick's desk that morning, I knew this would be one of those occasions; but, I was not sorry to have Mr. Jaggers and Wemmick together, as Wemmick would then hear for himself that I said nothing to compromise him.

My injured appearance, with my arm bandaged and my coat loose over my shoulders, worked to my advantage in meeting with him. Although I had sent Mr. Jaggers a brief account of the accident as soon as I had arrived in town, I hadn't yet given him all the details. The uniqueness of the occasion caused our talk to be less dry and hard, and less strictly regulated by the rules of evidence than it usually was. While I described the disaster, Mr. Jaggers stood, as usual, before the fire. Wemmick leaned back in his chair, staring at me, with his hands in the pockets of his trousers, and his pen put horizontally into his post office.

My narrative about the accident finished, and their questions exhausted, I then produced Miss Havisham's authority to receive the nine hundred pounds for Herbert. Mr. Jaggers's eyes retracted a little deeper into his head when I handed him her notes, but he presently handed them over to Wemmick with instructions to create the check for him to sign. While that was being done, I looked at Wemmick as he wrote, and Mr. Jaggers, poising and swaying himself on his well-polished boots, looked at me. "I am sorry, Pip," said he, as I put the check in my pocket when he had signed it, "that we do nothing for you."

"Miss Havisham was good enough to ask me," I returned, "whether she could do nothing for me, and I told her No."

"Everybody should know his own business," said Mr. Jaggers. And I saw Wemmick's lips form the words "portable property."

"I would not have told her No, if I had been you," said Mr. Jaggers, "but every man ought to know his own business best."

"Every man's business," said Wemmick, rather reproachfully towards me, "is portable property."

As I thought the time was now come for pursuing the theme I had at heart, I said, turning to Mr. Jaggers:

"I did ask something of Miss Havisham, however, sir. I asked her to give me some information relative to her adopted daughter, and she gave me all she possessed."

"Did she?" said Mr. Jaggers, bending forward to look at his boots and then straightening himself. "Hah! I don't think I would have done so, if I had been Miss Havisham. But she ought to know her own business best."

"I know more of the history of Miss Havisham's adopted child, than Miss Havisham herself does, sir. I know her mother."

Mr. Jaggers looked at me inquiringly, and repeated "Mother?"

"I have seen her mother within these three days."

"Yes?" said Mr. Jaggers.

"And so have you, sir. And you have seen her still more recently."

"Yes?" said Mr. Jaggers.

"Perhaps I know more of Estella's history than even you do," said I. "I know her father too."

A certain stop that Mr. Jaggers came to in his manner – he was too self-controlled to change his manner, but he could not help its being brought to an indefinably attentive stop – assured me that he did not know who her father was. This I had strongly suspected from Provis's account (as Herbert had repeated it) of his having kept himself dark and out of the way; which I pieced on to the fact that he himself was not Mr. Jaggers's client until some four years later, and when he would have no reason for claiming his connection to Estella's mother. But, I could not be sure that Mr. Jaggers did not know who her father was, though I was quite sure of it now.

"So! You know the young lady's father, Pip?" said Mr. Jaggers.

"Yes," I replied, "and his name is Provis – from New South Wales."

Even Mr. Jaggers started when I said those words. It was the slightest start that could escape a man, the most carefully repressed and the soonest checked, but he did start, though he made it a part of the action of taking out his pocket-handkerchief. How Wemmick received the announcement I am unable to say, for I was afraid to look at him just then, lest Mr. Jaggers's sharpness should detect that there had been some communication unknown to him between us.

"And on what evidence, Pip," asked Mr. Jaggers, very coolly, as he paused with his handkerchief half way to his nose, "does Provis make this claim?"

"He does not make it," said I, "and has never made it, and has no knowledge or belief that his daughter is alive."

For once, the powerful pocket-handkerchief failed. My reply was so unexpected that Mr. Jaggers put the handkerchief back into his pocket without completing the usual performance, folded his arms, and looked with stern attention at me, though with an immovable face.

Then I told him all I knew, and how I knew it; with the one reservation that I left him to assume that I knew from Miss Havisham the parts that I knew from Wemmick. I was very careful indeed about that. Nor did I look towards Wemmick until I had finished all I had to tell, and had been for some time silently meeting Mr. Jaggers's look. When I did at last turn my eyes in Wemmick's direction, I found that he had unposted his pen, and was staring intently upon the table before him.

"Well!" said Mr. Jaggers at last, as he moved towards the papers on the table, " - What item was it you were at, Wemmick, when Mr. Pip came in?"

But I would not be disregarded in that way, and I made a passionate, almost an angry, appeal to him to be more frank and manly with me. I reminded him of the false hopes into which I had fallen, how long they had lasted, and the discovery I had made. I hinted at the danger that weighed upon me. I said I must surely be worthy of some little confidence from him in return for the confidence I had just now shared with him. I said that I did not blame him, or suspect him, or mistrust him, but I wanted assurance of the truth from him. And if he asked me why I wanted it and why I thought I had any right to it, I would tell him, little as he cared for such poor dreams, that I had loved Estella dearly and long, and that, although I had lost her and must live a sad life, whatever concerned her was still nearer and dearer to me than anything else in the world.

Seeing that Mr. Jaggers stood quite still and silent, and apparently quite stubborn under this appeal, I turned to Wemmick, and said, "Wemmick, I know you to be a man with a gentle heart. I have seen your pleasant home, and your old father, and all the innocent cheerful playful ways with which you refresh your business life. And I entreat you to say a word for me to Mr. Jaggers, and to represent to him that, all circumstances considered, he ought to be more open with me!"

I have never seen two men look more oddly at one another than Mr. Jaggers and Wemmick did after this monologue of mine. At first, a misgiving crossed my mind that Wemmick would be instantly fired from his employment; but, it melted as I saw Mr. Jaggers relax into something like a smile, and Wemmick become bolder.

"What's all this?" said Mr. Jaggers. "You with an old father, and you with pleasant and playful ways?"

"Well!" returned Wemmick. "If I don't bring 'em here, what does it matter?"

"Pip," said Mr. Jaggers, laying his hand upon my arm, and smiling openly, "this man must be the most cunning impostor in all London."

"Not a bit of it," returned Wemmick, growing bolder and bolder. "I think you're another."

Again, they exchanged their former odd looks, each apparently still distrustful that the other was taking him in.

"You with a pleasant home?" said Mr. Jaggers.

"Since it don't interfere with business," returned Wemmick, "let it be so. Now, I look at you, sir, I shouldn't wonder if you might be planning and contriving to have a pleasant home of your own one of these days, when you're tired of all this work."

Mr. Jaggers nodded his head retrospectively two or three times, and actually sighed. "Pip," said he, "we won't talk about 'poor dreams;' you know more about such things than I, having much fresher experience of that kind. But now, about this other matter. I'll put a case to you. Mind! I admit nothing."

He waited for me to declare that I quite understood that he expressly said that he admitted nothing.

"Now, Pip," said Mr. Jaggers, "put this case. Put the case that a woman, under such circumstances as you have mentioned, was hiding her child, and had to communicate that fact to her legal adviser, who told her that he must know how the facts stood about that child so he could plan out her legal defense. Put the case that at the same time he held a trust to find a child for an eccentric rich lady to adopt and bring up."

"I follow you, sir."

"Put the case that this legal advisor lived in an atmosphere of evil, and that all he saw of children was that they were generated in great numbers for certain destruction. Put the case that he often saw children tried at a criminal court, where they were often made an example of. Put the case that he routinely knew of their being imprisoned, whipped, neglected, cast out, qualified in all ways for the hangman, and growing up to be hanged."

"I follow you, sir."

"Put the case, Pip, that here was one pretty little child out of the heap who could be saved. A child whom the father already believed dead, and consequently chose not to make a stir about for fear of the mother being convicted for its murder. A child whom, over the mother, the legal adviser had this power: "I know what you did, and how you did it. You came so and so, this was your manner of attack and this was the manner of resistance, and you did such and such things to divert suspicion. Now, part with the child, unless it should be necessary to produce it to clear you, and then it shall be produced. Give the child into my hands, and I will do my best to get you cleared. If you are saved, your child is saved too; if you are lost, your child is still saved." Put the case that the woman agreed to this, and that the woman was subsequently cleared."

"I understand you perfectly."

"But that I make no admissions?"

"That you make no admissions." And Wemmick repeated, "No admissions."

"Put the case, Pip, that passion and the terror of death had a little shaken the woman's mind, and that when she was set free, she was scared out of the ways of the world and went to her legal advisor to be sheltered. Put the case that he took her in, and that he kept down the old wild violent nature whenever he saw an inkling of its breaking out, by asserting his power over her in the old way. Do you comprehend the imaginary case?"

"Quite."

"Put the case that the child grew up, and was married for money. That the mother was still living. That the father was still living. That the mother and father, unknown to each other, were dwelling within several miles of one another. That the secret was still a secret, except that you had got wind of it. Put that last case to yourself very carefully."

"I do."

"I ask Wemmick to put it to himself very carefully."

And Wemmick said, "I do."

"For whose sake would you reveal the secret? For the father's? I think he would not be much the better for the mother. For the mother's?

I think if she had agreed to such a deed, she would be safer hidden where she was. For the daughter's? I think it would hardly be in her best interests to establish her parentage for the information of her husband, and to drag her back to disgrace after an escape of twenty years, pretty secure to last for life. But, add the case that you had loved her, Pip, and had made her the subject of those 'poor dreams' which have, at one time or another, been in the heads of more men than you'd believe. Then, I tell you that you had better – and would much sooner, too, when you had really thought about it – chop off that bandaged left hand of yours with your bandaged right hand than to spill the secret."

I looked at Wemmick, whose face was very serious. He gravely touched his lips with his forefinger. I did the same. Mr. Jaggers did the same. "Now, Wemmick," said the latter then, resuming his usual manner, "what item was it you were at, when Mr. Pip came in?"

Standing by for a little, while they were at work, I observed that the odd looks they had cast at one another were repeated several times, with this difference now, that each of them seemed suspicious of having shown himself in a weak and unprofessional light to the other. For this reason, I suppose, they were now inflexible with one another; Mr. Jaggers being highly dictatorial, and Wemmick obstinately justifying himself whenever there was the smallest deviation from strict fact. I had never seen them on such ill terms, for, generally, they got on very well together.

But, they were both happily relieved by the opportune appearance of Mike, the client with the fur cap whom I had seen on the very first day of my appearance within those walls. This individual, or a member of his family, seemed to be always in trouble with the law, and he stopped by to announce that his eldest daughter was arrested on suspicion of shop-lifting. As he shared this melancholy news to Wemmick, with Mr. Jaggers standing magisterially before the fire and not participating in the proceedings, Mike's eye happened to twinkle with a tear.

"What's that about?" demanded Wemmick, with the utmost scorn. "What do you come sniveling here for?"

"I didn't go and cry, Mr. Wemmick."

"You did," said Wemmick. "How dare you? You're not in a fit state to come here, if you can't come here without spluttering like a bad pen. What do you mean by it?"

"A man can't help his feelings, Mr. Wemmick," pleaded Mike.

"His what?" demanded Wemmick, quite savagely, "Say that again!"

"Now, look here my man," said Mr. Jaggers, advancing a step, and pointing to the door. "Get out of this office. I'll have no feelings here. Get out."

"It serves you right," said Wemmick, "Get out."

So, the unfortunate Mike very humbly left, and Mr. Jaggers and Wemmick appeared to have re-established their good understanding, and went to work again with an air of refreshment upon them as if they had just had lunch.

Chapter 52

From Mr. Jaggers' office, I went with my check in my pocket to Miss Skiffins' brother, the accountant; and he went straight to Clarriker's and brought him to me, and I had the great satisfaction of concluding that arrangement. It was the only good thing I had done, and the only completed thing I had done, since I was first informed of my great expectations.

Clarriker informed me on that occasion that the business was steadily growing; that he would now be able to start a small branch-house in the East which was much needed for the extension of the business, and that Herbert, in his new partnership capacity, would go out and take charge of it. So, I found that I would have had to prepare for a separation from my friend, even if my own affairs had been more settled. And now indeed I felt as if my last anchor were loosening its hold, and I should soon be driving with the winds and waves.

But, there was compensation in the joy with which Herbert would come home at night and tell me of these changes, little imagining that he told me nothing that I didn't already know, and would sketch airy pictures of himself conducting Clara Barley to the land of the Arabian Nights, and of me going out to join them (with a caravan of camels, I believe), and of our all going up the Nile and seeing wonders. I wasn't confident regarding my own part in these bright plans, but I at least felt that Herbert's future was clearing fast, and that old Bill Barley just had to stick to his pepper and rum and his daughter would soon be happily provided for.

We had now got into the month of March. My left arm, though it didn't look bad, took so long to heal that I was still unable to get a coat on. My right arm was tolerably restored; scarred, but fairly serviceable.

On a Monday morning, when Herbert and I were at breakfast, I received the following letter from Wemmick in the mail.

"Walworth. Burn this as soon as read. Early in the week, or say Wednesday, you might do what you know of, if you felt ready to try it. Now burn."

When I had shown this to Herbert and had put it in the fire – but not before we had both got it by heart – we considered what to do. For, of course my being disabled could now be no longer kept out of view.

"I have thought it over, again and again," said Herbert, "and I think I know a better course than hiring a Thames waterman. Let's take Startop. A good fellow, a skilled rower, fond of us, and enthusiastic and honourable."

I had thought of him as well, more than once.

"But how much would you tell him, Herbert?"

"It is necessary to tell him very little. Let him suppose it a mere freak, but a secret one, until the morning comes. Then, let him know that there is urgent reason for your getting Provis aboard and away. You go with him?"

"No doubt."

"Where?"

As much as I had anxiously thought about this, it didn't seem to matter what port we made for – Hamburg, Rotterdam, Antwerp – the place meant little, just so that he was got out of England. Any foreign steamer that we happened to come across, and that would pick us up, would do. I knew we had to get him most of the way down river before we got him on a boat; certainly well beyond Gravesend, which was a critical place for search or inquiry if suspicion were afoot. As foreign steamers would leave London at about the time of high-water, our plan would be to get down the river and lie by in some quiet spot until we could row out to a passing ship. The time when one would be due where we lay, wherever that might be, could be calculated pretty closely if we made schedule inquiries beforehand.

Herbert agreed to all this, and we went out immediately after breakfast to gather the information we needed. We found that a steamer for Hamburg was likely to suit our purpose best, and we crafted our plans chiefly around that vessel. But we noted down what other foreign steamers would leave London with the same tide, and we satisfied ourselves that we knew the build and colour of each. We then separated for a few hours; I, to go get any necessary passports; Herbert, to see Startop at his apartment. We both did what we had to do without any problems, and when we met again at one o'clock where we had split up near the port office, we reported it done. I, for my part, was prepared with passports; Herbert had seen Startop, and he was more than ready to join.

We decided that those two would pull a pair of oars and I would steer; our charge would be sitting quietly. As speed was not our goal, we should make our way easily enough. We arranged that Herbert should go straight to Mill Pond Bank that evening after work and get Provis ready to be picked up Wednesday when we approached in the boat. We decided that all the arrangements with Provis should be finished that night, on Monday, and that Herbert should not go there at all tomorrow evening, and that Provis should not be communicated with in any way until we took him on board the next day, on Wednesday.

These precautions well understood by both of us, I went home.

On opening the outer door of our apartment with my key, I found a letter in the box, addressed to me; a very dirty letter, though not badly written. It had been delivered by hand (of course since I left home), and it said:

"If you are not afraid to come to the old marshes tonight or tomorrow night at Nine, and to come to the little office by the limekiln, you had better come. If you want information regarding your uncle Provis, you had much better come and tell no one and lose no time. You must come alone. Bring this with you."

I had already had enough on my mind before receiving this strange letter. What to do now, I couldn't tell. And the worst part was that I must decide quickly, or I'd miss the afternoon coach which would take me down in time for tonight. I couldn't go tomorrow night, for it would be too close to the time of Provis' escape. And again, for anything I knew, the offered information might have some important relevance to the escape itself. I had hardly any time to think it over – my watch was showing me that the coach would leave within half an hour – so, I decided to go.

If I had had plenty of time to think it over, I believe I still would have gone anyway. I would not have gone, except for the reference to my Uncle Provis; that, and coming so soon after Wemmick's letter and the morning's busy preparation, swayed me to go.

It is difficult to absorb the contents of any letter in a hurry, and I had to read this mysterious note again, twice, before its direction to be secret got stuck into my mind. I left a note in pencil for Herbert, telling him that since I would be going away soon, and I didn't know for how long, that I had decided to hurry down to my old town to check how Miss Havisham was doing. I barely had time to put on my great-coat, lock up the apartment, and head to the coach office. I caught the coach just as it came out of the yard. I was the only inside passenger, and I finally had some time to collect my senses.

For, I really had not been myself since I got the letter. The morning's activity had been hurried and frantic, for, despite how long and anxiously I had waited for Wemmick's signal, it had still come as a surprise when it at last arrived. And now, I began to doubt that I had a good enough reason to be sitting there in that coach, and to consider whether I should get out and go back home, and if I should believe an anonymous note like that, and, in short, to go through all those phases of indecision to which I suppose most hurried people go through. Still, the reference to Provis by name conquered everything. I reasoned, in case any harm should happen to him because I didn't heed the note, how could I ever forgive myself!

It was dark before we got to my old town, and the journey seemed long and dreary to me. Avoiding the Blue Boar, I stayed at a less desirable inn down town, and ordered some dinner. While it was preparing, I went to Satis House and asked about Miss Havisham; she was still very ill, though doing a bit better.

I returned to the inn, and as I was not able to cut my own dinner with my arm in a sling, the old landlord with a shining bald head did it for me. This bringing us into conversation, he was so good as to entertain me with my own story – of course with the popular feature that Pumblechook was my earliest benefactor and the founder of my fortunes.

"Do you know the young man?" said I, knowing he didn't, since I was the young man.

"Know him!" repeated the landlord. "Yes, ever since he was – no height at all."

"Does he ever come back to this neighbourhood?"

"Ay, he comes back," said the landlord, "to his great friends, now and again, and gives the cold shoulder to the man that made him."

"What man is that?"

"Him that I speak of," said the landlord. "Mr. Pumblechook."

"Is he ungrateful to no one else?"

"No doubt he would be, if he could," returned the landlord, "but he can't. And why? Because Pumblechook done everything for him."

"Does Pumblechook say so?"

"Say so!" replied the landlord. "He doesn't need to say so."

"But does he say so?"

"It would turn a man's blood to white wine vinegar to hear him tell of it, sir," said the landlord.

I thought to myself, "Yet Joe, dear Joe, you never tell of it. Long-suffering and loving Joe, you never complain. Nor you, sweet-tempered Biddy!"

"Your appetite's been affected by your accident," said the landlord, glancing at the bandaged arm under my coat. "Try a tenderer bit of meat."

"No thank you," I replied, turning from the table to brood over the fire. "I can eat no more. Please take it away."

I had never been struck at so keenly for my thanklessness to Joe, as through the brazen impostor Pumblechook. The falser he, the truer Joe; the meaner he, the nobler Joe.

My heart was deeply and most deservedly humbled as I sat brooding over the fire for an hour or more. The time eventually came for me to leave for the mysterious meeting, and I got up and had my coat fastened around my neck, and went out. Earlier in the evening I had looked in my pockets for the letter, but I could not find it, and I was nervous that I must have dropped it in the coach. I knew very well, however, that the chosen place was the little office by the limekiln on the marshes, and the hour nine. Towards the marshes I now went straight, having no time to spare.

Chapter 53

It was a dark cloudy night with a melancholy wind, and the marshes were very dismal. A stranger would have found them unbearable, and even to me they were so oppressive that I hesitated, half inclined to go back. But I knew them well and could have found my way on a far darker night, and I had no excuse for returning, since I was already there. So, onward I went.

I knew the limekiln as well as I knew the old cannon mound, but they were miles apart, so that if a light had been burning at each point that night, there would have been a long strip of the blank horizon between the two bright specks. Nobody was around and I seemed to have the whole flats to myself.

It was another half-hour before I drew near to the kiln. The lime was burning with a sluggish stifling smell, and the fires were made up and left, but no workmen were visible. Nearby was a small stone-quarry. It lay directly in my way, and had been worked that day, as I saw by the tools and wheel barrows that were lying about.

Coming up again to the marsh level out of this pit – for the crude path I walked ran through it – I saw a light in the little old office house. I quickened my pace, and knocked at the door. Waiting for some reply, I looked around me, noticing how the house – made of wood with a tiled roof – would not hold up against the weather much longer, if it even did now. There was no answer, and I knocked again. No answer still, and I tried the latch.

It rose under my hand, and the door opened in. Standing in the doorway looking in, I saw a lighted candle on a table, a bench, and a mattress on a bed. As there was a loft up above, I called out, "Is there any one here?" but no voice answered. Then, I looked at my watch, and, finding that it was past nine, called again, "Is there any one here?" There was still no answer, and I turned around to face the night, unsure what to do, and it began to rain.

I figured that someone must have been there recently and must soon be coming back, or else the candle wouldn't be burning, and the idea came into my head to examine if the candle's wick was long. I turned around to do so, walked into the house and had picked up the candle, when it was extinguished by some violent shock, and the next thing I knew was that I had been caught in a strong noose thrown over my head from behind.

"Now," said a suppressed voice with an oath, "I've got you!"

"What's this?" I cried, struggling. "Who is it? Help, help, help!"

Not only were my arms pulled close to my sides, but the pressure on my bad arm caused me excruciating pain. Sometimes a strong man's hand, sometimes his chest, were pushed against my mouth to deaden my cries, and, with his hot breath always close to me, I struggled ineffectually in the dark while I was fastened tight to the wall. "And now," said the suppressed voice with another oath, "call for help again, and I'll make short work of you!"

Faint and sick with the pain of my injured arm, bewildered by the surprise, and yet aware of how easily this threat could be executed, I silenced myself, and tried to ease my arm were it ever so little. But, it was bound too tight for that. I felt as if my arm, having been burnt before, was now being boiled.

The man closed the window shutters and door, and the room became pitch black. After groping about for a little, he found the flint and steel he wanted and began to strike a flame to re-light the candle. I strained my eyes trying to get a look at his face as the sparks fell among the tinder he was trying to light, but I could only intermittently see his lips. The man was in no hurry, and struck again several times with the flint and steel. Eventually he succeeded, and a flare of light flashed up, showing me Orlick.

Whom I had looked for, I don't know. I had not looked for him. Seeing him, I felt that I was in a dangerous strait indeed, and I kept my eyes trained on him.

He lighted the candle from the flaring match with great deliberation, and dropped the match, and stepped on it to put it out. Then, he pushed the candle away from him on the table, so that he could see me, and sat with his arms folded on the table and looked at me. I saw that I was fastened to a strong perpendicular ladder a few inches from the wall, which was the way to get to the loft above.

"Now," said he, when we had surveyed one another for a few moments, "I've got you."

"Unbind me. Let me go!"

"Ah!" he returned, "I'll let you go. I'll let you go to the moon; I'll let you go to the stars. All in good time."

"Why have you lured me here?"

"Don't you know?" said he, with a deadly look.

"Why have you attacked me in the dark?"

"Because I mean to do it all myself. One keeps a secret better than two. Oh, you enemy, you enemy!"

His enjoyment of the spectacle I provided, as he sat with his arms folded on the table, shaking his head at me, had an evil hatred in it that made me tremble. As I watched him in silence, he put his hand into the corner at his side, and picked up a gun with a brass-bound stock.

"Do you know this?" said he, making as if he would take aim at me. "Do you know where you saw it before? Speak, wolf!"

"Yes," I answered, recognizing the gun from when he worked for Miss Havisham.

"You cost me that job. You did. Speak!"

"What else could I do?"

"You did that, and that would be enough, without more. How dared you to come betwixt me and a young woman I liked?"

"When did I?"

"When didn't you? It was you as always give Old Orlick a bad name to her."

"You gave it to yourself; I could have done you no harm if you had done yourself none."

"You're a liar! And 'you'll take any pains, and spend any money, to drive me out of this country', will you?" said he, repeating my words to Biddy in the last conversation I had with her. "Now, I'll tell you; it was never so well worth your while to get me out of this country as it is tonight. Ah! If it was all your money twenty times told, to the last brass farden!" As he shook his heavy hand at me, with his mouth snarling like a tiger's, I felt that it was true.

"What are you going to do to me?"

"I'm a-going," said he, bringing his fist down upon the table with a heavy blow, and rising as the blow fell, to give it greater force, "I'm a-going to have your life!"

He leaned forward staring at me, slowly unclenched his hand and drew it across his mouth as if it watered for me, and sat down again.

"You was always in Old Orlick's way, since ever you was a child. You goes out of his way tonight. He'll have no more of you. You're dead."

I felt that I had come to the edge of my grave. For a moment I looked wildly around my trap for any chance of escape, but there was none.

"More than that," said he, folding his arms on the table again, "There won't be a rag of you, or a bone of you, left on earth. I'll put your body in the kiln – I could carry two like it, on my shoulders – and let people suppose what they may of you, they'll never know nothing."

My mind, with inconceivable quickness, followed out all the consequences of such a horrible death. Provis would believe I had deserted him, he would be taken, and would die accusing me; even Herbert would doubt me, when he compared the letter I had left for him with the fact that I had called at Miss Havisham's gate for only a moment;

Joe and Biddy would never know how sorry I had been that night; nobody would ever know what I had suffered, how true I had meant to be, what an agony I had gone through. The death close before me was terrible, but far more terrible than death was the dread of being misremembered after death. And so quick were my thoughts, that I saw myself despised by unborn generations – Estella's children, and their children – while Orlick's words were yet still on his lips.

"Now, wolf," said he, "afore I kill you, like any other beast, I'll have a good look at you and a good goad at you. Oh, you enemy!"

It had passed through my thoughts to cry out for help again; though, few could know better than I the solitary nature of the spot, and the hopelessness of aid. But as he sat gloating over me, I was strengthened by a scornful loathing of him that sealed my lips. Above all things, I resolved that I would not plead with him, and that I would die making any last resistance to him that I could. My thoughts and heart were softened now, humbly begging pardon of Heaven and knowing that I had taken no farewell of those who were dear to me, or could ask for their forgiveness of my miserable errors. Still, even with all of that, if I could have killed him, even in dying, I would have done it.

He had been drinking, and his eyes were red and bloodshot. Around his neck was slung a tin bottle, as I had often seen his meat and drink slung about him in other days. He brought the bottle to his lips, and took a fiery drink from it; and I smelt the strong spirits that I saw flash into his face.

"Wolf!" said he, folding his arms again, "Old Orlick's a-going to tell you something. It was your fault what happened to your shrew sister."

Again, my mind quickly reviewed the whole subject of the attack upon my sister, her illness, and her death, before his slow and hesitating speech had formed these words.

"It was you, villain," said I.

"I tell you it was your doing – I tell you it was done through you," he retorted, catching up the gun, and making a blow with the stock at the air between us. "I come upon her from behind, as I come upon you tonight. I giv' it to her! I left her for dead, and if there had been a limekiln as near her as there is now near you, she wouldn't have come to life again. But it warn't Old Orlick as did it; it was you. You was favoured, and he was bullied and beat. Old Orlick bullied and beat, eh? Now you pays for it. You done it; now you pays for it."

He drank again, and became more ferocious. I saw by his tilting of the bottle that there was not a lot left in it. I distinctly understood that he was working himself up with its contents, to make an end of me. I knew that every drop it held, was a drop of my life. I knew that when he made an end of me that he would do as he must have had done in my sister's case – make all haste to the town, and be seen slouching about there, drinking at the ale-houses.

It was not only that my mind flashed years and years of time to me while he said a dozen words, but that what he did say presented pictures to me, and not just words. In the excited state of my brain, I could not think of a place without seeing it, or of persons without seeing them. It is impossible to over-state the vividness of these images, and yet I was so intent all the time upon him – who would not be intent on the tiger crouching to spring! – that I saw the slightest action of his fingers.

When he had drunk this second time, he rose from the bench on which he sat and pushed the table aside. Then, he picked up the candle, and shading it with his murderous hand so as to throw its light on me, came over and stood right in front of me, looking at me and enjoying the sight.

"You and her have pretty well hunted me out of this country, so far as getting a easy living in it goes, and I've took up with new companions, and new masters. Some of 'em writes my letters when I wants 'em wrote – do you listen? – writes my letters, wolf! I've had a firm mind and a firm will to have your life since you was down here at your sister's burying. I hadn't seen a way to get you safe, and I've watched you to know your ins and outs. For, says Old Orlick to himself, 'Somehow or another I'll have him!' And when I looks for you, I finds your uncle Provis, eh?"

Mill Pond Bank, so clear and plain in my mind! Provis in his rooms, the signal whose use was now over, pretty Clara, the good motherly woman, old Bill Barley on his back, all drifting by, as on the swift stream of my life fast running out to sea!

"You with a uncle too! Why, I know'd you at Gargery's when you was so small a wolf that I could have took your thin little neck between this finger and thumb and chucked you away dead, as I had thoughts o' doing when I'd see you loitering amongst the marshes on Sundays. And you hadn't found no uncles then. No, not you! But when Old Orlick learned that your uncle Provis had likely worn the leg-iron that Old Orlick had found on these marshes ever so many year ago, and that he kept by him till he dropped your sister with it, as he means to drop you – what do you think of that?--"

In his savage taunting, he flared the candle so close at me, that I turned my face aside, to save it from the flame.

"Ah!" he cried, laughing, after doing it again, "the burnt child dreads the fire! Old Orlick knowed you was burnt, Old Orlick knowed you was smuggling your uncle Provis away. Old Orlick's a match for you and know'd you'd come tonight! Now I'll tell you something more, wolf, and this ends it. There's a man that's as good a match for your uncle Provis as Old Orlick has been for you. There's a man that can't, and that won't, have Magwitch – yes, I know the name! – alive in the same land with him. There's a man that's had such sure information of Magwitch when he was living in another land, and kept tabs on him. Perhaps it's that man that writes my letters. Beware Compeyson, Magwitch, and the gallows!"

He flared the candle at me again, smoking my face and hair and for an instant blinding me, and turned his powerful back to me as he replaced the light on the table. I had thought a prayer, and had been with Joe and Biddy and Herbert, before he turned towards me again.

There was a clear space of a few feet between the table and the opposite wall. Within this space, he now slouched backwards and forwards. His great strength seemed to sit stronger upon him than ever before, as he did this with his hands hanging loose and heavy at his sides, and with his eyes scowling at me. I had no grain of hope left. I clearly understood that he never would have told me what he did unless I was within a few moments of dying by his hand.

Suddenly, he stopped, took the cork out of his bottle, and tossed it away. Light as it was, I heard it fall like a hammer. He swallowed slowly, tilting up the bottle, little and little, and now he looked at me no more. The last few drops of liquor he poured into the palm of his hand, and licked them up. Then, with a sudden hurry of violence and swearing horribly, he threw the tin bottle away, and stooped over to pick up a stone-hammer with a long heavy handle.

The resolution I had made did not desert me, for, without uttering one useless word of appeal to him, I shouted out with all my might, and struggled with all my might. It was only my head and my legs that I could move, but to that extent I struggled with all the force that was within me. In the same instant I heard answering shouts, saw figures and a gleam of light dash in at the door, heard voices and confusion, and I saw Orlick emerge from a struggle of men, and watched him jump over the table and run out into the night.

I passed out briefly, and when I came to I found that I was lying unbound, on the floor, in the same little shack, with my head on someone's knee. My eyes were fixed on the ladder against the wall, when there came a face between me and it. The face of Trabb's boy!

"I think he's all right!" said Trabb's boy, in a sober voice; "but ain't he just pale though!"

At these words, the face of him who supported me looked over into mine, and I saw my supporter to be--

"Herbert! Great Heaven!"

"Softly," said Herbert. "Gently, Handel. Don't be too eager."

"And our old comrade, Startop!" I cried, as he too bent over me.

"Remember what he is going to assist us in," said Herbert, "and be calm. You have all tomorrow to rest. What hurt have you got? Can you stand?"

"Yes, yes," said I, "I can walk. I have no hurt but in this throbbing arm."

They laid it bare, and did what they could. It was violently swollen and inflamed, and I could scarcely endure to have it touched. But, they tore up their handkerchiefs to make fresh bandages, and carefully replaced it in the sling until we could get to the town and get some cooling lotion to put on it. In a little while we had shut the door of the dark and empty limekiln shack, and were passing through the quarry on our way back. Trabb's boy – Trabb's overgrown young man now – led us with a lantern, which was the light I had seen come in at the door. But, the moon was a good two hours higher than when I had last seen the sky, and the night, though rainy, was much lighter. As I had thought a prayer before, I thought a thanksgiving now.

Begging Herbert to tell me how he had come to my rescue – which at first he had flatly refused to do, but had insisted on my remaining quiet – I learnt that in my hurry I had dropped the letter in our apartment, where he, coming home with Startop, whom he had met in the street on his way back, found it, very soon after I was gone. Its tone made him uneasy, and the more so because of the inconsistency between it and the hasty letter I had left for him. His uneasiness increasing instead of going away after a quarter of an hour's thought, he set off for the coach office with Startop, who volunteered his company, to ask when the next coach went down. Finding that the afternoon coach was gone, and finding that his uneasiness had grown into positive alarm as obstacles came in his way, he decided to follow me in a hired-out cart. So, he and Startop arrived at the Blue Boar, fully expecting to find me there, or news of me. Finding neither, they went on to Miss Havisham's, where they lost me. Then they went back to the Boar (doubtless at about the time when I was hearing the popular local version of my own story at the other inn), to refresh themselves and to get someone to guide them out on the marshes. Among the loungers under the Boar's archway happened to be Trabb's boy – true to his old habit of happening to be everywhere where he had no business – and Trabb's boy had seen me passing from Miss Havisham's in the direction of my dining-place.

Thus, Trabb's boy became their guide, and with him they went out to the limekiln house. As they went along, Herbert reflected that I might, after all, have been brought there on some genuine errand about Provis's safety. In that case, an interruption would be bad per the note's instructions, so he left his guide and Startop on the edge of the quarry and went on by himself, and quietly walked around the little house two or three times, trying to determine if everything was alright within. Since all he could hear were indistinct sounds of one deep rough voice, he began to doubt whether I was even in there, when suddenly I cried out loudly, and he answered the cries, and rushed in, closely followed by the other two.

When I told Herbert what had happened within the house, he wanted to immediately get the police and get out a warrant for Orlick's arrest. But, I had already considered that doing this might force us to be detained or to have to come back to town, and either of those outcomes could be fatal to Provis. There was no denying this difficulty, so we gave up all thoughts of pursuing Orlick at the time. Under the present circumstances, we decided it was wise to make rather light of the matter to Trabb's boy, who I am convinced would have been very disappointed if he had known that his help had saved me from the limekiln. Not that Trabb's boy was evil, but that it was in his nature to want variety and excitement at anybody's expense. When we parted, I gave him two pounds (which seemed to please him), and told him that I was sorry I ever had a bad opinion of him (which made no impression on him at all).

Wednesday being so close, we determined to go back to London that night, so we could be clear away from town before the night's adventure began to be talked of. Herbert got a large bottle of lotion, and by applying it to my arm all through the night I was just able to bear its pain on the journey. It was daylight when we reached our apartment, and I immediately went to bed, and stayed in bed all day.

My fear of falling ill and being unfit for tomorrow's escape was so troubling that I wonder it did not disable me by itself. It would have done so, pretty surely, coupled with the mental wear and tear I had suffered, except for the dreaded excitement I felt about tomorrow. So anxiously looked forward to, so full of consequences, and its results so unknown though so near at hand.

As I lay in bed all day, falling in and out of fretfully restless sleep, I had the strongest convictions that Provis had been discovered and caught, or that I had overslept and that tomorrow had come and gone, and with it, Provis's chance of escape. My burning arm throbbed, and my burning head throbbed. Herbert and Startop kept me quiet all day, kept my arm constantly dressed, and gave me cooling drinks. About midnight I at last fell soundly asleep.

Wednesday morning was dawning when I looked out the window. The winking lights on the bridges were already pale in the morning light, and the coming sun was like a marsh of fire on the horizon. The river, still dark and mysterious, was spanned by bridges that were turning coldly grey. As I watched the sun come up, a veil seemed to be drawn back from the river, and millions of sparkles burst out upon its waters. From me too, a veil seemed to be drawn back, and I felt strong and well.

Herbert lay asleep in his bed, and our old fellow-student lay asleep on the sofa. I made up the fire and got some coffee ready for them, and in good time they too woke up strong and well. We let the sharp morning air in at the windows, and looked at the river's tide that was still flowing towards us.

"When the tide turns at nine o'clock," said Herbert, cheerfully, "look out for us and stand ready, you over there at Mill Pond Bank!"

Chapter 54

It was one of those March days when the sun shines hot and the wind blows cold; when it is summer in the light, and winter in the shade. We had our heavy pea-coats with us, and I took a bag. Out of all my possessions I took no more than the few necessities that filled the bag. Where I might go, what I might do, or when I might return, were all questions with answers utterly unknown to me. I didn't even really think about them, for my mind was wholly concentrating on Provis's safety. I only wondered for a brief moment, as I stopped at my apartment door and looked back inside, what my life would be like the next time I saw those rooms, or if I ever would see them again.

We headed down to the stairs by the river, stowed our gear in my boat, and cast off; Herbert in the bow, and I steered. It was then about high tide – half-past eight in the morning.

Our plan was this. We'd row with the tide, which would begin to run down towards the sea near nine, and would be with us until three in the afternoon. We intended to creep on after it had turned to come back in, and row against it until dark. We should then be below Gravesend, between Kent and Essex, where the river is broad and solitary, where the waterside inhabitants are very few, where lone public-houses are scattered here and there, and we would choose one for a resting place for the night. The steamers for Hamburg and Rotterdam would leave London at about nine the next morning, on Thursday. We would know at what time to expect them based on where we were, and we would hail the first, so that if by any accident we were not taken aboard we should have another chance with the second steamer.

The relief of finally starting our plan, instead of anxiously worrying about it, was so great to me that I could hardly believe the condition I had been in just a few hours before. The crisp air, the sunlight, our movement on the river, and the moving river itself – the road that ran with us, seeming to sympathize with us and encourage us on – all refreshed me with new hope. I felt horrible to be so useless in the boat, but there were few better oarsmen than my two friends, and they rowed with a steady stroke that was to last all day.

Early as it was, there were plenty of rowers going here and there that morning, and plenty of barges heading down with the tide. We went downriver among them all, briskly. Old London Bridge was soon passed, along with several others, and we found ourselves coming up on Mill Pond Bank.

"Is he there?" said Herbert.

"Not yet."

"Right! He was not to come down till he saw us. Can you see his signal?"

"Not well from here; but I think I see it. - Now, I see him! Pull both. Easy, Herbert. Oars!"

We touched the stairs lightly for a single moment, and Provis stepped aboard and we were off again. He was wearing a boat-cloak and carried a black canvas bag, and he looked as much like a river-pilot as my heart could have wished. "Dear boy!" he said, putting his arm on my shoulder as he took his seat. "Faithful dear boy, well done. Thankye, thankye!"

At the stairs where we had taken him aboard, and since then, I had looked warily for any sign of our being suspected. I had seen none. We certainly had not been followed by any boat, and went without any appearance of trouble.

Provis, as I have said, looked like a natural part of the scene. It was remarkable (but perhaps it was because of the wretched life he had led) that he was the least anxious of any of us. He was not disinterested, for he told me that he hoped to live to see his gentleman be one of the best gentlemen in a foreign country. He had no notion of meeting danger half way; when it came upon him, he confronted it, but until then he didn't trouble himself.

"If you knowed, dear boy," he said to me, "what it is to sit here with my dear boy and have my smoke, after having been stuck day after day between four walls, you'd envy me. But you don't know what it is."

"I think I know the delights of freedom," I answered.

"Ah," said he, shaking his head gravely. "But you don't know it equal to me. You must have been under lock and key, dear boy, to know it equal to me – but I ain't a-going to be low."

"If all goes well," said I, "you will be perfectly free and safe again within a few hours."

"Well," he returned, drawing a long breath, "I hope so."

"And think so?"

He dipped his hand in the water over the boat's gunwale, and said, "Ay, I s'pose I think so, dear boy. We'd be puzzled to be more quiet and easy-going than we are at present. But I was a-thinking through my smoke just then that we can no more see to the bottom of the next few hours than we can see to the bottom of this river what I catches hold of. Also, we can't no more hold their tide than I can hold this water. And it's run through my fingers and gone, you see!" holding up his dripping hand.

"You sound like you're a little sad," said I.

"Not a bit of it, dear boy! My thoughts come from the river flowing on so quiet, and of that there rippling at the boat's head making a sort of

Sunday tune. Maybe I'm a-growing a trifle old besides." He put his pipe back in his mouth with an undisturbed expression of face, and sat as composed and contented as if we were already out of England.

The air felt cold upon the river, but it was a bright day, and the sunshine was very cheering. The tide ran strong, I took care to lose none of it, and our steady stroke carried us on thoroughly well. The tide was still with us when we made it to Gravesend. As our charge was wrapped in his cloak, I purposely passed within a boat or two's length of the floating Customs House, and so out to catch the stream, alongside two ships, and under the bow of a large transport with troops on it looking down at us. Soon the tide began to slacken, and the boats lying at anchor began to swing around the other way. The ships taking advantage of the incoming tide to get up to London began to crowd upon us in a fleet, so we kept close to the shore, as much out of the strength of the tide as we could, and stayed carefully off from low shallows and mudbanks.

Herbert and Startop were fresh from having occasionally let the boat drift with the tide for a minute or two, so only fifteen minutes was as much rest as they wanted. We got ashore among some slippery stones while we ate and drank what we had with us for lunch, and looked about. It was like my own marsh country, flat and monotonous, and with a dim horizon. The last of the fleet of ships was just passing round the last bend we had passed, and now, except for the river, everything seemed stranded and still. A little squat lighthouse on pilings stood crippled in the mud on its stilts and crutches; slimy stakes stuck out of the mud; slimy stones stuck out of the mud; red landmarks and tidemarks stuck out of the mud; an old dock and an old roofless building slipped into the mud; and all about us was stagnation and mud.

We pushed off again and made what way we could. It was much harder work now, fighting the incoming tide, but Herbert and Startop persevered and rowed, and rowed, and rowed, until the sun went down. By that time the river had lifted us a little, so that we could see above the bank. There was the red sun, on the low level of the shore, in a purple haze, quickly deepening into black. There was the solitary flat marsh, and far away there were the rising grounds, between which and us there seemed to be no life, except here and there a gull flew slowly by.

As the night was fast falling, and as the moon would not rise early, we held a little council; a short one, for clearly our course was to stop for the night at the first lonely riverside tavern we could find. So, they rowed once more, and I looked out for anything like a house. Thus we went on, speaking little, for four or five dull, cold miles. The night was as dark by this time as it would be until morning, and what light we had seemed to come more from the river than the sky, as the oars in their dipping struck at a few reflected stars.

At this dismal time we were all possessed by the idea that we were being followed, and we became paranoid and jumpy. Little waves would land on the shore making a louder noise than usual, and whenever such a sound came, one of us was sure to start and look in that direction. Here and there we passed little creeks, and we were all suspicious of such places and eyed them nervously. Sometimes, "What was that ripple?" one of us would say in a low voice. Or another, "Is that a boat yonder?" And afterwards we would fall into a dead silence, and I would sit impatiently thinking how loud the oars seemed to be grinding in their locks.

Eventually we saw a light and a roof, and soon afterwards ran alongside a little landing made of stones. Leaving the others in the boat, I stepped ashore, and found the light to be the window of a public-house. It was a dirty enough place, and I dare say not unknown to smugglers; but there was a good fire in the kitchen, and there were eggs and bacon to eat and various liquors to drink. Also, there were two double-bedded rooms - "such as they were," the landlord said. No other company was in the house than the landlord, his wife, and a grizzled male creature who was the Jack of the little boat landing and was as slimy and smeary as if he had been part of the low tide. He showed off a shabby looking pair of shoes he was wearing as a great treasure find of his, since he had found them on the feet of a dead seaman who had washed ashore a few days earlier.

With the Jack as my assistant, I went down to the boat again, and we all came ashore and brought out the oars, the rudder, the boat-hook, and everything else, and hauled her up for the night. We took our bags to the rooms, with Herbert and Startop in one, Provis and I in the other. We found the air in them stale, and there were more dirty clothes under the beds than I could believe the family owned. But, we made a very good meal by the kitchen fire and we considered ourselves well off, for a more solitary place we could not have found.

While we were comforting ourselves by the fire after our meal, the Jack asked me if we had seen a four-oared galley going up with the tide? When I told him No, he said she must have gone back down river then, and yet she headed up river when she left those premises earlier.

"They must have thought better of it for some reason or another," said the Jack, "and gone down river instead."

"A four-oared galley, did you say?" said I.

"A four, with two sitters," said the Jack in a slushy voice, as if much mud had washed into his throat.

"Did they come ashore here?"

"Yes, they stopped in for some beer. I'd have been glad to poison the beer, myself," said the Jack.

"Why?"

"I know why," said the Jack, without actually answering us.

"He thinks," said the landlord, a weakly pondering man with a pale eye, who seemed to rely greatly on his Jack, "he thinks they was, what they wasn't."

"I knows what I thinks," observed the Jack.

"You thinks they were police, Jack?" said the landlord.

"I do," said the Jack.

"Then you're wrong, Jack."

"Am I!"

In the infinite meaning of his reply and his boundless confidence in his views, the Jack took one of his old shoes off, looked into it, knocked a few stones out of it on the kitchen floor, and put it on again. He did this with the manner of a person who knew he was so right that he could afford to do anything he pleased.

"Why, what do you think that they done with their uniforms then, Jack?" asked the landlord, wavering weakly.

"Done with their uniforms?" returned the Jack. "Chucked 'em overboard. Swallered 'em!"

"Don't be cheeky, Jack," scolded the landlord, in a melancholy and pathetic way.

"A police officer knows what to do with his Uniform," said the Jack, repeating the obnoxious word with the greatest contempt, "when it comes between him and his job. A Four and two sitters don't go hanging and hovering around, up with one tide and down with another, and both with and against the tide, without there being Police at the bottom of it." After saying this, he left the room arrogantly; and the landlord, having no one to reply to, dropped the subject.

This conversation made us all uneasy, like we were caged and threatened. A four-oared galley hovering about in so unusual a way as to attract this attention was an ugly circumstance that I could not ignore. When I had convinced Provis to go to bed, I went outside with my two companions (Startop by this time knew what our mission was really about), and held another council. We discussed whether we should remain at the house until near the steamer's time, which would be about one in the afternoon, or whether we should head out early in the morning. On the whole we decided we were better off to stay at the pub until within an hour or so of the steamer's time, and then to get out in her track, and drift easily with the tide. Having settled to do this, we returned into the house and went to the two bedrooms for the night.

I lay down with most of my clothes on, and slept well for a few hours. When I awoke, the wind had risen and the sign of the house was creaking and banging about with noises that startled me. Rising softly, for Provis lay fast asleep, I looked out of the window. It looked out over the area where we had hauled up our boat, and, as my eyes adapted themselves to the light of the clouded moon, I saw two men looking into our boat. They passed by under the window, looking at nothing else, and they did not go down to the landing-place which I could see was empty, but instead headed out across the marsh in the direction of the mouth of the river.

My first impulse was to wake up Herbert and show him the two men going away. I turned to go, but I remembered that he and Startop had had a harder day than I and were fatigued, so I let him sleep. Turning back to my window, I could see the two men moving over the marsh. In that dark night, however, I soon lost them, and as I was feeling very cold, I lay down to think of the matter, and fell asleep again.

We were up early. As the four of us walked around before breakfast, I decided I had better tell them what I had seen. Again, Provis was the least anxious of the group. It was very likely that the men were Customs officers, he said quietly, and that they had no thought of us. I tried to persuade myself that it was so – as, indeed, it might easily be. However, I proposed that he and I should walk away together to a distant point we could see, and that Herbert and Startop should take us aboard there at about noon. This being considered a good precaution, soon after breakfast he and I set forth, without saying anything at the tavern.

He smoked his pipe as we went along, and sometimes stopped to clap me on the shoulder. One would have supposed that it was I who was in danger, not he, and that he was reassuring me. We spoke very little. As we approached the point, I begged him to remain in a sheltered place, while I went on to scout the area, for, it was towards it that the men had passed in the night. He complied, and I went on alone. There was no boat off the point, nor any boat drawn up anywhere near it, nor were there any signs of the men having left there. But, the tide was high, and there might have been some footprints under water.

When he looked out from his shelter in the distance, and saw that I waved my hat to him to come up, he rejoined me, and there we waited; sometimes lying on the bank wrapped in our coats, and sometimes moving about to warm ourselves, until we saw our boat coming round. We got aboard easily, and rowed out into the track of the steamer. By that time it was ten minutes to one o'clock, and we began to look out for her smoke.

But, it was half-past one before we saw her smoke, and soon afterwards we saw behind it the smoke of another steamer. As they were coming on at full speed, we got the two bags ready, and took that opportunity of saying good-bye to Herbert and Startop. We had all shaken hands cordially, and neither Herbert's eyes nor mine were quite dry, when I saw a four-oared galley shoot out from under the bank just a little way ahead of us, and row out into the same track.

The galley, which was very skillfully handled, had crossed us, let us come up with her, and fallen alongside. Leaving just enough room for the play of the oars, she kept alongside, drifting when we drifted, and pulling a stroke or two when we pulled. Of the two sitters one held the rudder lines, and looked at us attentively – as did all the rowers; the other sitter was wrapped up, much as Provis was, and seemed to shrink, and whisper some instruction to the steerer as he looked at us. Not a word was spoken in either boat.

Startop could make out, after a few minutes, which steamer was first, and gave me the word "Hamburg," in a low voice as we sat face to face. She was nearing us very fast, and the beating of her paddles grew louder and louder. I felt as if her shadow were absolutely upon us, when the galley hailed us.

"You have a fugitive from Australia there," said the man who held the lines. "That's the man, wrapped in the cloak. His name is Abel Magwitch, otherwise known as Provis. I apprehend that man and call upon him to surrender, and you to assist."

At the same moment, without giving any audible direction to his crew, he ran the galley alongside us. They had pulled one sudden stroke ahead, had got their oars in, and were holding on to the side of our boat before we knew what they were doing. This caused great confusion on board the steamer, and I heard them calling to us, and heard the order given to stop the paddles, and heard them stop, but felt her driving down upon us irresistibly. In the same moment, I saw the steersman of the galley lay his hand on Provis' shoulder, and saw that both boats were swinging round with the force of the tide, and saw that all hands on board the steamer were running forward quite frantically. Still in the same moment, I saw Provis start up, lean across his captor, and pull the cloak from the neck of the shrinking sitter in the galley. Still in the same moment, I saw that the revealed face was of Compeyson, the other convict from long ago. Still in the same moment, I saw him tilt backward with a white terror on it that I shall never forget, and heard a great cry on board the steamer and a loud splash in the water, and felt the boat sink from under me.

It was but for an instant that I seemed to struggle with a thousand mill-weirs and a thousand flashes of light; that instant past, I was taken on board the four-oared galley. Herbert and Startop were there; but our boat was gone, and the two convicts were gone.

The crew of the galley pulled away from the steamer and every man was looking silently and eagerly at the water astern of the steamer. Soon, a dark object was seen in it, heading towards us. No man spoke, but the steersman held up his hand, and the crew kept the boat straight and true before the object. As it came nearer, I saw it to be Magwitch, swimming, but not swimming strongly. He was taken on board, and instantly manacled at the wrists and ankles.

The galley was kept steady, and the silent eager look-out at the water was resumed. But, the Rotterdam steamer now came up, and apparently not understanding what had happened, came on at full speed. By the time she had been hailed and stopped, both steamers were drifting away from us, and we were rising and falling in a troubled wake of water. The look-out for Compeyson was kept long after the water was still again and the two steamers were gone, but, everybody knew that it was hopeless to find him alive now.

Eventually we gave it up, and pulled towards the tavern we had recently left, where we were received with no little surprise. Here, I was able to get some comforts for Magwitch – Provis no longer – who had received a very severe injury in the chest and a deep cut in the head.

He told me that he believed himself to have gone under the keel of the steamer, and to have been struck on the head in rising. The injury to his chest (which rendered his breathing extremely painful) he thought he had received against the side of the galley. He added that he did not pretend to say what he might or might not have done to Compeyson, but, that in the moment of his laying his hand on his cloak to identify him, that villain had staggered up and staggered back, and they had both gone overboard together. The sudden wrenching of Magwitch out of our boat, coupled with the effort of his captor to keep him in it, had capsized us. He told me in a whisper that they had gone down, fiercely locked in each other's arms, and that there had been a struggle under water, and that he had disengaged himself, struck out, and swum away.

I never had any reason to doubt the exact truth of what he told me. The officer who steered the galley gave the same account of their going overboard.

I got the officer's permission to change Magwitch's wet clothes by purchasing spare garments at the public-house, but he said that he must take charge of everything the prisoner had on him. So, Magwitch's pocketbook which had once been in my hands, passed into the officer's. He further said I could accompany the prisoner to London, but declined to give that option to my two friends.

The Jack of the tavern was instructed where the drowned man had gone down, and he undertook to search for the body in the places where it was likeliest to come ashore. His interest in its recovery seemed to be much increased when he heard that it had stockings on. It probably took about a dozen drowned men to fit him out completely, and that may have been the reason why the different articles of his clothes were in various stages of decay.

We remained at the public-house until the tide turned, and then Magwitch was carried down to the galley and put on board. Herbert and Startop were to get to London by land as soon as they could. We had a dejected parting, and when I took my place by Magwitch's side, I felt that that was my place from that time forward while he lived.

For now, my revulsion of him had all melted away, and in the hunted wounded shackled creature who held my hand in his, I only saw a man who had meant to be my benefactor, and who had felt affectionately, gratefully, and generously towards me with great loyalty through a series of years. Mainly, I saw in him a much better man than I had been to Joe.

His breathing became more difficult and painful as the night came on, and often he could not repress a groan. I tried to rest him on the arm I could use, in any easy position. I hated to think it, but it was unquestionably best that he should die from his injuries. That there were still people around who were willing and able to identify him, I could not doubt. That he would be leniently treated, I could not hope. He had been presented in the worst light at his trial, had since broken prison and had been tried again, had returned from banishment and a life sentence, and had contributed to the death of the man who was the cause of his arrest.

As we returned in the galley towards the setting sun we had yesterday left behind us, I told him how grieved I was to think that he had come home for my sake.

"Dear boy," he answered, "I'm quite content to take my chance. I've seen my boy, and he can be a gentleman without me."

No. I had thought about that, while we had been there side by side. No matter what my thoughts were on the subject, I understood Wemmick's hint now. I foresaw that, being convicted, his possessions would be confiscated by the Crown.

"Lookee here, dear boy," said he "Its best as a gentleman should not be knowed to be seen with me now. Only come to see me as if you come by chance with Wemmick. Sit where I can see you when I am swore to, for the last o' many times, and I don't ask no more."

"I will never stir from your side," said I, "when I am able to be near you. Please God, I will be as true to you as you have been to me!"

I felt his hand tremble as it held mine, and he turned his face away as he lay in the bottom of the boat, and I heard that old sound in his throat – softened now, like all the rest of him. It was a good thing that he had touched this point, for it put into my mind what I might not otherwise have thought of until too late: That he need never know how his hopes of enriching me had perished.

Chapter 55

He was taken to the Court the next day and would have been immediately committed for trial, except that it was necessary to send for an old officer of the prison-ship from which he had once escaped to confirm his identity. Nobody doubted who Magwitch was, but, Compeyson, who had meant to be the one to swear to it, was tumbling somewhere in the river, dead, and it happened that there was not at that time any prison officer in London who could give the required evidence. I had gone directly to Mr. Jaggers at his private house on my arrival in London to retain his assistance, and Mr. Jaggers on the prisoner's behalf would admit nothing. It was the sole recourse, for he told me that the case would be over in five minutes when the witness was there, and that no power on earth could prevent its going against us.

I let Mr. Jaggers know my desire to keep Magwitch ignorant regarding the fate of his wealth. Mr. Jaggers was angry with me for having "let it slip through my fingers," and said we must try anyway for some of it. But, he did not conceal from me that, although there are cases in which assets would not be seized by the Crown, there were no circumstances in this case to make it one of them. I understood that, very well. I was not related to the outlaw, or connected with him by any recognizable tie; he had not written any document designating me as an heir before his arrest, and to do so now would not carry any legal authority. I had no claim to his wealth, and I had resigned myself to that fact.

It appeared that Compeyson had hoped for a reward from Magwitch's estate forfeiture, for he had obtained some accurate knowledge of the man's wealth. When Compeyson's body was found, many miles from the scene of his death and so horribly disfigured that he was only identifiable by the contents of his pockets, there were some notes that were still legible, folded in a case he carried. Among these notes was the name of a bank in Australia where a sum of money was, along with the designation of certain lands of considerable value. This information matched a list that Magwitch, while in prison, gave to Mr. Jaggers, of the possessions he supposed I would inherit. His ignorance, poor fellow, at last served him; he believed my inheritance was quite safe with Mr. Jaggers' aid.

After three days delay, the witness from the prison-ship came, identified Magwitch, and completed the easy case. He was committed to take his trial at the next Sessions, which would come on in a month.

It was at this dark time of my life that Herbert returned home one evening, a good deal downcast, and said:

"My dear Handel, I fear I shall soon have to leave you."

His partner, Clarriker, having prepared me for that, I was less surprised than he thought.

"We shall lose a fine opportunity if I put off going to Cairo, and I am very much afraid I must go, Handel, when you most need me."

"Herbert, I shall always need you, because I shall always love you; but my need is no greater now than at another time."

"You will be so lonely."

"I don't have time to think of that," said I. "You know that I am always with Magwitch to the full extent of the time allowed, and that I would be with him all day long, if I could. And when I leave him, you know that my thoughts are with him."

The dreadful condition to which he was brought was so appalling to both of us that we could not refer to it in plainer words.

"My dear fellow," said Herbert, "let the near prospect of our separation – for, it is very near – be my justification for troubling you about yourself. Have you thought of your future?"

"No, for I have been afraid to think of any future."

"But yours cannot be dismissed, my dear Handel. I wish you would discuss it now, as far as a few friendly words go, with me."

"Alright, what is on your mind?" said I.

"In this branch house of ours, Handel, we must have a--"

I saw that his delicacy was avoiding the right word, so I said, "A clerk."

"A clerk. And I hope it is not at all unlikely that he may expand (as a certain clerk you know quite well has expanded) into a partner. Now, Handel – in short, my dear boy, will you come join us? Clara and I have talked about it again and again and the dear little thing begged me only this evening, with tears in her eyes, to say to you that if you will live with us when we're together over there that she will do her best to make you a happy addition to the family. We would get on so well, Handel!"

I thanked her heartily, and I thanked him heartily, but said I could not yet be sure of joining him as he so kindly offered. Firstly, my mind was too preoccupied to be able to take in the subject clearly. Secondly – Yes! Secondly, there was a vague something lingering in my thoughts that I will relay very near the end of this tale.

"But if you thought, Herbert, that you could, without doing any harm to your business, leave the question open for a little while--"

"For any while," cried Herbert. "Six months, a year!"

"Not so long as that," said I. "Two or three months at most."

Herbert was highly delighted when we shook hands on this arrangement, and said he could now take courage to tell me that he believed he must go away at the end of the week.

"And Clara?" said I.

"The dear little thing," returned Herbert, "holds dutifully to her father as long as he lives; but he won't last long. Mrs. Whimple confides to me that he is certainly going."

"Not to say an unkind thing," said I, "but, it would probably be for the best."

"I am afraid that must be admitted," said Herbert: "and then I shall come back for the dear little thing, and we'll walk quietly into the nearest church. Remember! The blessed darling comes of no family, and she never looked into my mother's title book, and hasn't a notion about her grandpapa. How fortunate for me!"

On the Saturday in that same week, Herbert left in a coach – full of bright hope, but sad and sorry to leave me. I was then left to my lonely home – if it deserved the name, for it was now no home to me, and I had no home anywhere.

On the stairs I encountered Wemmick, who was coming down from my landing, after an unsuccessful application of his knuckles to my door. I had not seen him alone since the disastrous attempted escape, and he had come, in his private and personal capacity, to say a few words of explanation regarding that failure.

"The late Compeyson," said Wemmick, "had by little and little figured out what was going on, and it was from the talk of some of his people in trouble (some of his people being always in trouble) that I heard what I did. I kept my ears open, seeming to have them shut, until I heard that he was out of town, and I thought that would be the best time for making the escape attempt. I can only suppose now that it was a part of his policy, as a very clever man, to deceive his own people, and that he really wasn't out of town. You don't blame me, I hope, Mr. Pip? I tried to serve you, with all my heart."

"I am as sure of that, Wemmick, as you can be, and I thank you most earnestly for all your interest and friendship."

"Thank you, thank you very much. It's a bad situation," said Wemmick, scratching his head, "and I assure you I haven't been so cut up for a long time. What I look at is the sacrifice of so much portable property. Dear me!"

"What I think of, Wemmick, is the poor owner of the property."

"Yes, to be sure," said Wemmick. "Of course, there can be no objection to your being sorry for him, and I'd put down a five-pound note myself to get him out of it. But what I look at is this: the late Compeyson, having been keeping tabs on him and his return to England, and being so determined to have him arrested, I do not think he could have been saved.

Whereas, the portable property certainly could have been saved. That's the difference between the property and the owner, don't you see?"

I invited Wemmick to come up-stairs, and refresh himself with a glass of grog before walking to Walworth, and he accepted the invitation. While he was drinking his moderate allowance, he said, with nothing to lead up to it, and after having appeared rather fidgety:

"What do you think of my taking a day off work on Monday, Mr. Pip?"

"Why, I suppose you have not done such a thing these past twelve months."

"These past twelve years, more likely," said Wemmick. "Yes. I'm going to take a day off. More than that; I'm going to take a walk. More than that; I'm going to ask you to take a walk with me, on Monday."

I was about to excuse myself as being a bad companion just then, when Wemmick anticipated me.

"I know your engagements," said he, "and I know you are out of sorts, Mr. Pip. But if you could oblige me, I should take it as a kindness. It ain't a long walk, and it's an early one. Say it might occupy you (including breakfast on the walk) from eight to twelve in the morning. Could you manage it?"

He had done so much for me at various times that this was very little to do for him. I said I could manage it, and he was so very much pleased by my agreement that I was pleased too. At his particular request, I said I'd be at his house at half-past eight on Monday morning, and so we parted for the time.

Punctual to my appointment, I rang at his Castle gate on Monday morning and was received by Wemmick himself, who struck me as looking a little more dapper than usual, and having a sleeker hat on. Inside, there were two glasses of rum-and-milk prepared, and two biscuits. The Aged must have been out back for a morning stroll around the grounds, for, glancing into his bedroom, I saw that his bed was empty.

After we had eaten breakfast, we set off on our walk. Wemmick informed me he wanted to go towards Camberwell Green, which suited me just fine. When we were near there, Wemmick said suddenly, "Halloa! Here's a church!"

There was nothing very surprising in that; but, I was rather surprised when he said, as if he were thrilled by a brilliant idea, "Let's go in!"

We went in, and looked all around. In the meantime, Wemmick was diving into his coat-pockets and pulling something out.

"Halloa!" said he. "Here're a couple pairs of gloves! Let's put 'em on!"

As the gloves were white kid gloves, and as the post-office was widened to its utmost extent into quite a smile, I now began to have some strong suspicions. They were strengthened into certainty when I saw the Aged enter at a side door, escorting a lady.

"Halloa!" said Wemmick. "Here's Miss Skiffins! Let's have a wedding."

That discreet damsel was dressed as usual, except that she was now engaged in substituting white kid gloves in place of her green ones. The Aged was likewise occupied in putting his white gloves on. However, the old gentleman experienced so much difficulty in doing so that Wemmick found it necessary to put him with his back against a pillar, and then to get behind the pillar himself and pull away at them, while I for my part held the old gentleman around the waist, that he might present an equal and safe resistance. By way of this ingenious scheme, the Aged's gloves were got on to perfection.

The clerk and clergyman then appearing, we were arranged in order at those fatal alter rails. True to his notion of seeming to do it all without preparation, I heard Wemmick say to himself as he took something out of his waistcoat-pocket before the service began, "Halloa! Here's a ring!"

I was best-man to the groom, while an elderly little usher lady took on the role of being the Maid of Honor to Miss Skiffins. The responsibility of giving the lady away fell to the Aged, which led to an unintentionally scandalous situation. When the clergyman said, "Who giveth this woman to be married to this man?" the Aged P., not in the least knowing what point of the ceremony we had arrived at, stood most happily smiling at the ten commandments over on the wall. Upon which, the clergyman said again, a bit louder, "Who giveth this woman to be married to this man?" The old gentleman being still in a state of complete unawareness, the groom cried out in his usual voice, "Now Aged P., you know who giveth?" To which the Aged replied with great briskness, before saying that he gave the lady away, "All right, John, all right, my boy!" And the clergyman came to so gloomy a pause there, that I had doubts for the moment whether we would get completely married that day.

It was completely done, though, and when we were leaving the church, Wemmick said, "Now, Mr. Pip, let me ask you whether anybody would suppose this to be a wedding-party!"

Breakfast had been ordered at a pleasant little tavern a mile or so away, and there were some board games in the room, in case we should desire to unbend our minds after the solemnity of the wedding. It was pleasant to observe that Mrs. Wemmick no longer unwound Wemmick's arm when it snuck itself around her waist.

We had an excellent breakfast, and when anyone declined anything on the table, Wemmick said, "Provided by contract, you know; don't be afraid of it!" I drank to the new couple, drank to the Aged, drank to the

Castle, saluted the bride at parting, and made myself as agreeable as I could.

Wemmick came down to the door with me, and I again shook hands with him and wished him joy.

"Thankee!" said Wemmick, rubbing his hands. "She's such a good manager of chickens, you have no idea. You shall have some eggs, and judge for yourself. I say, Mr. Pip!" calling me back, and speaking low. "This is altogether a Walworth sentiment, please."

“I understand. Not to be mentioned in Little Britain,” said I.

Wemmick nodded. “After what you let out the other day, Mr. Jaggers may as well not know of it. He might think my brain was softening, or something of the kind.”

Chapter 56

Magwitch lay in prison, very ill, during the whole time between his committal for trial and the trial itself. He had broken two ribs, and they in turn had wounded one of his lungs. He therefore breathed with great pain and difficulty, and each day he seemed to only get worse. Being far too ill to remain in the common prison, he was moved after the first day or so into the infirmary. This gave me opportunities of being with him that I could not otherwise have had. Due to his injuries, he spoke so quietly as to be barely audible, so, he spoke very little. But, he was ever ready to listen to me, and it became the first duty of my life to say to him, and read to him, what I knew he ought to hear.

The kind of submission or resignation that he showed was that of a man who was tired out. I sometimes got the impression from his manner, or from a whispered word or two which escaped him, that he wondered whether he might have been a better man under better circumstances. But, he never tried to justify himself or bend the past out of its eternal shape, and he never complained about anything.

When the trial came, Mr. Jaggers made an application to postpone it until the next session. It was obviously made with the assurance that Magwitch could not live so long, and was refused. The trial came on at once, and, when he was brought into court, he was seated in a chair. No objection was made to my getting close to him, and holding the hand that he stretched out to me.

The trial was very short and very clear. Such things as could be said for him were said – how he had adopted industrious habits and had lived lawfully and respectfully since being sent to Australia. But, nothing could negate the fact that he had returned to England in violation of his life sentence, and was sitting there in the presence of the Judge and Jury. It was impossible to accuse him of that, and find him anything other than Guilty.

At that time, it was the custom (as I learned from my terrible experience of that trial) to devote the last day to the passing of Sentences, and to make a finishing effect with the Sentence of Death. If it wasn't for the picture burned into my memory, I'd never believe that I saw thirty-two men and women lined up before the Judge to receive that sentence together. Foremost among them was Magwitch, seated, so that he might stay alive long enough for the sentence to be delivered and carried out.

I once again stood outside the line, but close enough to hold his hand. Some of the thirty-two men and women were defiant, some stricken with terror, some sobbing and weeping, some covering their faces, some staring gloomily about. The sheriffs with their great chains, other ornamental and worthless court employees, criers, ushers, a great gallery full of on-lookers – altogether making a large theatrical audience – looked on, as the thirty-two and the Judge solemnly confronted each other. Then, the Judge addressed them. Among the wretched creatures before him whom he must single out and make an example of, was one who almost from his infancy had been an offender against the laws; who, after repeated imprisonments and punishments, had been eventually sentenced to exile for a term of years; and who had made his escape years ago and been re-sentenced to exile for life. That miserable man seemed for a time to have learned from his errors while in exile, and to have lived a peaceable and honest life. But, in a fatal moment of weakness, he had left his haven of rest and repentance and had come back to the country from where he had been banished. He had for a time succeeded in evading the officers of Justice, but was eventually found out and arrested while in the act of escaping. While being arrested, he had resisted the officers and had – only he knows whether on purpose or not – caused the death of his accuser, to whom his whole criminal career was known. The required punishment for his return to England being Death, and his case being an aggravated one, he must prepare himself to Die.

Rising for a moment, the prisoner said, "My Lord, I have received my sentence of Death from the Almighty, but I bow to yours," and sat down again. There was some hushing, and the Judge went on with what he had to say to the rest. Then, they were all formally doomed, and some of them were supported out, some of them sauntered out with a haggard look of bravery, and a few nodded to the gallery of onlookers. He went last of all, because of having to be helped from his chair and to go very slowly. He held my hand while all the others were removed and while the audience got up (putting their dresses right, as they might at church) and pointed down at this criminal or at that, and most of all at him and me.

I earnestly hoped and prayed that he might die before the Recorder's Report was made, but, in the dread of his lingering on, I began that night to write out a petition to the Home Secretary of State, relating my knowledge of him and how it was that he had come back for my sake. I wrote it as passionately and pathetically as I could, and when I had finished it and sent it in, I wrote out other such petitions to similar men in authority that I hoped were the most merciful, and wrote one to the Crown itself. For several days and nights after he was sentenced, I took no rest except when I fell asleep in my chair, but was instead wholly absorbed in these appeals. And after I had sent them in, I could not keep away from those places and felt as if the appeals were more hopeful and less desperate when I was near them. In this unreasonable restless mental state I would roam the streets in the evening, wandering by those offices and houses where I had left the petitions.

The daily visits I could make him were shortened now, and he was more strictly kept. Seeing, or at least imagining, that I was suspected of carrying poison to him, I asked to be searched before I sat down at his bedside, and told the officer who was always there that I was willing to do anything that would assure him of my intentions. Nobody was hard with him, or with me; there was duty to be done, and it was done, but not harshly. The officer always gave me the assurance that Magwitch was steadily getting worse.

As the days went on, I noticed more and more that he would lie there quietly looking at the white ceiling, with an absence of light in his face, until some word of mine brightened it for an instant, and then it would subside again. Sometimes he was quite unable to speak; then, he would answer me with slight pressures on my hand, and I grew to understand his meaning very well.

The number of the days had risen to ten when I saw a greater change in him than I had seen yet. His eyes were turned towards the door, and lit up as I entered.

"Dear boy," he said, as I sat down by his bed, "I thought you was late. But I knowed you couldn't be that."

"It is just the time," said I. "I waited for it at the gate."

"You always waits at the gate; don't you, dear boy?"

"Yes. Not to lose a moment of the time."

"Thank'ee dear boy, thank'ee. God bless you! You've never deserted me, dear boy."

I pressed his hand in silence, for I could not forget that I had once meant to desert him.

"And what's best of all," he said, "is you've been more faithful with me since I was under a dark cloud than when the sun shone. That's best of all."

He lay on his back, breathing with great difficulty. Do what he would, and love me though he did, the light left his face ever and again, and a film came over his peaceful gaze at the white ceiling.

"Are you in much pain today?"

"I don't complain of none, dear boy."

"You never do complain."

He had spoken his last words. He smiled, and I understood his touch to mean that he wished to lift my hand and lay it on his chest. I laid it there, and he smiled again, and put both his hands upon it.

The allotted time ran out while we sat that way; but, looking around, I found the governor of the prison standing near me, and he whispered, "You needn't go yet." I thanked him gratefully, and asked, "Might I speak to him in private, if he can hear me?"

The governor stepped aside, and beckoned the officer away. The change, though it was made without noise, drew back the film from his gaze at the white ceiling, and he looked most affectionately at me.

"Dear Magwitch, I must tell you something, now at last. You understand what I say?"

A gentle pressure on my hand.

"You had a child once, whom you loved and lost."

A stronger pressure on my hand.

"She lived and found powerful friends. She is living now. She is a lady and very beautiful. And I love her!"

With a last faint effort, which would have been powerless but for my yielding to it and assisting it, he raised my hand to his lips. Then, he gently let it sink upon his chest again, with his own hands lying on it. His peaceful look at the white ceiling came back, and he passed away.

I knew there were no better words that I could say beside his bed, than "O Lord, be merciful to him, a sinner!"

Chapter 57

Now that I was left completely by myself, I gave notice of my intention to vacate the apartment in the Temple as soon as my time could legally end, and in the meanwhile to sub-let it. I immediately put rental ads up in the windows, for, I was in debt and had scarcely any money, and I began to be seriously alarmed by the state of my affairs. Actually, I should write that I would have been seriously alarmed by the state of my affairs if I had had enough energy to feel that way, when in actuality all I really noticed was that I was becoming very sick. The recent stress I had been under, that had an unfortunate (but definite) end in sight, had granted me the strength to fight off getting sick until Magwitch's situation was resolved. But now that it was, a sickness took hold of me in an iron grip, and I didn't even really care.

For a day or two I lay on the sofa or on the floor – wherever I happened to fall – with a heavy head, aching muscles, no purpose, and no energy. Then there came one feverish night which seemed to last forever, which was filled with real or imagined anxieties and horrors. In the morning I tried to sit up in my bed and sort it out, but I found I could not get up, so I just lay there and let my mind swirl.

I tried to think about whether I really had been outside last night groping around for the row boat that I thought was still there; whether I had found myself lighting the lamp in the hallway, positive that Magwitch was coming up the stairs, and that the lights had blown out; whether there had been an iron furnace in a dark corner of the room and a voice had called out over and over again that Miss Havisham was being burned within it. These were some of the things that I tried to settle with myself and get into some order as I lay that morning on my bed. But, the fever kept my wits scattered and I couldn't sort out what was real or not. Eventually though, I saw that two men were in my apartment, looking down at me.

"What do you want?" I asked in surprise, "I don't know you."

"Well, sir," returned one of them, bending down and touching me on the shoulder, "this is a matter that you'll soon arrange, I dare say, but you're arrested."

"What is the debt?"

"Hundred and twenty-three pound, fifteen, six. Jeweller's account, I think."

"What is to be done?"

"You had better come to my house," said the man. "I keep a very nice house."

I made some attempt to get up and dress myself, but I still lay there.

"You see my state," said I. "I would come with you if I could, but indeed I am quite unable. If you take me from here, I think I shall die on the way."

Perhaps they replied, or argued the point, or tried to encourage me to believe that I was better than I thought. I don't remember much, but I do know that they decided not to remove me.

The fever gripped me and I often lost my reason and was disoriented, and time seemed to have no meaning. I could tell that I sometimes struggled in a vain fight with real people, in the belief that they were murderers, but then I would all at once understand that they meant to do me good, and I would then sink exhausted into their arms and let them help me. But, above all, I knew that there was a constant tendency in all these people, whose faces morphed and changed with my fever, to sooner or later settle down into the likeness of Joe.

After I had turned the worst point of my illness, I began to notice that while all its other features changed, this one consistent feature did not change. Whoever came near me, still settled down into Joe. I opened my eyes in the night, and I saw in the great chair at the bedside, Joe. I opened my eyes in the day, and, sitting on the window-seat, smoking his pipe in the shaded open window, still I saw Joe. I asked for cooling drink, and the dear hand that gave it to me was Joe's. I sank back on my pillow after drinking, and the face that looked so hopefully and tenderly upon me was the face of Joe.

At last, one day, I took courage, and said, "Is it you, Joe?"

And the dear old home-voice answered, "Which it are, old chap."

"O Joe, you break my heart! Look angry at me, Joe. Strike me, Joe. Tell me of my ingratitude. Don't be so good to me!"

For, Joe had actually laid his head down on the pillow at my side and put his arm round my neck, in his joy that I recognized him.

"Which dear old Pip, old chap," said Joe, "you and me was ever friends. And when you're well enough to go out for a ride – what larks!"

After which, Joe withdrew to the window, and stood with his back towards me, wiping his eyes. And as my extreme weakness prevented me from getting up and going to him, I lay there, penitently whispering, "O God bless him! O God bless this gentle Christian man!"

Joe's eyes were red when I next found him beside me; but, I was holding his hand, and we both felt happy.

"How long, dear Joe?"

"Which you meantersay, Pip, how long have your illness lasted, dear old chap?"

"Yes, Joe."

"It's the end of May, Pip. Tomorrow is the first of June."

"And have you been here all that time, dear Joe?"

"Pretty much, old chap. For, as I says to Biddy when the news of your being ill were brought by letter, which it were brought by the mailman, and him being formerly single and now married, though underpaid for how much walking he has to do and shoes he wears through, but wealth were not an object on his part, and marriage were the great wish of his heart--"

"It is so delightful to hear you, Joe! But I interrupt you in what you said to Biddy."

"Which it were," said Joe, "that how you might be amongst strangers, and that how you and me having been ever friends, a visit at such a moment might not prove unacceptabobble. And Biddy, her word were, 'Go to him, without loss of time.' That," said Joe, summing up with his judicial air, "were the words of Biddy."

There Joe cut himself short and informed me that I was to be talked to sparingly, and that I was to take a little nourishment at regular intervals, whether I felt inclined to or not, and that I was to obey all his orders in my recovery. So, I kissed his hand, and lay quiet while he proceeded to compose a note to Biddy with my love in it.

Evidently, Biddy had taught Joe to write. As I lay in bed looking at him in my weak state, it made me cry again with pleasure to see the pride with which he set about writing his letter. My bed, with its curtains taken down, had been moved, with me in it, into the sitting room, as it was the airiest and largest. The carpet had been taken away and Joe kept the room always fresh and clean. At my own writing-table, pushed into a corner, Joe now sat down to his great work, first choosing a pen from the pen-tray as if it were a chest of large tools, and rolling up his sleeves as if he were going to wield a crowbar or sledgehammer. It was necessary for Joe to hold on heavily to the table with his left elbow and to stick his right leg well out behind him before he could begin. When he did begin, he made every down-stroke so slowly that it might have been six feet long, while at every up-stroke I could hear his pen spluttering extensively. He had a curious idea that the inkstand was on the side of him where it was not, and constantly dipped his pen into empty air, and seemed quite satisfied with the result. Overall, he got on very well indeed, and when he had signed his name he got up and hovered about the table, looking at his creation from various points of view as it lay there, with unbounded satisfaction.

Not to make Joe uneasy by talking too much, even if I had been able to, I waited to ask him about Miss Havisham until the next day. He shook his head when I asked him if she had recovered.

"Is she dead, Joe?"

"Why you see, old chap," said Joe, in a tone of subtlety, and by way of getting at the answer by degrees to lessen any impact on my health, "I wouldn't go so far as to say that, for that's a lot to say; but she ain't...."

"Alive, Joe?"

"That's closer to the answer," said Joe; "she ain't alive."

"Did she linger long, Joe?"

"After you was took ill, pretty much about what you might call a week," said Joe; still determined, for my benefit, to come at everything by degrees.

"Dear Joe, have you heard what becomes of her property?"

"Well, old chap," said Joe, "it does appear that she had settled most of it on Miss Estella. But she had wrote out a little addition to her will in her own hand a day or two before the accident, leaving a cool four thousand to Mr. Matthew Pocket. And why do you suppose, Pip, she left that cool four thousand to him? 'Because of Pip's account of him, the said Matthew.' I am told by Biddy that that is the writing," said Joe, repeating the legal phrase as if it did him infinite good, "'account of him, the said Matthew.' And a cool four thousand, Pip!"

I never discovered how Joe figured out the temperature of the four thousand pounds, but it appeared to make the amount of money more to him, and he had a clear love of insisting on its being cool.

This news gave me great joy, as it perfected the only good thing I had done. I asked Joe whether he had heard if any of the rest of her family had inherited anything?

"Miss Sarah," said Joe, "she have twenty-five pound for to buy pills, on account of being sickly. Miss Georgiana, she got twenty pounds. Mrs. - what's the name of them wild beasts with humps, old chap?"

"Camels?" said I, wondering why he could possibly want to know.

Joe nodded. "Mrs. Camels," by which I soon understood he meant Camilla, "she got five pounds for to buy candles to make her feel better when she wakes up in the night."

The appropriateness of these details gave me great confidence in Joe's information. "And now," said Joe, "one last piece of news for the day. Old Orlick, he got caught breaking into a house."

"Whose?" said I.

"Well, the victim's manners may be blusterous," said Joe, apologetically; "but still, a Englishman's house is his Castle, and castles must not be broken into except when done in wartime. And wotsumever the failings on his part, he were a corn and seedsman in his heart."

"Is it Pumblechook's house that has been broken into, then?"

"That's it, Pip," said Joe; "and they took his money, and they drinked his wine, and they ate his food, and they slapped his face, and they pulled his nose, and they tied him up to his bedpost, and they stuffed his mouth full of flowering annuals to prevent his crying out. But he knowed Orlick, and Orlick's in the county jail now."

By these approaches we arrived at normal conversation. I was slow to gain strength, but I did slowly and surely become less weak, and Joe stayed with me, and I fancied I was little Pip again.

He would sit and talk to me in the old simple and comforting way, so that I would half believe that all my life since my childhood was just one of the mental troubles of the fever. He did everything for me except the household work, for which he had hired a very decent woman, after paying off my laundress on his first arrival. "Which I do assure you, Pip," he would often say, in explanation of taking that liberty to fire her, "I found her tapping the spare bed like a cask of beer, and taking the feathers in a bucket to sell. Which she would have tapped your bed next, and taken the feathers out with you a laying on it. And she was carrying away your coals gradually in your dishes, and taking the wine and liquor away in your Wellington boots."

We looked forward to the day when I could go out for a ride, as we had once looked forward to the day of my apprenticeship. And when the day came, and an open carriage was brought round, Joe wrapped me up, took me in his arms, carried me down to it, and put me in, as if I were still the small helpless child to whom he had so abundantly given of the wealth of his great nature.

Joe got in beside me and we drove away together into the country, where the rich summer growth was already on the trees and on the grass, and sweet summer scents filled the air. The day happened to be Sunday, and when I looked at the loveliness around me and thought how the world had grown and changed since I was last outside, I felt that I was not nearly thankful enough – that I was too weak still, to be even that – and I laid my head on Joe's shoulder, as I had laid it long ago when he had taken me to the Fair and it was too much for my young senses.

I gained some strength during the day, and we talked like we used to talk when we laid on the grass at the old cannon mound back home. There was no change whatever in Joe; he was just as simply right and faithful as I remembered him to be.

When we got back to my apartment again, he lifted me out and easily carried me across the courtyard and up the stairs, reminding me of that eventful Christmas Day when he had carried me over the marshes. We had not yet discussed my change of fortune, nor did I know how much of my recent history he knew. I was so doubtful of myself now, and put so much trust in him, that I couldn't decide if I should bring it up or not. Later that evening, I decided I should.

"Have you heard, Joe," I asked him, as he smoked his pipe at the window, "who my patron was?"

"I heerd," returned Joe, "as it were not Miss Havisham, old chap."

"Did you hear who it was, Joe?"

"Well! I heerd it were the person that sent the man that gave you the two pound notes at the Jolly Bargemen, Pip."

"So it was."

"Astonishing," said Joe, in the most tranquil way.

I presently asked, with increasing hesitation, "Did you hear that he was dead, Joe?"

"Which? Him as sent the bank-notes, Pip?"

"Yes."

"I think," said Joe, after thinking a long time, and looking rather evasively at the window-seat, "I did hear that he were some way or another in that general direction."

"Did you hear anything about his circumstances, Joe?"

"Not partickler, Pip."

"If you would like to hear, Joe--" I was beginning, when Joe got up and came to my sofa.

"Lookee here, old chap," said Joe, bending over me. "Ever the best of friends, ain't us, Pip?"

I was ashamed to answer him.

"Very good, then," said Joe, as if I had answered, "that's all right, that's agreed upon. Then why go into subjects, old chap, which are unnecessary? There's subjects enough between us without needing unnecessary ones. Lord! To think of your poor sister and her Rampages! And don't you remember Tickler?"

"I do indeed, Joe."

"Lookee here, old chap," said Joe. "I done what I could to keep you and Tickler apart, but my ability were not always equal to my inclinations. For when your poor sister had a mind to drop into you, if I opposed her, I noticed that she dropped into you always heavier because of it. And when you got dropped into heavier because of me, then I naturally says to myself, 'What is the good that you are a-doing?'

"Similarly, old chap, supposing ever you kept any little matter to yourself when you was a little child; you kept it mostly because you know'd as J. Gargery's power to keep Tickler and you apart were not fully equal to his inclinations. Therefore, think no more of it between us, and do not let us talk about unnecessary subjects. Biddy gave herself a deal o' trouble with me afore I left (for I am most awful dull) to show me I should view it in this light, and, now viewing it in this light, I should likewise put it to you. Both of which now being done," said Joe, quite charmed with his logical arrangement, "now, from a true friend to you, I say that you mustn't go a-over-doing it, but you must have your supper and your wine-and-water, and you must be put to bed."

The delicacy with which Joe dismissed my long-held secret, and the sweet tact and kindness with which Biddy – who with her woman's wit had found me out so soon – had prepared him for it, made a deep impression on my mind. But whether Joe knew how poor I was and how my great expectations had all dissolved, I did not know.

Another thing in Joe that I could not understand when it first began to happen, but which I soon had a sad understanding of, was this: as I became stronger and better, Joe became less easy with me. In my weakness and entire dependence on him, the dear fellow had fallen into the old tone and called me by the old names; the dear "old Pip, old chap," that were now music to my ears. I too had fallen into the old ways, only happy and thankful that he let me. But, little by little, though I tried to hold onto those ways, Joe's hold upon them began to weaken.

I was confused at first, but I soon began to understand that the fault of it was all mine. Over the years, hadn't I given Joe plenty of reasons to doubt my loyalty, and to think that once I was back in prosperity that I would grow cold and cast him off again? Hadn't I given Joe plenty of cause to feel instinctively that as I got stronger, that his place in my heart would grow weaker, and that he had better loosen his attachment and let me go before that happened? I had to admit that the answer to both of those questions was Yes.

It was on the third or fourth occasion of my going out walking in the Temple Gardens, leaning on Joe's arm, that I saw this change in him very plainly. We had been sitting in the bright warm sunlight, looking at the river, and I chanced to say as we got up:

"See, Joe! I can walk quite strongly. Now, you shall see me walk back by myself."

"Which do not over-do it, Pip," said Joe, "but I shall be happy for to see you able, sir."

The last word grated on me; but how could I complain! I walked no further than the gate of the gardens, and then pretended to be weaker than I was, and asked Joe for his arm. Joe gave it to me, but was thoughtful about it.

I, for my part, was thoughtful too; for, I didn't know how to fix the damage I had done. I was ashamed to tell him exactly how my finances stood and what I had been reduced to, but, I hope my reluctance was not quite an unworthy one. I knew he would want to help me out of his little savings, and I knew that he shouldn't help me, and that I must not allow him to do it.

It was a quiet, introspective evening for both of us. But, before we went to bed, I had decided that I would wait during tomorrow (tomorrow being Sunday) and would begin my new plan with the new week. I decided that on Monday morning I would speak to Joe about this new course I had in mind; I would put aside the last bit of reserve I had and I would tell him what my plan was (that "Secondly", brought up earlier but not yet arrived at), and why I had not decided to go out to Herbert yet. However, as my plans solidified in my head, Joe must have been arriving at his own decisions, too.

We had a quiet day that Sunday, and we rode out into the country, and then walked in the fields.

"I feel thankful that I have been ill, Joe," I said.

"Dear old Pip, old chap, you're almost come round, sir."

"It has been a memorable time for me, Joe."

"Likeways for myself, sir," Joe returned.

"We have had a time together, Joe, that I can never forget. There were days once, I know, that I did for a while forget; but I never shall forget these."

"Pip," said Joe, appearing a little hurried and troubled, "there has been larks, and, dear sir, what's been between us – has been."

That night, when I had gone to bed, Joe came into my room, as he had done all through my recovery. He asked me if I felt sure that I was as well as in the morning?

"Yes, dear Joe, quite."

"And are always a-getting stronger, old chap?"

"Yes, dear Joe, steadily."

Joe patted the sheet on my shoulder with his great good hand, and said, in what I thought might have been a slightly choked up voice, "Good night!"

When I got up in the morning, refreshed and stronger yet, I was full of my resolution to tell Joe everything, without delay. I would tell him before breakfast. I would dress at once and go to his room and surprise him; for, it was the first day I had been up early. I went to his room, but he was not there. Not only was he not there, but his things were gone.

I hurried then to the breakfast table, and on it found a letter. These were its brief contents.

"Not wishful to intrude I have left for you are well again dear Pip and will do better without JO.

"P.S. Ever the best of friends."

Enclosed in the letter was a receipt for the debt and costs over which I had been arrested. Up until that moment I had vainly assumed that my creditor had suspended the case against me until I had recovered. I had never dreamed of Joe's having paid the money; but, Joe had paid it, and the receipt was in his name.

What was left for me now, but to follow him to the dear old forge and beg forgiveness for my past actions and to share my last desperate hope of a plan with him? That plan being the “Secondly”, which had begun as a vague something, but had by now formed into a solid intention.

That intention was, that I would go to Biddy and show her how humbled and sorry I was; that I would tell her how I had lost all I once hoped for; that I would remind her of our old closeness in my unhappy youth. Then, I would say to her, "Biddy, I think you once liked me very much. My heart, even when it strayed away from you, was quieter and more at peace with you than it ever has been since. If you can like me only half as well once more, if you can take me with all my faults and disappointments, then I hope I am a little worthier of you than I was – not much, but a little. And Biddy, it shall be up to you to say whether I shall work at the forge with Joe, or whether I shall try for a different occupation here in this country, or whether we shall go away to a distant land where an opportunity awaits me, which I set aside when it was offered until I knew your answer. And now, dear Biddy, if you can tell me that you will go through life with me, you will surely make it a better life for me, and me a better man for it, and I will try hard to make it a better life for you."

That was my plan. After three more days of recovery, I left London and went to the old forge to put my plan into execution, and how it unfolded is all I have left to tell.

Chapter 58

The news of my fall from great fortunes had reached my old village before I got there. I discovered the Blue Boar knew about it and that it made a big difference in that establishment's attitude towards me. Before, the Boar had done its best to impress me when I was coming into property; now, the Boar was not the least bit interested in me since I was going out of property.

It was evening when I arrived there, and I was very tired from the journey I had so often easily made before. The Boar could not put me in my usual bedroom, which was in use (probably by someone who had expectations), and could only assign me a very forgettable room among the pigeons and horse carts up the yard. But, I slept as soundly there as in the best room the Boar could have given me.

Early in the morning while my breakfast was getting ready, I took a walk by Satis House. There were printed announcements on the open gate advertising the sale by auction of the contents of the house next week. The House itself was to be sold as old building materials and torn down. LOT 1 was marked in whitewashed letters on the brew house; LOT 2 was on that part of the main building which had been so long shut up. I stepped in for a moment and looked around me with the uncomfortable manner of a stranger who had no business being there. I saw the auctioneer's clerk walking on the casks and counting them off for another clerk who was cataloguing the inventory. That second clerk had made a temporary desk out of the wheeled chair I had so often pushed Miss Havisham along in.

When I got back to my breakfast in the Boar's coffee-room, I found Mr. Pumblechook conversing with the landlord. Mr. Pumblechook (not improved in appearance by his recent encounter with Orlick) was waiting for me, and addressed me in the following terms.

"Young man, I am sorry to see you brought low. But, what else could be expected! What else could be expected!"

As he extended his hand with a magnificently forgiving air, and as I was feeling run down by my illness and had no desire to argue, I took it.

"William," said Mr. Pumblechook to the waiter, "put a muffin on the table. And has it come to this! Has it come to this!"

I frowningly sat down to my breakfast. Mr. Pumblechook stood over me and poured out my tea – before I could touch the teapot – in the manner of a benefactor who was resolved to be dedicated to the very end.

"William," said Mr. Pumblechook, mournfully, "put the salt on. In happier times," addressing me, "I think you took sugar. And did you take milk? You did. Sugar and milk. William, bring a watercress."

"Thank you," said I, shortly, "but I don't eat watercresses."

"You don't eat 'em," returned Mr. Pumblechook, sighing and nodding his head several times, as if he might have expected that, and as if not eating watercresses was consistent with my downfall. "True. The simple fruits of the earth. No. You needn't bring any, William."

I went on with my breakfast, and Mr. Pumblechook continued to stand over me, staring fishily and breathing noisily, as he always did.

"Little more than skin and bone!" mused Mr. Pumblechook, aloud. "And yet when he left here years ago (I may say, with my blessing), and I provided him with my humble bounty, he was as plump as a Peach!" He went on, handing me my bread-and-butter, "And are you a-going to Joseph?"

"In heaven's name," said I, getting fired up in spite of myself, "what does it matter to you where I am going? Leave that teapot alone."

It was the worst course I could have taken, because it gave Pumblechook the opportunity he wanted.

"Yes, young man," said he, releasing the handle of the pot and backing up a step or two from my table, and speaking so the landlord and waiter at the door could hear, "I will leave that teapot alone. You are right, young man. For once, you are right. I forget myself when I take such an interest in your breakfast, as to wish you wholesome nourishment. And yet," said Pumblechook, turning to the landlord and waiter, and pointing me out at arm's length, "this is him as I ever sported with in his days of happy youth! I tell you, this is him!"

A low murmur from the two replied. The waiter appeared to be particularly moved.

"This is him," said Pumblechook, "that I have driven around in my horse cart. This is him that I saw brought up by hand. This is him, the sister of whom I was uncle by marriage, as her name was Georgiana Maria from her own mother; let him deny it if he can!"

The waiter seemed convinced that I could not deny it, and that it gave the case a bad look.

"Young man," said Pumblechook, screwing his head at me like he used to and speaking in a superior tone, "you are a-going to Joseph. I will tell you what to say to Joseph. Here are Squires of the Boar present, known and respected in this town, and here is William, which his father's name was Potkins, if I am not mistaken."

"You are correct, sir," said William.

"In their presence," pursued Pumblechook, "I will tell you, young man, what to say to Joseph. Says you, 'Joseph, I have this day seen my earliest benefactor and the founder of my fortunes'."

"I swear I don't see him here," said I.

"Say that," retorted Pumblechook, "and even Joseph will probably be surprised."

"There you quite mistake him," said I. "I know better."

"Says you to Joseph," Pumblechook went on, "'I have seen Mr. Pumblechook, and that man has no bad feelings towards us. He knows your character, Joseph, and is well acquainted with your pig-headedness and ignorance; and he knows my character, Joseph, and he knows my lack of gratitude. Yes, Joseph,' says you," here Pumblechook shook his head and hand at me, "'Mr. Pumblechook knows my total lack of common human gratitude. He knows it, Joseph, as nobody else can. You do not know it, Joseph, having no reason to know it, but he does.'"

Windy donkey that he was, it really amazed me that he could have the nerve to speak this way to me.

"Says you, 'Joseph, Mr. Pumblechook gave me a message, which I will now repeat. It was, that in losing his fortune, Pip saw the light of day. Pip knew losing his fortune was his reward of ingratitude to his earliest benefactor, and founder of his fortune. But I do not regret what I had done for Pip, not at all. It was right to do it, it was kind to do it, and I would do it again. That is the message, Joseph'."

"It's a pity," said I, scornfully, as I finished my interrupted breakfast, "that Mr. Pumblechook did not say anything about what it was he had done and would do again."

"Squires of the Boar!" Pumblechook was now pompously addressing the landlord, "and William! I have no objections to your mentioning to your esteemed townsmen, if you happen to in passing, that it was right to do it, kind to do it, and that I would do it again."

With those words the Impostor shook them by the hand and left the Boar; still leaving me in the dark regarding what that certain "it" was that he had supposedly done for me.

I left the Boar shortly after him, and when I went down the market street I saw him preaching at his shop door to a select group of people, no doubt delivering a variant of the speech he had given me. They honored me with very unfavorable glances as I passed by on the opposite side of the street. But, it just made it all the more pleasant to turn towards the forge, and to Biddy and Joe, whose great patience shone even more brightly than before when compared to this shameless pretender.

The June weather was delicious. The sky was blue and the countryside looked more beautiful and peaceful than I had ever known it to be. In my mind I saw many pleasant pictures of the life that I would lead here, and of the change for the better that would come over me when I had Biddy by my side. She would be my guiding spirit with her simple faith and clear home-wisdom. I felt like someone who was trudging home barefoot from distant travels, and whose wanderings had lasted many years.

As I drew nearer to the forge, but still out of sight of it, I began listening for the clink of Joe's hammer. Long after I ought to have heard it, I realized I did not. I stopped to listen; the summer wind carried many sounds of the countryside to me, but Joe's hammer was not among them. I began to feel a tinge of worry without knowing quite why.

I turned the last corner and saw that the forge was closed. No gleam of fire, no glittering shower of sparks, no roar of the bellows; all closed up and still. But, the best parlour seemed to be in use, for the window was open and happily decorated with flowers and fluttering white curtains. I went softly towards it, meaning to peep over the flowers to see if all was alright, when the door opened and Joe and Biddy stood before me, arm in arm.

At first Biddy gave a cry, as if she thought it was my ghost, but in a moment she was hugging me. I wept to see her, and she wept to see me; I cried because she looked so fresh and pleasant; she cried because I looked so worn and weary.

"But dear Biddy, how pretty and dressed up you are!"

"Yes, dear Pip."

"And Joe, how handsomely dressed you are!"

"Yes, dear old Pip, old chap."

I looked at both of them, from one to the other, and then--

"It's my wedding-day," cried Biddy, in a burst of happiness, "and I am married to Joe!"

They took me into the kitchen and I laid my head down on the old table where Mr. Jaggers and I had conducted our first business. Biddy held one of my hands to her lips, and Joe's healing touch was on my shoulder. "Which he warn't strong enough, my dear, for to be surprised," said Joe. And Biddy said, "I ought to have thought of it, dear Joe, but I was too happy." They were both so overjoyed and proud to see me, and so delighted that I came by accident to make their day complete!

My first thought was one of immense thankfulness that I had never breathed this last desperate hope to Joe. How often while he was tending to my illness had it risen to my lips. How awfully irrevocable would have been his knowledge of it if he had stayed with me just another hour!

"Dear Biddy," said I, "you have the best husband in the whole world, and if you could have seen him by my bed you would have – But no, you couldn't love him better than you do."

"No, I couldn't indeed," said Biddy.

"And, dear Joe, you have the best wife in the whole world, and she will make you as happy as even you deserve to be, you dear, good, noble Joe!"

Joe looked at me with a quivering lip and touched his sleeve to his eyes.

"And Joe and Biddy both, please receive my humble thanks for all you have done for me, and all I have so ill repaid! I'm going away within the hour to go abroad, and I shall never rest until I have worked for the money with which you have kept me out of prison and send it to you. Even if I could repay it a thousand times over, I still couldn't cancel a bit of the debt I owe you, and I wouldn't even if I could!"

They were both melted by these words, and both begged me to say no more.

"But I must say a bit more. Dear Joe, I hope you will have children to love, and that some little fellow will sit in this chimney corner who may remind you of another little fellow gone out of it forever. Don't tell him, Joe, that I was thankless; don't tell him, Biddy, that I was ungenerous and unjust. Only tell him that I honored you both because you were both so good and true. And that, as your child, I said it would be natural for him to grow up a much better man than I did."

"I ain't a-going," said Joe, from behind his sleeve, "to tell him nothink o' that nature, Pip. Nor Biddy ain't. Nor yet no one ain't."

"And now, though I know you have already done it in your own kind hearts, please tell me, both, that you forgive me! Please let me hear you say the words, that I may carry the sound of them away with me. Then I shall be able to believe that you can trust me, and think better of me in the time to come!"

"O dear old Pip, old chap," said Joe. "God knows as I forgive you, if I have anythink to forgive!"

"Amen! And God knows I do!" echoed Biddy.

"Now let me go up and look at my old little room, and rest there a few minutes by myself, and then when I have eaten and drunk with you, please go with me as far as the finger-post, dear Joe and Biddy, before we say good-bye!"

And thus, we happily parted. I sold all I had, and put aside as much as I could, and set up a plan with my creditors – who gave me ample time to pay them in full – and I went out and joined Herbert. Within a month, I had left England, and within two months I was clerk to Clarriker and Co., and within four months I took on my first major responsibility. This was because Old Bill Barley was finally at peace, and Herbert had therefore gone back to England to marry Clara, and I was left in sole charge of the Eastern Branch until he brought her back.

Many years went by before I was a partner in the House. But, I lived happily and frugally with Herbert and his wife, I paid my debts, and I constantly stayed in touch by mail with Biddy and Joe. It was not until I became third in charge at the firm that Clarriker betrayed my secret to Herbert. But, he then declared that the secret of Herbert's partnership had been on his conscience long enough, and he must tell it. So, he told it, and Herbert was as much moved as he was amazed, and the dear fellow and I were no worse off for the long concealment.

We were never a large trading house, or made mints of money; but we had a good reputation, worked hard for our profits, and did well. We owed so much to Herbert's always cheerful attitude and readiness that I often wondered how I had ever thought up that old idea of his inability to succeed, until I was one day enlightened by the thought that perhaps that inability had never been in him at all, but had been in me.

Chapter 59

For eleven years I had been abroad and not seen Joe or Biddy, until one evening in December I laid my hand softly on the latch of the old kitchen door. I touched it so softly that I was not heard, and I looked in unseen. There, smoking his pipe in the old place by the kitchen firelight, as healthy and as strong as ever, though a little grey, sat Joe. And there, fenced into the corner with Joe's leg, and sitting on my own little stool looking at the fire, was – I again!

"We giv' him the name of Pip for your sake, dear old chap," said Joe, delighted when I took another stool by the child's side (but I did not rumple his hair), "and we hoped he might grow a little bit like you, and we think he do."

I thought so too, and I took him out for a walk the next morning, and we talked at great length, understanding one another perfectly. I took him down to the churchyard and set him on a certain tombstone there, and he showed me from that spot which head stone was sacred to the memory of Philip Pirrip and his wife, Georgiana.

"Biddy," said I, when I talked with her after dinner, as her little girl lay sleeping in her lap, "you must give Pip to me one of these days, or lend him, at least."

"No, no," said Biddy, gently. "You must marry."

"So Herbert and Clara say, but I don't think I shall, Biddy. I have so settled down in their home that it's not at all likely. I am already quite an old bachelor."

Biddy looked down at her child, and put its little hand to her lips, and then put the good matronly hand with which she had touched it into mine. There was something in the action and in the light pressure of Biddy's wedding-ring that had a very pretty expressiveness in it.

"Dear Pip," said Biddy, "you are sure you don't fret for her?"

"O no – I think not, Biddy."

"Tell me as an old, old friend. Have you quite forgotten her?

"My dear Biddy, I have forgotten nothing in my life that ever was important to me. But that poor dream, as I once used to call it, has all gone by, Biddy; all gone by!"

Nevertheless, I knew while I said those words that I secretly intended to revisit the site of the old house that evening, alone, for her sake. Yes even so. For Estella's sake.

I had heard of her as leading a most unhappy life, and as being separated from her husband, Drummle, who had been very cruel to her and who had, himself, become quite renowned as a combination of arrogance, cheapness, brutality, and meanness. And I had also heard of his death, from an accident due to his ill-treatment of a horse. This release had happened to her some two years before; for all I knew she was married again.

The early dinner-hour at Joe's left me plenty of time to walk over to the old spot before dark. But, what with loitering on the way, to look at old objects and to think of old times, the remainder of the day had grown quite short when I came to where Satis House was.

There was no house now, no brewery, no buildings left; just the wall of the old garden and small piles of ruin scattered here and there. The property had been enclosed with a rough fence, and a gate in it stood ajar; I pushed it open, and went in.

A cold silvery mist had veiled the early evening, and the moon was not yet up to scatter it, and it was not dark yet. I could trace out where every part of the old house had been, and where the brewery, gate, and casks had been. I was looking along the desolate garden walk, when I saw a solitary figure in it.

The figure showed itself aware of me, as I advanced. It had been moving towards me, but it now stood still. As I drew nearer, I saw it to be the figure of a woman. As I drew nearer yet, it was about to turn away, when it stopped, and let me come up with it. Then, it faltered, as if much surprised, and uttered my name, and I cried out:

"Estella!"

"I am greatly changed. I wonder you know me."

The freshness of her beauty was indeed gone, but its indescribable majesty and its indescribable charm remained. Those attractions in it, I had seen before; what was not there before was the saddened softened light of the once proud eyes; what I had never felt before was the friendly touch of the once unfeeling hand.

We sat down on a bench that was near, and I said, "After so many years, it is strange that we should meet like this, Estella, here where our first meeting was! Do you often come back?"

"I have never been here since."

"Nor I."

A white moon began to rise, and I thought of Magwitch's peaceful gaze at the white ceiling of the infirmary, and of the pressure on my hand when I had spoken the last words he had heard on earth.

Estella was the next to break the short silence between us.

"I have very often hoped and intended to come back, but have been prevented by many circumstances. Poor, poor old place!"

A few tears dropped from her eyes, and not knowing that I saw them, set herself to get the better of them. She said quietly, "Were you wondering, as you walked along, how it came to be left in this condition?"

"Yes, Estella."

"The ground belongs to me. It is the only possession I have not given up. Everything else has gone from me, little by little, but I have kept this. It was the subject of the only determined resistance I made in all the wretched years."

"Is it to be built on?"

"At last it is. I came here to take leave of it before its change. And you; you live abroad still?"

"Still."

"And do well, I am sure?"

"I work hard for a sufficient living, and therefore – Yes, I do well."

"I have often thought of you," said Estella.

"Have you?"

"Of late, very often. There was a long hard time when I pushed far from me the remembrance of what I had thrown away when I was quite ignorant of its worth. But, I have since given it a place in my heart."

"You have always held your place in my heart," I answered.

We were silent again, until she spoke.

"I little thought," said Estella, "that I should take leave of you in taking leave of this spot. I am very glad to do so."

"Glad to part again, Estella? To me, parting is a painful thing. To me, the memory of our last parting has been ever mournful and painful."

"But you said to me," returned Estella, very earnestly, 'God bless you, God forgive you!' And if you could say that to me then, please say that to me now – now, when suffering has been stronger than all other teaching, and has taught me to understand what your heart used to be. I have been bent and broken, but – I hope – into a better shape. Be as considerate and good to me now as you were then, and tell me we are friends."

"We are friends," said I, rising, as she rose from the bench.

"And will continue friends apart," said Estella.

I took her hand in mine, and we walked out of the ruined place. Long ago, when I first left the forge, the morning mists had risen and seemed to reveal the world and a grand future to me. Now, this evening, the mists were also rising, and in all the world they revealed to me, I saw no shadow of another parting from her.

Printed in Great Britain
by Amazon

18454063R10192